A Map of Glass

BOOKS BY JANE URQUHART

FICTION

The Whirlpool (1986)
Storm Glass (short stories, 1987)
Changing Heaven (1990)
Away (1993)
The Underpainter (1997)
The Stone Carvers (2001)
A Map of Glass (2005)

POETRY

I Am Walking in the Garden of His Imaginary Palace (1981)
False Shuffles (1982)
The Little Flowers of Madame de Montespan (1985)
Some Other Garden (2000)

JANE URQUHART

A Map of Glass

M&S

Library and Archives Canada Cataloguing in Publication

Urquhart, Jane
A map of glass / Jane Urquhart.

ISBN 0-7710-8727-6

I. Title.

PS8591.R68M36 2005   C813'.54   C2004-905952-1

We acknowledge the financial support of the Government of Canada through the
Book Publishing Industry Development Program and that of the Government of
Ontario through the Ontario Media Development Corporation's Ontario Book
Initiative. We further acknowledge the support of the Canada Council for the Arts
and the Ontario Arts Council for our publishing program.

This is a work of fiction, and the characters in it are solely the creation of the author.
Any resemblance to actual persons – with the exception of the historical figures – is
entirely coincidental. When historical figures consort with fictional characters,
the results are necessarily fiction. Similarly, some events and some geographies
have been created to serve fictional purposes.

The epigraph on page vii is taken from Robert Smithson's essay
"A Provisional Theory of Non-Sites" (1968), published in
Robert Smithson: The Collected Writings, edited by Jack Flam. Copyright © 1996.
Used by permission of the Estate and VAGA (Visual Artists and Galleries Association).

Typeset in Centaur by M&S, Toronto
Printed and bound in Canada

This book is printed on acid-free paper that is 100% recycled,
ancient-forest friendly (100% post-consumer recycled).

McClelland & Stewart Ltd.
The Canadian Publishers
481 University Avenue
Toronto, Ontario
M5G 2E9
www.mcclelland.com

1 2 3 4 5   09 08 07 06 05

For A.M. to the west of me
And A.M. to the east of me.
They encouraged and inspired.

"By drawing a diagram, a ground plan of a house, a street plan to the location of a site, or a topographic map, one draws a 'logical two dimensional picture.' A 'logical picture' differs from a natural or realistic picture in that it rarely looks like the thing it stands for."

— Robert Smithson, *The Collected Writings*

A Map of Glass

*H*e is an older man walking in winter. And he knows this. There is white everywhere and a peculiar, almost acidic smell that those who have passed through childhood in a northern country associate with new, freshly fallen snow. He recognizes the smell but cannot bring to mind the word *acidic*. *Snow, walking,* and *winter* are the best he can come up with – these few words – and then the word *older*, which is associated with *effort*. Effort is what he is making; the effort to place one foot in front of the other, the effort required to keep moving, to keep moving toward the island. It might have been more than an hour ago that he remembered, and then forgot, the word *island*. But even now, even though the word for island has gone, he believes he is walking toward a known place. He has a map of the shoreline in his brain; its docks and rundown wooden buildings, a few trees grown in the last century. Does he have the word for trees? Sometimes yes, but mostly no. He is better with landforms. *Island* – though it is gone at this moment – is a word that stays longer than most; *island, peninsula, hill, valley, moraine, escarpment, shoreline, river, lake* are all

1

words that have passed in and out of his mind in the course of the morning, along with the odd hesitant, fragmented attempt at his name, which has come to him only partially, once as what he previously would have called the article *An*, then later as the conjunction *And*.

Tears are sliding over the bones of his face, but these are tears caused by the dazzle of the sun in front of him, not by sorrow. Sorrow and the word for sorrow disappeared some months ago. Terror is the only emotion that visits him now, often accompanied by a transparent curtain of blinding gold, but even this is mercifully fleeting, often gone before he fully recognizes it. He does not remember the word *gold*. He does not remember that in the past he saw the real colours of the world.

He senses an unusually cluttered form in his immediate vicinity: "a fence," he once would have called it. It would have brought to mind the "path-masters" and surveyors of the past, but now he knows it only as something that has not grown out of the earth, something that is impeding his progress. As he stands bewildered near the fence, he looks at the intricate shadows of the wire created by sunlight on the snow in front of him and the word *tangle* slips into his mind. He walks right through the tangle of the shadow, but is not able to gain passage through the wires themselves.

He does not remember what to do with a fence, how to get over it, through it, past it, but his body makes a decision to run, to charge headlong into the confusion, and in fact this appears to have been the correct decision, for he has catapulted to the opposite side and has landed first on one shoulder, then on his stomach so that his face is in the snow. Snow, he thinks, and then, walking, which is what he must do to reach the island. He gropes for the word *island*, and has almost conquered it by the time he is back on his feet. But the shape and sound of it slips away again before he can grasp the meaning, slips away and is replaced by a phrase, and the phrase is *the place the water touches all around*.

He knows the island was the beginning — knows this in a vague way, not having the words for either island or beginning. He must get to the place that water touches all around because without the beginning he cannot understand this point in time, this walk in the snow, the breath that comes into his mouth and then departs in small clouds like the ghosts of all the words he can no longer recall. If he can arrive at this beginning, he believes he will remember what was born there, and what came into being later, and later again, and later again — a theorem that might lead him to the *now* of effort and snow.

He begins once again to move forward. Often he bumps against trees, but this does not worry him because he knows they are meant to be there, and will remain after he has passed by them. Like an animal, he is stepping by instinct through the trees, branch by branch, the smell of the destination on the edge of his consciousness. While he is among pines, an image of an enormous raft made of timber floats through his imagination and connects somehow, for an instant, with the word *glass*, which, in turn, connects again, for just an instant, with the word *ballroom*. In this daydream there are men with poles standing on the raft's surface. Sometimes they are dancing. Sometimes they are kneeling, praying.

When he comes to a break in the forest, he is perplexed by an area of openness that curls off to the left and to the right. Then, quite suddenly, inexplicably, he remembers a fact about winter rivers and their tributaries, how they become frozen, covered with snow. He is momentarily aware of some of the natural things he used to think about. He enunciates, quite clearly, the syllables of the word *watershed*, then straightens his shoulders, attentive to, and briefly suspicious of, the deep, bell-like sound of his own voice.

He walks for some time on the hard, pale river, his left sleeve now and then brushing against the arms of snow-laden pines. Eventually his body comes to know it is exhausted and takes the decision to lie on the smooth bed of ice and snow. By now the sun is gone; it is a deep winter night of great clarity and great beauty. He can see points of light that he knows are stars, and yet he no longer knows the word for stars. When he rolls his head to the left and then the right, the still, leafless branches of the trees on the bank move with him, black against a darkening sky. "Tributaries," he whispers, and the word fills him with comfort, and also with something larger, something that, were he able to recognize it, would resemble joy.

He sleeps for a long time. And when he wakens he discovers that his body has been covered by a thick, drifting blanket that is soft and cold and white. The whole unnamed world is so beautiful to him now that he is aware he has left behind vast, unremembered territories, certain faces, and a full orchestra of sounds that he has loved. With enormous difficulty he lifts his upper body from the frozen, snow-covered river and allows his arms to rest on the drift in front of him. The palms of his gloved hands are open to the sky as if he were silently requesting that the world come back to him, that the broken connections of heart and mind be mended, that language and the knowledge of a cherished place re-enter his consciousness. He remains alert for several moments, but eventually his spine relaxes and his head droops and he says, "I have lost everything."

This is his first full sentence in more than a month. These are his last spoken words. And there is nobody there to hear his voice, nobody at all.

The Revelations

$\mathcal{A}$t the northeastern end of Lake Ontario, toward the mouth of the wide St. Lawrence River, a number of islands begin to appear. Some of these are large enough to support several farms, a pattern of roads, perhaps a village, and are still serviced year-round by a modest flotilla of ferries that departs from and returns to Kingston Harbour. One or two minor islands are completely deserted in winter, having always been summer playgrounds rather than places of employment. There is a small, difficult-to-reach island, however, an island that a hundred years ago was busy with ships and lumber, that is now a retreat for visual artists and, for this reason, its single serviceable nineteenth-century building – a sail loft – has been renovated as a studio where an artist can live and work for a limited period of time, alone.

On the final leg of his journey from his Toronto studio to this sail loft, Jerome McNaughton had kept his back to the main-land view and had watched instead the skeletal trees and tilting grey buildings on the island grow in size and, behind them, the less definable evergreen forest enlarging, like a motionless black cloud, as the boat drew nearer. He had chosen the equinoctial period of late winter, early spring for his residency on the island, and he had chosen it because of the transience he associated with the heavy sinking snow, the dripping icicles of the season. The difficulty of arriving at the place when the ice was either uncertain or breaking up altogether – the enforced isolation brought about by these difficulties – had attracted him as well.

He had left Kingston Harbour on a Great Lakes coast guard icebreaker, onto the deck of which he had loaded a stack of firewood, enough food to last at least two weeks, a couple of bottles of wine, some whisky, camera equipment, and a backpack filled with winter clothing. Though it was only a mile or so from the city to the island, the men on board had thought him reckless to go out there alone in this season. They were somewhat mollified, however, when he admitted he had a cell-phone. "You'll be using it soon enough," the captain had ventured. "Pretty grim out there this time of year."

Grim was what Jerome was after. Grimness, uncertainty, difficulty of access – a hermit in a winter setting, the figure concentrated and small against the cold blues and whites and greys that made up the atmosphere of the landscape, the season.

Ordinarily, residencies were not permitted during the winter months, but the officials at the Arts Council were aware of his work, his growing reputation, knew from his *Fence Line Series* that he preferred to work with snow. A young woman whose voice had indicated that she was impressed by his dedication had made the arrangements with the coast guard and had speeded his application through the usual channels. In a matter of days he had found himself standing on the deck of the vessel, his whole body vibrating with the hum of the engine, then shuddering with the boat's frame as the bow broke through the ice. The wind had repeatedly punched the side of his face, and there was not much warmth in the late March sun, but Jerome had preferred to remain on the deck in order to dispel the impression that there was a look about him, a scent maybe, that suggested longing, dependence.

The captain was right though, he would be using the phone soon, to call Mira. He had to admit that he wanted to please the girl who had miraculously remained in his life for almost two years, that he felt concern for her and must honour her affection for him. In this way he had been able, so far, to slip easily around the disturbing truth of his own feelings, the pleasure he felt when thinking of her, and the ease with which he remained in her company. He was almost always thinking about her.

For the time being, however, he had stayed focused on his journey, intrigued by the dark, jagged path the boat had left in its wake as it moved through the ice. It would be a temporary incision, he knew, one that would likely be healed by the night's falling temperature, so he removed his camera from the case, then leaned against the railing and photographed the irregular channel. The opened water was like a slash of black paint on a stretched white canvas. *Breaking the river.* He liked the sound of the phrase and would remember to record it in his notebook once he got settled in the loft.

He himself would never be a painter, considered himself instead a sort of chronicler. He wanted to document a series of natural environments changed by the moods of the long winter. He wanted to mark the moment of metamorphosis, when something changed from what it had been in the past. He was drawn

to the abandoned scraps of any material: peeling paint, worn surfaces, sun bleaching, rust, rot, the effects of prolonged moisture,
as well as to the larger shifts of erosion and weather and season.
This island was situated at the mouth of the great river that
flowed out of Lake Ontario, then cut through the vast province
of Quebec before losing its shape to the sea. The idea that he
would be staying near the point where open water entered the
estuary excited him and made the pull of the island stronger.

Now, two days after he'd arrived, as he stood near the shore with
the camera around his neck and a snow shovel in his hand, the
phrase *breaking the river* was still fresh in his mind, and he had
decided that it would be the title of the first series he would
complete on the island. He observed, by looking at the shards
of ice along the shoreline, that, in effect, the river was broken by
the island. Arguably, this would be true even in summer in
that the island would break up the current of the water that
passed on either side of it. But it was the ice that interested
Jerome, the way it had heaved itself up on end and onto the
shore like some ancient species attempting to discard an aquatic
past. He plunged the handle of the shovel into a nearby drift,
where it remained upright like a dark road sign. Then he walked
away and began to search the surroundings for slim fallen
branches of a suitable length.

   He would use these branches as poles to mark out the
perimeter of the site, about twenty square feet comprising one
scrub bush, one small hawthorn, a sizable area of deep heavy
snow, and the ice along the shoreline. Much would happen here,

he knew, in the next week or so, some of it natural, some of it
caused by his own activities. When the poles were in place, he
began to record the site with his camera, first the whole area and
then the details, reducing the depth of field in stages until he was
able to capture a thorn on the small tree, a grey, cracked milkweed pod with one remaining seed attached, and the feathered
end of a tall weed stalk that had somehow not succumbed to the
weight of snow. He enjoyed these exercises in increasing intimacy
and was warmed by the knowledge that he would be able to
remain for a period of time in the vicinity of the natural references that would move him. He was also pleased by the remnants
of abandoned architecture that he had seen here and there on the
island, the way these weakened structures had held their ground
despite time and rot and the assault of a century of winters.

After Jerome and his family had drifted down from the north
in his early childhood, they had lived first in a small suburban
house and then in an apartment building perched on a cluttered
edge of Toronto, far away from such haphazard architecture as
tool sheds, chicken coops, stables. And yet, his otherwise solemn
and often angry father could be brought to levels of brief excitement in the vicinity of childhood projects such as the making of
kites, go-karts, tree houses, or forts in scrub lots slated for future
development. The engineer in him, Jerome now believed, that
part of him he had been forced to abandon when the mine
closed, could be miraculously, though falsely, shaken into wakefulness by something as simple as the placement of load-bearing
lumber in a tree. His enthusiasm waned quickly, however, as did
Jerome's, and these projects were almost always left unfinished,
slowly decaying on the margins of the property, until Jerome

returned to them later and took a renewed interest in their construction and eventual restoration. After the horror of his father's death, Jerome would call to mind the structures on the now residential lots, and he found that he would be able to recall almost exactly the way a tree house had creaked in the wind, one loose board knocking against a branch, or the way the large nails had looked in his father's palm, his mouth, and then the same nails after a year or so, exposed and rusting during the decline of winter. Once, as a young adult, Jerome had walked all over the low-rental housing development that occupied what had been the vacant land, looking for the tree near a dirty stream where one of these projects had begun to take shape. But both the stream and its culvert were gone. There was simply no way to place even the few scraps of memory he had retained. His first project, then, would be an attempt to rebuild what he thought of as the few good moments of his childhood and would take the form of temporary and incomplete structures – playhouses of a sort – that he made himself with torn plastic, discarded wood, and broken objects found in abandoned lots.

He remembered a journey he had taken a few years before on a train, a journey he was able to recall now only in terms of the images he had collected while staring out the window. Trains were vanishing from this vast cold province and were often half-empty, those who were there likely being too poor to afford the kind of cars he saw on the freeway that for part of the journey mirrored the path of the railway. He had been thinking about the early days, about vacations taken when his father was still relatively well, holidays that were spent in one provincial park or another, he and his parents crammed into a tent that his father

had bought at an army surplus store. He remembered the sight
of this tent, an ominous bundle strapped to the roof rack of
their deteriorating car along with the bicycle that his father had
given him and that he seldom rode. He also recalled the camp-
fires his father had taught him to make, the configurations of
which were named after architectural structures such as "the
teepee" or "the log cabin." It wasn't until years later that he realized that the ignition of these constructions, made so that air
might move more freely and carry fire farther, faster, was like the
burning of the history of the country in miniature, a sort of
exercise in forgetting first the Native peoples and then the settlers, whose arrival had been the demise of these peoples, settlers
in whose blood was carried the potential for his own existence.

He recollected the cool mornings of these not-quite-real
episodes in his childhood, how mist rose from the lake (though
he could not recall which lake) in long scarves, and how his
father, briefly enthusiastic, would insist on a dawn swim. As the
day unfolded, however, the mists would evaporate, other campers
and their hot dogs and radios would come into focus, and his
father's mood would shift down into irritability. He would begin
to compare the spot unfavourably with the camp life he had
known in the bush when the mine was still operating. "Is there
no place left?" Jerome had heard his father whisper once through
clenched teeth, just before he had begun to berate Jerome's
mother about the food she had brought, her recent haircut, the
way she looked in a swimsuit. Then everything about the trip —
the campground, the tense meal shared near a dwindling fire, his
mother standing quietly by the water with her imperfect flesh
exposed — became tawdry, embarrassing, something to be quickly

discarded and forgotten. He would always respond to his father's temperament in this way, would know that any attempt to create family joy would deteriorate in the face of his father's disapproval, anger, or indifference.

It was the indifference that Jerome would try to take into his own nature: the combination of brief infatuation followed by an apparently casual lack of care. This, and the solid knowledge of the mutability of a world that came into being and then dissolved around him before he was able to fully grasp what it was trying to be, what it had been.

When the tracks had swung away from the highway, Jerome had become aware of the fencelines of the fields that were passing, one after another, by the train window. It seemed to him that these frayed demarcations made up of rotting cedar rails, fieldstones, rusting wire, and scrub bush were the only delineating features in an otherwise neutered winter landscape. The sole survivors, he had thought, glimpsing the irregular gestures of stunted Manitoba maples and listing wooden posts. (*Is there no place left?*) All of it in a state of heartbreaking neglect, destined to become the wilderness of asphalt, of concrete that he associated with the landscape of his later childhood. He had reached for his sketchbook, had drawn a series of overlapping lines on three or four pages, had made some notes about how these lines might be transformed into a three-dimensional installation within the confines of a rectangular room, and had experienced, for the remainder of the journey, the restless buzz that often announced the beginnings of a new conception.

He quickly became obsessed by the ruined fences, and a few weeks later he had borrowed a car, driven out of the city, and begun to search out remnants of rails, boulders, and stumps, sometimes tramping for hours through swamps and scrub bush following a line of decaying posts or a path defined by rusting, broken wire. He began to think of fences as situations rather than structures. Like an act of God or a political uprising, they seemed to him to mark the boundaries of events rather than territories. And like events, he felt that these fences had come into being as a result of a great deal of energy, flourishing on the edges of labour for a few hard decades, then collapsing onto a ground whose only crop now was an acre of windblown weeds.

Reading anything he could find on the subject, he learned about wedges and stakes, and about the much-coveted long, true split of cedar that resulted in six good rails to a log. He learned about rails that rested on notched "sleepers" and how those rails were fixed in place by wire. He learned about strong fences withstanding the assault of bulls and about weak fences that had permitted entire herds to drift into a neighbour's alfalfa. For a time he wished he had been born in the nineteenth century and had been appointed to a team of official "fence-viewers."

He attempted to reconstruct the frail, disappearing remnants of the fences on the indoor/outdoor carpeting of a city art gallery, had lugged boulders and fence wire, branches and decaying rails into the space and had made six lines that moved from the entrance to the far end of the space. Made uncomfortable by any kind of verbal explanation, he had not stapled the customary lyrical passages to the walls so that beyond the announcement "Fence Lines," which the dealer had pasted on the front window of the gallery, there had been no verbal apology for the exhibition. The black-and-white photographs on the walls of what he privately called "similar structures in the wild" had sold to some private and, in a few cases, small public collections, and had been the making of his reputation as a young artist to watch. The sense of loss that he felt in the face of decay, of disappearance had gone unnoticed, uncommented upon by the critics. But it was this loss that he had taken with him on his latest trip out of the city, to the town of Kingston and across the ice-filled lake, the ice-choked mouth of the huge river, to the shores of Timber Island.

Jerome stood at the very edge of the island, looking at the ice, thinking of Robert Smithson's *Map of Broken Glass*, about how the legendary Smithson had transported pieces of glass to the New Jersey site he had chosen, had heaped them into a haphazard shape, then waited for the sun to come out so that the structure would leap into the vitality he knew existed when broken glass combined with piercing light. Smithson had been mostly concerned with mirrors at the time and yet had chosen glass rather than mirrors, as if he had decided to exclude rather than to reflect the natural world. According to something Jerome had read, however, Smithson had come to believe the glass structure he had created was shaped like the drowned continent of Atlantis. Perhaps this explained his need to use a material that would suggest the transparency of water. But Jerome was drawn to the brilliance and the feeling of danger in the piece: the shattering of experience and the sense that one cannot play with life without being cut, injured. The sight of ice at this moment and in this place, ice rearing up against the shore of the island, the disarray of the arbitrary constructions that were made by its breakup and migration, seemed like a gift to Jerome, as if something electrical beneath the earth were sending signals to the surfaces of everything he was looking at.

The temperature had clearly risen in the week preceding his arrival and the deep snow was gaining in weight and plasticity. Jerome's footsteps remained embedded, small blue pools in sodden drifts, semi-permanent paths could be made from place to place, and the white surface was punctured by emerging grasses and shrubs, the shadows of which were like maps of rivers drafted on a white sheet of paper. The trees, in which he knew the sap would soon begin to rise, were beautifully placed, their branches vivid against snow and sky, the abandoned nests of birds and squirrels clearly evident. One tree in particular held his attention — an enormous oak with a thick trunk supporting a number of twisted branches.

Although it was the end of winter, almost spring, there was something ripe and faintly autumnal in the soft glow of the light in the waning afternoon. A fine mist filled the air and gave a malleable look to shapes that one month earlier would have been so frozen and emplaced that interpretation might have been impossible. This cusp of a declining season, which held on not only to itself but also to the blackened twigs and stems and seed pods, to the bones of what had gone before, felt as exciting to Jerome as the uncovering of an ancient tomb. But it was not the quickening of nature that intrigued him, rather the idea of nature's memory and the way this unstable broken river had built itself briefly into another shape, another form, before collapsing back into what was expected of it.

When he was finished with the primary documentation, Jerome wedged the camera in the groin of the hawthorn, then laughed when he found that its odd appearance in that location made him want to photograph it. He removed the shovel from the drift in order to begin the first of the physical sessions of the project. Using the front edge of the shovel he drew a rectangular shape approximately eight feet long and three feet wide on the untouched surface of the snow, then he reached for the camera in order to photograph the lines he had drafted, which were wonderfully exaggerated at this moment by the angle of the low sun. He returned the camera to the tree and began to dig, creating an inner wall by using a plunging motion at the edges; then, with wide-sweeping gestures, he flung the excess snow away from the centre so that it would not disturb the surrounding surfaces. It was not easy going; the ice storms of the winter and every crust that had once been surface had formed a series of tough layers – like strata on a rock face – and often he was forced to turn the shovel around to use the handle as a pick or gouge. When he neared the frozen surface of the earth, he tossed the shovel aside so that he could hunker down and work more carefully with his hands. He wanted everything he was uncovering to remain in place, as it had remained in place since the first snowfall. Unlike some artists who had exposed the roots of trees, he would not call what he was doing "an uncovering," but rather would refer to the process as a revelation, and would entitle the photographs he would take of this area of the site *The Revelations*. As he was thinking about this title, a shadow near some small willows farther down the shore moved at the edge of his peripheral vision, and he sat back on his haunches to survey the outlying terrain. It was then that he saw the small carved angel emerging like an ice sculpture from the snow, and he tramped across the quarter-mile of white space that separated him from it. An old gravestone, he realized as he approached, most of which was still buried. Perhaps there was a modest graveyard waiting to be revealed by the spring melt. The angel looked like a solemn child, lost in contemplation and surrounded by a circle of fresh pawprints. It had not occurred to Jerome that there would be animals on an island only a mile long and half again as wide, but he supposed that the animal tracks must have been made by a muskrat or an otter, some kind of water's edge dweller shaken temporarily out of hibernation by the sun and the warmth of the day. Whatever it was, it had broken his concentration, made him aware of the declining light, and the sodden state of his gloves, and he returned to the site, plunged the shovel once again into the drift, and picked up the camera. When he reached the door of the sail loft, he turned toward the shore and photographed the site from a distance. Then he walked inside and carefully climbed the stairs, which were littered with an assortment of old tin cans, some filled with dried pigments, left behind, he assumed, by the previous resident.

Each time he entered the loft he was astonished by the wealth of space around him, the width and length of the enormous pine floorboards, the height of the sloping timbered ceiling. The building had the dimensions of a barn or a medieval granary but without the roughness of the former or the stonework of the latter, though the ground floor had a stone foundation, a barnlike odour, and was used to store all manner of tools and equipment;

some old, possibly original, some likely purchased recently by the
Arts Council for the convenience of the residents. At the south
wall there was a large window, a window that once might have
been a door where sails would have been pushed onto waiting
wagons. Jerome had read the historical pamphlet left on the table
for the edification of those visiting artists who, like himself,
would have no real knowledge of the island's past, and he knew
that the sails stored, mended, and occasionally fabricated in this
location were made for ships built in what would have been called
"the yard" outside and then launched near the spot where the
coast guard vessel had deposited him. There was little about the
single remaining quay that suggested the size and presence such
nineteenth-century mammoths must have demanded. He remembered that, as a child, he had tried to copy illustrations of such
vessels, but the time it took to render each line of rope, each
board and spar, each of the many sails on the various masts had
discouraged him and he had mostly left the drawings unfinished.
Thinking of these things, he realized that the disappearance of
such huge vessels from Kingston Harbour and from the quays at
Timber Island would have resulted in an absence so enormous it
would have been a kind of presence in itself. Gathered together
at docksides, tall masts made from virgin pines rocking in the
wind, the ships would have been like an afterimage of the forests
that were being removed from the country. And when the last of
the great trees vanished, this floating afterimage would vanish
with them.

    He walked across the loft to a counter on which rested a
hotplate, an electric kettle, and a microwave oven. He poured
some water into the kettle, plugged it in, and fished about in his

knapsack until he found the green tea that Mira, concerned about his well-being, had given him before he left the city. He would call her once he had a mug in his hand so he could tell her that he was drinking her tea and that he was thinking of her.

Jerome finished making the tea but did not call Mira right away. He stood instead at the window, looking out over the snow toward the frozen lake, wondering, if it might be possible, in summer, to see remnants of the old schooners through the waters of Back Bay, the location of the ships' graveyard. The wrecks were indicated on the map in the pamphlet as dark markings drawn in the shape of a schooner's deck. These flat, geometric forms immediately signalled obsolescence, just as the rectangular form he was digging into the snow, once he began to think about it, suggested a human grave. He was toying with the idea of making his excavations in the shape of a schooner's deck when he again noticed small animal tracks in the snow. Whatever had made these tracks had moved out of the scrub bush near the foundations of an abandoned, wooden house some fifty feet from the sail loft, had advanced in a westerly direction, then had changed its mind and looped around toward the junipers near the door of another abandoned building, which Jerome was able to identify as the old post office. Here a skirmish had evidently taken place and Jerome believed, even in this fading light and from this distance, he could make out traces of blood, traces of a kill.

How wonderful the snow was; every change of direction, each whim, even the compulsion of hunger was marked on its surface, like memory, for a brief season. He told Mira all of this when he called her, but forgot to mention the green tea and how it made him think of her.

That night Jerome was awakened by the noise of a tin can bouncing slowly down the stairs, followed by a dull, steady thumping. When he opened the door to the stairs, he found he was looking directly into the green eyes of a large orange cat whose fur was matted with burrs and whose expression was hostile. The animal hunched its back and exhaled a long hiss in Jerome's direction, then strolled calmly into the vast space of the loft and disappeared. Too filled with sleep to fully believe in this apparition, Jerome staggered back to the cot and did not open his eyes until morning when, sensing that he was being watched, he turned his head and again met the animal's angry green eyes. "Hello, puss," he said and was greeted with a low growl. He reached out a hand and the cat promptly attempted to bite him, despite the fact that it clearly had no intention of leaving his bedside and did not pay any attention to Jerome when he rose from the cot and dressed himself. Neither did it refuse the bowl of milk that Jerome offered while he was putting together his own breakfast.

Jerome pulled his cellphone from his pocket and called Mira again. "I'm drinking your tea," he told her, "and thinking of you."

"Good."

"And there's a cat that's come into the loft. Dirty orange. It's feral, I think, growls a lot."

"A cat on a deserted island?" said Mira, her tone almost skeptical.

"Summer people left him here, I suppose, so he's likely to have been on his own for less than a year. He would have some memory of being tame."

"And also a memory of being abandoned."

Jerome was silent.

"The lion," Mira said suddenly. "Saint Jerome in the wild with his lion."

Along with a tiny plaster figure of Krishna, Mira had tucked into his pack a small poster of Joachim Patinir's sixteenth-century *Saint Jerome in the Wilderness*, an image she always insisted Jerome take with him when he disappeared into what she called "the wild," which, to her mind, was located anywhere beyond the city limits. Brought up as a Hindu, she was fascinated by the Christian saints and their stories that were, for her, as distant and compellingly exotic as the various Hindu gods and warriors were to him. When they began to get to know each other, she had been delighted to discover that his mother and father had given him the name of a famous saint, though he assured her that religion would have been the last thing on his parents' mind.

After studying the image for a while, they had eventually come to understand that the several tiny lions in the vivid blue-and-green Patinir landscape they were so fond of — each lion engaged in a particular activity: chasing wolves, curled at the saint's feet, chumming around with a donkey, or standing in a field filled with sheep — represented only one lion and that the painting was episodic in nature, depicting a number of events from the saint's life. In the far distance the lion could be seen either conversing with, or preparing to attack, a gathering of people. Mira believed the lion was conversing. Jerome always insisted he was attacking. Mira had asked how he could be so certain that the lion was a male since it was so small it was difficult to tell. Jerome said the lion would not have been permitted to live in the monastery with Saint Jerome had he not been a male of the species. Mira had loved that phrase, *a male of the species*, and had begun to use it herself shortly after this discussion, often in reference to Jerome himself. "Because you are a male of the species . . . ," she would begin.

Jerome laughed now and looked at the cat. "This animal is as fierce as a lion, anyway."

"Tame him," said Mira, "and bring him back to the city."

Jerome had not given Mira a clear indication of when he would return to the city. He would not be pinned down in that way, wanting to retain both flexibility and control. "I don't think there is much chance of that," he said.

"No chance of bringing him back to the city?"

"No," he said, "not that, exactly. I just don't think he's going to co-operate when it comes to taming. Looks like he's been on the loose for a while. He won't give himself over so easily to trust, I think. He might feel that he needs to protect himself."

The cat kept his distance but followed Jerome everywhere. When he was working, the animal either sat on a tall bank of snow watching his efforts with what appeared to be mild disdain, or it coasted back and forth inside the areas Jerome was excavating with its head high in the air and an ominous growl in its throat any time Jerome came too near. These dugouts, as Jerome thought of them, were assuming the shape of a ship's deck. Sometimes, after he had drawn the outline of such a dugout on the surface of the snow, the cat lay down in the middle of the area he was hoping to excavate and refused to budge, spitting and lashing its tail when Jerome attempted gently to remove it with the shovel.

Once, when Jerome became angry, he dug under the cat and tossed it along with a load of snow onto a nearby bank, where the animal scrambled to a seated position and remained in place, scowling. Two or three times a day, without warning, the cat would dash off toward the copse at the east end of the island. It always returned, however, and Jerome was once interrupted in the midst of photographing an excavation by the sound of crunching coming from one of the dugouts behind him where the cat was crouched over the rapidly disappearing body of a bird. Later, while photographing the remains, Jerome determined by the tattered remnants of red and black plumage that the bird had likely been a robin, the harbinger of spring.

By now the ice, both in the river and in the lake, was beginning to completely break up: the water was rising and the floes that were passing the shore of the island looked like parade floats featuring non-representational sculpture. Late one afternoon when the light was particularly intense, Jerome photographed several of these ice forms with a colour film. Then, with the cat in tow, he walked back to the loft on the path he and the animal had tramped into the snow. On the stairs the cat was so constantly underfoot Jerome began to feel as if his ankles were being bound in a blur of orange wool. Because of the soundless fluidity of the animal's movements, Jerome had decided to call it Swimmer.

"Swimmer," he said now, "are you hungry?" and as he spoke he realized that he had begun to talk to the animal some time ago, that he had explained his work to it, scolded it, and occasionally used terms of endearment. "So this is what solitude does to you," he said to the animal when it reappeared, "you begin talking to unfriendly cats."

Swimmer growled in reply, and ran away from him.

That night, it started to snow and Swimmer sat looking almost picturesque near the large window, watching the flakes descend through the beams of the one outdoor light in the yard. Jerome had given him — he had decided that a cat this large must be a neutered male — a portion of the tinned tuna fish he had had for supper and this seemed to have put the cat in a more placid mood. Jerome himself was far from placid and angrily paced the loft floor, glancing now and then with irritation at the snow, worrying about the accumulation in what he now called his *Nine Revelations of Navigation*. He feared that, unless he scraped the interiors out with a shovel, it would take him hours by hand to bring the bottom of each shape back to what it had been earlier in the day. But, having never before broken the surface of the earth in his work, he would do his best to avoid the disturbance a shovel might cause to what he believed was the purity of scattered twigs and blackened leaves.

Eventually he stopped pacing and turned his attentions to the cat. What a mangy, rough-looking beast! Weren't cats supposed to clean themselves up? An idea struck him. He searched for and found his own comb, put on his leather gloves, and warily approached the cat, who, though suspicious and growling, did not turn around. Gently but firmly seizing him around the middle, he wrapped a towel around the cat's legs. Then positioning his knee against Swimmer's side so that he could free one hand, he began to drag the comb through the matted fur. The cat yowled, swung his head back and forth, and made every effort to bite the offending, gloved hands, but finally he gave up and submitted to the grooming.

It wasn't long before Jerome discovered the wound near the tail. Swimmer hissed and yowled more loudly when the comb neared the lesion and Jerome turned some greyish-yellow fur aside to explore the problem. The torn flesh was clearly infected and not in any way helped by the abundance of dirty fur that covered it. He let go of the animal and went to search for the antiseptic and a pair of scissors he had noticed in a kitchen drawer. After retrieving them, it took some time to locate the cat again, but at last Jerome discovered him crouching behind the shower curtain in the bathroom. He closed the door and ran some warm water onto a clean washcloth. Then he cornered the beast once again, cut away the fur near the infected spot with the scissors, and began tentatively to bathe the exposed skin. When, despite Swimmer's continuous growling, it was clear he would tolerate these ministrations, Jerome applied the antiseptic. When he was finished, Swimmer walked slowly across the room, lay down, and went to sleep.

The next morning, a warm front moved in, melting both the previous evening's precipitation and some of the old snow on which it had fallen, and Jerome was pleased to find that his markers were even more prominent than they had been the day before. The blackened maple leaves, twigs, and flattened weeds appeared to have been pasted to the floor of the excavations by the melt, and a rising mist once again softened the atmosphere. Jerome had brought his sketchbook with him, as well as several graphite pencils and a folding stool, for today he intended to draw the details of what he had exposed. He smiled when he thought of

some of his contemporaries who felt that the making of drawings was a stale, traditional way of exploring landscape, for this
type of rendering of the details of the physical world gave him
great pleasure. He had almost finished the third drawing when he
heard an unfamiliar sound, that of the cat's loud, sorrowful, and
repetitive meowing coming from somewhere close to the edge of
the lake. Realizing that this was the first time Swimmer had used
this noise so common to cats, and sensing some urgency, some
insistence in the tone, Jerome stood, placed the sketchbook and
pencils on the stool, and walked toward the tall brittle grasses
near the shore.

It took Jerome's mind some time to interpret the visual information being transmitted. Some of the smaller icebergs had moved
closer to the island during the night and were now lined up like
docked rowboats near the shore. He once again marvelled at their
mysterious, irregular shapes, but this time there was something
more. During their journey down streams and rivers, the icebergs
had picked up and incorporated into their structures twigs and
branches, as if consciously creating their own skeletons. Jerome
was intrigued by this, and was about to pull the camera from his
pocket when he noticed a large mass of ice that contained within
it a blurred bundle of cloth that seemed both enclosed in the ice
and emerging from it. Wondering if the ice had somehow
managed to trap a patchwork quilt or a collection of rags, he
moved closer, camera in hand, hoping for an interesting shot. The
slab of ice bumped against the shore and shifted slightly. It was

then that Jerome saw the outstretched hands, the bent head, the frozen wisps of grey hair, and he heard his own voice announcing the discovery. "A man!" he shouted to the air, to the nearby cat, to himself. "A man!" he shouted again. Then he spoke the word *dead*, just before he turned away and vomited into the snow.

One year later, in a small town thirty miles down the lakeshore, a woman woke early. There was no sound coming from the street below. Darkness was still pressed against her bedroom windows.

Her husband was sleeping and did not stir as she slid from the bed, crossed the room, and walked down the hall to the bathroom where she had laid out her clothes the night before: the dark wool suit and grey silk shirt, the string of small pearls, the black tights, white underwear, and conventional cream-coloured slip, the sombre costume that she believed would ensure that no one would look at her, or look at her for very long. She took no special precautions as she washed and dressed, running the taps and opening the drawers as she would have on any other morning. Malcolm had been out on a night call and had not returned until 3 a.m. He would be sleeping deeply and would not waken for at least two more hours. By then she would be on the train, part of the journey completed.

She stood for some time in front of the open medicine cabinet in the bathroom, gazing at the plastic containers that held her various pills. Then she closed the door and stared at her own face in the mirror. Her fair hair, some of it grey now, was pulled back, and her face, she was relieved to see, was composed, her grey eyes were clear. She could not say whether it was an attractive face that looked back at her. Someone had once told her she was lovely and not, in some ways, that long ago, but she knew that her features, her expression had altered since.

The previous morning, after Malcolm had left for the clinic, she had filled an old suitcase with stockings, one blue skirt and cardigan, underwear, a few cosmetics, two well-used green leather notebooks, a plastic bag containing squares of felt, scraps of fabric and wool, one antique album, and a worn hardcover book. Then she had lifted the bag from the bed where she had packed it and had placed it in the unused cupboard of the spare room. The interior of the case was pink and had elasticized compartments under the satin-lined lid where, at one time or another, some long-dead woman must have kept hairbrushes and clothes brushes, and perhaps a bottle filled with liquid detergent for washing silk stockings. That woman may very well have been her own mother, but she couldn't be certain because as far as she knew her mother had never been a traveller. The people who lived in this rural County stayed home. Year after year, generation after generation. The geography of the County discouraged travel; trains no longer visited any of the pleasant towns of the peninsula where she had lived her entire life. She would have to drive for almost an hour to reach Belleville, the larger mainland town where she would catch the train that would take her to the city. The word *city* had hissed in her mind all week long, first as an idea, then as a possibility, and, finally, now as a certain destination.

After washing and dressing she went into the spare room, removed the suitcase from the cupboard, and carried it with her down the unlit back stairs and into the kitchen where she placed it on the table. On a desk facing the large kitchen window was the tactile map she had been making for her friend Julia, its rhinestones, tinsel, and bits of folded aluminium foil glistening under the single lamp she lit. Placed carefully beside it were the several diagrams and drawings she had made of the location Julia next wanted to visit: an abandoned lighthouse on a seldom-used road at the very tip of the County. She glanced at the map, then looked through the window into the yard, which was partially illuminated by the kitchen lamp. It was the middle of a cold April and only recently had the thaw begun in earnest. At this moment everything beyond the kitchen windows appeared to be weeping; droplets were clinging to her clothes-line and shining on branches, and icicles that had disengaged themselves from the eaves were embedded like spears in the remaining heavy snow near the foundations of this house in which she had lived all her life. This is the anniversary of sorrow, she thought — everything moist, transitory, draining away, everything disappearing.

Her friend Julia, who had also lived all her life in one house, said that she could smell the beginnings of the spring melt on her farm long before those who were sighted were aware of its arrival. She could also smell the approach of storms on cloudless summer days and the presence of deer hidden deep in the cedar bush behind the barn. How she admired this in Julia, this sensory prescience; that and the calm that always filled her corner of the room like a soft light.

It was Julia who had sensed her grief, Julia who had suggested that she make the journey to the city. In the year since the newspaper article had appeared, she had mentioned it to her friend only twice, her voice as neutral as milk, the need to state the terrible fact of it perfectly disguised. The first time, Julia simply shook her head as she often did when presented with sad news items concerning strangers. The next time, however, in the midst of the retelling, Julia had suddenly straightened in her chair and had moved her hand across the space between them. "There's something here, Sylvia," she had said. "Something deep and private and important. I think you should meet this young man."

Sylvia had said nothing more, but in the silence that followed Julia's statement the idea of taking her story to the city had been planted.

She opened her suitcase again and placed the map, the sketches, two rectangular plastic containers — one filled with an assortment of threads, textured papers, and several ordinance survey maps, the other with string, twine, sequins, and rhinestones — into the interior. Then, once again, she quietly closed the lid, using her thumbs to ease the fasteners into place. She would take the materials with her and continue to work on the map. In this way she would keep the connection to Julia.

As she put on her outer clothing she wondered if she should leave a note and decided, finally, that she would. She took a pen from her purse and wrote the sentence *I have engagement* on the back of a grocery bill. The question that came into her mind at this point was one of placement. Where did people leave such messages: near the phone, under a magnet on the refrigerator, on the hall table? The kitchen, she concluded, would be no place to leave such a scrap of paper, to leave such a formal declaration, and so, after lifting the salt shaker from the table and dropping it into one of her pockets, she moved down the hall and went into her husband's study, his library. Selecting two volumes that dealt with medical syndromes, she placed one on top of the other in the centre of the desk, then glanced at the note on the top. "I have engagement," she smiled, testing the phrase. She reached for her husband's pen and added the article *an* to the sentence. Then underneath this she wrote, *Don't bother calling Julia, she has no idea where I am.*

In order to reach the front door she had to pass through the dining room, and as she did so she recalled that in the late afternoon, while the rest of the house darkened, the low light entering the room from the west window always caused the large oval of the table to shine like a lake, a lake with two silver candlesticks floating on its surface. She had watched this happen almost every day of her life, as long as she could remember, and it would continue to happen when she was not there: an abandoned table gathering light and her far away, not witnessing the ceremony.

Outside, she unlocked her car, hoisted the old suitcase into the front seat, climbed behind the wheel, and backed slowly, carefully away with this one piece of furniture still glowing, senselessly, in her mind.

The road that was taking her out of the County was lined by the homes of some of the earliest settlers in the province. Though it was still too dark to see clearly, she was aware that much of this old architecture was sad, neglected; some of the properties were completely abandoned. A few houses in the County had been restored by city people seeking charm, however, and always seemed to her to be unnaturally fresh and clean, as if the past had been scrubbed out of their interiors, then thrown carelessly out the door like a bucketful of soiled water. She knew the histories of the old settlers as well as she knew her own body. Better, in some ways. She knew the three-pronged ladders leaning against trees in autumn orchards, the arrival at barn doors of wagons filled with hay, the winter sleighs, the suppers held on draped tables outdoors in summer, the feuds over boundary lines, politics, family property, the arrival of the first motor car, the first telephone, the departure of young men for wars, the funeral processions departing from front parlours. She knew these things as well, as if they bore some weighty significance in her own life lived behind the brick walls of a house situated in the town.

A graveyard swept by the window near her right shoulder, scarred, decaying stones inscribed with names still common in her County. These tombs stood stark and pale in the early-morning light that lay in pools on the sooty snow surrounding the bases of the tombstones and in small snow-filled hollows scattered here and there in the fields. Trees were dark against the lightening sky, darker than they had been in midwinter when they often became frosted by a coating of snow. She loved the trees, their reliability, the fact that they had always been there on the boundaries of fields or along the edges of roads. She loved certain boulders for the same reason. And there were cairns left behind as a visual reminder of the past. These were some of the markers Andrew had spoken of. The old settlers, he had once told her, had left nothing behind but a statement of labour, nothing but a biography of stones.

Andrew's voice, telling her such things over and over, was inside her head almost all the time now. In the past she leaned toward his whisper, had once or twice heard him sing, and then, near the end, had heard the terrible noise of his weeping. A recording of the sounds he had made was always playing in her mind, but she was losing the shape of his face, the look of his legs and arms and hands, the way his body occupied a chair, or moved across a room toward the place where she stood, as she had always stood each time, waiting for him to touch her. She had never told Andrew how touch, until him, had been a catastrophe for her, how having leapt over the hurdle of touch, he would then become a part of her — without him ever being aware of this — how the idea of him would be like something she was carrying with her, like an animal, or a baby, or a schoolbag, or maybe something as simple and essential as this purse that rested on the passenger seat of the moving car.

Afterwards she would rise and dress, cross the orchard, walk to her car, and drive the concessions with the smell of him still on her, wanting to keep this with her, not bathing until minutes before Malcolm returned from the clinic.

And then would come the distant days, days when she would not, or could not, inhabit her own body, as if she had taken the decision to go with Andrew wherever he had gone, as if she were out of doors mapping the scant foundations of houses abandoned by vanished settlers, or following the vague line of an old, disused road, though she did not see such things in her imagination. Then, gradually, she would feel her self begin to return, tentatively, like a guest anxious not to take up too much of her time, and a certain taste or smell would connect her to the present for a moment or two: that, or something like the sight of poplar leaves flickering in an otherwise invisible breeze just beyond the glass of the kitchen window. If it were winter, she might become focused on the movement of flame, the snap of cedar kindling, and then the satisfaction one feels when a piece of hardwood surrenders itself, finally, to the inevitability of combustion.

It was Andrew's voice that now fuelled the engine of this car, his voice that pushed down on the accelerator, his voice that chose the distance, the speed, the direction.

She slept on the train, slept as she often did when confronted by noise and unfamiliarity, willing stimuli to move away from her until a curtain of dark dreamlessness closed across the scene. She awoke an hour or so later in a swaying interior to the sight of the tattered edges of the city under a cold blue sky. Sunlight was pushing past the dust on the window, covering her hands and lap, and making her uncomfortably warm in her good wool coat and her winter boots. Someone rustled a newspaper behind her. Someone else across the way was buttoning the coat of a squirming child. A uniformed man careered down the aisle shouting the name of the city as if, without this announcement, no one would notice it was there, as if it would slip by, ignored. The city was not something she was going to be able to ignore. She was going to have to enter it. She was going to have to manage.

After walking stiffly along the cement quay, her purse in one hand, her suitcase in the other, she descended a flight of marble stairs, then walked up a long, sloping ramp into the great hall of Union Station, remembering that as a child she had been led by

her mother into this overwhelming world for a series of appointments deep in the city, and that the child she had been had often
refused to move through the huge room until she had read, high
on its walls, all the carved names of places that did not exist on the
maps of her County. Vancouver, Saskatoon, Winnipeg: unfamiliar, foreign-sounding names that would be forever associated in her
mind with the disturbing cacophony of the trains and the porten-
tous, smooth atmosphere, the hushed tone of the appointments.

The doctor she was being taken to see had an office at Sick
Children's Hospital, an office in which he kept a dollhouse with
three dolls that he wanted her to play with. "Why not call the
lady doll Mommy," she remembered him saying, "and the man
doll Daddy? The littlest doll can be you." All of this had confused and disoriented her. She had never liked dolls and could
not understand why this man wanted her to pretend the small
figures were her parents or herself. She developed ways to shut
out the doctor, her mother, the dollhouse: she could think about
china horses, for instance, or the County atlas she had memorized, or she could let a succession of rhymes play in her mind.
Eventually she learned how to disregard the enormous hospital
itself and all the pyjama-clad children who lived there. "Sick
Kids," she had heard her mother call it when talking on the
phone. "Robert hopes the doctor at Sick Kids can do something,"
she would say, adding ominously but also almost hopefully, "She
might have to be admitted."

She had always believed that this admission had something
to do with confession, that the fact of her would have to be confessed, that she would have to be admitted to, or would herself
have to admit to some crime or another. And, indeed, once she

was in the presence of the doctor, his soft questions had always seemed like an interrogation, an attempt to pry from her some sort of dark revelation. She had remained resolutely silent, however; she hadn't admitted anything, even though she knew her punishment would be her mother's anger, her mother's refusal to look at her all the way home on the train. And later, when she lay in her room facing the wall, she would hear the adult argument begin, her own name tossed back and forth between her mother and father long into the night.

She was fifty-three years old now and had never been alone in a city before. Still, since childhood, she had been an expert map-reader and, after finding the name and address in the city phone-book kept in her town library, and marking the location on a map, she had believed that, at least in the matter of way-finding, she was prepared. And, of course, each year since adulthood, she had spent the odd day in one of the larger towns of the County, had been peripherally aware of people hurrying, going about their business. Still, now that she had entered the city, everything about it seemed exaggerated, overstated, and the din almost defeated her at first. Then she formed a fist around the salt shaker that she had placed that morning in her pocket, put her head down, and counted the three blocks that she knew she must walk in a westerly direction away from a central intersection she had found, first on the map and now in the world.

"I am now in the world," she had whispered to the squares of cement that were passing beneath her feet.

She found herself standing at an alley. On the brick wall to the left was a list of words, and some numbers had been painted in a rough hand. The name she was looking for was on this list along with a title or explanation that read "Conceptual Fragments." Staring at the wall she was aware of herself in ways she had rarely been in the past, aware of how odd she must look in her good wool coat and her boots with the ring of fake fur at the ankles, aware of the old suitcase she was carrying, and the large black leather handbag she was clasping under her right elbow. Suddenly a young man with strangely coloured hair emerged from one of the doors partway down the alley and swung swiftly past her, turning left on the street with one quick glance back in her direction. "Hello, Mom," he said, laughing, as he bolted down the street. She knew instinctively that he was not the young man she was looking for, but that, nevertheless, the young man she was looking for could quite possibly be of his kind.

After this thought, she lost the courage to enter the alley, at least for the time being. At any rate, she had a task to complete. She proceeded to walk down the street and when she found a mailbox, she took from her purse a stamped envelope addressed to her husband, an envelope that contained the keys to the car. On the back of the envelope she had written *at the station in Belleville.* Nothing more. She wondered how long it would take him to fetch the vehicle, having a car of his own. And it would not be his first concern. He would be frantic, she knew, would be arranging some kind of search. There might even be police involved and a suggestion that she was incapable of looking after herself, a suggestion that she was too fragile to survive in the outside world. But they wouldn't find her for a while. She had told no one she was going. She had not even told Julia that she intended to take this journey.

When she returned to the alley she read the spray-painted words and numbers until she once again found the name she had been looking for. Then she peered into the passageway that she could now see was lined with a series of industrial-looking entrances and the odd, forbidding steel garage door. Each of these had a number on its surface along with a mass of coloured swirls and scrawls that she remembered from magazine articles was something called graffiti. She turned from this in a kind of confusion but did not leave the spot, and almost immediately she found herself focusing on the texture of peeling paint on the metal drainpipe attached to the wall near her shoulder. Several curls of dark blue, and a scattering of rust that, when she placed her gloved hand on it, covered the fingers like orange pollen. She remembered pollen from the woods, how once, long ago, the legs of her slacks had been dusted with it. "Anemone," Andrew had said as she bent to brush the gold powder from the cotton. "You're helping it to reproduce."

Nearer the asphalt the paint was holding better, and yet layers emerged in small islands of colour. She was lost in this for some time, lost in looking at the patterns, until the idea of islands brought her back to herself. She was here because of an island. She was not going home. She began to walk forward, across the old, soiled patches of ice — islandlike themselves — that littered the ground leading to the door with the number five on its surface.

There was no sign of a bell so she slapped her palm against the metal several times. Noise came from the interior, a scrambling, followed by silence. The sun unexpectedly plunged into the alley and struck a mound of ice that had been made by leaking drains directly in front of the threshold. Dangerous, she thought, be careful. She was fingering the salt shaker in her pocket nervously.

"Just a minute," a male voice called from the interior. "Hold on."

She held on.

This was a door that, as far as Sylvia could tell, could not be opened from the outside. As she was thinking this, the door swung wide to reveal a pale young man of perhaps twenty-five or thirty years who was standing in the shaft of sun. He was wearing an old flannel shirt and baggy pants covered with a number of loops and straps. His dark hair stood straight up at the back, as if he had just been roused from sleep, but his brown eyes were intelligent and alert, and his white skin was smooth. He looked at her face with a hint of suspicion, and then with curiosity at the suitcase she was carrying.

She had her opening speech prepared. "My name is Sylvia Bradley. I'm sorry to disturb you," she began, "but I am a friend . . . I was a friend . . . of Andrew Woodman and I was hoping . . ."

"The man who died," said the young man.

"Yes," she said, knowing she was beginning to tremble, "and I was a friend of his and I wanted to talk to someone, to Jerome . . ." She paused, unable suddenly to come up with the last name.

"Jerome McNaughton," the young man prompted. "I am Jerome McNaughton. Are you from his family?"

Then this was the person she had been looking for, Sylvia thought. "No, not from his family," she said. For a few moments Sylvia looked at the wet ground where a rainbow of oil was moving across a small puddle. Then, without lifting her gaze, she added quietly, "I've come all this way to talk to you. Will you let me come in?"

Jerome was silent, his hand still on the door, and, during this pause, Sylvia began to believe that her request would be denied. Then a slim, dark-skinned girl, dressed entirely in black, slipped up behind the young man. She had been standing, a dim silhouette, in his shadow, and her presence had barely registered in Sylvia's brain.

"Let her in, Jerome," this phantom said.

At first Sylvia wondered whether she would be able to cope with the cavernous space she'd been led into by these young people. There was an odd kind of music playing and, worse, competing with this were several rows of fluorescent lights. She had always believed she could hear the sound of artificial light and, as a result, had only once ventured into a department store, where the dissonant, rasping sound of the light had proved to be too much for her. Here, however, there was only a dull hum, a kind of undertone to the music. There were stacking chairs placed randomly, it seemed, around the room, a long chipped counter with a sink in it and a toaster on it, a low table on which rested a few stained cups, an ancient refrigerator growling in the corner, and one old sofa covered by a blanket as well as by a considerable amount of orange cat hair. In a further room, created by a partition, she could see part of a mattress on the floor, and the dim flicker of a computer sitting against the opposite wall. At the end of the room in which she stood there was a red door in the centre of a wall made of cement blocks. On this door were the words *Conceptual Fragments*.

The girl had followed her gaze. "The studio's in there," she said. "Where Jerome works." She reached forward, gently took the suitcase from Sylvia's hand, then placed it on the floor beside the sofa. "I'm Mira, by the way. Would you like to sit down?"

Thinking of her coat, of the cat hair, Sylvia chose a chair. The young man and the girl sat on the sofa. For the first time Sylvia noticed the jewelled stud at the side of the young woman's perfectly shaped nose. She could have lost herself in the glint of that, and in the features of the girl's lovely face, but remembered her purpose and shut everything — the room, the girl, the light — out of her mind and turned her attention to Jerome. "I want to talk to you about Andrew Woodman," she began again, with great formality. "I read that you were the one who found him."

"He has nightmares," said the girl. "He might not want to talk about it." She moved protectively closer to the young man and softly touched the top of his head, his hair. Jerome pulled back slightly from her touch and looked at Sylvia. "No, Mira," he said, "Leave it. It's all right."

Not to be put off, the girl linked her arm through Jerome's and rubbed her cheek against his shoulder.

An echo of this gesture touched Sylvia's mind. A room, the warmth of skin, a wet mouth on the inside of an arm, long quiet avenues of intimate speech were permanently webbed across her memory. Into the texture of her mind were woven these inescapable memories of tenderness, memories that now brought her nothing but pain. There was no longer any escape available to her in the comfort of her known world, never mind in disorienting, unfamiliar interiors. The young people's faces were serious, almost shocked, and she knew how she appeared to them: a middle-aged, well-dressed woman in a brown wool coat, perched on the edge of her chair with her leather handbag balanced on her knee, a silk scarf at her throat, the ridiculous boots with the fake fur circling the ankles.

"Yes, I did find him," said Jerome. "I was trying to make some drawings so I was quite near the shore, but really it was the cat that led me toward the spot. If I hadn't been right there at that particular moment, I might not have seen anything. I wanted to photograph the ice, anyway, and because the cat —"

"Let her speak, Jerome," said the girl softly.

Jerome leaned toward Sylvia. "Sorry," he said. "Just take your time. There's no hurry."

Sylvia found that she was unable to respond, was almost undone by this suggestion of sympathy.

The girl was the first to break the uncomfortable silence. She rose from the couch and disappeared into what must have been a bathroom at the far end of the room, emerging seconds later with a tissue in her hand and a large orange cat at her heels. "Here," she said, offering the tissue, "take this." Then, glancing at the suitcase, she asked, "Have you come from far away?"

"I'm a doctor's wife," Sylvia replied, "from Prince Edward County. I left there this morning."

"Eastern Ontario . . . ," Jerome offered, "not far from —"

"No, not far from Timber Island, not far from there."

"I was on the island to work," Jerome explained to Sylvia. "The moment between seasons, nature in transition, full of possibilities . . ."

Overhead a complicated series of pipes and wires snaked toward each of the four walls. Some of the pipes travelled down to the floor, where they connected with a couple of radiators, which had been painted white. Sylvia's eyes followed the pipes for a moment or two, then came to rest on several framed diagrams that were on the wall at the opposite end of the room. She thought she could identify a rock face in the drawings, and maybe the leaves and branches of a tree, but most of the surface seemed to be given over to a quantity of measurements scribbled in pencil. For a period as a girl, she herself had been very attached to measurements. She remembered an old metal measuring tape, originally belonging to her grandfather, which, as a child, she had liked to carry around with her from room to room and sometimes even when she ventured out of doors. Eventually she had tabled the measurements of almost everything in and around the house in a series of notebooks not unlike the one she now carried with her. One summer she had measured the yard, the growth of bushes from one week to the next, the diameter of flowers that had appeared overnight. If there was going to be change, change she could not control, she wanted at least to be aware of it, of what shape it was taking. There had been a small brass lever that when turned would retract the inches, in order to stop measuring. When had she last removed that essential object from a drawer, and then replaced it? When had she stopped measuring?

The cat was sitting in front of Sylvia, regarding her with a fixed but neutral gaze. She hoped it would not try to jump up onto her lap. She could not tell what Jerome might be thinking but, like the cat, he was regarding her quietly.

"I've lived," she said, "all my life in the same house. And my father's people lived there before me." An image of the oval table slid across her mind. The late-afternoon light would be on it now, and she not there to see it.

Jerome looked at her with interest. "Really?" he said. "Then you are settled," he continued, "a settler." He looked at the girl beside him. "We haven't lived together two years yet, and we've moved three times."

Sylvia could not imagine these moves, this drifting from one place to another. What, she wondered, had they been leaving behind?

"It's very hard," said Mira. "Very hard to find good studio space." She waved one arm in the direction of the red door Sylvia had noticed earlier. "This was just luck, really, that and word of mouth. When you hear about something, you have to act fast."

The sound of a siren pierced the room and Sylvia found herself becoming conscious of the vastness of the city, of people talking — *word of mouth* — of plans being made and carried out, of accidents taking place, of events unfolding while she sat in a white room with two young people she had never met before. Finding it cruel in its arbitrariness and impossible for her to control, the multiplicity of places and relationships connected to other people's lives was something she tried to avoid thinking about. Now the fact of all this interaction seemed overwhelming, and, for a moment or two, she had to fight back the urge to go back to the station, to board the train that would return her to the place she had come from. "I'll stay somewhere nearby," she said, reaching down to touch the handle of the suitcase. "Is there somewhere near . . . ?"

"The Tilbury," said Mira, looking briefly at Jerome, "but it's not posh."

"I'll stay there then." She had removed only eight hundred dollars from the joint account before leaving. And she would need to eat. She didn't know what the cost of a hotel might be, but couldn't bring herself to ask.

Jerome had moved away from the girl now and was standing near the door, shifting nervously from one foot to the other. He moved his hand through his hair, but said nothing.

"I'd like to be able to talk to you," Sylvia said again.

"I am involved with my work all day long," Jerome began, reasonably. "And then at night Mira and I sometimes go out, do things. It's not that I'm not interested in what you have to say, but I just don't see what I can do, how I can help. And, anyway, I'm not much good at listening." He smiled at the girl. "Mira can vouch for that."

Mira bristled slightly. "That's not what I said, Jerome, I said that you weren't much good at talking. There's a difference."

The fluorescent light emitted a kind of soft, grinding roar, as if someone in a distant part of the building were using a drill or a sander. Sylvia glanced around the room, searching for an advocate. "I had hoped," she said.

"I just don't know," said Jerome.

Mira had her knees pulled up under her chin, and her arms wrapped around her legs. "Why not let her come back, Jerome? You're not up to much at the moment. You haven't got a specific project, or at least not anything I've heard about."

"You found him," Sylvia said quietly. "You can't have forgotten that." She rose from the chair, then bent to lift the suitcase. "And because of that you brought him back to me."

Jerome was standing with his hands in his pockets now, but his spine was straighter and his expression less ambiguous than before. He looked as though he might be about to take a stand, to bargain. "I just don't know about the time," he said with a certain amount of assurance. "I need to concentrate, and I'm not sure that this is what I am supposed to be thinking about."

As she had many times in the past, Sylvia wondered how it was that other people were so easily able to control what they thought about, how they purposefully moved their minds from one subject to another.

"Could you come back in a couple of days?" asked Jerome suddenly.

Sylvia felt a combination of hope and panic stirring somewhere near her heart. A couple of days. She remembered the kind of bargaining for time that she had been forced to engage in with Andrew on phones and at the thresholds of departure, the faint air of irritation — or was it pity? — that would enter his voice or his expression when she asked for something sooner or something more. She was well acquainted with bargaining. She looked down before speaking. "Please," she said, "please let me start before then."

Jerome glanced toward Mira. "All right," he said. "Tomorrow. But not until the afternoon. I'm not fit for company in the morning."

A wave of relief passed over her. "I'll be here at two," she said, pushing on the metal bar that opened the door to the outside. She glanced back at the girl. "Which way is the hotel?"

"Turn left at the end of the alley. Then left again, and two blocks south."

She was about to say thank you but found herself in the dimness of the late afternoon on the opposite side of the door.

$\mathcal{S}$ylvia had never experienced the bought neutrality of rented rooms and so had no idea what would be expected of her when, with a pounding heart, she approached the desk at the end of a lobby decorated with potted plastic plants, glass tables, and a few oversized black leather chairs. She managed to ask for a room but the demand, in return, for a credit card was even more unnerving. She decided to produce the partner card Malcolm had given her for household items, realizing that using it might prove to be the key to her whereabouts. "We keep the details on file while you are here," the clerk told her, "but you can pay with cash if you wish when you leave."

"In five days," she said. She might need a full week. She could bargain later.

Once inside the room she took stock of her surroundings, wanting to learn the objects with which she would live. Thankfully, there was not much to know: stuccoed walls painted off-white, a coffee maker with a small collection of tea and coffee supplies beside it, a television hidden behind the doors of a cupboard, a desk on which rested a leather folder containing information about the hotel, writing paper, a pen, and a few envelopes. Three chairs, a bed, two bedside tables, a telephone. In the bathroom were towels, washcloths, some tiny plastic bottles that she discovered were filled with shampoo, conditioner, and moisturizing cream. Tub, toilet, washbasin. Back in the room, she unpacked the album, the two green notebooks, and the hardcover book, and put away her clothes, but left the mapping materials in the suitcase. Then she walked across the floor to the opposite end of the room. Lined drapes covered a window that looked out to a brick wall. So, there would be no view to contend with and for this she was grateful: she knew she couldn't digest the panorama quickly enough for her to be comfortable with it. She opened the folder on the desk to the section entitled "Room Service." Sylvia knew about room service. When Malcolm had been away at medical conventions, the arrival of room service at the door of his room had sometimes interrupted the early-morning call he always made to her, to find out how she was managing alone. She managed well alone in the house with which she was so familiar, everything in it measured and learned years ago.

She would have to summon this room service — she hadn't eaten since the morning. Placing the order was another anxiety that would have to be dealt with, but she felt, somehow, she could manage if she did this right away with hunger gnawing at her stomach. She lifted the receiver, pushed a button beside the words *Room Service*, and talked to the woman who answered. When the meal arrived, fifteen long minutes later, the girl carrying it seemed flustered, overheated, and, to Sylvia's relief, not much interested in her. "Just leave the tray outside the door when

you're finished," the girl said as she left the room. Sylvia consumed the meal quickly, without thinking about the patterns on
the plates, the shape of the cutlery.

The cutlery she used each day in her house was engraved
with the flowing initials of long-dead ancestors, and the plates
were ringed with flowers, the names of which she had insisted on
knowing as a child. In the centre of some plates, entire landscapes had been painted, the odd shepherdess too, or a herd of
cows. At first as a very young child she hadn't liked these scenes,
the animals, the people, and often wouldn't eat if she knew such
things were hidden under the food. Gradually, after she had seen
them over and over again, she came to be quite fond of them.

Here in the hotel, when she had eaten everything she could,
she stood up and went over to the bed, removed the coverlet and
lay down, remembering how hungry she had always been when
she was with Andrew, even toward the end when the food
he brought was often impossible — a bunch of not very new
radishes, taken, she assumed, from his home refrigerator along
with a tub of sour cream and a breadstick or two — and then at
what would turn out to be their very last meeting when she
had asked if there was anything to eat, he had backed away, had
looked at her with suspicion, and had asked her exactly what she
meant by the question. She had approached him then with the
kind of comforting sounds that, in the past, she would have
reserved for herself when she lay huddled, alone in a room, and
had led him back to the bed where she opened his shirt and placed
her ear above the frantic hammering of his heart, one hand on the
side of his face, wanting to bring him to a state of rest, a state of
calm, wanting to pull his grey head toward her own chest, so that

he could weep and ask, out loud, where he was. So she could answer, "With me, love. Where you should be, with me."

Sometimes in those final weeks, because it had seemed that the only way to bring him back into the room was to escort him toward the sensations of his own body, she'd had to find new ways of giving him pleasure. And even in the midst of this, even when his response was charged with heat or laced with desperation, she would feel him begin to forget her as if the act in which they were engaged were unprecedented and terrifying. There were few words between them by then, and no laughter. His silences were huge, mythical almost, and, to her mind, full of portent. Everything about him, even when they were inches apart, suggested disappearance. When she said that she loved him, he appeared to be confused by the phrase, then embarrassed, then fearful – a man locked in a room with a stranger who was being inappropriately intimate. She loved him harder then for everything they had said and done together. For all the years they had been together, then apart, and then together once more. For everything she knew they were, again, going to lose.

She rose from the bed and moved over to the small desk where she had eaten her meal. She lifted the tray and, after opening the door, slid the object onto the carpeted floor of the hallway, glad to be rid of the clutter it contained. Walking around the room, she touched and then named aloud each piece of furniture several times. "Bed," she said, "table, table, lamp one, lamp two, chair, another chair." When she became tired of doing this she approached the bed, folded back the blanket, and lay slowly down on her back with her arms by her sides. Andrew's voice came into her mind, his gentle voice, the long sentences, the pause of punctuation. Then his broken voice, the quick frightened breath, his awful weeping. She closed her eyes and willed herself back to the bubblelike world of her childhood, a world whose skin had not yet been pierced, broken by the shock of connection, of feeling.

She remembered that when she was very young, before she had learned how to read, a story had been brought to her awareness in an unexpected way. On the bottom shelf of a bookcase in one of the downstairs parlours she had discovered a gift that had been abandoned years before by a child long dead: an album with a variety of large animal decals. The child in question (*To Mamie* was printed on the flyleaf) had evidently quickly lost interest in this volume as only three or four of the decals had been pasted into the book. The rest were still loose, tucked between the last page and the back cover. There were birds and horses and kittens and dogs dressed disturbingly in an assortment of human costumes, animals masquerading as sailors, police officers, scholars, bakers, but all exhibiting an innocent, unthreatening lack of expression. Then, inserted between the pages at the very middle of the book was a collection of large, square decals, depicting vibrantly coloured scenes, birds perched on branches and among grasses and flowers of streamside foliage.

She had begun to turn the pages of the book. Oh the berries and the feathers and the flowers – pure delight – and yet, and yet something was terribly wrong. The first decal portrayed a beautiful robin, his wings limp, falling back toward the earth because an arrow had pierced his side, producing one bright bead of blood.

On the shaft of the arrow, looking intently at the bird, was a large fly. In the next scene a fish rose from the stream with a saucer in his mouth, and into the saucer streamed the robin's blood. Off in the distance, a small sparrow was flying away, while at the end of a garden path sat a beetle sewing a white garment.

Then there was an owl standing with his spade near the large rectangular hole he had dug into the dark soft earth of the river-bank. A rook wearing spectacles on his beak and a pale flowing robe over his black feathers read from a long scroll of paper while a lark gazed steadily at an open book that rested on a pedestal. The next scene depicted a strange and upsetting bird she did not rec-ognize with a brown, oblong box strapped to his back. This was followed by a chicken and a wren carrying the box down a distant, winding road. The last was a decal Sylvia had looked at only once, for the normally expressionless faces of the birds were now filled with grief. An extraordinary dove in the foreground hung her head and allowed her tears to fall into the cavity the owl had created.

Until those paper decals resting inside a child's album, those birds, that riverbank, Sylvia had remained uninterested in the stories her parents had tried to tell her, not understanding the idea of sequence, believing all living things were as attached to their singularity as she was to hers. She had looked at picture-books, of course – mostly those that concerned animals – but the images in those books had seemed to her to be self-contained, static: a horse in a field, a spider on a web – nothing that suggested one scene related to another. Now, quite suddenly, she had come to understand that the blood dripping from the robin's neck and the flight of the departing sparrow were connected, and that from this blood, this flight, came both spontaneous events and

planned ceremonies, though she wouldn't have known the words
for such things at the time. And she had understood as well, that
from such a chain of images, from action and reaction, there
came the depth of feeling that was portrayed on the final illustration. A suggestion of this feeling seemed to be moving out
from the page and into her own mind in the same way that, in
winter, something her parents called electricity sparked from her
sweater onto her skin when she was dressing.

Years later, as a young adult, she had come across the poem:
the words that interpreted those images that she had so carefully
examined, then shunned. One verse stayed with her always.

Who'll be the chief mourner?
I, said the Dove, I'll mourn for my love
I'll be the chief mourner.

$\mathcal{J}$erome leaned against the door frame, the large orange cat in his arms. Mira was bent over the sink washing her face. He knew she had not registered his proximity, was not aware of his gaze. How lovely the back of her neck was; how lovely, and how vulnerable. And this ordinary, daily gesture, this lifting of a drenched cloth up to the face with both hands, the water falling like rain through the slim, brown fingers, how oddly it suggested weeping, mimicked grief. When she was finished she looked at herself in the mirror, staring it would seem into her own eyes as if to find the answer to a question there, while the liquid chugged slowly down the old drain. What did she see? he wondered. Beauty, or some minor imperfection he had never glimpsed? He thought that he was likely in love with her, but he also knew that at moments like this she could almost be unknown to him. She turned finally, met his gaze, then approached and punched him gently on the shoulder as she walked out of the bathroom. "You're just like Swimmer," she said, "so quiet I hardly know you're there."

❧

That night before going to sleep, Jerome looked at Mira's profile, the black fringe of lashes, the jewel in her nose, blue now in the light from the computer screen. It was never, he thought, fully dark in this room. He rolled over on his back and examined the ceiling. "This woman," he said, "she seems so . . . troubled . . . not shell-shocked exactly, but wounded somehow."

"She lost her lover, Jerome, no wonder she's wounded." Mira ran her hand over her eyes, trying to fight sleep.

"How do you know they were lovers? And anyway, it's something else I'm picking up, or at least something more." He smiled at Mira and touched her arm, knowing she would object to the suggestion that there could be something more than love. "I think that she is afraid . . . afraid of almost everything."

"But not too afraid to come here," said Mira.

"It wasn't easy, though. It was hard for her. I could see that."

"Yes, I could see that too. But they were lovers, Jerome. Believe me."

After Mira had fallen asleep, Jerome continued to think about the woman who had arrived so unexpectedly at his door, of her sudden intrusion into his life. He felt a certain sympathy toward her now, but it was laced with anxiety. An image of the frozen man came into his mind. The upper part of the body had been leaning forward, the motionless arms and open hands resting on the surface of the iceberg while the hips and legs remained encased. There had been frost in the hair and on the eyebrows and lashes and a sad, puzzled expression on the face. How could he possibly tell the woman about that? As usual lately, he had no idea what was going to be expected of him, no idea what to expect of himself.

For almost a year he had longed for a new site, a new project to capture his interest. He was still reluctant to develop the films from his time at the island — as if he believed the dead man he had found might appear in the wavering images that swam into focus in the darkroom — so he could not say how he was spending his time in the studio while Mira was at work. He had tacked a few drawings on the wall, he had shot several rolls of film, he had done some reading, but not much else. Long walks through the streets and alleyways of his neighbourhood had yielded only a new admiration for the miniature front gardens of the Italian and Portuguese immigrants who had settled in this part of the city, and the suspicion that on their small piece of ground in front of their houses, these people were working on projects more creative and useful than anything he had undertaken so far. He had photographed the gardens in the lushness of late summer, and then again during their decline in the fall, and had thought that he might somehow reproduce them — or at least the idea of them — in shadow boxes, but nothing tangible had come from any of this. It put him in mind of his father, how, once, during the last chaotic weeks of his life, he had inexplicably made a brief attempt to grow parsley in a pot near the door to the balcony of their apartment, and how the plant had withered from lack of water after his death. Anyway, they were Mira's gardens really, she being the one who first insisted that he look at them, whereas every other image he had worked with had been his own discovery. Lately there had been no real discoveries. And yet, the daylight hours had passed quickly enough while he waited for

the sound of her key in the door. Just last week he became aware
that the sound of a key entering a lock could be anticipated with
pleasure, rather than the dread he remembered from certain
nights in his childhood. He lay on his back now and listened to
Mira's even breathing, then turned on his side and placed one
hand on the bone of her hip. How small she was, how small, and
how strong, and how rooted she was in the changing world.

She had taken a different path than he had into the world of
art and, being the Canadian-born daughter of first-generation
immigrants with high hopes for the future of their children, her
choice, in some ways, had involved more personal risk. She had
told him that in the beginning she had followed the practical,
educational route suggested by her parents, and had never
allowed even the thought of disappointing them enter her mind.
But somehow she had stumbled into a fine arts class at her university, a class taught by a young woman interested in using
fabrics and thread, costumes and performance as an expression
of high art. Mira had been more intrigued by all this than she
had thought she would be when the nature of the class first made
itself known to her. (Jerome hadn't told Mira his own opinion
about this form of expression.) At the time he met her, she had
been making soft protective coverings for a variety of solid
objects: toasters, books, bicycle pumps, even, eventually, and
much to her parents' bafflement as she always delighted in telling
him, for her father's lawn mower. At first she had called her works
"cosies," having taken the idea from the gorgeously embroidered
covering for a teapot that her mother had brought to the New
World when she left Delhi. But later, when Mira's fascination
with all things Christian had taken hold, she changed the name

of her creation to "swaddles," a tip of the hat to the swaddling clothes she was told had wrapped the Baby Jesus in his manger. "I like the word. The sound of it," she had told Jerome when he had gently suggested that the whole notion seemed a bit bizarre. She had exhibited some of these in the gallery where she now worked part-time, the same gallery where she had first met Jerome. In the three years or so since they had been together, however, she had moved toward performance work, using the fabric either to cover herself or to create changing patterns on the floor, and Jerome could see she was really coming into her own.

When he looked at her now, he could hardly believe that she had once been merely a businesslike voice on the phone, a polite, efficient presence in the gallery where he showed his work. What amazed him most was how all of this formality could be softened by degrees simply by walking side by side down a street, sharing a meal, a conversation, eventually a touch, and now this most intimate of experiences, one impossible to imagine in the past, this lying side by side in the dark, allowing unconsciousness to wash over them, carry them toward the morning. There had been women in the past, of course, and occasionally he had found himself in their beds in the morning, but he had always rolled away, rather than toward them, had been courteous and discreet in what he knew was, and would remain, their territory, and had always felt a flicker of relief when, on the street, he had turned a corner, out of range of their windows.

Now he was warmed by the knowledge that Mira's calm face would be the first image that he looked at each morning. Her certainty in the face of his own lack of it. Until her, nothing in him had fully experienced either the anticipation of reunion, or the hollowness of separation. To him it had all been a great surprise, this combination of comfort and tenderness, pleasure and then the shared quiet aftermath of pleasure, and there were still moments when he was mistrustful, suspicious almost, of the ease with which he had walked into the partnership. In the past he had wanted not even the faintest suggestion of reliance to be a part of his character. For him, the implications of dependence teetered – always – on the edge of addiction and so he would often change, though never fully abandon certain social networks in the city. So far nothing and no one had kept him for long, curiosity being the only mood he fully trusted. But, as far as he could tell, for her, his entrance into her life was as natural as the air she softly inhaled and exhaled beside him here in this room that she insisted on calling a bedroom despite the pipes on the ceiling, the stacked cartons used to store clothing, the glow from the computer, the functional futon.

He recalled the spare rigidity of his parents' bedroom, the twin white headboards, so disturbingly like tombstones on adjacent plots, the matching polyester spreads, faded by repeated washing, the decorative lampshades and doilies that were his mother's sad attempt to bring some intimacy and joy into this corner of her life. He remembered quite vividly his mother's two or three good dresses hanging in the closet and her one pair of party shoes, so out of fashion, so seldom worn, and the stale boozy smell on his father's jackets overpowering the lighter smell of his mother's cologne. He also remembered the nights when his father was out late alone and everything – even the furniture – seemed to be anxiously listening for the sound of his key in the lock, nights when his father would return angry, accusatory,

smashing everything in his path. By the time Jerome was an ado-
lescent, the sight of his father's undershirts and shorts in the
laundry hamper, or his black rubbers by the front door, had dis-
gusted him. And then there was the inexplicable guilt he had felt
after his father's death, a guilt he could resurrect right here, right
now, without ever being able to make any sense of it. Sometimes
when Mira questioned him about that part of his past, he would
feel the buzz of anger rising in him, and not wanting to go
toward that, he would change the subject or make an excuse to
leave the room. Occasionally he left the room abruptly, without
making excuses.

She was the last person who deserved his anger. And he did
not want to leave her. But he would not let Mira within fifty miles
of his childhood, wanted none of it to touch her, to touch them.

$\mathcal{S}$ylvia jerked nervously into wakefulness but had no difficulty determining where she had been sleeping. The room was dark: the only evidence of morning was a narrow channel of light plunging toward the floor from a space between the curtains, a quantity of dust motes trapped within it. A river alive with molecular activity. She switched on the bedside light, then lay back against the pillows, thinking first, as always, about Andrew, and then allowing her thoughts to turn to Malcolm, who would be, by now, quite desperate with worry. She decided to telephone the clinic, which would not yet be open at this hour. She would speak to an answering machine, tell it that she was fine, and no one, nothing, would demand an explanation for her behaviour, a description of her whereabouts. Knowing this, she was able, quite calmly, to make the call, speak the required words. She realized as she did this that she had not undressed the night before, had fallen asleep on top of the bed fully clothed, exhausted.

In the bath she became agitated about what she would say when she met with Jerome. She had next to no experience

with meetings outside of those that, over and over, she and
Andrew had so carefully arranged in the preceding years. The
plastic flowers and the Formica tabletop of the restaurant where
they had sometimes shared a coffee took shape in her mind, and,
suddenly filled with anguish, she pulled her legs toward her chest
and placed her forehead against her knees. When she had been
with him, everything – the trees outside the window, the paper
napkins in their shining dispenser, the plastic bread basket on the
table – had been charged with the significance of his presence
and had therefore been impossible to look at without feeling, and
impossible to remember later without suffering. Now she opened
her eyes and focused on the chain of silver beads attached to the
bathtub plug. She knew that each tiny metallic orb would be
filled with reflections almost too small to see and that in each of
these miniature reflections there would be replicas of herself –
crouching, cowed under an assault of feeling. She thought about
the chain until her breathing became more even. Then she rose
from the tub, dried herself with the hotel towels, left the bathroom, and began to dress.

She went over to the desk and, with Julia in mind, sat down,
opened the folder, and took out the pen and two sheets of hotel
stationery. *I'll send the map to you as soon as I can,* she wrote. *You won't
be able to get out to the point for a while anyway . . . too wet.* She thought
for a moment. Others would have to read this letter to Julia, as
always. She made a one-inch fold at the top of the letter, tore the
paper along the seam, discarded the printed hotel address in
the wastebasket under the desk, and resumed writing. *I've gone on
a little trip, myself,* she wrote, *thanks to you.* Then remembering the
worn, echoing floorboards of the farmhouse where Julia and her

aging parents lived, she added, *Where I am there is carpet everywhere except in the bathrooms. I have the materials with me, however, and intend to work on the map. I'll use something else (haven't decided what . . . any suggestions?) for the water this time because it's quite exposed out there. The lighthouse is on the end of a point so the water can be quite rough. And the air smells different as well, or at least it will smell different by the time you get there later in the spring.*

Sylvia could not finish the letter. All that she would have to talk about later in the day was gathered like humid weather in her mind. This intensity of focus was not new but saying what was on her mind was something she had shied away from most of her life. She had almost confessed, however, to Julia, she'd felt so desperate the first time she had lost Andrew. But in the end she had lacked the courage. All that she had permitted herself to tell her friend was that she knew a man whose profession allowed him to explore not only geological phenomena but also the traces of human activity that were left behind on the textured surface of the earth. Julia had been delighted by this. "I understand that," she told Sylvia. "The whole world is a kind of Braille, if you consider things from that perspective."

"I'm a curious person," Julia had once said as they sat facing each other on either side of the kitchen table at the farm. "I want to know exactly what you look like."

Sylvia hadn't replied, but hadn't stood to leave either as she might have had she been elsewhere.

"I'll never learn your face because I know you don't like to be touched." Julia was smiling as she said this.

"How do you know I don't like to be touched?" Sylvia had been somewhat taken aback, though Julia's smile had told her

that the remark was not an accusation. On the wooden table
between them lay the tactile landscape Julia had wanted: a view
across Barley Bay from the wharf at Cutnersville; that and a
tactile of the route from the bus station to the end of the wharf.
It had only been recently that Julia had explained that, in spite of
her blindness, she was interested in views, in vistas. "Panoramas,"
she had said, motioning Sylvia to follow her into the parlour
where she ran her hand across the glass that covered a narrow
framed picture of cows grazing near a river. She not only wanted
to know how to get to a place, she had explained, she wanted to
be able to see what was in the vicinity.

"I know by the sound of your footsteps coming up the
stairs," Julia said, "and by the way you place your teacup in
the saucer. By the way you remain stiff, motionless in your chair.
I know that you are one of those people who don't like physical
contact. You're shocked," she continued, laughing. "You had no
idea how much of yourself you give away."

Julia had been the only person whom Sylvia had made an
effort to visit, until Andrew. At first she had driven out to the
farm at Malcolm's suggestion, to deliver the maps that he had
encouraged her to make, maps that described the things in the
physical world that Julia couldn't see. Later, she made the trip
simply because Julia interested her and because she had felt so
comfortable in the company of someone who was unable to look
at her. These had been her first purely social encounters and she
was surprised by how much she enjoyed them.

"The problem," she had begun uncertainly, "is just that I
can't ever classify touch, can't seem to understand degrees of
contact. All accidents, all injuries, involve contact, impact, don't

they? What is the difference, really, between touch and collision?"

"But, of course, there's a difference," Julia had said.

"I know that, but often it doesn't seem that way to me."

Julia's hands had moved across the surface of the pine table as if testing the familiarity of the grain. Her irises were soft, opaque, as beautiful and distant as planets. "There is being touched, and then there is touching, and attached to both of these things there is intention."

"But how do you know for sure what is intended?" As a child Sylvia had been certain that her mother's few attempts at embraces had been meant to restrain her, to cause her to stop doing something, or to move her in a direction other than the one she had wanted to take. "I like," Sylvia began, "to count on things being the same way they were the last time I saw them. Sometimes I think that the world is just too crowded, too full of people rearranging things, touching each other, making changes."

"It's like that for the newly sighted," Julia said quietly, then added, "or so I've heard. They are sometimes unable to cope with the profuseness of whatever is out there in the perceived world. Many of them apparently want to go back . . . back to blindness." She paused, thinking. "Perhaps there is something comforting about being able to choose a view rather than having it thrust upon you, to choose a view and then to touch a map. Maybe I'm more fortunate than I know."

Sylvia had watched as Julia sat back and relaxed in her chair. How wonderful she had looked right then, sitting beside the kitchen window, her blond hair and translucent skin and eyes making her seem ageless despite her forty-some years. She had been the first person Sylvia had wanted to spend time with, the first person, apart from Malcolm, with whom she had felt safe.

When Sylvia stood at the door that day preparing to leave, Julia had lifted one of her pale arms and had asked Sylvia to touch it. "Put your hand there," she had said, "just above my wrist." Sylvia hesitated. Then she placed her palm on the milk-white skin. "See how naturally your fingers curl around the shape?" Julia continued. "Human beings were made to touch one another."

Sylvia was surprised by the smoothness and warmth of her friend's arm. But then everything about Julia was soft, pliable. As she walked away from the farmhouse she thought about how Julia navigated through life. There were the maps, of course, and the cane, the tools she used for unfamiliar places. But the way she moved around the furniture, the obstacles in the rooms of her house, was so fluid, so filled with grace it was as if the structure of her body were made of some other substance altogether, something more forgiving than bone.

✗⌐

Malcolm had taught Sylvia about conversation. The introduction of a new piece of information usually requires that a question be asked, he had explained, even if the information comes about as a result of a previous question. This was an idea that the then much younger Sylvia had found to be absurd in theory and exhausting in practise. She had never let go of her fear of questioning but tried, anyway, to follow Malcolm's advice when they were in social situations. Later, when she had been with Julia, or Andrew, she had learned about the pleasure of conversation, the comfort of listening and being listened to, and in time she'd been able, quite naturally, to choose one path or another into long episodes of talk. There must have been questions, but she couldn't recall them, only how easily the pattern of speech and silence had fallen into place between them, until that pattern had begun to alter, break apart, become unrecognizable.

Now in midafternoon, with a series of frantic city images still present in her mind, she stood again in the alley at the industrial door of Jerome's studio wondering what they would say to each other. Jerome answered immediately when she knocked, opened the door wide, and then, without speaking, moved to one side to allow Sylvia in. As she stepped over the threshold, the large orange cat escaped into the alley.

"Swimmer!" Jerome called after the departing animal. "Oh well, we'll hear him when he comes back."

"I'm sorry, should I have tried to stop him?"

"No, no. He doesn't know the city all that well, but he's learning. He'll survive. He's used to the outdoors. I found him on the island, just before . . ."

"Just before you found Andrew."

"Yes," Jerome stood stiffly near the couch for a moment or two. Then he motioned to the chair Sylvia had occupied the previous day, "Maybe we should sit down."

Sylvia sat, then shrugged off her coat and let it fall over the back of the chair. Melting slush from the street pooled on the cement floor around her fur-topped boots. Only one bank of fluorescent lights was on today and through a window a wealth of sunlight was streaming. "Much warmer today," she said. This was one of the many climate-related remarks that Malcolm had suggested she use when he was trying to teach her the skills of

social interaction. She had learned many things about weather
during this period, had developed a fascination for it in fact,
watching reports on the television and reading books about
meteorology until her insistence that it should become the focus
of any conversation had led to Malcolm's banning of the subject
altogether. She smiled, remembering this, seeing the humour in
it now.

"Yes," said Jerome, settling himself onto the old couch,
"warmer."

The space between them became silent. Sylvia was aware of
a vacancy. "Your girlfriend?" she asked.

"She's at the gallery. An art gallery, where she works." Jerome
paused. "Her name is Mira," he offered.

"Yes, she told me. Mira," Sylvia repeated the name. "Almost
like mirror," she added.

"Almost. I hadn't thought of that." Jerome leaned against the
back of the couch, placed one ankle on his bent knee. Then suddenly he was on his feet again. "Are you comfortable?" he asked
"Warm enough? These old rads . . . but there is a thermostat. I
can turn it up if you like."

His nervousness made Sylvia aware of the tension develop-
ing in her own body. "No, no," she said, "this is fine."

Jerome sat down again and looked at her with what could
have been either pity or curiosity.

"I sometimes can't recall his face," Sylvia said. She hesitated
for a moment, then continued, "When I knew about you, I
thought that —"

"Don't forget that I didn't know him," Jerome interjected. "I
want to help but, because I didn't know him, I'm not sure what —"

"You . . . you came across him accidentally and so . . . so did I, and I've come to believe that without these accidents there really is nothing, nothing to life at all." How could it be that something unexpected, what she had in the past feared, had been what introduced her to Andrew? All this year, after his death, when she had been reading and rereading everything he had written in his notebooks, she knew she was attempting to make the accidental solid. Much of what he had told her was recorded there, but there was more. Was it Andrew's reconstruction that had filled in the gaps, or had his memory already grown so thin that imaginary events began to appear on the page? It had been impossible for Sylvia to find the solidity she sought.

"Tell me," said Jerome. "Tell me about Andrew Woodman, how you came to know him."

The evenness of his tone did not discourage her, made her, in fact, feel more relaxed than any degree of eagerness. Eagerness implied expectation and she had never been at ease with expectation.

And so she began to talk in a room with a steel door, cement walls, and no comforts, a room that had not been conceived with conversation in mind. She talked about the County, its farms and lakeside villages, its graveyards and ancient houses, its churches and meeting halls. She described Andrew, a tall man with an angular face, one who liked to be alone and who had never married; a man who had believed that domesticity would soften the focused attention he needed to give to the physical details of the earth. Outside was the constant hum of the city, the unknown world. Inside the young man shifted his position now and then on the old couch, leaning forward, or nodding to indicate that he was listening. Sylvia found herself speaking slowly and carefully, as if rehearsing a speech she had memorized.

"The day that you found Andrew you became the present, the end of the story, the end of my story, the reply to the last unanswered question," she told him. "And you were the end of Andrew's story as well. You were, in a way, the last thing he told me. Toward the end, one of the very last things he said aloud was something about a hook of the past sewing us together. By then it was difficult to grasp what he was talking about. I've always pictured the kind of needle sailors used for making sails. I saw these in the museum . . . the museum where I sometimes do volunteer work." She paused. "They look a bit like long silver question marks."

Andrew had gone to the museum to see the needles after she had told him about them, but he had gone on a day when he was certain she would not be there. It was she who had insisted on this, unable by then to bear the idea of seeing him in a place that was not entirely their own. *The whole room between them.* She had read that line in a book somewhere and had never forgotten it. The room was never between them when they met privately. The room was a part of them then, an extension of the story Andrew was building, sentence by sentence, the long journey through the tangled highways of his family's past.

"Memories are fixed, aren't they?" she said. "They might diminish, they might fade, but they don't change, become something else. I am now, you see, his memory." She sat forward in her chair. "Andrew thought he *was* the history that his forebears created, he felt responsible for that history, I think, and for those people. They are my responsibility now."

Jerome glanced at her. Then he looked quickly away as if he felt suddenly shy or embarrassed. Sylvia couldn't tell by the expression on his face what he was thinking.

"I'm not certain that what you said about memory is correct," he said. "I think it *can* change."

"Can it? Perhaps it only becomes stronger, purer." What she wanted was to sharpen her memories of Andrew, memories she feared were beginning to separate themselves from her. She had never before felt separate from Andrew. No, that was not quite accurate. There had been times when she had wanted to remain apart even in her imagination, times when she would spend an entire day examining, one by one, the goblets and candlesticks and wineglasses of her mother's cranberry glass collection rather than think of him at all, because the slightest shadow of him in her mind brought with it too much pain. But once she had seen him again, she would begin to crave inclusion, the encircling arm, the connection. She had never felt anything like it before. She began to believe that she could feel him moving toward her and then turning away from her, even when they were hundreds of miles apart. Such was her affliction. Despite her parents' care, despite her husband's love, she believed that the only family she had had until him was the family of the dead. Objects, maps, and vanished children.

"What kind of a young man found Andrew, I wondered," she said to Jerome now. "How would what he saw have affected him?" Because she read that he was an artist, she suspected that he might have been looking for a way to become haunted, by something, anything, and that being the case, this event might have entered his psyche like a dark, permanent gift. "All I really knew about you was that you were a painter."

"Actually, I am not a painter," offered Jerome. "I've never been a painter, really. What I do is more sculptural . . . involves three-dimensional space."

Sylvia hesitated at this point. Then, after a few moments of silence, she began to speak again. "Andrew felt that he had been destined to become a historical geographer," she said. "He told me that the mistakes of his ancestors had made this a kind of dynastic necessity. Unlike his forebears, you see, he paid careful attention to landscape, to its present and to the past embedded in its present."

Sylvia studied the face of the young man she was speaking to, his smooth wide forehead, full lips, and clean dark hair. He appeared to be thoughtful, serious, and yet somehow benignly detached. She was thankful for this detachment. She smiled at him and continued.

"Andrew never forgot his ancestors: they were always with him. One of the first stories he told me was about the dunes at the end of the peninsula, dunes that were strongly associated with his family. We barely knew each other, yet I had driven out there with him. I had said that I wanted these lovely, soft mountains of sand to remain in place forever. He maintained that these were a mistake, a man-made mistake, that the dunes were not natural, were, instead the result of human carelessness. You see, Branwell Woodman, Andrew's great-grandfather and the son of old Joseph Woodman, the timber merchant, had bought a hotel near there, a hotel that became entirely engulfed by sand."

Andrew had been looking across a billow of sand that sloped
down to the edge of the water when he spoke of this. Sylvia
remembered distinctly now, his light brown, slightly greying hair,
the perturbed, almost angry expression of his face in profile. He
had lifted his left arm to point in the direction of the long-
vanished hotel. There was an ordinance survey map twitching in
the wind at the end of his right hand. Abruptly he had turned
toward her, his face for the first time collapsing toward softness,
tenderness. And then his left hand had moved toward her hair.
"Still, some mistakes can be beautiful," he had said.

Sylvia held this inner picture for as long as she could, but
then, as always, it began to dissolve. She could still see the dunes
but not Andrew, not his hair, not his hand. "Everything," she said
to Jerome, "almost everything seems to disappear in one way or
another." Emerging slightly from her open handbag, the spines of
the two green notebooks shone in the afternoon light. She leaned
forward to touch them, then twisted around in her chair, having
heard the sound of the door opening. The girl called Mira walked
into the space in the company of the cat who was circling around
her feet and rubbing up against her legs. "Hello," she said, placing
two bulging plastic bags on the floor. "What's been going on?"

Sylvia tightened the scarf she was wearing around her throat.
"I scarcely know," she said. "I seem to have just gone on and on.
I should probably go now." She pushed one arm and then another
into the sleeves of her coat.

"We were just talking about memory," Jerome said, "about
memory and change. Where did you find Swimmer? He shot out
of the door like an arrow, no stopping him."

"I barely know," Sylvia continued, "whether I made any sense. I've been told that there are often times when I make no sense."

Mira turned to Jerome. "I tried to call you, but you didn't answer. I spent the whole afternoon with that client I told you about. The one who takes paintings home on approval, then always brings them back. I wonder if he'll ever really buy anything. Maybe he secretly hates art."

"The phone was turned off," said Jerome. Sylvia could see that the young man had brightened just looking at the girl. The intimacy between them included a kind of electrical awakening, even with the introduction of such an ordinary subject as a cat or a telephone. As she rose to go, both young people turned to look at her as if for the first time.

"Shall I come back tomorrow?" she asked, surprised that she was addressing this question to the girl.

"Oh yes," said Mira, "I think all this is good for him." She smiled at Jerome, then reached into one of the grocery bags, pulled out an orange, and tossed it in his direction. "Vitamin C," she said, then laughed as Jerome, having missed the catch, chased the fruit across the room.

The girl stretched her arms into the air then, keeping her back straight, bent at the waist, and swung her arms behind her where they remained extended like wings.

Sylvia thought about this odd gesture as she walked down the alley toward the street. The light was beginning to decline. She buttoned her coat against the cold.

Sylvia began to think of her husband, of the way he came into her life. A good young doctor, her father had said, feeling fortunate to have enticed him away from the city and into the backwater that was their County in order to join the practice. He had been speaking, of course, to her mother, not to her. He attempted to converse with Sylvia only occasionally, and when he did, he used the tone one reserves for a very young child. Sylvia was twenty at the time, but had not often left the house since she had completed high school and had walked forever away from a world where – despite her anxiety and confusion in the face of anything social, answering only when spoken to – she had felt almost happy when lost in the satisfying task of learning facts. There had been no talk about university, though her grades had always been exceptional: there were no universities in the County and both parents had accepted that their daughter would never leave home. And she hadn't left home, had not been "admitted," despite her mother's frequent threats when she was a child, and had not gone away for the suggested stint at a summer camp for "special" children. It had been her quiet father who had protected her from such departures, his grim silence eventually winning out over her mother's desperate requests, her mother's arguments.

The good doctor had been invited to dinner soon after his arrival in town. This customary courtesy when taking on a new locum or partner had been endured by Sylvia two or three times in the past. A stranger in the house could cause almost anything to happen to her: utter paralysis, a loss of motor skills, total withdrawal, awkwardness, collisions with furniture, or, at best, rote behaviour of a more or less civilized kind. Still her father had not wanted to exclude her. He had accepted, and expected others to accept, her disability, though no one had been able to identify the affliction.

She wondered now how she had been explained to Malcolm. What exactly did her father say about the strange daughter in order to prepare the young man for her presence? *My daughter is disabled* was a sentence she had heard him use on more than one occasion, often in her presence as if she hadn't been there at all, or as if she were locked in an adjoining room. If the person he was speaking to was a stranger, he or she would often look her over in a puzzled sort of way, seeking the flaw, and when unable to find it, no one had had the courage to make an inquiry. Only one very elderly and courtly man, whom she and her father had encountered while out walking, a man revisiting the town of his youth, had been able to come up with an interesting reply. "Your daughter," he had said with sadness, "is disabled by her beauty." Sylvia would always remember this, and often whispered it to herself at night before going to sleep though she had never been able to fully understand what the word *beauty* meant, at least in reference to her own physical self.

Malcolm had spent most of the visit gazing at her with an eager, frank curiosity, while she fidgeted under his scrutiny. She had left the dinner table in mid-meal in order to be closer to the three china horses that stood on a table in the corner of the dining room. Her parents had once or twice tried to introduce a pet, a kitten or a dog, into her life, but the unpredictability of live animals had disoriented her, though she had always been and remained delighted by the notion of animals. She preferred the stillness, the sheen, of the three miniature beasts on this table. There had once been four horses, but her mother, cleaning, had broken one. Sylvia had mourned for several months.

Unlike any other guest, Malcolm had put down his knife and fork and had come across the room to stand beside her. "Oh, please continue with your meal," her mother had said brightly. "Sylvia just likes to get up now and then to look at the horses, don't you, darling? Nothing to be concerned about." But Malcolm had been concerned. To Sylvia's great discomfort, he had stood beside her and lifted one of the china animals from the polished mahogany. "They're lovely horses," he said, and then, "Do you have names for them?" He held the blond horse in his fingers as he spoke.

"No," she had whispered. Then with her hand atop his she gently eased the horse back to the tabletop. "They don't like to be touched, to be changed," she had said quietly just before she turned and left the room for the night, her eyes on the floor as she walked silently away. In her room she listened to the murmur of the continuing dinner, though she could not make out the words that were spoken. And later, she heard the door close behind the stranger, the sound of his footsteps moving away, the creak of the old wrought-iron gate at the front of the garden.

She could visualize the path he would take, past the Petersons' white house with the tower, past the Redners' brick house with the tall, nodding hollyhocks in the garden. As she had done each time she went to school, he would walk over the one broken sidewalk square and, at the corner, over the square that had the words *Brunswick Block 1906* incised into its surface. The drugstore, the five-and-dime store, the Queen's Hotel, an outdoor bench no one sat on, a tree that was surrounded by a bent iron cage, the war memorial with its steady stone soldier and the names of the dead boys who had made the mistake of leaving home. Several years later she would make a tactile map of all this for Julia. "The curb, the surface of Willow Road, another curb, Church Street," she would say while her friend's fingers brushed the surfaces of the textures Sylvia had glued onto a rectangular piece of cardboard. "This is your world," Julia had said. "How built it is, how different than my farm." Malcolm would walk up the gravel path to the Morris apartments where he said he was staying. She would not have followed him through the door there. Only her own interior rooms and the cold halls and classrooms of the two schools she had attended were known to her at the time in any intimate sort of way.

The next time Malcolm came for dinner, he brought her a china horse.

For the first six months, the horses were all they spoke about, with Malcolm doing most of the speaking. Then, gradually, she began to show him the rest of the house, the particular objects she had animated in one way or another; her grandfather's important-looking shaving stand with its shining mirror the exact size of a face, a low footstool crouching near a Morris chair. Malcolm had pretended to be interested in all this, or perhaps he had really been interested. His tone when he talked was unthreatening, pleasing, careful. It was not unlike the tone her father had used to coax her out of bed, down the stairs, off to school in the past, except that, unlike her father, Malcolm seemed to want to enter her own world and to discuss what it might be that intrigued her there.

He did not shut her out of his world either, often describing an appealing child or a colourful adult who had come into the office, or making reference to a picturesque part of the County he had visited when making a housecall. Sometimes, when her parents were in the room, he complained a little about paperwork, how it never seemed to end. There was only one nurse-receptionist in the office: it seemed unfair to expect her to do it all. Maybe, he suggested, Sylvia could come in for a couple of afternoons a week, just to ease the load.

Her father seemed pleased; her mother had looked irritated, doubtful. "Sylvia will never be able to maintain a job," she said.

Malcolm had bristled. "She could most certainly maintain a part-time job," he said, "even after she is married."

"Good Lord," her mother had replied briskly. "Who on earth would ever have the patience for that?" She was not referring to the job.

Sylvia stared across the room and into the hall where she could see a painting of Niagara Falls. She concentrated on the white, indistinct cloud of steam at the bottom of the cataract and the way the river opened out from this spot, purposefully, with some other destination in mind.

"I would," Malcolm had said as he reached across the table for the hand that Sylvia immediately withdrew. "I would have the patience for that."

Her parents had made a faint attempt to discourage Malcolm, had used words like *sacrifice* while he had used words of love. Secretly, however, Sylvia knew that they considered the young doctor to be a miraculous blessing, a gift of luck visiting their unlucky home. When it was obvious that he was serious — determined in fact — her father had told her that if she married Malcolm, the young doctor had agreed that he would come to live in the house. "And you'll never have to leave," he said, knowing that that would be what she wanted. He was right, that was what she wanted although, until that moment, it had never occurred to her that the house, its objects and corners and stories, might be removed from her life.

After that, as if repeating a line he had been told he would be expected to say, her father asked if she'd thought about whether she wanted to marry Malcolm.

She had said nothing; none of it seemed to have much to do with her.

Her mother had spoken to her harshly one night in the kitchen shortly after Malcolm had left the house. She had spun around angrily from her place at the sink, suds and water dripping from her hands. "You'll have to let him touch you," she had hissed in the direction of her daughter. "You'll have to let him touch you in ways you can't even imagine. And you have never, never let me, your father, or anyone else touch you. You won't be able to do it, and he will leave and we'll all be worse off than before." But neither the outburst nor what her mother said worried Sylvia. She knew exactly what her mother was talking about. And Malcolm had assured her, had promised her with his hand on the old family Bible. "I will not touch you," he swore, "until you want me to." She was never going to want him to; there was never going to be a problem.

There was a story about the four horses: the three horses and the one that had been broken by her mother. There would likely be a story about the new horse that Malcolm had brought into the house, but it had not yet become known to Sylvia at the time of her marriage. In the original story, the four horses had always lived together in the brown field that was the top of the mahogany occasional table that sat under the wall clock. The pendulum was a kind of brass moon to them, swaying in skies that were given to storms punctuated by the thunderous resonance of the gong. Normal weather was just a rhythm, a solemn, steady ticking or sometimes a creaking as if someone were slowly descending a flight of stairs. There was no time at all in the brown pasture, just weather and changing light. The four horses were grouped together because there was a calm love that existed among them, with no variation in it: it neither gained nor faltered in intensity. That and the fact that as long as they were grouped together there could be no arrivals, no departures, no accidents. The horses could prevent things from happening by staying close to one another without ever touching. Touch, Sylvia knew, caused fracture, and horses should never, never fracture. Horses had to be shot if anything about them was broken. Her father had told her that. Her mother, in the story, had shot the one horse, and still, while Sylvia slept, the weather of the clock ticked on and the storms boomed out into the night, and then continued to mark the mornings when she was awake, and when she was at school while school was still a part of her life. These were the kind of things she liked to think about at the time that Malcolm first came into her life: unnamed china horses.

Sylvia also liked to think about a piece of Staffordshire china that had been in the house for as long as she could remember. As a young child, she had asked her father when "the girl and the dog and the bird who were all joined together by the tree" had come to the house, and he had told her from the beginning, as far as he knew. And so, for her, the grouping became a kind of symbol of the Creation, one of "my first things," as she liked to call these pieces of china at the time. This term had nothing to do with ownership, rather it concerned the connection she believed existed between her and the shape such a thing would hold on to, unchangingly, forever. Often without laying one finger on it, she would whisper to the piece, "There was a girl and a dog and a bird and they were all joined together, forever, by a tree." The girl wore a pink dress, a white apron, and had a green ribbon round her neck and, on her head, a hat adorned with feathers. The dog was spotted and had delicate whiskers and nails made by the finest lines of paint. The bird was brown and black and was resting on a limb of the tree. They remained discrete, separate, attached only to and by the tree – a leafless tree, a tree that knew no seasons. A kind of security and contentment emanated from the grouping, as if the players in the tableaux knew who they were, what their role was, where they belonged. They were stable. They had no moods. They displayed no disturbing behaviour.

How charmed Malcolm had been by such things when he had finally persuaded her that it was safe to tell him about them. "I am safe, Syl," he would say, and then as if to indicate that he understood what mattered to her, "I am as safe as houses." It was then that she decided to show him the large 1878 County atlas with its old pictures of shops and houses and farms that had since fallen into disrepair or, in some cases, had disappeared completely from the roads on which they had stood. "These are safe too," she had told him, pointing to one building after another. And when he had asked her why they were safe, she had said, "Because everything that was going to happen to them, in them, has already happened. There will be no more changes. They are here," she placed her hand flat on a page, "just like this, forever."

"'And, little town,'" he had said, looking at a depiction of a village street, "'thy streets for evermore will silent be.'"

She had smiled at him then and had, for the first time, looked fully into his face. He knew about the poem that she had carried with her in her mind since Grade Twelve and he had assumed that she would know as well. He had not explained, had not said the words "Ode on a Grecian Urn," or "John Keats," as almost anyone else would have done, condescending to her "disability," her "condition." She relaxed almost completely then, concluded that he was someone she could like.

Oh Malcolm, she thought now, as she walked through the door of the hotel, you were safe. It was I who was never safe, for beneath the serene appearance of my house, there was always a story that I was making in my mind. No matter how carefully still the horses stood, in the end, even they couldn't stop things from happening. They couldn't stop the time that marched so noisily over their heads. They couldn't prevent me from leaving the room, walking down the hall, out the door. Neither you, nor your goodness, nor china horses could keep me forever away from the arms of the world.

❧

The hotel room had felt almost familiar when Sylvia re-entered it; the only change since she'd left a few hours earlier was the stack of fresh towels placed in the bathroom and a further straightening of the bed she had made before leaving. Her few cosmetics were lined up near the sink just the way she had left them, and the leather portfolio remained in perfect alignment with the right-hand corner of the desk. Her suitcase stood near the wall, the curtains were closed. I am going to be able to manage this, she thought. I am going to be able to be calm here.

When she was a child, there had been — apart from other people — two things that particularly separated her from calmness:

wind in a room and outdoor mirrors. She could still call up the fear she had felt when, one morning in June, she had walked into the dining room to discover the sheer curtains moving like sleeves toward her, and a bouquet of flowers that had been dead and still the previous day bending and shaking in the breeze that entered through the open window. She had become accustomed to the fact that the air moved when she was outside, but she believed the interior of the house was the realm of stillness, so that when she became aware of the wind in the room it seemed to her that something alien and disturbing had begun to animate all that she had relied on to be quiet and in place.

After that she would let neither her father nor her mother open her bedroom window at night and would inquire repeatedly about all the other windows in the house before climbing carefully into bed. In spite of her parents' assurances, she would worry that while she lay motionless between white sheets the long, draped arms of the curtains would be rising and falling as if conducting music she would never be able to hear, and would not be able to bear had she been able to hear it. These indoor currents and suspicions of music had caused her anxiety during her first years with Malcolm as well, but almost all of that was gone by the time she began to meet Andrew. And yet she had never been entirely comfortable in summer when Andrew wanted the front door of the cottage left open. She liked the idea of the two of them being closed in together; she liked the idea of shutting everything else out.

When she had been about twelve, her father had taken her to a country auction, thinking that it would be a pleasant outing for her after two days of tension in the house. A bad spell, he had said, referring to her mother's mood that had been an unspoken but dark and pulsing presence. Sylvia had not responded well to anything about the auction: not to the jabbering man on the platform, not to the displaced furniture and household goods arranged on the grass, and certainly not to the more delicate items — sheets and doilies and tablecloths being pawed through by those she knew had no right to touch them. But when she had passed by a row of mirrors and had seen herself reflected in them — herself drenched in sunshine with the hem of her dress moving, grass under her shoes, barns and trees, hills and clouds behind her — she had begun to cry and had not stopped crying until her father was forced to take her home. When questioned, all she could say was that nothing was where it should be. What she had meant, she realized much later, was that the mirrors had shown her that there was no controlling what might enter the frame of experience, that the whole world might bully its way into a quiet interior, and that there would be no way of keeping it out.

It comforted her that the mirrors in her own house were hung in locations where windows and all that moved outside of windows could not be duplicated on their surfaces, and each day when she passed them the same reflected furniture stood, reversed it is true, but stoically and reassuringly in place. Nothing about the three mirrors in this hotel room could startle or betray her either. In the one that hung over the dresser she saw herself reflected, from the waist up, against the background of the bed, bedside tables, and lamps, and when she closed the bathroom door, she saw the whole woman she had become: angular, slightly stooped, vague grey eyes, the veins of the hands that hung by her hips, the sharp shin bones that travelled from the hem of her skirt down to her narrow feet, the grey-blond hair that was pulled back from her face, and behind all this just the blankness of a wall.

On one of the bedside tables, beside the two notebooks, *The Relations of History and Geography* remained unopened where she had placed it the previous day. She had brought the book with her to the city, hoping that she might be able to begin to reread it when she was in a new place, as she had not had the courage to do so over the previous year. She had picked it up on occasion, had opened it, and had turned it on an angle to the light to search for the incised lines that would indicate that Andrew had marked a particular passage with his thumbnail. Then she had lightly touched with her fingers this practically invisible, frail trace of him on the printed text. But she could not read the passages that had interested him: not yet, not so far.

The book had been Andrew's last gift to her at a time when his gifts could take any shape at all – an empty shoebox, an oddly shaped stick, and once a Sears Catalogue from 1976. He would rise in the middle of a conversation, sometimes in the middle of a sentence, cross the room, rummage through the bookshelves or the box near the fire, and return to her with some object or another in his hands. "Please take it," he would say. "It would mean so much to me if you did." Once, he had approached her with a loaf of bread in his hands. "Please accept this bouquet," he had said. And when she had laughed, he had laughed with her, and then had spoken the word *joy* while removing her blouse. This book, then, was the final offering from his hand, and she had kept it near her in the hope that, when she could bring herself to read it, there might be some message from him encoded in its chapters, though she knew this to be irrational, wishful thinking. Andrew was not the kind of man who sent symbolic messages, not even the younger Andrew, twenty years before. No, all of the messages she had read – in the objects that were near him or in the cloud formations that passed over him, even, sometimes, in the expressions that visited his face – were often, she now acknowledged, envisioned by her alone, invented by her need. She reached for the book, let it fall open to a page near the back, and forced herself to read a thumbnail-marked quotation by a man named York Powell:

> *The country was to him a living being, developing under his eyes, and the history of its past was to be discovered from the conditions of its present. . . . He could read much of the palimpsest before him. He was keen to note the survivals that are the key to so much that has now disappeared but that once existed.*

She lifted her eyes from the page and stared at a small red light below the television that was beating soundlessly like something alive. She had not heard of the author who had written these lines or the scholar to whom the quotation referred, but the words described Andrew so accurately they stirred her heart and awakened her grief and she turned her face to one side, closed the book, and placed it back on the table.

The next afternoon at two o'clock, as Sylvia approached Jerome's door, she saw that it was held open by a broken piece of timber. Timber, she thought, no one uses the word any more, a light, musical word, so much better than lumber or wood. As a teenager she had often whispered to herself a sentence that sounded to her like poetry: *My house is made of timber and of glass.* The sentence had comforted her, especially when she found herself outside the house walking to school. Now as she stepped over the threshold of this interior that was so new to her, Sylvia found that she was in an empty room: no sign of Jerome and no fluorescent light either. "I'm in here," the young man called from the adjoining space. "I'll be with you in a moment." He emerged a few seconds later looking distracted, distant.

"Is something wrong?" Sylvia asked and then, by habit, made a mental note that she had read the expression of another, the way Malcolm had taught her to do.

Jerome glanced in her direction, then lowered his gaze. "No, nothing, I was just looking at some drawings, some things I haven't finished yet."

Sylvia wondered if she should ask to see these drawings but decided against making the request. She seated herself in the customary chair. Jerome walked over to the wall, flicked some switches, and looked up as two banks of fluorescent lights quivered toward full illumination. Then he walked across the room and leaned against the counter near the sink. "Would you like some tea?" he asked. "Mira has green tea. I could make some."

"No, I'm fine," said Sylvia. "I've had lunch." The restaurant had been one geared toward sandwiches; the variety of contents displayed behind the glass counter had almost driven her back out to the street until she realized she could simply mimic the choices of the customer who preceded her. Sylvia was beginning to appreciate the neutrality of the city, the fact that its inhabitants had absolutely no interest in her. Perhaps her life would have been easier to manage had she always been a stranger.

"Okay then." Jerome walked quietly over to the couch and slowly sat down, as if he felt that any sudden movement might be too disruptive, might startle her.

He believes I am a problem, thought Sylvia, much like everyone else. She found this oddly unsettling, as if she had wanted to impress this young man and had failed somehow. Still, she had come this far and was not going to retreat into silence. She placed her handbag on the floor by her feet, removed her coat, and began to speak.

"My father was a doctor and I married my father's partner, a man called Malcolm Bradley. I married a kind man who came into my father's life as a locum. Malcolm, who wanted to look after me."

She smiled after she said this, and Jerome smiled as well, out of politeness probably, for where was the joke? What she had said should not have been spoken lightly, she realized. Sometimes in recent years when she had stood in the evenings unnoticed at the doorway of Malcolm's office, watching him turn the pages of the books that might or might not have described her condition, her heart nearly broke in the face of his need to believe in the purity of diagnosis. He was so innocent at these moments, this man who felt that everything deserved what he called "the dignity of a scientific explanation." Had he taken her character through the several stages of the scientific method, spent months making observations, before carefully, deliberately, drawing his conclusion? Had he in fact married his conclusion?

" 'She will have a good life,' he assured my parents, 'a good life with me. I understand her.' "

Sylvia sat very still, fearing that Jerome might ask what was wrong with her. It was the inquiry she dreaded more than anything, this question. When it was clear that he was not going to do so, she relaxed and said, "Did they tell you that Andrew Woodman was a landscape geographer?" she asked.

"No," said Jerome, sitting back against the couch, "I think I read about that . . . afterwards, in the newspaper." He cleared his throat. "And you told me as well."

"Did I? He claimed that everywhere he went he found evidence of the behaviour of his forebears: rail fences, limestone foundations, lilac bushes blooming on otherwise abandoned farmsteads, an arcade of trees leading to a house that is no longer there." She looked down. Her hands lying in her lap looked to her like two dead birds "All that sad refuse, Andrew used to say. And that island, of course . . . your island . . . abandoned by those ancestors a century before. He recorded everything that was left behind there, each sunken wreck, the remains of pilings, iron pulleys, cables, broken axels. You must have seen remnants . . . something?"

The young man nodded. "There were empty buildings and a couple of smaller sheds that had collapsed. And one huge anchor near the jetty. But I never saw the wrecks. I was hoping that the ice would clear enough for me to catch sight of one or two, but then . . ." He placed his elbow on his bent knee and ran his hand through his hair, not looking at her.

What is he seeing in his mind? Sylvia wondered. Certainly not Andrew. He wouldn't want to remember that, wouldn't want to think about it. Jerome's hand was still in his hair, cupping the shape of his skull as if he were attempting to prevent the image of Andrew, or some other image, from entering his mind. As a younger woman Sylvia had been baffled by the gestures of others. She could never understand, for example, why people raised their hands when they spoke. The sudden lifting of arms and hands in the middle of speech had seemed to her to be aggressive, imposing, a ceremonial display of weapons by warriors preparing for battle. But here, now, this simple gesture seemed to her to suggest frailty, vulnerability, and she found she was moved by it.

When Jerome eventually glanced in her direction, she locked eyes for a moment with him. Then she looked away and continued, "Andrew's great-great-grandfather, the first Woodman to come to Canada in the nineteenth century, settled on the island as a timber merchant," she said. "Before that he had been in Ireland briefly as one of several engineers sent out by the British government to investigate, then to map and file reports on the state of the bogs of Ireland. County Kerry mostly." She ran one hand up and down the sleeve of her cardigan. "According to Andrew," she said, "Joseph Woodman had a complicated relationship with Ireland – the people, the landscape."

"A complicated relationship with landscape," Jerome repeated. "How could that be?"

Sylvia looked up now and studied the young man she was talking to, his smooth forehead and long perfect hands, his thoughtful, serious expression. It seemed she had never really seen anyone this young, and she doubted she had ever looked this young herself. "He wanted, or at least Andrew said he wanted, to drain everything: the lakes, the rivers, the streamlets, and every acre of bog. Andrew always said that old Joseph Woodman wanted to squeeze all moisture out of the County of Kerry, as if it were a dishrag. He was convinced, you see, that with proper drainage, fields of wheat could be made to replace the bogs. When he presented his report to the British Crown, his ideas were utterly dismissed. One month later he immigrated to Canada in a full-blown fit of pique, a man still young enough – and ambitious enough, Andrew claimed – to cause serious damage. Thousands of acres of forests would be floated to his docks on Timber Island, so that the logs could be assembled into rafts. Then the rafts would be poled downriver to the quays at Quebec, where the timber was loaded onto ships bound for

Britain. This went on for years and years, until all of the forests were gone."

"But he couldn't have been the only timber merchant."

"No, no, of course not. But Andrew never forgot that his own family was involved. He could never let go of the picture of a raped landscape. He didn't forget this, at least he didn't forget for a very long time." Sylvia twisted the ring on her left hand. "Forgetting would come later."

Sitting in silence, she wondered if Jerome would ask her a question, would in some way begin to interview her. She would not have liked it if he had.

"Sometimes," he began, "it's best just to let them go, family things. Otherwise . . . well, what's the point? There's nothing you can do anyway." He was looking at the wall behind and slightly above Sylvia's head. "But this would be a sort of ecological forgetting, another kind of letting go, I suppose . . ."

Jerome's angle of vision remained unchanged, and Sylvia felt an urge to turn in her chair and follow his gaze. She suppressed this, however, and spoke again. "All those years ago when we first began to meet – began to know each other – that inherited memory of destruction was still in Andrew's mind," she said. "He spoke to me about it." She paused again, catching just a glimpse of Andrew's face in her memory, the expressive mouth, the sad eyes. "That we should have been alive at the same time," she said to Jerome, "that we should have somehow walked from such distance toward each other, and that he would speak to me about the things that troubled him . . . all this seemed miraculous to me. I took everything he told me and kept it deep inside me – so deep that I could hear him speaking when he was not there.

And the truth is, he was most often not with me, not there. We were not able to meet with any kind of frequency, and sometimes there were months when he was travelling, months when we were not able to meet at all."

He had become, in spite of his absences, or perhaps, she thought now, because of his absences, the vital centre of her inner world. Her daily life had strutted around her like theatre, like a performance needing neither her participation nor her attention. Even during painful, disorienting times – her father's sudden heart attack and death and, years later, her mother's stroke – she could bring the curtain down and permit Andrew's distant light to dominate. Because he had spoken about the wind from the lake, there was no longer anything neutral about the wind from lake; because they had talked together on the dunes, a child's sandbox glimpsed in a neighbour's yard brought with it the idea of Andrew as palpably as if it were a letter written by his hand. But there were no letters written by his hand; often he didn't communicate with her for weeks, or would make the briefest, the most perfunctory, of calls during the empty hours of the day.

"During these periods of absence, of withdrawal," she told Jerome, "I would believe that he was communicating with me through dreams, or thoughts, or omens, a belief I maintained during this last, this final absence."

"Yes," said Jerome, leaning forward to pick up the cat near his feet. "It's odd how people who die come into your dreams. My father's been gone for more than ten years, and still I have these dreams. About him." He watched as the cat leapt back to the floor. "I never dream about my mother. Never about her, and never about them together."

Sylvia tried to envisage Jerome's parents, the people who had given birth to the earnest young man who sat opposite her. They would have a familiar domestic life, she imagined, not unlike, in some ways, her and Malcolm's, a shared daily space, but with room for a child, of course. There would be that difference and other differences as well. But all of it, the rooms, the partnership, would be there on a daily basis.

She began to think about the first time she entered the place where for twenty years she and Andrew would meet and part, and meet and part. An old cottage, almost deserted, situated on a wooded hill thirty miles or so down the lakeshore from where she lived on property left to Andrew by his father because no one else wanted it. In the summer the cottage smelled of racoons and damp. In the winter the wood stove's fire barely penetrated the cold. It had been winter that first time, and during her walk from the car, deep snow had fallen over the tops of her boots, burning her legs when it melted against the skin. There had been no talk, at least not at first. It had been far too cold to undress, and as they had fumbled through layers of clothing in order to touch, fear had set off its sirens in her brain. But she overcame this, barely knowing what was taking place, only that she could not stop it. She had learned next to nothing that first winter about Andrew's long, angular body, the bones and ligaments and pale, faintly bluish skin that would become so familiar to her. So familiar that, as the years passed, she would sometimes confuse it with her own. Unlike the awkward disruption of Malcolm's sad, brief attempts to establish a physical relationship with her, there would come to be nothing foreign or invasive about Andrew's lovemaking, just the comfort, the consolation of full embrace.

It wasn't until months after their first meeting — when the summer heat began — that they had seen each other whole. They had been relatively young then and Sylvia had been amazed by the fact of their flesh — hers as much as his, as she had never paid any attention before to her own nakedness, though she said nothing at all about this. He had pulled back and had looked at her for what seemed to be a long, long, time, one hand moving over her breasts and stomach. Then he had lifted her legs and groaned as he entered her.

Always, afterwards, they would remain silent for some time, as if making a focused journey over a dangerous and beautiful terrain, a journey requiring rapt attention and great care. And then when they began to talk, they spoke about the land: her County, the objects in her house, and the stories of his ancestors on the island where the lake became the river. They did not then, and would never, speak of love. Only about geography, the townscapes she had just hours before left behind, the house she would return to, and the tapestry of fields and fences that tumbled away from the place where they lay.

"Even when we were far, far apart," she told Jerome, "Andrew rolled through my mind like active weather." She smiled, pleased with her description, then, suddenly embarrassed, straightened her hair with her hand and tugged her skirt farther down over her knees. "And when I wasn't with him, I was waiting."

"My mother was like that," said Jerome, a shadow sliding over his face and a faint trace of anger in his voice. "She was always, always waiting."

This abrupt confession startled Sylvia somewhat. "What was she waiting for?"

"Change. For my father: for him to change. He didn't, of course." Jerome coughed. "No, that's not quite true," he added. "He got even worse, became even more impossible."

Sylvia would not ask about his father's condition, what it might be. "I'm sorry," she said.

"It doesn't matter. Or, at least it doesn't matter to me." Jerome got up and walked back to the counter, where a bowl filled with Mira's oranges sat near the toaster. He picked up one perfect orange and offered it to Sylvia, but she shook her head, so he returned to the couch and began to peel the fruit for himself, slowly, and with what appeared to be great concentration. Sylvia found herself drawn to the vibrancy of the colour as if she had never seen orange before.

"You know," she said, "Andrew always maintained that all married couples seemed to him to be placed for the purposes of determining scale in a painted landscape. Tiny anonymous figures that Victorians referred to as the 'argument' of the picture." She paused. "He liked the pun, the word *argument*. Marriage, for him you see, would have been an argument. He told me he couldn't imagine using the word *we* all the time in reference to thoughts, or even actions." They had been curled together on the bed and his mouth had been against the back of her neck when he had spoken about this — she had been able to feel the slight motion of his lips. "But here we are," he had said later. "Here we are lying on the shoreline of the ancient lake. This whole ridge is like negative space, like a physical memory." He had explained that braided in the limestone around the Great Lake were the fossils of life forms whose narrow sessions of animation had been silenced forever. Such brief, simple narratives,

such unobserved histories, he had said, permanently halted by a
wall of ice. Sometimes, he'd said, you could see the direction the
animal intended to take. With others – those who were born to
a spiral shape for instance – they seemed to have already accepted
their fate.

In what season had he spoken those words? What year? She
didn't, she couldn't remember. Only that she had been lying on
her side and that he was curled around her like a shell, his hand
circling the wrist of her left arm, their clothing tangled together
on a chair near the bed. Flannel and corduroy, silk and linen
caught on a lathed armrest or falling over the torn rush webbing
of a chair seat woven a hundred years ago in innocence. Corduroy,
she had whispered once, removing his old brown jacket. From the
French, he had joked. The threads of the king. Then he had
run his hands through her hair, had looked at her and said,
"Sylvaculture, the encouragement of trees."

She had told him, once, that in the first half of the nineteenth century there was scarcely a pioneer family in her County
that hadn't lost one or two of their young men to the whims
of the Great Lake as boy after boy joined the crews of schooners
that carried goods from settlement to settlement along the
Canadian shores. Often these tragedies took place within sight of
home, as the peninsula itself was the most dangerous feature
of the lake. Storms gestated there, lake currents became confused, and then there were the limestone outcroppings set like
teeth across the eastern and southern edge of the land. The scattered fragments of the wreck, the light brown sails draped like
huge shrouds on the surface of the water, or tangled by rigging
and filled with sand; yards and yards of fabric lolling in the froth.

"It's always difficult," Jerome said, "two people and all the things between them. That's one thing even I know is true."

Sylvia folded her hands on her lap, looked toward the window, then said quietly, "In time, everything that should have been joy between Andrew and me became too painful. And when for a period of time we stopped, stopped meeting, stopped talking, I spent endless afternoons driving through the landscapes he had described to me. I wept, and when I was finished with weeping I believed something had gone dead inside me. But, as I was to discover later, there is a difference, a difference between death and dormancy. We had stopped, but we would start again, seven years later, impossible though that may seem." Her voice began to falter. "When you are reacquainted with love in middle age," she murmured as if speaking to herself, "it is more critical, almost an emergency. You can see the end of it. The conclusion is always with you in the room." The empty, unheated cottage appeared in Sylvia's mind, the smell of the cold, the scent of absence. She closed her eyes, willing the image to disappear.

Slowly, slowly her attention returned to Jerome, who was sitting stiffly on the edge of the couch, with the partly peeled orange in his hands and his elbows on his knees as if he were poised for flight. The late-afternoon sun had come in through the window and a pale ribbon of light cut through the air between them. It occurred to Sylvia that perhaps she had gone too far, had revealed too much of her grief, which had been with her so constantly it now no longer seemed to her like unusual pain, seemed more like breathing or sleep or walking. Of course Jerome could never understand this and would instinctively resist entering that dark world. If she continued in this vein she would lose this young man, he would want to remove himself. In fact, even now, she sensed his wanting to be elsewhere. "Should we talk about something else for a while?" she asked and, when he didn't answer, "What were your favourite things when you were a child?"

"Forts," he answered with surprising suddenness, leaning forward to drop an orange peel onto the table. "Tree forts, mostly." He paused, thought a moment, looking around the room. "For a while, until quite recently, really, I made structures in my studio that were like tree houses." Then he looked cha-grined, as if he knew she wouldn't or couldn't comprehend, or as if he wanted to change the subject in order to avoid having to explain. "Those old buildings on the island, they had been houses I think, but they were falling down and covered with ivy and moss. I thought I might be able to recreate them in another way."

Sylvia had not yet been able to grasp the ideas behind Jerome's art, but she was struck once again by the awareness that she wished the conversation to continue. "But those forts, or the houses on the island, how could you build them in a room?" she heard herself ask. Whenever she was reading, it had seemed absolutely right to her that the mark at the end of a question was shaped like a hook designed to snare someone intent on just passing by. Here, however, such a sentence seemed almost natural, and she could tell that the young man had relaxed now that the subject of their talk had shifted.

Jerome leaned back against the couch and folded his arms. "I don't know," he said, "I had done a lot of work based on man-made structures in the past — huts and the like. I was fascinated, on the island, by the idea of built things going back to nature, you know, at least the beginnings of nature . . . germination. But I couldn't figure out a way to get that to work in a gallery space. Nothing would grow fast enough for me to get the point across." He laughed. "Maybe fertilizer would have been helpful."

"Those would have been the workers' cottages, I suppose." Sylvia remembered Andrew saying that there had been a row of labourers' dwellings on the island's one street, and then, of course, there was the big house at the top. She was silent for a moment or two, lost in the act of removing small woollen balls from the sleeve of her cardigan. "They would be houses for the men who worked in the shipyards. Those who manned the rafts came and went . . . and only in the months when the river was open and there was no ice."

"Vikings were pushed out into the icy sea on rafts when they died," offered Jerome. He paused and his face reddened with embarrassment. "Oh sorry," he said, "I shouldn't have said that."

"It's all right," said Sylvia, not looking up from her sleeve, "it's with me all the time, his death, the knowledge of it is always with me. It is impossible for anyone, anything to remind me of it." She was quiet for a moment. "It is a comfort to be able to say that aloud." Suddenly her gaze shifted to the left and rested on a very old chair, minus one leg, tilting in a corner near Jerome and the couch. "Did you know," she said, "that in this light you can see the imprint of the stencilling on the back of that chair? Under all that paint! Andrew would have loved that, would have called it evidence of the chair's history. My friend Julia too. She likes to be able to trace what has happened to things. She told me once that she could feel the difference between new and old knife cuts on a breadboard."

Jerome looked at the chair. "I've never noticed that before," he said. "A history written in paint, pentimento on a chair back."

"It seems to me now," Sylvia said slowly, "that during my own childhood, everything around me was connected to history: a knowable and therefore a safe history. Surely there must have been new toys, new clothes but, if there were, they meant so little to me that I can't remember these gifts. What I recall instead were the Christmas and birthday gifts given to children long dead; gifts given to my father and his sister, to his father and his father's father, for everything had been so carefully organized and preserved in the house — stored away in the spare room or in the attic — that it was all quite easily retrievable."

She had been fairly ambivalent about the dolls, which had been grouped together like a fragile wide-eyed congregation at one end of the large attic. They were still there, but she had covered them some time ago, with sheeting. The cars and tractors and toy trains that had belonged to boy children had interested her more, the fact that they were in no way attempting to be human, were content instead to pretend to be the large machines they were drawn from. Sometimes she had found a faded Christmas tag stuck to one or another of these objects. *To Charlie, Xmas 1888*, it might read, still existing after the small Charlie had passed through adulthood on his journey toward death. *To Charlie from his loving Mama.* When she was older, she came to realize that the tag wouldn't have remained attached to the toy were it not for the way that other children — children not like her — were so easily diverted from the things that surrounded them by the episodic nature of their small, vibrant lives. The world had probably handed them an invitation, and, unlike her, they had been able – joyfully – to accept the offer to participate.

"When I was small," she said, "I distrusted the human face and all the changes of expression that the human face invariably brought with it. Animals were somehow less threatening, though I suppose it is possible to read a change of mood or disposition in the face of an animal, particularly if one looks directly into its eyes."

Both Sylvia and Jerome turned toward Swimmer as if to test this theory. The cat, who was sitting on a high table with his back to them, and who was staring out of the window, remained totally unaware of their attention.

"I came to love the poem called 'The Death and Burial of Cock Robin,'" Sylvia said.

"I don't remember many picturebooks from my childhood," said Jerome. "Not too many poems either. My mother tried to teach me a few songs, though, told me that what she remembered most about being small was that she seemed always to be singing – you know, in class, or in church, or even in the play-ground. Girls' skipping songs and all that. But I was embarrassed by singing. I don't remember any of those songs now."

Sylvia recalled the imaginary music she had so dreaded during her own childhood. "Your mother's girlhood must have been lovely if it was filled with singing," she said to Jerome. "Serene almost . . . and happy. My husband's youth was like that as well, but I can't imagine that Andrew's was, though he never talked about that. I knew so little about him, really, his parents, his schooldays."

The expression on the young man's face tightened. "Serenity and joy are not things I would associate with my mother." He looked at the floor for a moment or two, then glanced at his wrist.

"Is it time for me to go?" Sylvia asked, then reddened. It occurred to her that she had not said these words since she had been with Andrew.

"No, no, it's fine, not yet," said Jerome. He had begun to fiddle with his watch. "It's old, this watch . . . belonged to my father. I should probably get a new one." He rearranged his sleeve, looked up. "You know, I had a tendency to forget about time altogether when I was out there alone on the island. I just worked all day and went back to the sail loft when I felt I had done enough or when the light began to dim. It was quite wonderful, the sail loft."

"The men who worked with the sails were mostly French, I think." Sylvia tilted her head to one side, remembering. "Andrew told me that the island was divided – quite amicably – but divided nevertheless between French and English notions of how things should be. Not just because of language: it had a lot to do with waterways. The English knew the lake, you see, and the French, the French would be more familiar with the river."

"Yes," said Jerome. "Yes, I like that idea. Geographical allegiances. Allegiances to bodies of water."

The huge wet shroud of a schooner's sail moving in lake water and the drowned nineteenth-century boys surfaced in Sylvia's imagination. "Sometimes human beings are confined by geography," she said, "and sometimes," she added, "they are overwhelmed, destroyed by it."

$\mathcal{J}$erome told Mira that he was not sure about using the woman's given name, that he had not yet decided how to address her. The woman had used his own first name on occasion, but still he found it difficult to say the word *Sylvia* when she was with him in the room. She was so obviously from another generation, he was tempted to call her Mrs. Bradley. But the intimacy of what she had been telling him made the formality of that seem somewhat absurd. "And yes," he said to Mira, "they were lovers, just as you suspected."

"I didn't suspect, as you may remember," said Mira. "I knew."

Jerome ignored this clarification and changed the subject. "She told me that no one so far had really determined if that island belonged to the lake or the river. The French said it was a river island, the English maintained it belonged to the lake . . . and so on." He pondered this. "I thought about that too," he said. "When I was there. I'd like to go back in summer and look at the geography . . . the geology. Maybe," he said, "we could answer the question."

This was the first time he had made reference to the possibility of returning and, quite suddenly, he became aware that, if this were to take place, he would not want to be on his own. He could see himself standing on the shore, alone with the new knowledge of the woman's grief and, almost before the picture had fully taken shape, he turned his mind away from it.

"She also talked about a poem from her childhood, Cock Robin, of all things," he said.

"Cock Robin?" Mira did not look up from her knitting. She was making a "swaddle" for the rusted galvanized pail she had found in the alley the previous weekend, a pail that, once it was covered, she would use as a prop in her next performance piece. The wool she was using was pink mohair, and particles of it clung to her dark sweater along with cat hair from Swimmer, who had recently spent some time in her arms. It was often only in the evenings now that she had time for such things, the gallery taking up many of the daylight hours. Just recently she had been told that she would be working on Sunday afternoons.

Jerome sat up straight, became more attentive and formal as he always did when it became clear to him that there was something he could explain to her. He was struck, suddenly, by the familiar pleasure he felt when he knew there was something, even a kindergarten poem, that he could unravel for her. It gave him an edge, a brief flush of superiority. "Robin" he told her, "the bird. From a nursery rhyme."

Jerome watched as the girl bent to unwind a skein of wool from a large pink shape – rather like candy floss – that rested near her left foot. Sometimes all he wanted to do was sit across the room and look at her. He, who had always been so prone to activity, so dependent on plans, so restless and so easily bored, now found himself becalmed, happy to float in the vicinity of a knitting girl. Her beautiful arms, the tilt of her head. Over and over he was surprised by such things.

"'Who killed Cock Robin? I, said the sparrow, with my bow and arrow, *I* killed Cock Robin,'" he quoted. And all at once he wondered how it was that the rhyme had been implanted in his own memory since he had never seen it in a book. Had his tired mother recited it to him? It seemed unlikely. How, then, had this bird-filled children's dirge entered his family's suburban world of freeways and strip malls and cement apartment buildings on the edges of the city? A world conducive to neither birds nor children. The memory of his bicycle came again into his mind, the sight of it rusting in dirty snow on the winter balcony of their apartment, then twisted and broken in a drift ten storeys below. He had stopped riding it once they began to live in the apartment — too humiliated by the journey in the elevator with the bicycle resting uselessly against his hip, too shy of the inevitable adult who would enter the elevator and ask, as if it were not utterly obvious, if he intended to go for a ride.

Mira looked up from her work and gazed at the cat, who was ambling toward her like a sleepwalker. "There were many rhymes, many stories when I was growing up, stories about animals who wouldn't be able to survive in this climate. Some of the animals in the stories were Gods — Ganesh, for example — so I believed that all tropical animals were deities and that's why I figured I didn't see them hanging around the neighbourhood."

"It would be wonderful, though, to find Ganesh strolling through the streets of this city," Jerome said.

"How about Saint Jerome's lion? He has certainly taken to the streets . . . particularly in the alley in the vicinity of garbage pails."

"Just like an autumn bee." Jerome stood now and moved to the back of Mira's chair, then placed his hands on her shoulders, allowing his fingers to rest in the twin hollows between the muscles of her upper back and her collar bones. He bent toward her ear. "I think that in your previous life you were most likely a bee," he whispered. "Or was it a wasp?"

Jerome was intrigued by the fact that Mira was fascinated by bees and had once even taken a course in beekeeping. She liked their colour, their shape, their commitment to labour. Most of all, she was impressed by the way they enthusiastically constructed the hives she referred to as "paper houses." Unlike any other woman Jerome had known, Mira would announce the presence of a bee with joy rather than with terror. There was something oddly beelike about her, Jerome had concluded; she was so industrious, so alert she almost buzzed, and often when she was near him, walking through the galleries, shopping at the market, her presence felt focused, airborne, as if she were hovering above flowers. He was tremendously attracted to her at such moments, when she was absorbed by some task or when her attention shifted to things in the material world. There was an admirable adaptability about her, a generosity toward the beginnings of things. Thinking of this, he studied her busy hands, the frown of concentration on her downcast face. A part of her was gone from him, and yet she was still tantalizingly within reach.

She stopped knitting, rested her head on the back of the chair, and looked up at him, the wool a pink pool on her lap. It occurred to Jerome that he had no idea whether people knitted in India, a country, he now realized, that was difficult to associate with wool, but he didn't want to ask her, show his ignorance, and anyway he was more interested in her smooth shoulders, her beautiful arms. He was aware that even after three years of intimacy there was always a moment or two when she hesitated, but he also knew that these moments passed. She would respond once he was able to touch her, to touch her and to use the word *love*. Then her arms would lift, encircle his neck.

"Probably," she said, "probably I *was* a bee. And if so I would have liked peonies best."

He thought of how she would stand entirely still, mesmerized by the small front gardens in their neighbourhood. Once or twice she had remained long enough that an owner had emerged from inside the house to ask if she needed assistance. Jerome had never seen anyone examine all of the external world with such care. Sometimes she became so absorbed by one thing or another he felt she had completely forgotten he was there. How was it possible, he wondered, that with all the other concerns and interests that fought for space in her mind, work and art and the whole complicated network of family and friends that she attended to, at the end of each day she calmly took the decision to return to the place where he was waiting in order to share his evening meal, his bed? Equally mysterious to him was the fact that he himself was always there when she arrived.

"Please?" he said now.

There it was, that moment of hesitation. Then she stood, placed the wool on the kitchen counter, turned, lowered her eyes, and took his hand.

⁂

The man behind the desk always looked up when Sylvia entered but never said anything. She too remained silent, her key, which had been recently removed from her handbag, dangling in her gloved hand, the salt shaker clinking slightly against the loose change in her coat pocket as she crossed the tile floor.

It had been three days since her train had departed from Belleville Station, three days since she had mailed the car keys back to Malcolm, three days since she had left the message on the answering machine at his office. Soon Malcolm would discover where she was and would come to fetch her home. Sometimes, here in the hotel when she closed her eyes just before sleep, she saw him in his study, focused on the texts that might give him a description of this new, this inexplicable dance of disappearance she had undertaken. The protective side of him touched her in an odd way at such moments, and she wondered if what she was feeling might be what someone else might call pity. It was, however, a feeling that she experienced only in relation to his faithful attachment to her disability, if that is what it was, a disability. That and the fact that he had chosen to come so completely into the physical spaces that made up her ancestral history. Her father's desk, her great-grandmother's china. The antique marriage bed that would have been, on more than one occasion, a deathbed: all the details that made up what she thought of as her known and knowable place had been fully accepted by him, incorporated into his life's work. Her in her natural habitat. His life's work.

Andrew had believed that the cells of humans, like those of birds and animals, were programmed to recognize the smells and sights and sounds of their natural habitat. Even if he had not been born in Italy, for example, a New Yorker whose grandparents had been Tuscan might experience a sense of familiarity with, say, the hills around Arezzo when first stepping onto the soil of that region. "In a particular kind of light in certain landscapes," he had told her, "all you can see are ruins, all you can feel is the past, your own ancestry or that of someone else." She understood this, although in her case, until Andrew opened the door of the world for her, the physicality of the past was mostly brought toward her by objects stored like relics inside her family home.

Whenever she entered the hotel room, she would remove the two green leather journals from her handbag, place them on the desk, then, using the hotel stationery, she would write for an hour or so. Today, however, pulling back to look at the sheet of paper in front of her, she found she was slightly startled by the appearance of her own handwriting, which was tight and dark on the page, and which was coming in and out of focus before her eyes. Knowing she was tired, she rose and walked over to the pristine bed and, without removing the coverlet, she lay down.

Soon she began to go through the inventory of the house she had left behind, an inventory she had made in early childhood and had never forgotten. Even here, even during these uncertain days, it was a comfort to her. Mentally opening the door with the key she had learned to use when she was seven, she walked into the front hall, past the umbrella stand, with its diamond-shaped mirror, and the walnut table whose bird's-eye maple drawers were filled with flowered calling cards engraved a century ago with the names of neighbours, neighbours whose years of birth and death had since grown indistinct under the rain that had washed over their marble grave markers. On the wall above the table hung a print of the Niagara River rendered downstream from the famous cataract. There is a print of that river on the wall of my house, she would say when Andrew told her, once, that he was going there to record the remnants of a trolley line abandoned since the 1920s. It is a print I know well, she told him as if this knowledge of lines on a piece of paper could connect her more closely with him and his life without her. But she did know it well; each tree, the rocks, and the small, solitary human figure staring into the current, the cliffs on each side.

The hall led into the dining room (the domain of horses) if one walked straight ahead, or into her father's office (now Malcolm's study) if one turned to the right, or off to the realm of the vast double parlour if one turned to the left. What huge, multidimensional worlds those parlours had seemed to her when she was a child, and sometimes later as well; Africa and Asia couldn't have been larger, more filled with changing light and shades of colour, with the sudden rumble of a furnace hidden beneath the boards of oaken floors polished to such a degree the furniture was reflected in them like architecture placed at the edge of vast golden lakes. There were the carpets and the confusing, mesmerizing patterns of the carpets, the different paws and hooves of chair legs lurking near the fringed edges of the carpets. The two round mirrors with the child, and then the girl, and now the mature woman in them, always with the same carved eagle on the frame

hovering over her head, benignly some days, and on others
hunting, about to unfurl its talons, wanting to carry off her brain.

Sylvia, lying now on the bed in a modern, urban hotel room,
ran all these things through her memory. She knew the contents
of the drawers: twelve knives, eleven soup spoons, twelve forks,
one serving fork, or fourteen folded linen napkins, and the small,
silver tongs with tiny hands fashioned like maple leaves. The
napkin rings with the names of previous children of the family
etched into them in flowing script; Ronnie, Teddy, Addie, the
names old-fashioned, tender in the use of the diminutive.
Platters depicting the wildflowers of England or France dwelt
inside a cumbersome mahogany sideboard beside a set of plates
depicting the rivers and mountains and pavilions and bridges of
the Orient in shades of blue, and one large dish that must have
been much loved by Addie and Ronnie, a plate with a fully decorated Victorian Christmas tree painted on its surface, toys like
those now occupying the attic placed under its boughs. And
everywhere, in all the rooms of the house, stood the china
figurines, the horses and the Creation piece, of course, but shep-
herdesses as well, and horsemen and dancers and soldiers whose
relationships had kept Sylvia busy with gossip when she was little
and at certain times – before Andrew – as an adult.

Sometimes, however, she had been prone to exhaustion.
When she had been unable to give weight or order to the variety
of sounds and sights and smells that were near her, she had been
convinced that each impression she received was insisting on its
own importance. Like a series of ego-driven guests, the fold of a
sheet, the sound of a dripping tap, the click of a closing door,
her shoes huddled together in the closet all demanded equal

attention. It was at these times that she would begin to shut
down, to disappear. She was surprised to realize now that it had
been Jerome, not her, who had seemed occasionally to be absent
while they had been talking, and she wondered whether it had
been her, or something else, perhaps some fear she was unaware
of, that had caused him to drift and then come back again. Did
he have a collection of objects from his childhood he could go
to at such times? She thought not, knowing by now that such
peculiarities of character were certain to be hers alone.

She got up and went over to the closet and took the salt
shaker out of her coat pocket. Then she crossed the room and
placed it on the desk beside the journals. How intimate she had
been all her life with things like this. As she again allowed the
objects in her house to appear, one after another, in her imagination, here in this room in the city, she did not question whether
she had left them behind. There was their world and her world
and the times of day when both worlds intersected. Sometimes,
as now, as dusk entered the city that was not her home, the intersection took place simply in a state of recall. But there were other
times when she could lift the ceramic figures from the furniture
that sheltered or displayed them, lift them up to the light, and
then hold them for a few comforting moments in her hands.

The following day when Sylvia knocked on the steel door and Jerome opened it and beckoned her inside, she was ushered into a space filled with sound and movement. The young man with the orange hair that she had seen when she first approached the alley was seated on the couch playing a guitar while someone else — someone oddly dressed — was executing a series of awkward gestures in the centre of the room. The floor beneath the performer's feet was covered with a coating of sand into which several circular patterns had been incised by a pointed toe. Sylvia, unnerved by this pantomime, felt as if she was intruding on an act of great secrecy, one that by rights should be enacted in utter privacy, and she was suddenly unsure of the permission she had been granted to be in this place.

Jerome placed his finger on his lips, then opened his palm in a gesture that Sylvia knew was meant both to silence her and to placate her. Then he raised a small movie camera to his face and turned it in the direction of the performer, who bent at the waist and lifted both arms behind his or her back, then crouched near the floor, hands sweeping through sand. After a few uncomfortable moments during which Sylvia was acutely aware of the buzzing noise of the camera, the music stopped, Jerome placed the camera on the counter beside the sink, and Mira removed the veil from her head.

"Sorry," the girl said to Sylvia, "we were just finishing up."

The sound of clicking buckles. The orange-haired boy was noisily packing up his guitar. He stood, zipped up an old leather jacket, and lifted the tattered black case from the floor. "I'm off then," he said.

"Please," said Sylvia, "not because I —"

"Nope," he said. "Don't worry . . . got to go to work." He glanced at her as he walked out the door, but Sylvia could see that there was no recognition in the look. He would not, this time, call her "Mom" in that condescending tone that was an acknowledgement of her age and demeanour. Not here. Not now that she was known by these young people, now that she was inside.

"That was Geoff," said Mira after the door had closed. "He works at the music shop down the street, repairing instruments — guitars mostly, some violins."

Jerome had moved to the edge of the sand and was now filming the patterns left there by Mira's dance steps — if that is what they were. Mira was massaging her head, lifting the short, dark hair that had been pasted to her skull by the headgear.

"A performance piece," the girl explained, "though, at the moment I'm still working on it. I have no idea where it's going."

"Where might it be going?" asked Sylvia.

Mira smiled. "I mean, where it will end up. How it will turn out. We had to repeat it a couple of times because of Swimmer.

He kept rubbing up against my legs." She walked toward the door of the place she called the bedroom, opened it, and released the cat. "We had to lock him up in the end."

Today Sylvia would talk about how she met Andrew. She had imagined revealing this episode to Jerome the night before, had envisaged herself in the chair, him on the couch, the story a thread between them. Mira had not been in the picture she had seen in her mind and she began to worry about how she would be able to talk with the girl in the room, with the two of them together and the bond that existed between them so visible, so obvious to her.

Mira, as if sensing this, pulled her scarf and coat from a hook on the wall, then paused and stood still for a moment. "I wish I could stay," she said, "but I guess I'll leave you two alone now."

"Poor Mira," said Jerome. "Off to the salt mines."

Mira wound the scarf around her neck. "Yes, the salt mines," she said. "Though in some ways I suspect the real salt mines might be more interesting."

"Smithson would have agreed with that," said Jerome. "He loved mines, loved excavation of any kind, in fact. Even . . . no, maybe especially, industrial excavation. He wanted to know about everything."

Mira opened the door. "I want to know about everything too," she said, turning to look at Jerome. "I always have."

When Mira had gone, Sylvia told Jerome about the tactile maps she made for her friend Julia. "She's blind," Sylvia explained, "but touching a map is one of the ways she is able to see. I didn't think I could do it at first, didn't think I could translate landscape into texture on a board. But then I know the County so well; I suppose that made it easier." She shifted in her chair. "I came to love making the maps," she confessed. "In fact, I am working on one, right now, in the hotel."

"You're making art yourself when you do that," he said, "taking what you see in your own County and reproducing it on a flat space."

Sylvia rejected the suggestion but found that she was somewhat flattered nonetheless.

"Andrew and I first encountered one another on the only busy street in the County," she began when she could no longer remain separate from the idea of him. "The only thoroughfare that sustained anything that resembled what a city person might think of as traffic." She described the town of Picton, its sidewalks, walls, and old windows, and as she did so she each square inch of that town's surfaces presented itself in her mind, as if she were walking, right then, on one of the familiar streets. As always, she took quite a lot of pleasure from doing this, this long walk back to the subject of Andrew.

"I was carrying on a conversation with myself, or revisiting a scene from my childhood, or perhaps I was bringing something I'd seen — a pebble on a path, the grain of a fenceboard — back into being in my mind. I was walking down this busy street in the centre of a town two or three times larger than the town in which I live, but in my mind I was, as I so often was, somewhere else, following the thread of a story that had nothing to do with the street, the errand I was performing. This ability to be absent was really the only unique skill I had managed to master, though I could clean a house, cook a passable meal, drive a car, participate in a prescribed set of ordinary social activities."

"Sounds like what we all do," said Jerome. "I spend half my life daydreaming."

She couldn't recall the season because seasons were only important to her when they brought about discomfort and distraction in the form of extreme heat or cold. She'd been aware of neither of these states so it must have been autumn or spring, an unobtrusive climate that would not have caused her to apply or remove a layer of clothing, to unfurl an umbrella, to turn her face from the wind, or to watch her step on a slippery surface. "I would have seemed, to anyone watching, a thin, unremarkable, young woman," she said, "dressed conservatively, going about my daily tasks, likely about to enter a drugstore or a stationery shop, preoccupied perhaps.

"I had, I suppose, stepped from the curb without looking, without thinking. I almost believed at the time that everything that surrounded me appeared because I was walking through it, and when I had moved on, it withdrew until I had need of it again. I counted on this neutrality; it was the key to my freedom, my singularity, and, as I would later come to understand, it was my charm against sorrow."

Though she was not looking at him, Sylvia could sense Jerome's clear, focused gaze.

"He came toward me from somewhere just behind my peripheral vision so that my first impression was that I was being assaulted, my arms pinned to my side, my feet lifted off the ground, that and the blue blur and slight wind of the car that swept by inches in front of my knees. Then I looked down, saw the wool sleeves – tweed, I think – one atop the other across my sweater, the slightly freckled wrists, and felt the elbows – his or mine – digging into my ribs. I didn't make a sound. Neither did he, at first. Then he spoke some sentences that included the words *might have been killed.*" Back on the curb they had faced each other and he had laughed. She had thanked him, said that he had saved her life. She was shaken, not by the proximity of death, but by the accident of this sudden, purposeful embrace.

"'A conditioned response,' he told me when I thanked him for rescuing me. Then he looked at me more closely. 'I've seen you before. You're the doctor's wife,' he said, 'from Blennerville.' When the light turned green, he nodded toward the other side of the street. 'All clear now,' he said. I began dutifully to cross, my face burning as if I had been slapped out of a shock or out of hysteria though, in the course of my entire life, I had been visited by no emotion powerful enough to cause such a response. I stopped on the opposite side, turned back, and watched him walk away. He was a tall, awkward man, with a slight stoop and light brown hair, greying slightly at the sides, though I had been able to tell by his face that he was still fairly young."

A conditioned response, a conditioned response. She remembered that the phrase had kept repeating itself at the centre of her mind as she watched him climb the four steps of the County Archives. She saw the shadowed carving of the stone mullions around the arched windows of that building, the reflections in the glass, petunias in the flowerbeds beside the steps, and, even from that distance, the curve of his shoulders, the worn heels of his shoes.

"Well, the truth was he had broken into my calm like a burglar then and, like a burglar, had gone casually on his way. But what had he stolen, apart from my detachment. My heart? No, that would come later. The poor man. He had no idea what he had done."

"Well, what had he done?" said Jerome. "Other than save you from a speeding car? That seems like a good thing to me."

"No," said Sylvia. "You don't understand. I have an odd mind. There are times when I can't move it around, can't take it to a new subject of concentration. It sticks . . . it sticks to things, things that I've come to understand other people have little, sometimes no interest in at all."

"You're not alone in that," said Jerome. "Once, I thought about old, decaying fences for an entire year. And then, there are other times when I think about absolutely nothing . . . nothing at all. I hate it when someone asks what's going on in my mind. Often, quite often in fact, it's a blank slate."

"A blank slate," Sylvia repeated and looked around the room. "But my own strangeness, I think, is that perhaps I have lived too long in the same place, too long in the same house, thinking about sofas no one sits on, cupboards no one opens filled with silver and china and linen no one ever uses. Any more. There are also Bibles no one reads and ancient photo albums no one ever looks at, old letters no one ever glances at. Except for me, of course, except for me. It is as if I were an extinct species mysteriously catapulted into the beginning of the twentieth-first century out of a childhood where boys stood on the burning deck when all but they had fled and captains lashed their daughters to the masts of sinking ships."

"'The boy stood on the burning deck when all but he had fled,'" Jerome said quietly. He turned to Sylvia. "I haven't a clue how I came to know that."

"Could you have learned it at school?"

"Doubtful."

"They don't memorize poems in school any more, then." Sylvia had been particularly good at memory work. When called upon, however, she had been unable to rise to her feet, unable to recite the required lines.

"Not in the school I went to," said Jerome.

"In the beginning, at least, we seemed so alike, Andrew and I, so much a part of the same vanishing species with our pioneer ancestors and a shared focus that drifted to the past. He often stood on burning decks of one kind or another when all but he had fled. And I . . . I seemed to be constantly lashed to the mast by those who had, for my own safety — or was it for theirs? — tied me there."

Jerome, Sylvia noted now, had leaned back against the arm of the couch and had lit a cigarette. "Don't tell Mira," he said. "She thinks I've quit." Smoke rose from his hand, then twisted in the air above him. "Well, at least you know something about your past. Not much of that in my life. In fact I know next to nothing about my family's past."

"Oh yes," said Sylvia. "I know about the past, all about the past. I can list from memory the entire genealogy of my father's family and have been able to do so since I was six, seven years old: also, the townships of my County, backwards and forwards, in rapid succession." She smiled, remembering. "I can tell you the names of all the constellations and I can relate their exact distance from Earth. I can tell you where each Georgian house in the County is situated and I can describe what it looked like when it was in its prime — what was cultivated in its flower beds and vegetable gardens, whether the clapboard was painted, where the original log house was placed, when the magnificent barns were built, the full name of the earliest settler and that of his wife, and how many of his children died during the first winter, and where they are buried.

"I can describe each line on Andrew's face, the one brown eye that is fractionally larger than the other, the dip of his temples and the smooth, moist creases of his eyelids. The way his hair changed from light brownish grey to white before my own eyes, how when it is brushed back the growth pattern of this hair reveals an uneven widow's peak. I can describe this the way a child describes a set of facts given to him in school, but now there are times when I can't visualize anything at all about Andrew's face."

His hands had been soft, not the hands of a labourer. There had been a place on his leg where the thigh muscle eased like a beach onto the hard bone of the knee. There was a particular vein that stood out on his forehead, and a small oval-shaped birthmark on the back of his neck. Sylvia knew all this and yet, when she closed her eyes, she could not see him.

"But, you met him again . . . somehow, somewhere."

"Yes," she said, "I saw him again, but not until I became interested in the buried hotel, the hotel that sleeps, quietly, under the dunes. I was working part-time as a volunteer at the village museum by then, amassing my own peculiar collection and demonstrating that I could be successful in turning my obsessions to good use." She sat back in her chair and described the

village museum, her odd choices for the collection: a rendering
of a family tomb made from human hair, a painting of a dog
mourning the recently drowned body of a young child, cumbersome pieces of machinery that resembled instruments of torture,
stuffed and boxed birds and animals, and all those ominous-
looking porcelain dolls that she honestly believed had survived
for a century or so because no child really wanted to touch them.
There were certain hats, as well, hats that appeared to her to be
mistakes of creation, as if some God hadn't been able to decide
whether He wanted to make a reptile or a bird or a clump of turf.

Jerome laughed. "I think I would like to see those hats."

"Andrew had heard about the museum's efforts to try to pre-
serve the dunes," Sylvia continued, "to prevent a cement company
from carting away more and more truckloads of sand. He just
came by to see if there were any old photographs in the collection, or any information at all about the hotel that had belonged
to his great-grandfather, and I, I of all people, I took him out to
the dunes. We drove the fifteen miles out to the very tip of the
County." She remembered the tension in the car, the sand shifting under their feet, his hand moving toward her hair, and the
almost unbearable silence on the way back.

"So there really was a hotel buried by sand?"

Sylvia smiled. "You didn't believe me," she said.

Jerome did not answer. He leaned forward to crush the half-
finished cigarette into an empty cat food tin on the table in front
of him.

"Malcolm taught me to drive . . . another miracle, much
celebrated by him. He taught me how to drive and, once he was
certain that I had mastered this skill, he bought me a small car

and set me free to explore the roads and architecture of the
County. The roads were easy to negotiate, and had been well
known by me ever since I had memorized the County atlas when
I was a child. The shops were more difficult because once I
entered them I would be forced to engage in conversation, and
this alone would heighten my awareness of the oddness of situations where people had no foreknowledge of my condition. It
was in such a shop, however – a shop near the dunes – where an
old man had told me about the hotel. He had played in the attic
of this building as a child, or at least he claimed to have done
this, at a time when the rest of the hotel was already buried by
sand. By the time he was a young man only the roof was visible,
and then, not much later, the building disappeared forever."

As she said this Sylvia remembered listening to the old man
speak. She had been examining a butter press where a pattern of
oak leaves and acorns had been carved into a block of pine about
four inches square. The shop was dark and full of cobwebs, and
had in a previous life been a milk house or stable. Dusty windows,
grey light. She had picked up the object and paid for it while the
old man scrabbled through a collection of paper bags in which
he was going to wrap it. And all the time he had been talking,
Sylvia had been seeing the faded, stained wallpaper of the rooms
in which the old man had played, the sun coming through broken
mullions, the sand surrounding it.

"I went home that day with one butter press, two bags
of groceries, and knowledge of the very thing that – though of
course I did not know this – would lead me to Andrew. The
hotel, then, became my sole preoccupation for several months of
that year. At dinner I told Malcolm stories connected with it,

stories about the old man as a child playing there until he could no longer squeeze through the windows because of the rising sand. Stories about how the owner of the hotel awoke one morning to find sand in the corner of his lavish garden, a small pile that became noticeably larger each day until the flowers wilted and the grass died and the guests began to discover sand in the corners of their rooms, on their plates at dinner-time, and constantly under their feet as they walked down the long, planked halls."

"I can almost see," said Jerome, a hint of surprise in his voice, "everything you say. Everything you're talking about."

Sylvia was thinking that much of what she had said about the hotel had been, in some way, triggered by Mira's performance, and that here in this room she had for the first time actually seen sand covering a floor. "Mira . . . ," she began, then stopped. She was about to say something about Mira's piece but thought better of it. Malcolm, instructing her in the finer points of social inter-action, had told her to try, as much as possible, to stick to topics that she knew something about. Then he had laughed, remem-bering her tendency to lecture, to repeat, her tendency to get stuck on the topics that she knew far too much about.

"You were going to say something about Mira," Jerome prompted.

"She seems so vital, somehow, so" – Sylvia searched for the word – "so awake."

"She's attentive," said Jerome, "curious. She pays attention to almost everything." He glanced toward the door as if he expected the girl to walk into the room. "About your hotel," he added, "Mira would have said it was like a children's story. In a children's story anything at all can happen," he said with surprising conviction. "The most impossible things and" – he looked at Sylvia – "as long as the story is being told, we believe everything. Or at least I always believed everything."

"That may be why I loved childhood so much," Sylvia said, "because of the larger belief, and because . . ."

"But your childhood –" Jerome interjected.

"I was very content, unless I was interfered with, unless I was interrupted, unless someone else stood in my path and blocked my view of my private world. I wonder why they couldn't understand that, apart from this, I was content?"

"The world is so full of a number of things," said Jerome, "I'm sure we should all be as happy as kings."

"Yes," said Sylvia. She reached into the pocket of the coat she had draped over the chair, pulled out the salt shaker, and held it in front of her. She had never done this before, had never let anyone know what she carried with her. "If you hold on to it long enough," she told him, "it becomes warm in your hands."

He leaned forward to look at the shaker, then reached over and lightly touched the top of it.

"Perhaps it was because I had no friends," Sylvia continued. "Maybe that's why they thought I wasn't happy. All through high school, you see, I kept at a distance. Once or twice a year a boy would try to speak to me, or a girl who was not part of the crowd would attempt to form a friendship. But it was not possible. Either I wanted nothing to do with those who approached me or I watched them constantly, learned the buttons on their coats, the part in their hair, a freckle on an elbow, wanting all the details of their lives. When they began to withdraw, as they always did, it was a relief in a way. I could lose myself in the schoolwork, which was a safe haven, an achievable goal. Teachers, on the whole, approved of me, but I had no friends, until Julia of course."

The high-pitched ringing of a cellphone burst into the room, causing Sylvia to jump in her chair as if she had been shaken from a trance. Jerome stood, excused himself, fumbled in his pocket for the phone. Then he turned his back and walked away, speaking quietly.

"That was just Mira telling me that she'll be late," he said when he returned to the couch. "They're installing a sculpture show at the gallery. Metal trees apparently." He smiled. "Sounds like there is a complete forest of them."

"Forests," said Sylvia. "The cottage where we met was surrounded by one of the few forests that still contained some old-growth trees, though Andrew never pointed out the oldest, most important ones. And I, I was afraid to ask, frightened of my own ignorance. I was so awkwardly vulnerable, so stupid. People like me are supposed to have next to no attention span. But, in fact, in my case, quite the opposite is true: my attention span is limitless; it's just a matter of where my focus settles: a buried hotel, a butter press, the salt shaker, the County atlas, the genealogy and then, and then him, him, him. The idea of him, you see, kept its arm around my shoulders, just as my peninsula kept its arm around the lake, protected me, and kept me safely distant from everyone else. The distance, of course, was not new, but the phantom encircling arm was a surprise until it became a habit, until it became like breathing or like pulse."

Sylvia began to move the salt shaker around in her lap as if it were a toy and she a child. Then, becoming aware of herself, she stopped, and without looking at her companion, turned and dropped the object back into her coat pocket.

"He left me after years of infrequent meetings," she said finally. "He met me in a restaurant on the edge of Picton and told me that we had to stop." Sylvia was silent for some time, revisiting his serious voice and recalling also how passive she had been. She had never fought and would never fight for anything she wanted simply because she did not know which weapons to carry or how to use them. Instead she had turned inward, away, looked out the window at a bird trembling on a branch. Andrew was saying words such as *work, commitment,* and *distraction,* and then something about Malcolm. She was looking at a bird and trying to imagine what kind of avian emergency had caused its terror. She believed that Andrew had discovered the flaw in her, that he now knew about the condition. At the very least, he had sensed something missing, something lacking. No, she could not fight.

So this was the heart-torn present, she remembered thinking at the time. This is the collision with pain. She told Jerome that after Andrew had gone from her life, there was a period during which she became convinced that almost everything was poisoned: the colossal dark chambers of rotting barns, the ghosts of vanished forests, polluted water flowing under roads through culverts, sand dunes comprising smashed shells and the bones of deformed fish pushing inland from the lake. "So this was my known, my benign world," she said. "Everything was in a state of decay." All of the ancestry she had so carefully learned was under the altered ground, bones turning to powder. There was nothing beautiful about the traces of human endeavour, despite what Andrew believed, all was unravelling as quickly as it was knit. Her

own strained face when she examined it in the mirror was a collection of dead cells. The love they had made was barren, had
resulted in no quickening, no quickening at all except this
newborn capacity of hers to see things the way they really were,
that and the ability to feel pain.

"I was grateful for that," she said aloud. "I still am grateful
for that."

In the silence that followed the orange cat strolled majesti-
cally, almost theatrically, across the room, tail high in the air. For
several moments he became the centre of attention, as if he had
planned it that way.

"What was it," asked Jerome, "what was it you were grateful
for?"

"I don't think I'd ever really felt anything before . . . before
him." Sylvia said. She paused. "And then there were the stories he
told about his family, his ancestors." She leaned over and reached
into the bag at her feet, running her fingers for a moment over
the smooth leather of one of the journals. "They were like a gift,
really, those stories, a gift from him to me."

Jerome nodded. "That's a lovely thought."

"You know," she said suddenly, "there was a picture on the
wall of the cottage where we met. It was painted by Andrew's
great-aunt Annabelle and, as Andrew pointed out, it depicted a
panorama she could not possibly have seen, one that may have
been a compilation of everything she had learned how to draw,
how to paint I guess, perhaps partially copied from the kind of
steel engravings you see in nineteenth-century books. Some of it
came, of course, from the various ships that would have been —

at all hours of the day — part of her view at Timber Island. In the upper background of the picture perched on the edge of an improbable-looking escarpment was a castle in a state of ruin. Below this — engulfed by a magnificent fire — was a beached schooner in front of which, for reasons impossible to explain, a man leads two horses and a cart into the waves."

This was the scene she had stared at while Andrew slept after their lovemaking, while Andrew slept and late-afternoon light entered the cottage. Her first landscape after love. Afterwards she would step outside the door of the cottage, walk past the foundations of the house that had once stood on the hill, and, before climbing into the car, would look into the far distance. The long arm of the peninsula where she lived would be visible, and the pale blemishes at the southern end of it which were the dunes. Sometimes she could see the small white finger of a lighthouse on the lakeshore. And then, under the surface of the lake, she would sense the presence of wrecked schooners — some of them launched a hundred and fifty years ago at Timber Island.

Sylvia removed the two journals. She turned to Jerome. "Perhaps," she said quietly, "you might be interested in these."

Jerome looked at the notebooks in Sylvia's slightly trembling hands. "What are they?" he asked.

"A record," Sylvia said, "a story. Everything that Andrew wrote about Timber Island, the story of his family. But, you may not be interested, you may not have time, or . . ." She hesitated, was worried suddenly that the stories that had engaged her, the sentences that had so affected her, might not be understood by this young man, might not be understandable.

Jerome reached forward to accept the notebooks from her.

Once, she had included Timber Island on a map she had made for Julia when her friend was going to visit the famous Thousand Islands scattered throughout the river downstream from Kingston, the same islands that the Woodman timber rafts would have sailed by on their journey to Quebec. Technically Timber Island need not have been on the map at all, but it had given her private pleasure to include it. "This is where the river begins," she had to her friend, drawing her hand toward the spot on the map, "right here where this small island is situated." She had made Timber Island from a piece of fabric quite different than that which she used for the vast anthology of islands down-river in the same way that she had used cotton for the lake and then linen for the river. "Will I be near this small island?" Julia had asked, and when Sylvia had replied in the negative Julia had added "then you must have put it here for some other reason altogether. Maybe someday you will tell me why."

She stared at the notebooks resting now on the crate that Jerome used for a coffee table. How odd, Sylvia thought, to see them here, in this place, a place that neither she nor Andrew could have ever imagined.

Later, as she walked out of the alley and down the street toward the hotel, her anxiety lifted somewhat. She could not lose the writing, really: she could recall, almost exactly, every word Andrew had used. In the beginning, it hadn't occurred to her that she would want the young man who found him to read Andrew's words. But later, after the idea of the trip to the city had taken hold of her, she had become aware of the hope that this would happen. It was the body, she supposed, the physical fact of Andrew's anatomy, so carefully learned by her, and now presented to this young person in such a shocking, unforgettable way that made this, to her mind, something she needed to do. She wanted Jerome to know Andrew, the man he had been.

As this thought entered her, she was rocked by a wave of grief so intense it caused her to stop walking, to stand quite still on the sidewalk, with a river of strangers passing swiftly on either side of her.

Timber Island is situated at the spot where the Great Lake Ontario begins to narrow, she thought, allowing the sentence to unfurl in her mind, *so that it can enter the St. Lawrence River.*

By the time Sylvia had passed through the glass doors that lead to the lobby of the hotel, she had mentally turned seven or eight pages of the first notebook. She saw the shape that the paragraphs made on the lined paper, the different colours of ink Andrew had used, the places where he had angrily stricken imperfect phrases from the record. All this — every flaw, each hesitation, his changes of mind and mood, his humour, his diagrams of interiors, his efforts to depict emotion — would be evident now to someone other than herself. *"The last raft of the season was being constructed in the small harbour,"* she whispered to herself, and then, *"continued to paint the burning hulks and smashed schooners of which she was so fond."*

Just after the elevator doors closed she spoke the sentence *"They walked with the horse out of the darkness of the stable and into the vivid autumn light."* Often in the past six months she had risen at two or three in the morning, had descended the stairs, and had read and reread the journals with such concentration that when she paused to look at the kitchen clock, two or three hours would have passed. Several hours of exhausted sleep would most times follow this, so that when she awoke late in the morning she would be unsure if the world she had entered on the page hadn't been one built by a dream. And then, the following day, when she was alone, Sylvia would say certain sentences aloud, knowing that by doing so she could evoke a scene quite different than the one in which she stood or walked, could make her own kitchen disappear, for instance, and cause the shadow of a barn door on sandy ground, the glint of lake, leaves twisting in a breeze appear in its place.

$\mathcal{J}$erome was stretched out on the futon, but he was not asleep. In the semi-darkness of the early evening he was listening to Mira describe the three vows that a monk must take upon becoming part of a religious community. Lately she had been reading Thomas Merton.

Was his namesake, Saint Jerome, a Benedictine? he wanted to know. He was lying on his back, staring at the ceiling. They had been dressing to go to a party in another area of the city but had found themselves making love instead. It was quite early in the evening: the intention to leave the studio was still with them, but it was fading fast.

"No" she told him, "Saint Benedict was the famous Benedictine. He founded the Benedictine order." She was curled on her side, facing him, with both small arms wrapped around his larger one. He could feel her lips moving near his shoulder, the way her torso shook in a soft explosion of silent laughter. So this had nothing to do with him, these were not vows that she secretly hoped he would take.

"There is the vow of stability," she was saying. "That means that you must stop, once you have entered a community, you must stop imagining that there is a monastery somewhere else that would be better than the one you are living in, stop thinking that you would be happier in another place. You must enter fully and completely each day of the life you have chosen, or the one that has been assigned to you." She paused. Jerome said nothing, but he knew she could sense his attention in the dark. "Then there is the vow of the Convergence of Life."

"Wait," he said, "that last vow. Smithson said in an interview that one pebble moving six inches over the period of four million years was enough for him, enough to keep him interested."

"He would have made a good Hindu."

"Not sure . . . probably a meat eater. The other vow?"

Mira had rolled away from him now onto her left side, and he adjusted himself so that he could put one arm over her waist, their thighs touching, his kneecaps pressing slightly into the smooth hollows of her bent legs. "The next vow," she corrected, "the Convergence of Life. I think it might mean that, while you remain stable, you must also accept that the world will change around you, and that you should remain open to and aware of those changes, though it also suggests that your life will converge with God's, or something along those lines."

Jerome remembered Sylvia's suggestion that the relentless stability of her surroundings might have somehow caused her mysterious condition, that and what she said about being trapped, imprisoned by geography. "Aren't those two vows contradictory?" he asked.

"A bit. But I've thought about that and they seem to work together somehow. The first vow has to do with what can be controlled – you can control yourself – the second is about accepting what you can't control."

Grant me the serenity, Jerome remembered, *to accept things I can't change, the courage to change things I can, and the wisdom to know the difference.* His father, returning from a meeting, had told Jerome about this. At the time this directive had seemed to the fourteen-year-old boy to be a miraculous solution to the chaos of a family made miserable by his father's binges. He had allowed himself to become certain, as he had been so many times in the past, that his father would stop drinking forever, that sanity and predictability would visit their household even though, by then, he had forgotten – if he ever knew – what sanity and predictability looked like, what form they took, how they would feel. But, in the end, the prayer was of little use anyway. Within weeks his father had entered the prolonged bout of inebriation that would be his last. Jerome could recall the horror; the older man weeping, or shouting in anger, his own terror when he was wakened in the night by the sounds of retching in the bathroom, the terrible accusations, the furious silences. "What was the third vow?" he asked.

"Oh, that," she said, and he could again feel the tremor of her laughter, "is the vow of chastity."

"Too late for that now."

"Yes," she agreed, "far too late."

His father had used those words. "It's too late," he had shouted when Jerome's mother had begged him to stop. "It's far too late to stop." Jerome, wakened by the argument, had stood trembling with rage in a pair of old flannelette pyjamas that, in the past year, had tightened around his chest and thighs in the same way that the apartment, his parents' drama, and all the cheap furniture of their lives had tightened around him. His father had turned to him then and had said in a voice suddenly calm and cold, "It's too late for you too, pal. Don't think that you are immune. Don't think for a second that you are exempt, you judgmental little shit."

There had been nothing left to break in the room, nothing that didn't already bear the mark of his father's anger, nothing of his own, so Jerome had wrenched open the glass door and had gone out onto the freezing balcony in his bare feet. He had dug with his hands though layers of snow, then had pulled the frozen, rusted bicycle from the corner where it lay and, only peripherally aware of his father's attempts to restrain him, had tried to smash up this final piece of evidence of his childhood with his fists.

As he thought about this, an image of his mother's ashen face and wide eyes came into his mind, but he willed himself away from the memory, turned instead back to the girl and placed his forehead against the warm skin on her back. He could tell by the small, involuntary twitches that passed through her body that Mira was asleep, and soon he began to drift into a dream where it was his father, not Andrew Woodman, that he found trapped in the ice near the docks of Timber Island, trapped but still alive. On his ravaged features was an expression of such tenderness that Jerome reached forward to touch the frost-covered face. But when his fingers made contact with his father's cheek, the whole head fragmented, collapsing into a confusion of thin transparent pieces on a flat surface, and suddenly he was looking at Smithson's

Map of Broken Glass. Each shard reflected something he remembered about his father: a signet ring, a belt buckle, a dark green package of cigarettes, an eye, a cufflink, the back of his hand, and Jerome knew his father was broken, smashed. The toe of a shoe, a plaid sleeve, the seam of a pair of pants, an Adam's apple. In the dream this was satisfying rather than distressing. In the dream it seemed that this alteration in his father was what he had wanted all along. And yet, when he awoke in the dark, he was weeping.

✗

That evening, after adding a few more sentences to the sheet of paper on the desk, Sylvia worked on the map of the route to the lighthouse, an occupation that she hoped would both soothe her and permit her partly to overlook the fact that Andrew's journals – his thoughts, his memories, his imaginings – were no longer close at hand. Jerome might even now be reading the words, the way she had read them night after night while Malcolm slept and rain or snow fell through the ochre path cast into the yard by the kitchen light. When she returned to bed those early mornings just before dawn, she would close her eyes and envision a world made up of islands, a world dependent on flotation. Andrew had written that on each island there had been a spot called Signal Point and that when significant messages needed to be sent quickly down the lake or up the river a fire would be lit on the shore of one island after another, a sort of telegraph of flame. Marriages and deaths were often announced this way, particularly during late fall and early spring, times when the ice was too dangerous for navigation yet not strong enough to support a horse.

There had been no such fires lit for her. The answer to the final question, the source of her grief, had been presented to her in an impersonal way on a flimsy sheet of newsprint destined for the recycling box.

"It presents in a very odd way," Malcolm had often said, referring to some disease or another, and she remembered thinking that diseases were almost always in the present, in the now, unless they were cured, or unless they were in remission waiting to recur. Her own incurable love had been like that; it had shocked her with its insistence on the present, and with its persistence, how it had presented itself, and continued — along with the grief — to present itself to her each morning when she woke. It had always been and continued to be one of her few connections to the present tense.

When she was busy with a map, however, she fully entered the landscape she was translating to touch, was able to see in her mind the rough edges of the road, the grass growing in the centre, potholes here and there, sumac bending just beyond the verge. She cut a piece of pine veneer, now, into three octagonal shapes, each slightly smaller than the last, and pasted them one atop the other in a spot near the lake where the lighthouse would be situated, then knowing that Julia would want to walk beside the water, she decided that she must find some way to let her friend know that the beach was filled with small, smooth stones.

Landscapes are unreliable, Sylvia thought, as she rummaged through her fabric bag, looking for something to define stoniness. Landscapes are subject to change. But shorelines are even less stable, shorelines are constantly changing.

When designing a map, there was always the problem of the periphery. A person blind from birth is one dependent on intimacy, Sylvia had thought, the reach of one arm defining for them the extent of the known world. When she spoke about this to Julia, however, her friend had disagreed, had reminded Sylvia that she could identify and name distant sounds and could smell things – animals, various crops, a wind that has passed over the Great Lake, the approach of a storm – from very far away. Sitting in a kitchen she knew when the apples were ripe in an orchard that would not have been visible from that kitchen. So what does a location mean to you, Sylvia had asked, how much of a place do you want to know?

"More than you," Julia had replied, "I want to know it all. I want much, much more than you can possibly fit on a map. Just give me the centre and I will move out from there, in the spirit if not in the flesh. Soon I'll know all of the County by heart."

Thinking of this, Sylvia put on her coat and began to walk back and forth across the room. Each aspect of the County – her own territory – had been named, filled, emptied, ploughed and planted long ago; all harvests belonged to the dead who insisted on their entitlement. "I cut the trees, built the mills, sawed the boards, made the roads, fenced the fields, raised the barns," they had told her in the dark of her childhood bedroom. *I, said the sparrow, with my bow and arrow.* "I drew up the deeds, made the laws, drafted the plans, invented the history, prescribed the curriculum," the dead whispered. *I, said the rook, with my little book.* They beat out a telegraph in her blood, one that read, "I fought the wars, buried the dead, carved the tombstones." *I, said the fish, with my little dish, And I caught the blood.*

Sylvia opened the curtains and looked at the concrete wall stained a mustard yellow by the muted, artificial light that gathered democratically in all the corners of the city at night. *I, said the lark, if it's not in the dark.* At this instant she found in herself the desire to walk in the city at night, the desire to be of the moment, time-bound. She looked at her watch. Nine-thirty. She decided she could be absent from the hotel for exactly one hour.

She buttoned up her coat, switched off the lights, left the room.

Once she was on the street, Sylvia stood for a while in front of a shop window behind which a variety of television sets was displayed, each relaying the same image of a well-dressed man energetically speaking and moving his hands. She was interested in his gestures, in the way his forehead wrinkled then smoothed again and how his shoulders moved up and down. He was like Malcolm during the period when he was teaching her the art of expression and she was forced, now, to suppress an impulse to copy his actions.

The next window was filled with medical supplies: basins, pumps, walkers, wheelchairs – clean, shining – patiently anticipating a whole range of infirmities. Mannequins absorbed her in subsequent windows, their stillness and that of their clothing. No wind to move fabric, no weather at all to respond to. She liked that. The damp cement sidewalk glittered faintly beneath her boots, which were now at home on that surface. Behind her, brightly lit traffic rolled on patched pavement. No one paid any attention to her, and she knew then that the city had opened its indifferent arms to her, that she could move or stand entirely still, respond, or refrain from responding, and a strange calmness came over her. The feeling was not foreign, not new to her, but here in the city she did not recognize it for the contentment that it was. It was not happiness; she had experienced that particular exhausting state of alert only three or four times, always in the company of Andrew. Now in the midst of the kind of constantly altering stimuli she had believed she could never incorporate into her life she knew only something she had always known: that this kind of tranquility could never be brought to her in the hands of others.

When she returned to the hotel and walked into the lobby, the desk clerk caught her eye, then glanced toward the black leather chairs that, after the first day, Sylvia had always ignored. She recognized the trench coat first, the hat resting on a knee the coat covered, then, as the figure rose to his feet, the face, and the weary, tolerant expression on the face. Her husband spoke her name, then, "Syl," he said quietly while moving toward her, taking her arm, "Syl, I've come to take you home."

The Bog Commissioners

$\mathcal{T}$imber Island is situated at the spot where the Great Lake Ontario begins to narrow so that it can enter the St. Lawrence River. Scattered islands with odd names appear at this point, islands that are premonitions of the famous Thousand Islands downstream where there is no longer any question about the water one looks at being that of the river. But one hundred and fifty years ago there was much discussion among the residents of my great-great-grandfather's Timber Island empire as to whether the surrounding water belonged to the lake or to the river. The ferocious swells of late-autumn squalls ought to have put the argument to rest, but despite the evidence the populace had such definite opinions on the subject that they formed themselves into two camps, called "lakers" and "streamers." Sports teams and spelling bees were said to have been assembled in this manner: "lakers" to the left, "streamers" to the right. The "streamers" were most often French: children of the coureurs du bois, or the raft makers, or the rivermen themselves. My father believed that they probably felt more at home with idea of the river that had

153

so influenced their lives touching this island territory. And from the point of view of geology a good case could be made. The west end of the island is made up of Lake Ontario limestone, the east end of the kind of granite rock that lines the river. It could be argued that the island was a child of both the lake and of the river. And certainly the industry that flourished there made extensive use of both and could not have survived without either.

Shortly before he emigrated to Canada to set up business on Timber Island, my ambitious great-great-grandfather, Joseph Woodman, an engineer by training, was hired by the Crown (along with five or six other men) as part of a commission whose job it would be to investigate and report on the state of the bogs in Ireland. The commissioners were dispatched to the various Irish counties and, as a result, Joseph Woodman was stationed on the Iveragh Peninsula in County Kerry for close to half a year.

According to my father, the fact that the only commerce in this bog-ridden district involved the carrying of butter on a footpath over Knockanaguish Mountain dozens of miles to Cork City had greatly irritated his forebear. He had been appalled to learn that, among other things, there was not a single road in the district capable of supporting a simple donkey cart, and bridges only of the rudest sort, so that the people of the region were often seen carrying baskets of turf, furniture, sacks of potatoes and cabbages, and sometimes even coffins on their backs. Something in him must have rebelled at the very size and scope of a landscape so undeveloped that it supported only scattered potato patches and hard-won fields occupied by few very poor cows. And, of course, the expanse of the bogs in the region, bogs from which men removed turf for their hearths with long, narrow handmade spades that Joseph Woodman would have considered to be almost comical. He wanted the people of Kerry to put down their spades, pick up some good English shovels, and begin the task of draining the bogs so that these murky territories could be replaced with fields of golden grain. But, on the other hand, he wondered if the Irish were capable of completing such a task. Paying little attention to the damp climate and rough geography with which Kerry farmers had always had to contend, he likely ascribed the persistence of the bogs to what he would have seen as the laziness of the men of the district. Yes, my great-great-grandfather was blind to almost everything about the people and the landscape of County Kerry, and yet, for the rest of his days, that landscape had never lost its hold on his imagination. When he returned to England with his report, he did so with the hope that he would be going back to the Iveragh in the company of a vast team of English labourers who would dig the required ditches with proper shovels. He wanted, you understand, to squeeze all moisture out of County Kerry, as if it were a dishrag, but parliamentarians more aware of climate and expense than he apparently was utterly rejected his suggestions. For his efforts, he was dismissed from the commission but granted a small island at the eastern end of Canada's Lake Ontario. Filled with humiliation, he gathered together a few possessions and his wife and, one month later, set sail for that location.

A few years later, when he gave his Canadian-born son the Irish name of Bran (which he extended to Branwell to make it seem more English), there were those who were surprised by the notion that Joseph Woodman would commemorate the dissolute brother of the by then famous Brontë sisters as he had never, to anyone's knowledge, read a work of fiction. But, in fact, as family lore would have it, he knew nothing at all about the Brontës, had named his son instead after a magical dog in an intriguing story he'd heard from an old man with a ridiculous spade while they had been standing ankle-deep in a bog near a mountain pass named Ballagh Oisin in the old Irish Gaelic, a name that had been just recently and, to Woodman's mind, sensibly changed by a British surveyor to the more easily pronounceable Ballagasheen.

In time this son, my great-grandfather, Branwell Woodman, would be sent by his now widowed father to Paris to study painting. How his father justified this in a society that must have believed his artistic interests were pure foolishness was never properly explained, but it likely had something to do with getting the young man out of the way. There was whispered mention of a pregnant parlour maid who had been banished from the island once her condition was known. Branwell, however, may not have been eager to give the young woman up, and his father may have wanted an ocean between the pair. Perhaps studying art had been considered simply the lesser of two evils. Besides, the boy had talent – not as much as his sister, Annabelle, but enough that sending him to Paris for a year or two would not seem unusual in the eyes of the few families of quality with whom Joseph Woodman was acquainted and from whom the secret of his son's indiscretion had to be kept.

So Branwell took the boat to Le Havre and went to Paris, a city I myself have visited a number of times. Branwell remained in France for a year or two, living the bohemian life of a young

art student, while back in Canada his father cursed the steam-
boats that were replacing schooners in the Great Lakes ("the
ugliest species of watercraft ever to diversify a marine landscape!" he was said to have thundered), cursed the steel that was
replacing wood, and watched his fortunes slowly recede. When
they had receded further, he cut back Branwell's allowance and
demanded that the young man return. But by this time Branwell
had seen one of his paintings hung in an "exposition," had had
a taste, a crumb, of artistic triumph, enough that he was able to
at least imagine, if not devour, the whole cake, and, under-
standably, he did not immediately want to separate himself from
a life warmed by these few small victories. Moreover, it seems
that he had been quite close to his mother, who had been dead
for only three years. Perhaps the memory of his father's stern-
ness, combined with the absence of both mother and lover,
made the prospect of returning to the island simply too gloomy
for a twenty-year-old boy.

This was not the first time that Branwell had been away from
home. From the age of about eleven onwards, while his mother
was still alive, he had been sent to one of the English-style boarding schools that were beginning to spring up in a few places in
the colonies. There he would have suffered, at least for a time,
from unbearable homesickness and from the bullying of older
boys until he himself learned to be a bully and learned as well to
at least pretend to care about cricket. During the holidays, as an
addendum to his education, his father insisted that he keep a
journal, a nautical record of any and all of the variations of the
wind that bore down on his island home, as well as a listing of
the subjects of the sermons delivered by the various visiting

Methodist clergymen. My father inherited this journal, which contained many personal references as well, usually written when the boy was miserably unhappy or terribly bored. Those particular entries were mostly about the progress Branwell had been making in the construction of a wind-driven iceboat in the winter and a small sloop in the summer. As for the sermons the young man dutifully recorded, my father could recite the titles of some of them verbatim. I can recall only two: "An Invitation – Incorruptible, Undefiled, and that Fadeth not Away" and "If Sinners Entice Thee Consent Thou Not." The latter was, in Branwell's words, delivered by "a real ranter" bent on giving his audience "a real raking up." The journal (which has, sadly, disappeared) lapsed during Branwell's seventeenth year and was only taken up again when he reached Paris.

While he was overseas, his sister, Annabelle, stayed at home where she would remain for life, keeping house (now that both her mother and the maid were gone) for her father, and occasionally painting burning schooners or schooners smashed to kindling on shores that bore no resemblance to those of the Great Lakes. And yet it was not entirely unthinkable that the ships she was surrounded by would meet their end on the rocks at the base of foreign cliffs. Often, after they were launched at the quays of the island, and if they were not to be used for the timber trade, they set sail for the wider world, travelling sometimes as far as Australia or Ceylon, carrying an unimaginable variety of objects in their hold, as if at that time it was deemed necessary to displace all the objects of the known world.

Branwell undoubtedly took up with several women in Paris – it would have been expected that this would be the case – in an attempt to forget about the hired girl altogether. Hers was a different story, her story and the story of their child.

Branwell, after a long night in Paris, perhaps a night of debauchery, had risen one day at noon and had decided to do penance by investigating the museums that would augment his scant knowledge of French history. He had already spent as much time as was required of any self-respecting art student in the Louvre and in the various churches and cathedrals famous for their art. Now he wanted war, he wanted Napoleon and his tomb, he wanted Les Invalides and the Musée de L'Armée. So, after his footsteps had echoed in the Pantheon, he entered the cool halls of Les Invalides with its rotting battle standards and its ancient swords and cumbersome suits of armour. He gazed for a while, no doubt, at Napoleon's assorted costumes, and with a sort of grisly fascination at the great man's two deathbeds. (It has been rumoured that two camp cots were required during the emperor's demise as he moved, albeit with great difficulty and in great pain, back and forth from one to the other.) Eventually, somewhat bored and wandering aimlessly past the detritus of battle after battle, Branwell, upon climbing to the third floor, came to a low wooden door with the words *Défense d'entrer* written on it, and the early recklessness, which later disappeared completely from his personality, caused him without hesitation to walk through the forbidden portal and up a flight of poorly lit narrow stairs.

Les Invalides is a large, imposing building, festooned with heraldic carving, originally built to house mutilated soldiers from a never-ending series of wars. Branwell, evidently well aware of

this, soon found himself in the vast dark attic of what he would
in upcoming days describe in his journal as the architecture of
misery, architecture built to house war and wounds and illness, a
museum of distress. Shining through the otherwise smoke-
coloured air were the silver discs of the *oeil-de-boeuf* windows that,
upon approaching the building, he had admired from the
outside. Gradually as his eyes adjusted to the lack of light he
began to discern lumpy, abstract shapes on pedestals placed
seemingly at random throughout the huge room. When he drew
closer he could see that the shapes were tiny papier mâché towns
and villages, stone walls in good repair, drawbridges pulled
firmly up, now evenly coated with several centuries of dust.
Branwell, without knowing it, had stumbled across the whole of
fortified France in miniature, made, according to the few old
labels he could decipher, so that Louis the XIV might survey his
territory at a glance, a territory fearful of strangers and constantly prepared for strife. This, Branwell commented in his
journal, was "the architecture of fear, housed in the unused brain
of the architecture of misery."

Each tree in a village square, the shutters on a town hall, walls
surmounted by crenulations, the sculptured facade of a church or
cathedral, cobblestones on a *ruelle* were wonderfully and faithfully
rendered, but this may not have made much of an impression on
Branwell at the time. It might very well have been this view of all
of fortified France that made him decide at that moment to
leave Europe, for that is exactly what he did. Perhaps there was
simply too much of it: too much art, too much architecture, and
too much history that included too much war. He must have
recalled – and with uncharacteristic fondness – his island

boyhood and everything that had delighted him about it. His father's tyrannical ways may suddenly have felt sane to him, sane and firm, and rooted in a world large enough to include the limits of the family's island empire as well as all the ships and rafts that set sail from its quays. The ships, the rafts likely appeared in his mind, and then the verdant shores of the St. Lawrence River dotted with discrete, undefended villages. Home, he would have known, was now what he really wanted.

A few days later, canvases unstretched, rolled, and packed, he sailed, taking with him two memories: the darkness of Les Invalides and an unshakeable desire to reproduce a particular turquoise painting in the Louvre, by a long-dead northern European artist.

So after a visit to the attic of Les Invalides, Branwell left behind European civilization and returned to his home on the island where everything for a time probably appeared to him to be not pastoral and bucolic as he had preferred to recall it, but raw and unfinished and in what looked to be a state of complete destruction. Felled and ruined trees were being floated down the lake to his father's docks. Raw and unfinished timber was being hastily assembled in order to construct the merchant ships that would litter the lake's surface, ships that would eventually carry not only timber but also animals, barrels, china, furniture, food, bolts and nails, cast-iron cooking utensils, shotguns, salt, axes, hacksaws, looking glasses, bolts of cloth, cannons, cannonballs, and human beings. For a time, the sails that surmounted these vessels might have seemed too crisp to Branwell, too free of the patina of age, and the ships themselves too attached to greed and commerce. Still, all of this would have been preferable to the cities that crouched in the dusty attic of Les Invalides, cities in which, it appeared, each activity, every thought, and all spoken words could only have been a preparation for conflict.

His distracted father had been — in the beginning — quite pleased to see him: he believed that his son had taken on an air of sophistication as a result of his European adventure and said as much to him during a welcoming dinner cooked by his sister. After a couple of weeks, however, Woodman Senior became uneasy about this sophistication that seemed to be manifesting itself in an attitude of bored listlessness and the inability to take to any form of useful employment.

His sister, a year younger, much less beautiful, and in some ways even odder than Branwell, continued to paint the burning hulks and smashed schooners of which she was so fond but he, the educated one who had gone abroad to study art, painted nothing at all. What was his father to make of this? He offered himself as a subject for a portrait and Branwell complied in order to please him, but Joseph Woodman proved incapable of sitting still long enough for his son to make a creditable likeness (more-over, staring at his father made the painter nervous and his subject even more irritable than usual).

"It isn't what you want," his sister had told him. "Paint something you want to paint, ships for example."

But, of course, that wasn't what he wanted either.

He finished the portrait. It was hung above the mantel in the parlour where it remained for several decades until his father, in ill-tempered old age, demanded of Annabelle that it be taken down.

As the months passed, Branwell was constantly urged by his father to enter into the family business as a clerk in the office. "All he's good for," he told Annabelle, time and again, when she questioned this. Branwell resisted, claiming that had he a female model his artistic prowess would return. This revived earlier fears about his libertinism and made his father long to confine him to a room in which there was nothing but a desk and an inkpot and a ledger. He was twenty-two. It was high time he was making a living.

Annabelle knocked on Branwell's door one evening shortly after one of these conversations with her father. Her brother, who had been lying on the counterpane staring at the ceiling, rose from his bed and opened the door. He had let the fire go out and the siblings could see their breath as they spoke.

"I will be here forever," she told him, "but you can do something. You can get out."

When he said nothing, she asked, "What did you see in Paris that you still see in your mind?"

The awful miniature cities almost took shape in his memory, but he shook them off. "Frescoes?" he said uncertainly. He didn't like to mention naked models to his unmarried sister.

"Frescoes," she said, bending down to nurse a leg rendered almost useless by a childhood bout of tuberculosis, "that's good. I've never seen a fresco. Wall paintings. What else? There must have been something else."

He thought of the painting that had so impressed him in the Louvre. From the Flemish school of the sixteenth century, it was the only picture he could recall in accurate detail despite days spent walking on squeaky parquet past large-bottomed goddesses, blood-soaked battles, bored or anemic princelings, spoiled dogs, dead rabbits, and rotting fruit, saints suffering under the hands of torturers, Madonnas, *Pietàs*, baptisms, and the inevitable crucifixions. He had stopped in front of this painting because at first glance it had seemed to be about nothing at all except pure landscape and glorious shades of colour: turquoise and grey and emerald green with a touch, here and there, of rose. All of this was surprising, almost shocking, in the midst of the jaundiced yellows and bog browns that darkening varnish had leant to the other masterpieces in the room. There was light in this painting and it wasn't candlelight, or firelight, or torchlight. It was daylight. It was fresh air.

"There was a painting," he ventured, "done long ago, I think, by a Dutchman."

"Yes?" said Annabelle encouragingly. She had a cast in one eye and it seemed at this moment as if she were eyeing her brother with amusement. In fact, she was looking at the collar of one of his shirts and thinking that it needed washing. But she was far from uninterested in what he had to say. "What was the subject of the painting?"

Branwell suspected that she was secretly hoping for ships. "Not ships," he said, "no, wait, perhaps one, but far off, far off in the distance." He paused, remembering. "There were great distances in the painting, Annabelle, rivers winding off and around, mountains and towns and many caves." He had shuddered a little when he mentioned the towns, but mentioning the caves had helped him steady his nerves. "There were fields too, and orchards, all miles and miles away. At first I thought that there was nothing but air in the painting but, in fact everything was in it, the whole world." Branwell was warming to his subject.

Annabelle now had the shirt tucked firmly under her arm.

"There was a saint. Very small," Branwell continued. "You might not have noticed him at all. And the lion was even smaller but visible, doing this and that in the wilderness, sometimes chasing a wolf, I think."

Annabelle had always been intrigued by dangerous wild animals, frightened and fascinated at the same time. She exchanged a glance with her brother when he mentioned the wolf. It almost looked as if he were about to say something but decided against it and instead, as she turned to leave the room, he announced, "I want to use these colours, I want to paint these distances, but not on a panel like the Dutchman, on walls." He rose from the bed where he had been lying, took a couple of steps, and caught Annabelle by the arm. "I want to make frescoes, but how on earth am I to do that? Father would never put up with me splashing colour all over this house. He would call it unseemly."

"That's just it," said Annabelle, glancing over her shoulder at her brother. "You'll be forced to travel. You will become itinerant." She paused and then repeated the word *itinerant*, as if she had just discovered it, and maybe she had. "This is how you will get out," she added as Branwell released his grip on her arm. "Think about that."

What Branwell did not know about the papier mâché towns that had so affected him was that itinerancy was central to their creation. Itinerate draftsmen had been dispatched to the farthest reaches of France to draw the details of each house, public building, garden shed, crumbling wall, broken window, piggery, chicken coop, struggling fruit tree. Some were sent farther afield to the coveted borderlands of Belgium and Prussia, where they

innocently measured and recorded the length of streets and
alleys, town gates and fortifications, then plotted the dimensions
of adjacent outcroppings and caves. They returned to Paris with
their leather satchels and portfolios overflowing with accurate
drawings of the pristine palaces of the rich, collapsing hovels of
the poor, markets, barns, bridges, and towers, and the varying
textures of the surrounding fields and fortified or unfortified
farms; everything that was needed for craftsmen to reproduce the
world in miniature in order to facilitate the battles of a king.

Later that night Annabelle slowly descended the back stairs into
the now darkened kitchen and abandoned her brother's shirt on a
chair beside the door. Moonlight entered the place through two
large windows and settled on the objects in the room as if by
design – several pitchers, one large bowl, and three pale onions
shone. Annabelle always noticed images such as these, but even
though, on nights like this, she would sometimes stop and gaze at
one dramatically lit object or another, it was only the ships that she
chose to capture in her paintings. Apart from these vessels her art
was almost entirely innocent of the actual. Still, even as she limped
across a kitchen that had moonlight on the walls and firelight on
the floor, the masts of her father's ships were visible through the
windows, and on the ceiling swam a river of silver light.

You might think that with all this reference to moonlight and
water and wreckage that Annabelle had a romantic soul, but you
would be very wrong. In fact, she read no novels and brooked no
nonsense, and was an astute and unsentimental judge of character,
particularly the character of her bog-draining, forest-plundering

father. She suspected that were Branwell to linger too long here on the island he too would become the object of drainage and plunder of one kind or another and she wanted, as much as possible, to save him from that.

And so, the next day, after a morning spent with the apple-peeling machine and a bushel of apples, a morning during which she noted that the peels falling from the fruit resembled gold and crimson ribbons tumbling to the floor and knowing that she had no desire to paint them, she washed her hands, placed a bonnet on her head, and a shawl on her shoulders, and moved as quickly as she was able across the yard to her father's offices.

What a masculine world Annabelle would have had to tramp through in order to reach her father! There was wood everywhere. Logs were being unloaded from the hulls of the two ungainly timber ships that had recently arrived from the northern lakes, and scattered here and there were the stacks of planked lumber that would eventually make their way to the opposite side of the island to be used to build schooners and clippers. The first timber raft of the season was being assembled in the small harbour and this was a noisy French business all round: men were cursing and shouting at each other in a language Annabelle pretended to ignore though she knew the vocabulary well. The enormous dram, or unit of the raft, sixty feet wide and almost two hundred and fifty feet long, had just been completed and the rivermen were now poling sticks of oak timber (along with some pine to ensure buoyancy) into the first crib, which had been fastened by withes and toggles to its neighbour. Annabelle's favourite part of the raft, the temporary frame bunkhouse where the men slept and ate, would not be constructed until later when all of the cribs were filled and the floor of the raft was secure. Then, as a final touch, a mast with a sail attached to it and a recently felled small pine would be erected in the very centre of the dram. No one had ever properly explained the presence of the pine to Annabelle, but she secretly believed that it must be an offering of sorts to the wounded spirit of the plundered forests.

The Frenchmen — for that matter, the Englishmen — who worked for her father paid no attention to Annabelle, having intuited early on that one glance in her direction might result in an abrupt termination of their employment. She wasn't much to look at anyway, with her flat chest, her lameness, her long face, and her severe dark clothing. Annabelle believed that the French thought of nothing but sex, a distasteful subject that never entered her own mind unless she was in earshot of those men, that language.

Her father's whiskers had always looked to Annabelle like a feathered headdress (worn upside down, as if it were a bib) and this headdress had always been white. Moreover, he had always resembled certain powerful Old Testament leaders: the temperamental Isaacs and Noahs and Abrahams — even Jehovah himself — an angry potentate whose tantrums were kept only temporarily beneath the surface of his character as the result of an enormous act of self-control. As far as she knew, her father smiled only on the occasion of a launching of a ship and even then he appeared to be showing his crooked and oddly pointed teeth rather than displaying any real signs of good humour. He was much admired for his firmness and for the latent ferocity that everyone sensed in him. And, as owner of Timber Island and everything on it, he was considered to be honest and fair by all the men whose lives he controlled. Women were of no consequence to him – beyond their ability to cook food and procreate – and so he mostly ignored all wives and female children, his own wife included when she was alive. But Annabelle was another matter. She was not afraid of him. And he knew it.

"What is it?" he asked, not looking up from his papers, recognizing his daughter's footsteps as she entered his office. The top of his head shone in the low light. The grate was without fuel. "I haven't much time," he went on, without giving his daughter a chance to speak, "that vile Gilderson over on the mainland has now built a steamship of all things! The ugliest species of watercraft ever to diversify a marine landscape, I'll wager! He has had the infernal nerve to invite me to the launching Saturday next, even asked if I'd like to send a small flotilla of sloops to attend the monstrosity's progress out of the harbour. I certainly will not provide anything of the sort and am writing him at this moment to say just that. The fool!"

Despite the fact, or perhaps because of the fact, that he was ten years his junior, Oran Gilderson was Joseph Woodman's chief competitor in the local shipbuilding trade. They were locked together by envy and a not inconsiderable amount of loathing and, as a result, invariably issued handwritten invitations to each other on the occasion of the launching of a ship, savouring the opportunity for potential humiliations of one kind or another.

Annabelle untied her bonnet, removed it from her head, and placed it on the oak desk directly in front of her. She shifted her weight onto her good leg. There was only one chair in the office and her father was occupying it. "Branwell isn't happy," she blurted. "Your son. He wants to paint walls, to do something that is all his own."

Her father looked up now in irritated astonishment. "Whatever can you mean?" he asked. He had no time for frivolous interior decoration. A succession of mainland drawing rooms of various hues might have passed through his mind, drawing rooms in which he would have been ill at ease, bored, and overheated.

"He wants to make frescoes, to paint landscapes in hallways."

"Landscapes? Hallways?" Joseph Woodman removed his reading spectacles and peered at his daughter. "For heaven's sake, why?"

"To give the people here more scenery." Annabelle drew herself up into her nearest approximation of good posture. "Some trees, perhaps . . ."

"I'll show them trees," said her father testily.

"Live trees," continued Annabelle. "Mountains . . . waterfalls."

Her father placed his hands flat on the desk and leaned forward. "Don't be foolish," he said. "No one will want these walls. No one at all. Paris was clearly a mistake. It's time he became a man, took some responsibility, and got over his fancy French ways." This declaration was followed by an ominous, angry silence. Then he said, "Has his mind been destroyed by drink, by absinthe?" Joseph Woodman had no doubt heard about the unsavoury side of the Parisian art world but had overlooked these rumours in favour of removing his son from the vicinity of the hired girl. "Well," he continued, "did he? Has he?"

It was well known that Joseph Woodman permitted no liquor of any kind to be unloaded on the island in order to prevent the Frenchmen from infecting the more serious workers of Scots and English descent with their fondness for the grape. Since any reference to Ireland brought with it a tinge of remembered frustration and humiliation, no Irishmen were tolerated on the island either, thereby removing that particular brand of alcoholic danger. Joseph Woodman insisted that Timber Island remain a parched community.

"Of course not," Annabelle said. She had read enough about Paris to know that wine, at the very least, would have been imbibed regularly. She didn't know anything at all about absinthe, but was certain that, regardless of what he may have consumed, her brother's mind, though filled with melancholy, was completely intact.

"Well, I won't have it, this business of decorating parlours . . ."

"Hallways," Annabelle corrected.

"Parlours, hallways, it's all the same and I won't have it." Both of his fists were clenched now as if he were preparing to do battle with these parlours, these hallways, and his face was reddening as his blood pressure rose. Joseph Woodman had been in a particularly foul temper in recent months. The entire treasury of his beloved Orange Lodge (he had been ardently anti-papist ever since his Irish adventure) had been spent in Kingston on a marvellous triumphal arch that had been erected in anticipation of a royal tour. The Prince of Wales, however, tired of the wretched

Irish question, had refused to dock at Kingston at all, forcing schoolchildren to enter boats in order to serenade him with their patriotic songs. These boats could be seen quite clearly from the shores of Timber Island, and the sweet voices of the youngsters could be heard by Mr. Woodman as he sat seething in his office. "Branwell should stick to portraits," he told Annabelle now, "if he insists on art as a profession. Portraits are what people want." He looked past her shoulder. "But in truth," he said, pointing one long finger in the direction of the outer office, "what he should undertake instead is gainful employment with Cummings."

Cummings was a thin, sallow-faced clerk of indeterminate age who had been a fixture of the outer office for years. Although he was timid and withdrawn, he had nevertheless once, and only once, summoned the courage to leer at Annabelle as she passed by his desk. No man had ever looked at her that way before, and she was determined that no man would ever look at her that way again. She had, therefore, since that day resolutely refused to speak to Cummings for any reason at all, though she did not tell her father about the incident.

"That will never happen," said Annabelle. "It's not what he, what Branwell, wants to do. It's not what Branwell *should* be doing."

No woman, not even Annabelle, was going to give Woodman advice. "I'll be the judge of what he should or shouldn't do," he thundered. "And I say that he starts in that office Monday next."

Annabelle placed her bonnet back on her head and tied the ribbons under her chin. The bow looked like dark bird's wings on either side of her narrow face. She gave her father a determined look, which was all the more unnerving because of the one wayward eye. Then she turned, left the room, walked through the outer office, and into the noise and disarray of the yard.

A half an hour later Annabelle found herself in Back Bay, or, as it was sometimes called, Wreck Bay or Graveyard Bay, one of her favourite island locations. It was a shallow, muddy, weed-fringed spot where annulled ships were brought to die, and several vessels that had been recently towed there were now in the process of doing just that. Others, having been stripped of anything considered useful, had already sunk beneath the surface of the water. In summer, Annabelle liked to glide across the bay in a rowboat in order to peer down at the vague shapes of scuttled ships wavering at the bottom of the lake, but today she would remain on the shore. As always, she carried her sketchbook with her in her apron pocket, though, at this moment, she had removed neither it nor her pencil. She sat on a remnant beam near the water, dressed in her dark outfit, dwarfed by a collection of broken masts, frayed ropes, ragged sails, and water-stained hulls in varying stages of decay and levels of submersion. Booms groaned in the increasing wind, chains clanked and knocked against rotting timbers, but Annabelle took no notice of these sounds. She was thinking about Marie. And she was thinking about the baby. If it had been born alive, it would be just two years old by now.

It is a sad fact that into any individual's life there will stroll only a very few irreplaceable fellow creatures, friends who, when they are absent, leave one bereft, awash in one's own solitariness.

For the islanded Annabelle, whose dealings with the outside world were severely restricted by her gender and by her geography, there had been her brother, who was largely unconscious of the magnitude of his importance in her life, and there had been Marie. When Marie had been sent away from Branwell, he had suffered from her absence and Annabelle had been denied the companionship of her dearest friend. Marie, at least, like Branwell, had been sent away, had been given a change of scene, however grim that scene might turn out to be. But Annabelle had been left behind in the silent, empty house. This echoing, vacant region, she had concluded, was to be her territory, her prison. She would bang up against its walls as long as she breathed while, mere steps from her window, all those wonderful cathedral-like ships moved soundlessly, like floating works of art, away from her shore. It is sometimes difficult to believe in Annabelle's fondness for all the schooners and sloops and privateers that were moored at the docks of Timber Island, or which cut through the waves of the lake, or whose sails dipped and flashed on the horizon, and yet, despite all the paintings she made of the demise of such vessels, she couldn't help but be affected by their beauty.

Joseph Woodman had told his children that the word *schooner* came into being as the result of a young man shouting into the crowd at the launching of such a vessel, "See how she schoons!" What could it mean, this verb *to schoon*? To lean into the wind and move swiftly forward, Annabelle had concluded. She had been known to use the verb now and then when describing the activities of another person, most often, because of her friend's vitality, in relation to Marie.

If Marie had been with her at this moment, she and
Annabelle would have been engaging in one of their favourite
pastimes: discussing what was wrong with Branwell. They never
tired of this topic, which they had approached from every imag-
inable angle and related to which they had considered the most
improbable questions. Why, for instance, would he not eat broc-
coli, or raw tomatoes, or any of the cook's delightful relishes?
What made him want the crusts cut off his bread? He could talk
at length when enthusing about his iceboats and then refuse to
reveal anything about the inner torment that the girls were
certain resided in his soul. Why would he not confess his adoration for Marie when it was clear to both the object of that
adoration and to his sister that that adoration existed? Would
he never want to be a soldier and fight wolves and Americans
and other enemies? How was it that he could think of nothing?
(When they asked him what he was thinking about, he always
said, "Nothing.") If Marie were here now, the question Annabelle
would ask to open the conversation would have been something
like, "Why did I have to make it clear to him, and to my father,
that he wants to paint hallways?" And then she would have
added, "Doesn't he know how fortunate he is to be a boy who
can, with or without parent approval, do what he wants with
his life, who can become itinerant, who can get away?" In the
end, though, she would have softened. Poor Branwell, she
might have said, trapped in a world where the expectation was
that, regardless of the detours of his youth, the road he walked
would eventually lead him back to the grinding routine of the
family business.

Annabelle took the pencil and the small sketchbook out of the pocket of her skirt, stared for a while at one blank page, and began to draw the outline of a raft from memory. She had considerable trouble with the perspective. Having never before attempted to render something so thoroughly horizontal, she was unable to make the structure look as if it were lying flat in the water. Frustrated by this, she concluded that this was not to be a day during which the making of drawings was possible, so she returned the sketchbook and the pencil to her pocket, rose to her feet, and began to walk back to the house.

Passing the quay, she noticed that several of the men were on their hands and knees testing the withes that held the timbers in place. The raft was nearing completion. Soon it would begin its journey down the river, past a scattering of villages and a quantity of islands, moving through the shallows and rapids out into the world.

$\mathcal{A}$nnabelle could recall quite vividly the March day in her twelfth year when Marie had been brought across the ice, how she had been transported and then delivered like a package during the least negotiable month when, because of rising temperatures, it was necessary for islanders to make use of a contraption – half canoe, half sleigh – in order to make the journey back and forth to the mainland. This vehicle either slid with great difficulty (pushed by its passengers) over frozen bumps and cracks, or it floated in constant slush and broken ice through frigid and partly thawed waters. The girl, who from a distance appeared to be paralyzed either by fear or by frost, sat upright in the bow, not moving when the other passengers climbed out onto the ice to push, as they made their slow progress from Kingston Harbour to the island.

Annabelle was not a pretty child, and there were moments when, despite her almost complete lack of vanity, she felt a twinge of resentment at the injustice of this arbitrary fact of nature. That March morning, looking through the watery glass of one of the parlour windows toward the partly frozen lake, however, she'd had the odd, inexplicable notion that the small, distant girl in the boat was her other, her more beautiful self being conveyed to her, and that when this girl eventually stepped into her house their two bodies would overlap and become three-dimensional like the twinned images on the photo cards she slipped into the stereoscope on Sunday afternoons. She was mad with excitement, convinced that the girl's imminent arrival would be more of a longed-for reunion than a first encounter. She stood by the window, transfixed, as the skipper heaved the brown mail sacks onto the dock, then held out a hand to the child who had not moved one inch. The man made no effort to escort the girl, but pointed instead at the big house where Annabelle waited.

Branwell, who was then in his thirteenth year, and home for late-winter holidays, joined Annabelle at the window. As he watched the girl limp toward the house, he said disapprovingly, "She'll never do, she's too thin. And, look, she's lame."

Annabelle, who was thinking of her own damaged leg, said nothing at first, then whispered, "I think she will be beautiful."

"Doesn't she know that she's supposed to come to the kitchen door?"

The girl's pale face was visible now. She was about to climb the front steps. Branwell rapped on the glass to get her attention and Annabelle saw two startled dark eyes glance toward the window. "Next door down," Branwell shouted with more volume than was necessary. "Not here."

The girl looked at them for some time — long enough to cause discomfort — and the look combined curiosity and a not insignificant amount of contempt. Then, quite suddenly, she stuck out her tongue before moving toward the appropriate door. Annabelle and Branwell racketed through the intervening rooms of the house to the kitchen. They had both fallen hopelessly in love. But at that moment Annabelle was the only one of them who knew this.

Inside the kitchen Annabelle and Branwell grabbed each other's arms and pulled at each other's clothing, each wanting to be the one who opened the door to the stranger. When Branwell advanced, Annabelle kicked him in the left shin and he swore and lost his grip on the porcelain knob. "Damn," he said in a tone much like his father's, and then again when he saw that his sister was drawing the girl into the room by the sleeve of her tattered coat.

"Leave go of me," the girl hissed. She jerked her arm out of reach, then sat on the floor and began hastily untying her boots, ignoring altogether, it would seem, the presence of the other two children in the room. Annabelle withdrew slightly and took in the girl's costume: a soiled bonnet, worn overcoat, and grey lisle stockings with holes in the knees. Some kind of pinafore was visible where the coat fell open over one raised leg, then the other. Once the boots were off, two white hands covered the dark grey cloth on the feet. She's not lame at all, thought Annabelle with a rush of disappointment, just frostbitten. The sodden boots lay like small dead animals near the fire. Tears of pain gleamed on the girl's eyelashes, eyelashes that were dark and plentiful. The sight of those wonderful lashes was to be among the first of many things about Marie that Annabelle's mind would retain indefinitely.

"Well," said Branwell in the condescending tones of an adult, "what's your name then, girl?"

The child sat clutching her toes. She stared at Branwell but did not answer him. Then she sniffed, looked away, and announced, "I don't have to tell you that. I've only got to tell things to the Missus." She scanned the kitchen, as if she expected to find this person hidden in a shadowed corner.

"My mother is in bed," said Branwell truthfully. "She stays there all the time," he added. This was somewhat of an exaggeration. Mrs. Woodman was prone to bouts of migraine – more prone in winter than in summer – and withdrew for days at a time. But in fair weather, and sometimes even in the coldest season, she would be a more or less cheerful if somewhat vague and occasional presence in the kitchen.

"She stays in bed all the time," continued Branwell with an air of authority, "so you'll have to wait on her and I'll be the one telling you what to do."

"No he won't," said Annabelle indignantly. "He's good for nothing. My father says so."

Just then, the cook, a tiny woman with a disproportionately large face marked by two fierce black eyes, entered the room. "What's this?" she asked, surveying the still-huddled child. "Oh, yes, the girl from Orphan Island." She shot a look in the direction of Branwell and Annabelle. "What are you two up to?" she asked and, without waiting for a reply, turned again to the recent arrival. "We don't sit on the floor here," she offered and then, "I expect you're far from clean."

"*Far* from clean," echoed Branwell.

"No one asked for your opinion," said the woman testily. "In fact, no one asked for you – either of you – to be in here at all. Both of you – back into the house!"

The siblings reluctantly withdrew, but not before Annabelle and the girl had exchanged a brief complicitous look.

How forbidden Marie was! Annabelle's father had made it clear to her and to her brother that they were not to consort with this girl who was an orphan who would therefore have come from God knows where, the progeny, most likely, of a drunken lout and a shameless hussy. Furthermore, she was there to work, not to lollygag about with the likes of them. Mackenzie, the cook, who up until that time had tolerated the children's presence in the kitchen only occasionally, now barred them completely from the premises on the grounds that they were too much of a distraction. Banishments and admonishments did nothing to dispel the air of romance and mystery that Annabelle believed was attached to the girl, and, as the days went by, she thought about little else. Often she found herself standing behind the open kitchen door, watching Marie through the space between the hinges while the girl went about her various tasks and was, more or less, bossed and pushed around by Mackenzie, who eventually softened somewhat under the influence of Marie's stubborn pride and unquestionable beauty.

One day, while Annabelle stood in the V-shaped shadow behind the door, Marie, who was scrubbing the floor, began to crawl toward the spot with brush and suds and pail until Annabelle could see quite clearly her small, soapy knuckles and thin, damp wrists. She hunkered down and reached into her apron pocket for a pencil and one of the small pieces of butcher paper she always kept with her in case she might want to make a sketch. Squinting in the gloom, she wrote a message that told the girl to come to her room late at night for a secret that would be told.

Annabelle wondered if the girl could read, doubted, in fact, that she could, but had made the decision, nonetheless, to make this attempt to communicate with her.

At first the girl ignored the scrap of pinkish-brown paper as if its sudden appearance in her line of vision had caused her no curiosity whatsoever. Then, quite abruptly, she snatched the paper from the floor and crammed it into the pocket of her pinafore. Mackenzie said something about the fire, the oven, and then something else about the length of time it was taking Marie to finish the floor. The girl did not look up from the brush in her hands, glanced neither toward the door nor toward the cook stove, and even when Mackenzie left the room, she did not remove the paper from her pocket. Just as I thought, she can't read, Annabelle concluded and having thus concluded did not bother to invent a secret.

Still, believing the girl to be illiterate had no diminishing effect upon her fascination, and the following day Annabelle was back at her post. She had the odd sense that her already small world had in fact shrunk, and now included only the dimensions of this triangle of shadow and the limited view that could be seen from it. A spider shared this space with her, but it didn't disturb her at all. Branwell might have screamed and run away, but not her. She wasn't afraid of spiders, and even had she been, there was theatre on the other side of the door crack and she was able to watch it all day long for months and months if she chose to do so. She was not required, as Branwell was, to participate in any formal kind of education because she was a girl so, even when her brother returned to school, she would be able to remain in close proximity to Marie. When she told Branwell about her luck he repeated his father's words about the drunken lout and the shameless hussy and predicted that Annabelle would catch cooties from the girl if she didn't keep her distance.

Her mother, though as listless and seemingly preoccupied as always, made the odd appearance. Occasionally, she would drift into the kitchen, where she would look at Marie — not with curiosity exactly — but with detached puzzlement until Mackenzie explained, for the fourth or fifth time, who Marie was and what she was doing there. Annabelle squirmed in embarrassment behind the door at these moments. What was it, she wondered with some impatience, her mother thought about all day, what made her seem so absent even when she chose to leave her room and be among them? Though Annabelle didn't know this, the truth was that Mrs. Woodman had never successfully managed to emigrate from England in her mind, and even as she stood in these rooms and gazed out the windows of this house, a landscape of a very different kind lit her imagination. Only Branwell would listen with any interest when their mother described stone villages and picturesque fields. Annabelle had no time for this rhapsodizing about distant places, places she doubted she would ever see and knew her mother would never see again.

"The girl from Orphan Island," Mackenzie would say, and Annabelle's mother would reply, "Oh yes, of course," then move vaguely around the kitchen touching a pewter jug, an earthenware bowl, as if she hoped that something in the kitchenware's insistence on being solid might pull her back from the lost green landscapes of the past and into the overheated interiors of the present.

On one of these days, shortly after Mrs. Woodman had floated out of the kitchen to wander aimlessly through the other rooms of the house, Marie was commanded by Mackenzie to once again scrub the floor while the cook went to fetch a brisket of beef at the island's butcher shop. What a thin back she has, thought Annabelle, looking at the nearby labouring figure. Her clothing, which was not finely tailored as Annabelle's, fell away from her spine toward the floor and appeared to be much too big for her frame. She watched the girl's muscles move under her cotton clothing and, as she was watching, one arm shot out from the body and shoved a familiar piece of butcher's paper under the door. Annabelle stooped to retrieve it and, in the gloom, read her own message. Then she turned the paper over in her hands and was confronted with a one-word message: *No.*

It wasn't as if Annabelle was unaccustomed to this word: her father often shouted it across the shipyards, or yelled it in the direction of Branwell and her when they were making demands. It wasn't that she hadn't seen it scrawled in two large characters across various letters of request on her father's desk. But to have the negative emerge from such a small, such a powerless source shocked her deeply and hurt her in a way she hadn't been hurt before. What could it mean, this refusal, this annulment?

Annabelle crumpled the paper in her fist, then walked into the parlour where she stood looking out the window at late-spring snow falling on vessels that had remained useless and dry-docked all winter long. In the corner of the room the recently fed Quebec stove roared as it devoured wood. Overhead she heard Branwell's quick steps progressing along the floorboards of the upper hall toward the back stairs, along with the clicking sounds made by the dog's nails. Soon, from the direction of the kitchen, Annabelle could make out the sound of Branwell's voice demanding that Skipper perform the one trick he had managed to teach him. "Roll over," he said and, shortly after, and much to her chagrin, she heard Marie's laughter followed by some light scolding about dog hair on the floor, and then the sound of Branwell and the dog beating a hasty retreat when Mackenzie must have been coming up the walk.

Nothing was ever going to happen to her, Annabelle suddenly knew. Plenty was going to happen to Branwell, she suspected. A great deal had undoubtedly already happened to the rejecting Marie, but she, Annabelle, was never going to be granted access to that intriguing history. She felt as if she were now and would be forever outside of everything, forced to dwell in the shadows, witnessing only a fraction of the world through a thin crack of light. With this feeling came a considerable amount of resentment.

Why should she remain invisible to this hired person? How dare she pretend that Annabelle was not close at hand, breathing the same air, walking up and down the same staircases? Did she not have two legs — one shorter than the other, it was true — and a nose, and hands and a heart, just like this other girl? She was determined to exist, to take up some space — whether wanted or not — in Marie's mind, along with memories of Orphan Island, of her journey to that destination, throngs of other splendidly independent orphans, children with no fathers obsessed by nautical calculations and the distribution of timber, and no distant mothers bent under the weight of the memory of green fields too far away to matter. She would have murdered her parents at that moment had it guaranteed a nod of approval from the girl, had it guaranteed an entry into the brotherhood, the sisterhood of those fortunate enough to be orphaned.

But that moment passed and Annabelle realized that a less dramatic method of gaining the girl's attention and approval would have to be discovered. Late afternoon found her a solitary, bundled creature engaged in frantic activity mere feet beyond the kitchen window. She lay on the ground, scissoring arms and legs, making angels in the snow deposited by a late March squall. She created snow men and women, hurled snowballs, lifted armloads of snow from the ground and flung them toward the sky, creating her own private, contained blizzard. As it grew darker the kitchen became a colourful, warmly lit stage where the girl, Marie, carried out her tasks under the instructions of Mackenzie or, when the cook left the room, on her own. During one of these latter periods Annabelle threw a snowball at the kitchen window. The girl gave absolutely no indication that she had heard the sound of the impact.

Then, just as Annabelle was thinking of re-entering the house, Marie approached the kitchen window with a saucepan of hot water in her left hand. When the glass was sufficiently clouded, she extended her free hand and with one thin finger wrote the words *No I will not* on the steamy surface. Infuriatingly, Marie wrote the words backwards so that Annabelle would have no trouble reading them, and even more infuriatingly, she never once looked in Annabelle's direction.

Annabelle marched inside and tramped snow all over the house looking for her brother. When she found him in his room upstairs, she said indignantly, "That girl downstairs can read, and she can write backwards and forwards. How about that?"

"So what," Bran said, not looking up from a novel entitled *Ralph, the Train Dispatcher.* He did not seem interested in the least. But he was absently pulling on his ear, a nervous habit he had developed in early childhood, and Annabelle knew, therefore, that any information concerning Marie was not something he was likely to forget.

The attic where Marie slept was not heated like the rest of the house by fireplaces and Quebec stoves, but it was made almost habitable by the fact that the two huge chimneys, through which the smoke of the half-dozen hardwood fires passed, were fully exposed and their bricks were warm. Despite this, one night, after everyone else in the house was asleep, while Annabelle ascended the steep stairs with a combination of anticipation and mis-givings, her entire body was covered with goosebumps as the cold slipped under her nightgown and up her legs. It was dark as pitch on the stairs and she believed that she had not made one sound, yet when she emerged into the attic, which was partially lit by a quarter moon, she could see that Marie was sitting up in her bed.

"Get in here," the girl said. "Get in here or you'll freeze."

Annabelle made her way quickly across the room, then scrambled under the covers. Marie shifted to one side to allow some space and Annabelle was aware, for the first time in her life, of the warmth that the recent presence of another body lends to flannel sheets. "Have you been to sleep yet?" she asked.

Marie shook her head.

"Nor me. But, then, I knew I was coming up here later."

"I knew that too."

Annabelle was surprised by this revelation but decided not to let on. "What's your favourite thing?" she asked.

"Night," said Marie, "now. My bed is all that is mine."

"But it's not yours," said Annabelle, proprietorship igniting briefly in her small self. Didn't her father own the whole house and everything that was in it? For that matter, didn't her father own the whole island and everyone on it, and all the ships that were built there and sailed to and from it, and all the timber that was rafted down the river? There was something unfair about this distribution of ownership and Annabelle knew it, even then. Still she added, "Your bed belongs to my father," then to associate herself with this awesome power, "to my family."

"But I am the only one here and I like that. And after I come up to bed at night and lie down, nobody tells me what to do."

"I'm here with you now," Annabelle persisted, "and if I told you to do something you'd have to do it."

"I would not," said the girl. "I would not because I'd say no."

Annabelle believed that that was precisely what the girl *would* say and decided to pursue the notion of superiority no further. In truth she was relieved that she had been allowed entrance into the girl's world, not sent away as she had suspected she might be.

Marie had the whole pillow. *Her* pillow, thought Annabelle. "Maybe," she ventured, "if I asked nicely you would do it."

"Maybe. What would you ask?"

"I would ask you about the orphanage."

The nuns have no money, Marie told Annabelle; all the money goes to the monasteries where "there is nothing but men."

Some of the boy children in the orphanage would eventually enter monasteries themselves, hoping to experience comfort. It was a very good idea, if you were a boy, to pretend to have received a "call" from God, instructing you to become a monk or a priest. That way you wouldn't have to be a farmhand owned by a mean farmer. It was not, however, a good idea to pretend to have received a "call" if you were a girl "because nothing would change except your clothes and those for the worse."

Annabelle had paid very little attention to these details. "But how did you become an orphan?" she asked.

Marie was silent, staring at the ceiling. Then she rolled over on her side to face Annabelle, her dark head in the angle of her arm. "It was a wolf," she said.

Annabelle doubted this. "All the woods are chopped," she announced. "Father says so. They're chopped all the way to Lake Superior so there can't be any wolves here. All the timbers come down on boats from Lake Superior."

"Yes, this wolf came on a boat with the timbers and he came dressed as a soldier so no one could know. Then he got to our house and ate my mother all up and killed my father." Marie was silent for a few moments and Annabelle feared that this wolf was the only part of the story that she was going to tell. Then the girl added, "He was a royal wolf with blue eyes, and he had medals from the wolf kingdom."

"And he made you his orphan," murmured Annabelle. Drowsy now, it seemed to her that this change of status from daughter to orphan would be like a sort of marriage, would necessarily involve ceremony and a long significant pause in the action when the blue eyes would lock with yours and tokens would be exchanged. Perhaps even a kiss. Then orphanhood. And, yes, then beauty.

Annabelle wanted something to dream about, something that was all hers, an orphanhood, a wolf of her own.

"The wolf made you beautiful," she said, drunk with a combination of this thought and approaching slumber. "Where is he now?" she asked, her voice thick with sleep.

"He's here. He swam beside the boat to the island," said Marie. "He's always with me. He bought me when he killed my parents. He owns me."

Both girls began to fall seriously into sleep. "He's come down with the timbers, he's just outside the house," said Annabelle, who was already dreaming of a flash of blue eyes caught in moonlight and large, formal pawprints in the snow.

Annabelle, thinking of Marie, began that spring to light fires during the day at the Signal Point of Timber Island – or so the story goes. This was the method of communication usually used by islanders for weddings and funerals and other newsworthy events, and was a kind of throwback to the bonfires lit on significant holidays in the distant British Isles from which many labourers in her father's empire had emigrated. However, Annabelle, had she been asked to explain it, wouldn't have been sure what she was trying to accomplish by doing this. Not knowing for certain where Marie was, she had little hope that a message would reach her friend, and so, eventually, she simply settled in to enjoy the flames. She loved to paint fire, and she loved to watch it.

Branwell, who despite Annabelle's best efforts was by now spending his days working with Cummings, was sent out by his father to Signal Point to see what on earth his sister was doing, but she never confessed to him her original intentions, which, by the end of the first week, she had realized were quite futile, at least in respect to the messages being sent by the blaze.

Her brother, not anxious to return to account books and columns of figures, sometimes took to doing "the ranges": an exercise in establishing a sort of mental aerial perspective. As he had explained earlier in his journal, and as he undoubtedly now explained to Annabelle, this involved the sorting of landscape by distance, beginning with the shore of the next island, followed by the intervening water, then the shore of the mainland, the barracks of the military school, the taller buildings and steeples of Kingston, and then the far-off deep purple of the now completely deforested hills to the north. Why ranges? Annabelle might well have asked. Like rows of mountains, her brother would have replied, one range behind another. Better would have been the sails of ships placed side by side in a harbour and looked at from the end of a peninsula, she had thought, but did not say so aloud. Instead she asked about Marie, about whether her brother ever thought about what might have become of her.

Branwell, to Annabelle's annoyance, probably would have continued to squint into the distance, and even more maddening from Annabelle's point of view the young man probably would have been making all those self-conscious gestures with thumbs and fingers at right angles, gestures that suggest that artists are intending to frame one view or another. Stop doing that, Annabelle very likely would have said, judging from her character, stop doing that and answer my question. What he answered we will never know. In fact we will never know whether the question was posed, though my father seemed to think that it would have been, that it had been, because shortly after this Branwell began to write in his journal again. One of the entries for that spring included not only the direction and speed of the winds and breezes but also the fact that Annabelle had been lighting a great number of unnecessary fires, and that she had asked him a question that had caused his mind to become troubled in the extreme.

Annabelle, meanwhile, had been visited by an unshakeable notion. The river was free of ice by now and each day ships docked at the island's quays and unloaded an enormous quantity of timber onto the island – if it were to be used for shipbuilding – or into the bay opposite to that of the nautical graveyard if it were to be poled downstream to Quebec. Teams of Frenchmen were to be seen busily assembling timber rafts, leaping from log to log like frantic squirrels, and shouting a variety of curses and commands that seemed neither to be directed at any particular individual nor related to a specific task. Still, the rafts, which were like islands themselves, sprang into being and sprouted small bunkhouses on their surfaces with remarkable swiftness, and they could be seen moving away, like large swimming animals, into the current of the river, heading east, as they had for as long as Annabelle could remember whenever the river was open to navigation.

Branwell's father had informed him that, in order to better learn the business, and to familiarize himself with the timber merchants in Quebec City, he would be required to make several journeys on board these rafts over the course of the season. When he complained about this to Annabelle, one afternoon on Signal Point, she announced that when their father was safely away on business in Toronto or visiting the remaining forests of the upper Great Lakes, she would be boarding a raft herself, going with him out on the river.

Her brother laughed, of course, at this ridiculous suggestion and told her, as he confessed in his journal, that she had taken leave of her senses. "There is something that needs to be done," she apparently said to him, "something you will come to understand." Her last fire would have been collapsing into embers as she said this, and the water that surrounded the island would have been lively with sails, the harbour bristling with masts. She had made her decision. Her fires had been on the wrong side of the island after all. Her brother was weak. He needed direction. He needed looking after.

❧

Annabelle recalled that the night Branwell had first visited Marie's bed, she herself had been out in the yard until midnight painting the ships across the water in Kingston Harbour by the light of the August moon. Branwell had said that if she added fire to the scene its light would compete with that of the moon to bad effect. She had paid no attention to his advice. How am I to see the schooners at night if not by the light of the moon? she asked. You could slip across the water and set them alight, her brother had teased in response. And all the time he was thinking of Marie, of how to draw nearer to her.

In the five years since Marie's arrival in their household, whenever Branwell was home from boarding school, Annabelle had watched him try various means to catch and hold the hired girl's attention. He had taunted her unmercifully, and when she did not respond with enough vehemence to the suggestion, for instance, that her attic was filled with bats, or the kitchen alive with mice, he had taken to making jokes, usually on the subject of her French heritage. Sometime later, he occasionally refused to eat the appetizing and decorative pies and pastries Mackenzie allowed Marie to make, culinary creations for which the girl seemed to have a special gift and ones that she presented with pride at family dinners. Annabelle suspected that Branwell barely knew what he was up to, and half-despised himself when he did this. It hadn't escaped Annabelle's notice that when he trailed around after Marie while she was straightening up the house, or criticized her work, or now and then tugged on the one black braid that hung down her back, the bewildered expression on his face in no way matched the authoritarian tone of voice he was attempting to achieve. In the past year or so, though, her brother's behaviour had ameliorated somewhat in relation to Marie: he had become quiet, almost thoughtful in her presence, and could be seen smiling at the girl in a wistful way across a room. And then, one Saturday afternoon, when she and Marie were busy with sewing, Annabelle had followed the direction of Branwell's focused gaze and had realized that he was staring, with a considerable amount of intensity, at Marie's downcast face.

Their mother had been dead for a year. No one – not even the parade of doctors called in to examine her – had been able to say precisely what was wrong with her. It had been very apparent to everyone that the woman was dying – but of what exactly? She became weaker and weaker, her small frame diminishing, her vague expression changing to one of sorrow and resignation. Near the end, she had been brought each day to the parlour where she could see from the window the oak sapling she had planted years before, a sapling that by now had become a flourishing young tree.

She could watch its trembling leaves lose green, gain gold, look at its thin arms bending in the autumn wind. Because he listened with real interest, she had described to Branwell the ancient oak that had grown near her old home in Suffolk. "Hundreds and hundreds of years old," Annabelle had heard her mother tell him repeatedly. "If your father destroys it, I insist that you kill him," she invariably added. It had never been entirely clear to Annabelle whether she was referring to the young oak on Timber Island or the old oak in Suffolk. Perhaps, she had thought, her mother meant both. "That will not take place," was all Branwell had managed to say in reply.

The tree remained after her death, had gained in height and breadth. If Joseph Woodman had ever detected an oak in his yard, he had made no comment on it. Unnoticed, the tree would be safe from the axe, Annabelle concluded, so Branwell would not have that reason to kill his father – though she didn't doubt that there would be others. She knew that her brother was shattered by the loss of their mother, and she suspected that he resented the way their father was able to conduct business the day after the funeral and all subsequent days as if nothing on his island had altered at all.

Annabelle remembered that on the night Branwell had first ventured to Marie's room to give comfort, and perhaps to receive it, their father had rampaged through the house like a confused bear, shouting at Marie, who, with some help from Annabelle, had by now assumed most of the domestic duties therein, Mackenzie having decamped with her French husband. Equating all betrayals, imagined and real, with Ireland, Joseph Woodman believed the pair had gone to that country. "They'll be drowned,

I'm telling you," he had said to Annabelle. "They'll be ruined. They'll be out on edge of Dereen Bog, they'll be stuck beside Loch Acoose with nothing but a ludicrous turf spade between the two of them and enough moisture to turn their flesh to water." When he stopped lambasting Ireland, he turned to Marie for whatever had gone wrong, and everything he had lost. Annabelle had shouted at him to stop, but Marie, her face flaming, had finally run up the two flights of stairs to her attic to be rid of the hullabaloo, an Irish word that Annabelle knew she had learned as a result of living in this house.

When Annabelle, confronted by her father's temper, had been taken by the desire to paint burning ships by moonlight, Branwell had likely seen his way clear. Soon their father, exhausted by ill humour, would have been snoring angrily in his bed. Annabelle would be gone for an hour or more. Branwell had likely made his way toward the staircase.

Looking back now with affection, Annabelle imagined Marie sitting up in bed, hearing Branwell's footsteps, perhaps seeing his shadow on the wall, and she imagined that Marie would have opened her arms to the boy, even before he stepped into the room. She could not, and did not, imagine what happened next, but remembered the warmth of that bed and the pleasure of intimate talk in the place that was Marie's alone.

✠

As you float on the lake away from Timber Island, then enter the mouth of the St. Lawrence River, the islands thicken until eventually you are aware of a number of shorelines composed of great rocks and tall trees moving soundlessly past the watercraft on which you stand. Sometimes you feel that you are not moving at all and that it is the islands themselves that are adrift, like icebergs sailing purposefully toward open waters. Branwell, however, trapped on the river by his father, was, at this stage, quite impervious to the beauty that surrounded him. Occasionally he would read to Annabelle a poem or two he had attempted in his journal to vent his frustration:

> *Oh solitude where are they charms*
> *That Sages say they have seen in they face*
> *Better to live in the midst of alarms*
> *Than to dwell in this terrible place*

> *The wind was from the east this week*
> *It blew hard all the day*
> *The raft was stopped at Batiseau*
> *And there now do we stay*

Amused by her brother's lack of literary prowess, Annabelle told him he was in no danger of becoming a poet, but suggested that there must be wonderful things to sketch all along the river. Branwell allowed that while this might very well be the case, he was in no mood to avail himself of these opportunities. "All I can think of," he said, "is getting onto dry land. But it seems the minute I get back, before I can even catch my breath, I'm back at work again. My whole life is just raft after raft after raft."

Timber rafts were the most temporary of constructed worlds and seem to have been constantly engaged in the artificial evolutionary process that was thrust upon them. What once was part of a great forest became for the span of a few days the platform of a small village where people worked and ate and slept and overcame the sequence of difficulties that made up the course of the river, difficulties so dramatic that even Branwell felt compelled to comment in his journal that the sight of turbulent rapids frothing over the edges of the raft, not five feet from where he stood, "filled the spirit with awe." Once the rafts successfully reached their destination, they were, of course, dismantled, their several parts dispatched to England, where eventually the wood that made up their construction might re-emerge in the shape of furniture in a multitude of Victorian parlours or, if the timbers were oak — and large and long enough — as masts on the decks of the pugnacious vessels of the Admiralty. One thing was certain, however, no raft ever made the return journey upriver, and Annabelle, knowing this, would have thought a raft to be the perfect vessel for the deliverance of her brother into the arms of the future she wanted for him.

✒

Annabelle worked up the nerve to get herself on board a raft in mid-July and was, oddly enough, able to do so with her father's permission. It wasn't entirely out of the question for a sightseer or two to be taken on board, especially in the warmer months, as it was well known that this was by far the best way to experience the thrilling power of the rapids. Furthermore, because his mind was almost always fully occupied with business, any curiosity shown in some aspect of how it worked by one of his offspring —

especially in the face of Branwell's obvious disinterest – pleased
Joseph Woodman even more than Annabelle had anticipated that
it might. And she *had* anticipated that it might, had spent the previous evening, in fact, composing the following speech. "I just
want to understand the business," she had said to him, "how the
rafts are taken down to Quebec. I just want to see what Branwell
does when he is on the river."

On this midsummer day, once the raft moved away from the
booms that held it, she grabbed her brother by the arm and
began to dance with him, awkwardly, it's true, because of her
lameness and because her brother was an unwilling partner. "I
don't understand what has got into you," he might have said to
her as he disentangled himself from her embrace. He would have
been irritated too, because now the journey was going to be
longer than the usual three or four days. The raft would have to
haul up in odd places along the river where lodgings could be
found with families known to their father, there being no question of Annabelle spending the night on board with the men.
Branwell would likely also be invited inside for an evening meal
out of politeness, and the thought of this may have put his teeth
on edge for he was becoming more and more unsociable as his
unhappiness deepened. His bemusement regarding his sister's
behaviour would be exaggerated by the fact that, although in the
past she had been suspicious and evasive about Frenchmen, she
had now apparently developed a certain camaraderie with them,
and before the raft was five miles downriver, she was laughing and
conversing with them, and showing them the watercolours she
was making of the river and the trees. His own artistic endeav-
ours at the time were confined to the penmanship he practised

while keeping the log — great, flourishing capital letters, for
example, at the beginning of each entry, and the odd mechanical
drawing of an iceboat or a sloop.

When, on the second day, Orphan Island hove into view and
the raft moved toward it, Branwell would have thought nothing
of it, as the French, who were both sentimental and pious, sometimes left a box of food or a bag of coal on the dock there out
of respect for the nuns and the orphans in their care. He watched
his sister step ashore and, searching the dock, was slightly
puzzled by the sight of her nightcase resting there. Then he was
seized from behind by two coureurs du bois who deposited him
unceremoniously at the spot where Annabelle waited and who,
after shouting orders to their comrades, swiftly poled the raft
back into the current of the river. When he called to the men,
they waved their caps and called back to him, "Bonne chance!"
and "Vive l'amour!"

By the time Branwell had collected himself enough to turn
angrily to his sister in search of an explanation, Annabelle was
running, as fast as she could with her bad leg, up the slope toward
the large forbidding facade of the orphanage where a woman with
a young child clinging to her skirts had come out to see who had
arrived. He watched, dumbfounded, as the two women embraced
so fiercely that they fell laughing to the ground, surprising the
child, who began to howl. And Branwell, shaken by his arrival at
the island and by the unhappiness draining out of him at the sight
of his lost love, began to weep as well. He might have seen himself
then as one of the minor characters in the painting he had admired
in Paris; perhaps one of the wolves in the far distance; not one
of the seductive wolves Marie had told him about one night as

he lay in her bed but a wolf with neither ferocity nor charm.

The orphanage that Marie and her child stood in front of was a large, unpainted, decaying pile of timber and clapboard, grey with neglect and adorned with many plain, ill-repaired, sagging porches. Grey might not be the appropriate word to describe its colour, for it would have been darkened by time, becoming almost as black as the habits of the nuns who cared for the orphans in its dusty rooms. Its windows were plentiful, but, by Branwell's count, at least six panes in these windows had vanished and were replaced by waxed paper. The sight of the opaque windows, the dark walls, awakened a sense of shame in him. Why had he acquiesced so completely to his father's wishes, which had resulted in consigning Marie to this dismal place? Why had he not insisted on marrying her, something he now knew he had always wanted? He was a distant, cringing wolf; a wolf without courage, he thought, and thinking this decided on the change that would determine the course of the rest of his life.

For most men a reunion after desire, then intimacy, then distance, and finally an ocean of time is a terrifying proposition, one that often causes them to avoid allowing even the possibility of the encounter to fully form in the mind. Annabelle, having had absolutely no experience with romance, and unlikely to ever have any experience with romance, would have nevertheless known all this instinctively. But how did she know where Marie was? This part of the story was never explained. Perhaps she was visited by a lucky guess, or perhaps she was told of Marie's whereabouts by the Frenchmen, who would have been well aware of the telegraph of rumours running up and down the river. Whatever the case, she would have walked toward her brother and, taking his hand, she would have drawn him toward his lover and the child who would become my grandfather. As they walked up the slope she would have told him that she always knew what he wanted, even if he didn't know. And Branwell would have nothing to say for he would have known in his heart that she was right.

✗o

After a week of Catholic instruction by the nuns, a week made somewhat easier by the marginal knowledge of Latin that Branwell had acquired while at boarding school, a visiting priest married him to Marie in the chapel of the orphanage. The ceremony was attended by a choir of orphans, a dozen nuns, Annabelle, and the small boy called Maurice, whose original status in life had been made legitimate by a ceremony of candles, incense, and chant, and who now had a full-blown temper tantrum just as vows were being exchanged and had to be taken from the room. Annabelle would never forget the sound of the boy's cries echoing through the wooden halls of the dark building after one of the nuns had lifted him up and carried him away. These howls, to her mind, did not presage a happy life, and, in fact, her predictions would prove to be accurate. For although Maurice would become inordinately successful, he would never be particularly happy, would never, in fact, develop the capacity for happiness, and would eventually come to grief as a result of a combination of serial fixations, greed, and bad weather.

But that day young Maurice recovered from his tantrum in time for the wedding supper and even submitted to being held, for a few tense moments, first by his father and then by his aunt, who repeatedly identified herself to him as such. Annabelle was enthusiastic in her new role; Branwell, fully attentive to his reawakened love for Marie, less so in his. He wanted all of his bride's attention and was a bit nonplussed by the notion that any other living creature could be in a position to make demands of her. Moreover, the child had become accustomed to occupying that most coveted spot by Marie's side in the warmth of her bed and, even during the first few days after the wedding, several discussions took place about this matter.

Marie seemed filled with joy, not only by her marriage to Branwell, but also by Annabelle's reappearance in her life, and, the day after the wedding, so that Branwell could spend some time alone with his son, she offered to take her friend on a tour of the home that had preceded her long and lively tenure in the Timber Island attic and that had provided her shelter since. There were fewer orphans in the dormitories now, Marie told her friend. "Not so many wolves, I suppose," Annabelle commented. Marie showed Annabelle the cot at the end of a long dormitory, the place that had been hers before she made the journey to the island. "I've always loved beds," she said as they left the room. "They are nests, really, a small space you burrow into, a space that comes to know your shape."

Annabelle's astonishing scrapbook – a scrapbook that would contain only one paper scrap – was begun during this tour of the orphanage, or at least the first relic to be placed in it was plucked from the rough surface of the rickety front steps of that structure as she and Marie walked out the front door to stroll around the property. Annabelle had long been intrigued by the idea of relics. A French riverman had once showed her a splinter of "le vrai croix," which he said he kept always on his person and which he claimed had been entirely responsible for the safe passage through rapids of every raft on which he had laboured. Should not, then, a splinter of this piece of architecture that had harboured her friend be kept by her as a magic charm?

That was the beginning, and as soon as she had the splinter tucked safely inside her sleeve, she regretted not having plucked a similar specimen from the delivering raft.

Eventually, Annabelle's book of relics, her splinter book, as Branwell would come to call it, would contain samples from any number of wooden constructions: a splinter from an assortment of sad, decomposing vessels in Wreck Bay, for instance, shavings from the floor of the shop where ships were being conceived, bits of bark from a delivery of rough timber – all dated, identified, and catalogued. She also included several ominous-looking charred wooden matches that, according to their labels, had been used quite innocently to light candles and oil lamps in the house on significant occasions of one kind or another. There would be fabric in the book, square inches of canvas and short lengths of rope from the sail loft, given to her by Monsieur Marcel Guerin, the sail master. But the only paper scrap in the book was the small half-inch of waxed paper she tore from the edge of one of the orphanage windows.

Marie also showed Annabelle the graveyard, an area surrounded by a white picket fence and filled with twenty or thirty small limestone pillars each topped by a lovely stone angel. An Italian monument maker in the town on the shore of the river had donated his services, she told Annabelle, and had carved an angel each time a child died. "I knew some of these children," Marie said, "not all, of course, but some. They almost all died quietly in the midst of some epidemic or another. Death seemed so romantic, somehow, to an orphan. You got attention, you got prayers with your name in them, and then a religious service just for you. Everyone thought about you for days and days. And," she paused, "and you got your own angel." To children with no possessions that angel must have seemed like a special gift, that and your own name carved on the stone beneath it. "In the winter after a storm," Marie said, "it looks as if there is a choir of miniature angels advancing like an army across the top of the snow."

Annabelle looked at the graveyard for quite a while, then, just before turning back toward the convent, she plucked a painted splinter from a tilting picket. "But you weren't the dying type," she said to Marie.

"No," laughed Marie, turning back toward the convent, "I certainly was not."

A few days later the small family (in the company of Aunt Annabelle, as she now liked to call herself) entered a rowboat skippered by a sturdy nun just as the morning sun rose over the river. On the mainland they caught a coach to Kingston and a skiff to Timber Island, arriving late in the afternoon. They knew that Joseph Woodman would still be at work at this time and so, with some trepidation, they approached the modest, unpainted building that he used as an office. Soon they were gathered in

front of his large desk. The old man neither stood to greet
them nor looked up from the account book he pretended to be
studying, and, when he finally spoke, he talked only to his daughter, whom he accused of high treason and "Irish behaviour."

Annabelle did not flinch. "This is Maurice," she told him,
placing her hand on the top of the boy's small head. "You are
his grandfather."

"I remember a certain Fitzmaurice from Ireland. Bog Irish
and a complete fool. Maurice . . . an Irish name if I ever heard
one." Woodman eyed the boy suspiciously.

"You know very well it is not an Irish name," Annabelle
replied. "You are perfectly aware that it is a French name. On the
other hand, let me remind you that Branwell *is* an Irish name, and
you were the one who chose it."

"Indeed," said Joseph Woodman, "and we can all see
what that brought him." This remark was delivered without
sarcasm. The patriarch had not the sense of humour to engage
in sarcasm.

Then, in the midst of the hollow silence that followed this
declaration, to everyone's amazement, Maurice, who had neither
spoken nor smiled throughout the journey or the week that had
preceded it, beamed at his grandfather, disengaged himself from
his mother's hand, and scrambled onto the old man's lap.

Joseph Woodman stiffened, but did not put the child down.
The small boy settled into the crook of one unyielding arm, then
reached up and touched the white beard. He looked with adoration into the stern face. "Monsieur Dieu," he said, smiling first
at his grandfather and then at his surprised mother, "Monsieur
Dieu . . . il est là."

This was to be one of the first of Maurice's fixations on per-
sonalities more powerful than his own, fixations that would rule
his life. Maurice would always be drawn to those more certain
than himself of how they wanted the world to operate, and these
attachments would be the source of both his occasional joy and
his chronic unhappiness. But that day, his deification of his
grandfather was to be the key that unlocked his family's future.
No one is immune to the flattery of adoration, and Joseph
Woodman was not to be an exception to this rule. Once Maurice
was fully established on the man's lap, the timber baron's expression gradually changed from irritated astonishment to a kind of
bewildered tenderness. "What is this clamouring all over me?" he
was said to have remarked in a tone that was now a mere parody
of bad temper. "It feels like a rat. Or is it perhaps a badger?"

From that day on "Badger" was the name that his grandfather
used, both when he spoke to Maurice privately and when he called
to him from a distance as he often did when returning to the
house for his evening meal. Sometimes he had a treat for the boy,
a candy he had purchased at the island store, or one of the baker's
sticky buns, and no amount of scolding on the part of Marie
could dissuade him from letting his grandson devour these sweets
right before supper. The boy, for his part, followed the old man
everywhere he could. He trailed around after him, from room to
room, down the road to the office, sometimes even into the old
man's private chamber. "Badger, be gone!" was a teasing command
that was often heard booming through the house. Sometimes the
boy, anxious for the morning reunion, would be up at dawn,
standing by Joseph Woodman's bed, waiting for the levee. On one

of these occasions, Joseph Woodman leapt from his bed and, still clothed in his nightgown and cap, chased his squealing grandson all over the house. It was obvious to Branwell, Marie, and Annabelle that the old man had come, quite quickly, to love the child and that this love was to be, at least for the time being, the bond connecting all the adults in the family.

Marie resumed her duties in the house with much enthusiasm now that her legitimacy afforded her the status of junior mistress rather than that of servant. Golden soufflés with one perfect crack down the middle and beautiful cakes with fruit slices arranged to represent bouquets emerged often from her ovens along with the more ordinary daily fare. She slept in Branwell's room now in a brass double bed bought for the couple by Woodman Senior in a moment of weakness that could only be viewed as a complete surrender to the very turn of events that he had taken such pains to prevent from happening.

On certain quiet afternoons Marie and Annabelle would retire to the old bed in the attic in order to talk, just as they had done when they were young girls. Their conversations mostly concerned Branwell. His virtues and his shortcomings, his various infirmities, and his mysterious inability to express himself continued to absorb them. Various theories about what he was thinking or how he was feeling were articulated, mulled over, dissected. Several conflicting conclusions were drawn, then reversed the next day or the following week. Branwell, unaware of all this, and thinking about nothing in particular, was, in fact, happier than he had ever been in his life. He went — albeit somewhat unwillingly — each day to the office and, once summer came, even more unwillingly out on the river with the rafts, but his marriage to Marie pleased and calmed him and made his tasks easier to manage, though the idea of painted hallways remained in his imagination.

Still, both women tended to believe that, underneath it all, Branwell was tortured. This made him more mysterious, more interesting. Long, speculative discussions about what might be torturing him took place in the attic while Branwell was yawning in the vicinity of account books or while he was stretched out on a cot gazing at the temporary ceiling of a moored raft. He wasn't tortured, he was just bored by duty. He wanted to embellish stark hallways with turquoise landscapes. Eventually he confessed his desire to his wife, who, in turn, brought up the subject with Annabelle. "It's what he is meant to be doing," Annabelle apparently announced, this time to a sympathetic listener, "and, in time, I expect, he'll be given his chance." Marie agreed and told Annabelle that she wanted pure contentment for the man who had made her so happy that even now, when she woke beside him each morning, she could hardly believe her good fortune.

Annabelle, whose domestic work had all but disappeared now that Marie was back, took up the thankless task of educating her little nephew until it became obvious that the lessons in poetry and drawing did not hold his attention the way the columns of numbers in his grandfather's office did. The old man eventually took over in the matter of Maurice's schooling, teaching him accounting and bookkeeping. By the age of ten, the boy was a businessman to be reckoned with and knew enough about how to extract money from others that his grandfather determined that he should be sent to board at Upper Canada College in Toronto, the perfect place, the old man knew, for the Badger to become acquainted with the kind of boys who, when grown, would inherit the fortunes he hoped his grandson would find a way to benefit from.

✗o

By the time Maurice, uniformed and capped, departed for school a few years later, his mother and father had moved away from Timber Island and, with the help of the elder Woodman, had purchased an inexpensive two-storey clapboard hotel on the sandy beach at the end of the nearby peninsular County. The rafts had dwindled to a trickle by now, Old Woodman had retired, and Cummings had taken over what remained of the much-diminished business, a business in which, to Branwell's relief, there was no longer any room for him. Annabelle and her father remained in the big house, she eventually nursing the cranky old man. The Badger, still devoted to his grandfather, would make the day trip from the hotel by way of his own sailboat in the summer or an iceboat he had constructed at the Christmas break.

Branwell, who had painted a number of landscapes in the upstairs and downstairs halls of the inn, was being encouraged by the more prosperous families in the County to decorate their homes. He completed these commissions in the winters when the dry heat thrown by the wood stoves would cause the paint to set, and when there were no guests at the inn. The summers brought a number of city families to the shores of the lake and the verandas of the inn, some from Toronto and Montreal, some from as far away as Albany or Chicago. In spite of his father's annoyance, Branwell had called the inn "The Ballagh Oisin," after the mountain pass in Ireland, the story of which had given rise to his name. "It's a mountain pass," he would tell inquisitive guests, "in Ireland." At one point he had staged an evening contest to see who among the visitors could pronounce the name properly. Branwell was a jovial host, much given to jesting. His disposition was greatly improved now that he had left the timber business and had in his life almost everything that his sister had known all along he wanted: Marie, the painted hallways, and an open view of the lake uncluttered by islands of commerce.

$\mathcal{D}$uring their third or fourth year at the hotel a letter arrived for Branwell from a fellow-innkeeper in a distant part of Ontario known as the Huron Tract. This was a portion of Upper Canada that had been considered quite useless by Joseph Woodman in that it was situated too far from the Great Lakes – or any other navigable body of water – to make it suitable for timbering, despite rumours of incredible hardwood trees, many of which were twelve to fifteen feet in diameter. A couple of decades before Woodman Senior had established his island empire in close proximity to the relatively civilized town of Kingston, however, a hundred-mile-long inland trail known as the Huron Road was being hacked, sawed, chopped, and burnt through this forest under the direction of the Canada Company, which comprised a group of British and Scottish entrepreneurs, several of whom were named after the wild animals they had killed in other corners of the Commonwealth. Tiger Dunlop is someone who comes immediately to mind, but likely there were other colourful monikers as well – Rhinoceros Smith, Polar Bear MacLeod,

Lion McGillivray. The trail ended at the Lake Huron port of Goderich into which the sorry, fly-bitten, half-starved party of blazers and engineers, axemen and surveyors had staggered in the autumn of 1828 after months of exhausting labour and bouts of swamp fever, only to be bullied by the company into making the trek back in the opposite direction in order that improvements might be made to the new road and the land surveyed and divided into saleable plots for would-be settlers.

A few years later, once the settlers started to arrive, several inns were established by the Canada Company at various points along the road – inns whose fortunes would suffer dramatically when, some years later, another company of entrepreneurs established a railway from the centre of the province to the port on the lake. The innkeepers, or their offspring, managed, somehow, to keep the doors of their solid brick Georgian buildings open for a year or two afterwards – though it was clear that their trade had suffered and there was no telling how long their businesses would survive.

Branwell's letter was from such an innkeeper, a certain Mister Sebastien Fryfogel Esquire, proprietor of Fryfogel's Tavern, which was situated on the Huron Road between the town of Berlin and the hamlet of Stratford. He had heard about the colourful murals of the Ballagh Oisin from a traveller who had stayed there, and he felt that paintings of this nature might enhance the rooms of his inn. Would Branwell consider making the voyage to the west? Fryfogel allowed that he normally had no time for the thieves and rogues that roamed the roads of Upper Canada plying their various trades. He listed

tinkers, medicine sellers, horse traders, dancers and singers,
and itinerant painters as being among the most disreputable
and offensive members of that already defective species of the
animal kingdom known as human beings. But he had it on the
best authority that Mister Branwell Woodman was, like himself,
primarily an honest innkeeper, though one who occasionally
painted pristine landscapes with no people – and, in particular,
no shapely, sinful women in them. His own inn needed dressing
up. Would Branwell oblige?

The letter arrived in early January when funds from the
summer had all but dried up and the commissions from mainland locals had slowed to a trickle. Branwell hated the idea of the
journey: he had heard the rumours (broken axels, mud, and
malaria in summer, overturned sleighs, ghastly blizzards, frost-
bite, and pneumonia in winter) that circulated about this distant
road, and he had no wish to test the accuracy of such rumours.
But Marie, who wanted not only to feed her small family but to
experiment as well with expensive French dishes in anticipation
of hungry and appreciative summer patrons, insisted that he take
the commission. "Not much money in it, I'll wager," he said,
pushing the letter across the table so that Marie could read it.

"More money than we've got here," she replied but in a philo-
sophic tone, with neither judgment nor malice in her voice.

"More money than we have got here," echoed young Maurice,
who was home for Christmas vacation. There was a touch of
malice in *his* voice.

And so, clothed in fur and rugs, Branwell rode in the back of
a sleigh bound for the mainland town of Belleville, where he

would board the train headed for Toronto, where he would make yet another westbound connection. Mister Fryfogel had written a second letter to say that if Mister Woodman intended to use such an unholy method of transportation as the railroad, it was no business of his and added that he himself, having been almost ruined by the railroad, was only too aware of the double meaning of that phrase. Baden was the name of the stop, he wrote, "a most unpleasant village, born recently as a result of the cursed railroad." He assured Branwell that he would be able to hire a sleigh at the station and, if conditions were favourable, he would be at the tavern in less than an hour. Sometimes, the innkeeper wrote, there were storms, storms that could make the going a little rough.

When he alighted at Baden, it became clear to Branwell that conditions were considerably less than favourable. Not a sleigh in sight and there was a biting wind, with a velocity higher than any of the ferocious currents he had recorded in his Timber Island journal, which tore at his coat and tossed the beaver hat from his head. Though it was not yet dark, the air was filled with such a quantity of snow that he could see nothing at all beyond the walls of the small wooden building that served as the apparently deserted station. Then, just as he was giving up hope, a man could be seen walking in his direction across the platform. "Nice day," the stranger said and was about to continue walking when Branwell caught him by the sleeve of his overcoat and told him his destination.

"I need to hire a sleigh to get out there today," he said.

"Not likely," said the man. "Not today, not tomorrow, probably not the day after that."

"For heaven's sake, why not?"

"Road's closed. Road's almost always closed. Snow in winter. Mud in summer. Waste of time if you ask me . . . roads."

Branwell was speechless.

"But," the stranger offered, "judging by the good weather, you might get out there on snowshoes if you've got 'em. Not today though. Too late. You'll have to put up at Kelterborn's Bar. Dreadful rooms, but good beer. Thanks to the railroad." He touched his head and for the first time Branwell noticed the railway cap.

The wind rose and the station master disappeared, enveloped by a shroud of white. "At least it's not snowing," the man said. "Nice sunny day."

"Not snowing?" said Branwell as the wind abated somewhat and the man came, once again, partially into view.

"This stuff is just blowing around. There's a storm coming through, though. We're proud of our storms here." The currents of air, the station master cheerfully explained, coming from the far-off Great Lakes encountered one another directly over this region and, "By Jesus," he slapped his gloved hands together, "don't we get snow!" He took Branwell's arm. "No more trains today," he said. "Let's go for a drink."

That night, as Branwell lay on a straw mattress in a room above the bar, his sleep was interrupted by the wind rattling the windows and a strange, vigorous thumping. "Just the ghost," Kelterborn told him when he inquired the following morning.

"We've asked him to keep it down, but he won't. He hates being imprisoned here, prefers to wander."

Kelterborn was a large, pink German fellow who presided over his bar with an air of pompous dignity mixed with that of boredom and mild disapproval. Branwell had already learned that his taciturn host was not inclined to give advice of any kind – political, elemental, spiritual – and he declined with a shrug to discuss the state of the road. He refused, in effect, to commit to anything beyond the price of the drink in your hand, or that of your bed for the night. His smooth, broad forehead glowed. The bottles behind him on the shelf shone. The Quebec heater roared. And, as the station master had said, his beer was good. Branwell was not, in fact, much of a drinker, but he had consumed enough beer the previous night to produce both a morning headache and a general sense of unreality into which the notion of the ghost fit nicely.

"Like you," Kelterborn offered, "the ghost has been trying to get out to Fryfogel's. Been here for a couple of weeks at least, might be here all winter."

Branwell rose at this point and, eager for some oxygen, headed for the porch, which, like the rest of the structure where he was sheltering, was made of rough-hewn logs. When he was finally able to push the front door open against the wind, it became evident that several Great Lake currents had collided during the night. A prodigious quantity of snow was falling from the sky, adding inches to the deep white sea that stretched off in all directions over the acres of townships that Branwell knew were named after the entrepreneurs who had cut them clean, divided them up, and sold them off. Everything else was named after European towns and villages. How absurd, he thought, that the spot where he now stood, a place where nothing happened but a succession of blizzards as far as he could tell, should be named after a tourist spa situated in a picturesque corner of the Austrian Alps. Even more absurd that the collection of squatters shanties and jagged stumps that he had heard existed farther west was apparently called London, and that the two major rivers in the vicinity became, therefore, the Thames and the Little Thames. Did this not show a singular lack of imagination? Branwell thought that it did.

When a few moments later he went back inside he was introduced to the ghost, a certain G. Shromanov, whose unpronounceable Slovakian first name had been long ago contracted to "Ghost," and who, according to his own admission, was primarily a stableman. Being born to love horses, he had worked at all three inns on the road, until the railway made the full-time care of horses almost completely unnecessary. Fortunately, however, he was also a rope-maker, a kettlesmith, and had been for at least a year roving through these parts searching for bears as a would-be bear trainer. He proudly confessed that, although he had been born in Europe, he could also read and write in English, and was occasionally able to acquire extra income by writing business letters, sometimes even love letters, for those who had never mastered the alphabet. Added to all this, he confided, he could mend pots, make medicine, tell fortunes, administer spells and curses, sing while accompanying himself on the mandolin, and perform a sort of speedy Spanish stomp that required much night practice to keep it up to the mark —

hence the thumping that had interrupted Branwell's sleep. With much clapping of hands on either side of his head, Ghost demonstrated several noisy staccato steps. The floor shook, the bottles behind the bar clanked, Branwell's headache throbbed.

"Fryfogel's his best customer," Kelterborn announced.

For what? Branwell wondered. Bear training? Cursing? He couldn't help but remember Fryfogel's remarks about the people who worked the road.

"Best customer," Ghost agreed. "He'll pay any amount of cash to get his fortune told, he'll pour any amount of whisky. I already predicted that his walls wouldn't be decorated, that you wouldn't be arriving for damn near twenty years."

"Well," said Branwell, "you were wrong about that because here I am." He lifted the wooden valise that served as his paint-box as proof of his trade.

"Oh, you're here all right." Ghost settled into the chair nearest to Branwell. "You're here, but you're not there, if you catch my meaning. Let me see your palm."

Branwell offered his hand to Ghost and then bestowed an amused smile on the other patrons in the bar.

"No, sir," said Ghost. "Not a sign of the Fryfogel in the immediate future. In fact, I see no trace of the walls of an inn at all . . . which is odd because I *can* see the Tavern Brook out the window. And wait . . . beside the window there *is* a painted wall — but it's far, far in the future — and, even so, there is nothing about an inn in these parts, nothing about a tavern, wait, no, there is something about a tavern, but not that tavern, there's a painted *ceiling*, of all things." He glanced quizzically at Branwell. "Wouldn't you go blind doing that? Wouldn't you all the time have paint dripping in your eyes?"

Branwell had no idea. "I never paint ceilings," he said.

"No you don't," said Ghost, "not yet. But, there's no doubt about it, you will."

Five days later, in the midst of one of the continuing squalls, Branwell trudged through the snow to the station. He had not been able to reach Fryfogel's Tavern; in fact, the weather had been so consistently bad that at times it seemed impossible to believe that beyond the somewhat greasy interior and smoky ambience of Kelterborn's log establishment, a village of some sort existed. He had done absolutely nothing during the course of the preceding days except inquire repeatedly about meteorological conditions in hopes that he might be able to wait out the storm and listen to Ghost – whom he had discovered was a voracious reader of newspapers when he could get his hands on them – tell more tales than he cared to hear about Tiger Dunlop, John Galt, and some other confident tycoon called Talbot who was in full control of all the lands at the western end of the lakes. These much-talked-about capitalists were both resented and admired by frequenters of the tavern, a combining of emotions that generally lead to ill temper and barroom brawls. Branwell had written twice to Marie describing all this and lamenting the lack of palatable food – a state of affairs that he knew would gain her sympathy. The day before, when he had made the trek to the station in order to post the letters, the station master told him that word had it that no one could determine, any more, where the road was situated. In the old days, the man added, you could identify a road in winter by the cut it made through the forest. "Forest is all gone now," he said, "and the stumps is all under the drifts."

Branwell had immediately laid down the last of his money in order to purchase a ticket home.

In Branwell's company now, and moving considerably faster than he was because of the snowshoes on his feet, was Ghost, who just that morning had announced that he would soon be stabling horses for a hotel situated on a sandy point near water. Branwell had done his best to discourage him, had made a prediction himself of no room, no board, no money, but Ghost was not to be put off. "One does not argue with destiny," he told his new friend, "for destiny always wins one way or another. I see horses again in my future. There were horses in my past as well, but since the railroad their numbers have diminished in these parts. I'm your man for horses."

Branwell, who was moderately alarmed, realized that it had been a mistake to tell Ghost that there was no railway in his County and therefore many horses. "You won't find any bears there," he said now, hoping to settle the matter. "There may be horses, but I've never seen a bear."

"No bears here either," Ghost said. "No forest, no bears . . . that's the way it is. Used to be bears, and there used to be horses, but it all went to hell around here faster than you could say knife." He pulled from his pocket a train ticket that he claimed to have found late one night on the barroom floor and looked at it closely. "Only good until Toronto," he said. "After that I'll be in the baggage car. I'll meet you at the other end. Did I tell you I saw a woman in my future too? And I saw plenty of good food . . . interesting food, not just your ordinary grub."

Poor Marie, thought Branwell. She wasn't likely to be happy about this, though he did recall that the previous summer she had said that they needed someone to look after the state of the stables and the visitors' horses.

*A*nnabelle was destined to witness her father's decline and fall, his body weakening, his mind beginning to shed parts of the past. As if he no longer had any use for them, he sometimes forgot that he had married and sired children, but more often he forgot that his wife was dead. Annabelle wondered if perhaps this was because her mother had been so indistinct, so listless, that absence seemed a permanent quality of her character even when she was alive. "Where *is* that woman?" her father would ask. "Down with a migraine again?" When reminded of her death, he appeared to be surprised rather than shocked or grief-stricken. "Well, I'll be bogged!" he would exclaim. "Why on earth didn't anyone tell me?" On the rare occasions when he remembered Branwell at all, he forgot that his son was no longer in residence. "Out on the rafts, I suppose," he would say when Branwell's name came up. Or, more suspiciously, "Upstairs in bed with that Irish girl, I'll wager."

Her father also failed to recall that not one serviceable tree remained in the vicinity of the tributaries and rivers that flowed into the Great Lakes and that, in consequence, his business was all but defunct. At least once a week he would rise much earlier than Annabelle, don his suit coat and hat, and depart for the office. Sometimes she found him in the sail loft angrily insisting that the long-gone sail master show himself and account for the lack of sails. Sometimes she found him standing, small and confused, under the gorgeous cathedral ceiling of the huge, vacant shed in which parts of his ships had once been constructed. It hurt Annabelle to tell her father, once again, that all the building and sailing and shipping was finished. "Finished? What do you mean finished?" he would demand. And when she told there were no more trees, he turned away from her, shook his fist at the sky, and reminded God that he had tried to tell both Him and everyone else this would happen if those damnable bogs were not drained. Her father's brain had grown confused, and she began to think that this confusion was not unlike the rapidly spreading moss on the sagging roof of his daily place of employment.

Annabelle began to feel that not only had the circumstances of the present changed utterly and irrevocably but that the facts of her own past were slipping away. When solidity and certainty began to slide away from her father, she herself was left feeling altered and disoriented. For the first time she realized that a very different Timber Island had existed before the Woodman empire had cluttered up its acreage and set sail from its shores. But, more disturbing, she could feel the indifferent future – a future that would have nothing to do with her or her family – stirring like a subtle tremor just below the surfaces of everything that until now had represented permanence.

One by one, the outbuildings on the island began to fall into disrepair. Cummings had retired: there was little work for him to do in any case. The white paint on the clapboard was all but gone by the time he locked the door of the office for the last time and made his final journey toward the waterlogged pier, a journey that Annabelle watched, in some ways without regret, from her kitchen window. The empty smithy was next to show signs of succumbing to January's howling winds and an unusually heavy weight of snow, and at this point Annabelle saw that her father's arthritis had worsened, making it difficult for him to stand erect. When the huge, splendid building where the ships had been born was blown down by a March gale, and the beams of its vaulted ceiling lay scattered like the bones of a huge extinct animal, Annabelle knew that her father's collapse would likely follow suit. And she was right. He took to his bed that May and after a few weeks of fever and delirium, he began to repeat the phrase *devil's steamships* over and over again. Then, one early morning, he clutched Annabelle's arm, told her that Gilderson would certainly attempt to steal the lake. Before she could ask him what he meant by this warning, he died. At the funeral only Maurice, her father's beloved Badger, wept openly, though his sorrow was to abate somewhat when he discovered that he was to inherit the lion's share of his grandfather's still sizable though admittedly diminished fortune. The remaining sum would go to Branwell and Marie and would be used for improvements to their hotel. Annabelle would become sole heir to the empty, changed world of the island: the deteriorating

architecture, the dwindling resources, the broken ships lying
under the waters of Back Bay.

Three or four weeks after her father's death, on an afternoon in
early June, Annabelle decided to take on the task of organizing
and cleaning the sagging, and now structurally unsound, office.
In contrast to the sparse furnishings and generally stark appearance of this interior, the lacquered wooden shelves that lined the
four walls of the large inner office were overflowing with a pro-
fusion of loose papers, ledger books, cardboard and wooden
boxes, rolled maps tied with frayed cords, charts, and an assortment of small dusty wax models for what might or might not
have become ships' figureheads. There were several stacks of
scribblers; each one, according to the labels carefully pasted on
the cover, was an account of the journey of a raft down the river
to Quebec. The first hundred or so of these logs were written in
the hand of Annabelle's father, the rest in the hand of her brother.

This is all that remains, thought Annabelle, of the efforts of
her father and those like him. She had no idea what to keep and
what to throw away and though she had brought several burlap
bags with her for trash, she had not as yet deposited a single
object in any of them. Instead, she found herself removing great
heaps of paper from the shelves, placing these in piles on the
floor, moving them to no apparent end back and forth across
the room while dust rose around her like smoke. It was while she
was engaged in this random and ultimately unsuccessful attempt
to organize her father's voluminous archive that she discovered
twelve maps of the bogs.

They were drawn on parchment and were so old and stiff they were almost impossible to unroll. When, by securing their corners with heavy ledger books, Annabelle managed to prevent the maps from snapping back into tight scrolls, the varnish that had covered them cracked and lifted like a caramel glaze on one of Marie's delicious desserts. Each time she unfurled another bog Annabelle gasped with pleasure, for these were beautiful works of art. Executed in what must have been hundreds of shades of brown that bled at the edges of the bog in question into infinitely varied shades of green, and occasionally criss-crossed by the tiniest of blue lines, intended, she supposed, to represent streams, these territories were drafted with such exquisite care they could only have been made with love. The calligraphy that spelled out the remarkable names of the bogs, and those of the arable green areas called cooms that sometimes existed in the centre of the bogs and the surrounding lakes and mountains, was also of the highest calibre. Coomaspeara, Coomavoher, Coomnahorna, Coomnakilla, Coomshana, and Knocknagantee, Knockmoyle, Knocknacusha, Knocklomena. Annabelle would remember always the shock and wonder she experienced when, at the bottom of each map, it was her father's signature that she found. Then a terrible sadness came over her. She realized that the artist in him was someone he had never permitted her to meet.

Annabelle walked to the east window and stared out at the vacant shipyard. She tried, without much success, to solve the puzzle that had been presented to her. How was it possible that her father could render the very landscape that had been the source of his humiliation with such meticulous affection? There was something wistful and tender about the maps, and Annabelle, strolling once again among them, began to understand that her father must have been bruised by experience or filled with longing at one time or another. None of this made any sense at all in the face of the tyrant he had been in his prime, or even the confused old man he had turned into later, and yet there was no denying that the younger man who had made these maps was one with vision and heart. The loss she felt in the face of this was more intense in that it was the loss of a gift she had never been given. She felt overcome with shame that she had not known all this before. She could not bring herself to remove the maps from the floor, to roll them back up, return them to the shelves. Before she left the office she sat slowly down on the hard chair behind her father's hard desk, put her face in her hands, and wept for the first time in years.

Summer after summer, beyond the bright windows of the Ballagh Oisin, the Great Lake roared or whispered against a sand beach on which visiting children made miniature towns, elaborate castles, or complicated drainage systems. Cumulus clouds bloomed like distant white forests far out over the lake, but never ventured inland to disturb the sunny afternoons. At night the constellations moved above the waves against a clear black background, and sometimes, in the very early mornings, or just before sunset, the water became entirely still as if intent on merging with the sky. Gulls rode the wind, ducks practised flight patterns for future migrations, and each year, on one spectacular July day, a flotilla of enormous arctic swans sailed regally past.

What a place it was! Perched on the very last finger of the arm of the peninsular County, the hotel was like a sturdy wooden ship that had come into port after a long journey, leaving fields and farmhouses and woodlots in its wake . . . almost as if it had created or had given birth to such things. The exterior of the building was painted bright white, as were the rocking chairs on

230

the porch. Guests emerging from its doors wore white as well, the unspoken dress code of the place. Women in pastel skirts drifted down halls past Branwell's turquoise landscapes, eager to enter the piercing light of the long summer days.

The natural talents that Marie had first begun to show evidence of in Mackenzie's kitchen on the island had now blossomed to such an extent that her culinary accomplishments were acquiring a reputation. Her lemon meringue pies and decorated cakes, for instance, were famous as far away as Toronto and Montreal, and her sauces for fresh lake trout were discussed well into the winter. The guests gorged themselves three times a day in the pale blue dining room while the darker blue of the Great Lake swell heaved beyond the panes of a multitude of windows and the Tremble Point lighthouse shone on a sandbar islet offshore.

There were walks in the evenings along the sandy shore or inland though a wood of flickering poplar and birch, then into a meadow filled with daisies, black-eyed Susans, and the soft blue flowers called bachelor button. Later, Ghost would be called in from the stables to dance and sing. (Marie, though fond of Ghost, was superstitious, and insisted one had to go *out* to the stables, in daylight, to have one's fortune told.) Even one or two of the guests could be persuaded to entertain: Mr. McIntyre, a bank manager from Grimsby, might sing a song, one of the young ladies might play the old piano (which could never be kept in tune because of the humidity), and inevitably someone would recite a poem by Mr. Tennyson. If this took place during the summer of 1889, just after the great poet had published "Crossing the Bar," one of the company would inevitably deliver the mournful lines and everyone's eyes would fill with tears. Everyone's eyes, that is, except for Annabelle's, if she happened to be in residence on her yearly visit. She considered the laureate to be a pretentious romantic and therefore she had always disliked his poetry. One June evening she announced to the guests, all of whom had removed their handkerchiefs during a shoe salesman's particularly sensitive recitation of "The Lady of Shallot," that, in her opinion, the girl in question was a simple-minded infant who had undoubtedly died of starvation rather than a broken heart since, beyond a brief reference to barley, there had been mention of neither food nor drink in the story, unless one took into account her name, which, if Annabelle remembered her French correctly, had something to do with onions. This had shocked the gathering so thoroughly that Branwell had found it necessary later in the evening to upbraid his sister in private concerning her frankness.

"What can it possibly matter to you what Tennyson says or doesn't say about romance?" he asked. "Why would you care enough to state your case so vehemently?"

"Well, what would you have me say?" she reportedly replied. "That his 'Lady' made the right decision? She should have stuck to her loom, or, better still, she should have gone outdoors into the fresh air and got some exercise. Reaping barley with the other early reapers would have been a much wiser choice than dying for the likes of Lancelot." In truth, she thought that the line "only reapers, reaping early in among the bearded barley" was quite beautiful, but she was far too stubborn to admit this.

She wondered, suddenly, how her brother saw her at this moment. As an aging, ill-tempered spinster, undoubtedly, an eccentric maiden aunt. Allowing such a thought to form in her mind increased her irritation in any number of ways. She decided she would spend the following day away from the Ballagh Oisin and asked Branwell to hire a carriage and driver for her so that she could make a tour of the County. She travelled along shore roads near bays and inlets filled with fishing boats, moved slowly down the main streets of a several towns where hardware and grocery stores were doing a brisk business, and passed by cultivated fields that would soon be ripe with the barley that was rapidly becoming the staple crop of the region. All this evidence of industry and practicality soothed her wounded spirits somewhat, though she couldn't say just why, and she returned to the hotel at twilight in much better humour.

A few days later, while helping Marie roll pastry dough in the kitchen, Annabelle glanced out the window and was the first to spot the arrival of her nephew at the end of the leafy lane that led to the hotel. The arrival itself was not unexpected; he often spent some of the summer there with his parents, though, by this time, he had little in common with them and was mildly embarrassed by their station in life, which, to his mind, was entirely defined by their position as innkeepers. What *was* surprising was the letter that preceded him, a letter in which he had stated his intention to stay for a considerable length of time – long enough to oversee the completion of a house nearby. Maurice, it would seem, had decided to become a gentleman farmer. Neither his parents nor Annabelle could quite fathom this; Maurice, to their knowledge, had shown not the slightest interest in the natural world. In fact, Maurice had shown interest in next to nothing

beyond his employment as assistant manager of the Bank of
Commerce in Kingston. Added to this was a further surprise.
Seated beside him in the approaching buggy was a fair-haired
woman. Annabelle, who was standing by the kitchen window
watching the couple disembark from the buggy, knew by the
woman's unmistakably commanding gestures, and by her nephew's
obvious attention to those gestures, that this woman had the devil
in her as big as a woodchuck. There is going to be trouble here, she
thought. She considered returning to Timber Island in order to
avoid the drama she sensed was about to take place, but her curiosity got the better of her.

It wasn't long before she came to know that the trouble she
had intuited was not to be of a short duration, for the Badger, as
it turned out, had married it. "My name is Caroline Woodman,"
the young woman announced as she entered the hall and began
removing the pins from her hat. "Maurice and I are married."
Maurice, who was at that very moment struggling with hatboxes
and suitcases, and a variety of assorted pieces of feminine
luggage, looked uncharacteristically sheepish at the mention of
his marriage, but said nothing. "He would have written to you,"
the woman called Caroline continued, "but I thought he should
tell you in person. After all, I had to tell my papa in person and
that was not an easy thing to do, I can assure you." Having delivered this piece of information, the young woman swept past the
small assembly, entered the sitting room, and collapsed on one of
the chairs, throwing her feathered hat onto one of the sidetables
as she did so.

Annabelle followed the girl into the sitting room in order to
observe her more closely. The eyes, she decided, were too small

and too close together. There were too many freckles on her otherwise milk-white skin and, by the look of her, she might fatten as she grew older. These were the only physical deformities that Annabelle could find on the person of Maurice's bride, but they would have to do for now.

"Maurice," the young woman called in the direction of the hall where her husband and his parents were still standing as if frozen to the floorboards, "come in here and introduce me to this elderly lady. Is she a relation of yours? And who were all those people on the porch?"

Maurice walked into the room and sat down by Caroline's side. "She is my Aunt Annabelle," he said. "But," he added, vaguely embarrassed, "those people we passed on the veranda, those people are the summer patrons." He seemed to have forgotten altogether about his parents, who were now standing quietly in the doorway. "I am Maurice's father," Branwell offered. He put his arm around Marie. "And this is his mother."

"I'm not elderly," said Annabelle, glancing at Marie. "Not quite yet."

"Was it a Catholic ceremony?" Marie asked her son.

Caroline began to laugh. She put her hand on Maurice's arm. "The state father was in . . . can you imagine what he would have said had we been married by a papist?"

"We were married secretly," Branwell said, "by the first minister we could find. A Presbyterian, I think."

"Lutheran," Caroline corrected. "A German. Papa wasn't too happy about that either. He's always said that he runs a good Methodist business in a good Methodist town, and that all his ships are good Methodist ships manned by good Methodist men."

Marie, much to Annabelle's astonishment, had brightened somewhat. "You're not really married then," she said to her son, "if there was no priest." She turned to Caroline. "If your father doesn't approve, you could tell him that because Maurice was baptized a Catholic, you're not really married. He might be pleased to hear that."

Maurice continued to gaze at his bride. "No," he said, "we are most certainly husband and wife. And, anyway, Mister Gilderson cheered up a bit once we began to talk about the barley."

"Gilderson?" said Annabelle. "Can you possibly mean Oran Gilderson?"

Maurice nodded.

"Of course," said Caroline. "I don't believe there is another Gilderson in the vicinity."

It took Annabelle a moment to digest this information. Oran Gilderson had been writing letters to her of late, letters in which he had offered to be of assistance with the salvage operations of what remained of the Woodman empire. Annabelle, remembering her father's distrust of his primary competitor, had grave suspicions about these missives. What exactly had this gentleman in mind for the diminished business toward which she had developed a surprising protectiveness. Thank God Father is dead, she thought, recalling his last words. She was about to say something but changed her mind. "What's all this about barley?" she asked instead.

The land that Maurice had purchased with his grandfather's money comprised one hundred acres, the narrowest, easternmost parameters of which touched the grounds of his parents' hotel just at the spot where the grass tennis court ended and the poplar woods began. The western edge joined a further hundred acres — acres that were under cultivation and that had been given to him, reluctantly to be sure, by his new father-in-law. Their house would be built on the far side of the woods and was to be, as his bride explained, made of brick and very modern. A great many bay windows and round towers and oddly shaped windows were to be seen in the plans Maurice pulled from a suitcase and unrolled at their feet. The meadow was to be ploughed and the poplar woods cut down.

"Why would you want to do that?" Annabelle was genuinely incredulous.

"Barley," Caroline said before Maurice had a chance to respond. She went on to explain that there were already ten acres of barley on the property, but they wanted more.

"That's all very well," said Branwell to his son, "but what will you have to look at if you are surrounded by nothing but fields of barley?"

"Look at?" asked Caroline. "Why should we need something to look at? We'll have a view of the lake, after all, and even barley can be quite lovely when the crop is high."

Annabelle noted that the young woman had stiffened in her chair. She had the defensive air of one who was vaguely frightened by the company and was asserting herself as a result. Her eyelashes, Annabelle noted, were almost as thick as Marie's but of a lighter hue, offsetting, quite beautifully, the blue of her eyes and the gold of her hair. Annabelle could see that the young woman was very attractive, but would not have called her pretty. There was something significant missing, and suddenly Annabelle knew what it was. Caroline gave off no light. She did not glow. Rather, in the manner of a coal fire, she smouldered and seemed, somehow, to be just on the edge of emitting a poisonous, though odourless, gas.

"Barley," said Maurice, "is very profitable. It is right now selling to the Americans at eighty cents a bushel and —"

"Eighty cents a bushel," interjected young Caroline eagerly, "and bound to go higher and higher. The Americans have a great thirst for beer and other spirits. They simply can't get enough barley."

"I fear," said Annabelle, who was once again wondering about Oran Gilderson's business plans, "that reapers, 'reaping early in among the bearded barley' are more likely to reap profits than those who appear later in the day." All of this, she thought, might very well be interpreted as the beginnings of the robbery of the lake.

Caroline looked confused.

"Tennyson," said Annabelle.

"We shall become very rich, Aunt," said Maurice. "You'll see."

Now it was Maurice who became the focus of Annabelle and Marie's ongoing inquiry into the bewildering nature of the male psyche. When they were once again alone together in the kitchen, the subject of Badger and what he had been thinking when he decided to marry this spoiled young woman was instantly raised. Although Annabelle had become aware early on that, because he was a son, not a husband or lover, Maurice's character was one that should be discussed with great delicacy, this seemed not to matter in the present circumstances. Normally, when Marie praised the boy, it was best that one nod in agreement. When she complained about her son's faults and weaknesses, it was best to disagree, the more vehemently the better. But now, when Marie angrily suggested that the catastrophe had occurred because Maurice was quite simply trying to improve his standing in life, was, in fact, like the girl or loathe her, marrying money, or "marrying up" as she put it, Annabelle agreed that, indeed, cold ambition had likely played a large part. "But, there is something else," she said. "He seems stunned, entranced. I suspect he is actually in love with her."

Marie looked horrified. "Sacré Dieu," she said, crossing herself and turning toward the wall.

"And as for ambition," Annabelle continued, "it will be Caroline's ambition that will rule the day, not that of poor Maurice, her besotted husband."

"He should run like a deer," said Marie.

"Where would he run to? Back to the bank? I've heard a lot about this man Gilderson. He would likely have him shot. And, as I said before, Marie, Maurice is smitten. He's a goner. From now on his life will be all bricks and barley."

What neither woman said, but both knew, was that come early autumn just before the harvest of the last crop of barley, the entire peninsula would be transformed into various shades of yellow: the poplars, the maples, and the field after field after field of barley, bordered near the water by the paler yellow banner of the sand. Moving through this landscape they had likely felt surrounded by radiance at one time or another: golden September sun, golden apples in the orchards (which were becoming scarce now because of the spread of barley,) golden clouds of sunset coming earlier and earlier to the sky, glasses filled with the dark gold of whisky in the evenings, or the bright gold of beer in the late afternoon. Sometimes in August, before the harvest, the fields of barley would turn a peculiar shade of lavender at twi-light, mysterious, unfathomable, the deep purple shadows of the maples that edged the fencelines like pools or clouds. The prosperity of the previous decade had been both directly and indirectly connected to the increasing production of this crop, a fact that would, in the future, cause the whole epoch to be referred to by citizens of the County as the Barley Days.

These Barley Days might just as well have been called the Brick Days, for central to the years when barley was making people rich was the building of larger and larger brick houses, houses much like the one that rose with alarming swiftness a quarter of a mile from the clapboard hotel. During the early stages of its construction, when the frame of the nuptial home was being erected, the noise of the carpenters' hammers dis-turbed the guests, as later did the sound of poplars and birches crashing to the ground. By the time the bricklayers arrived the half-finished skeleton of the house was clearly visible from the upper veranda.

Teams of oxen removed the ruined trunks and roots of trees and, not much later, a steam-powered tractor churned up the earth. Hedgerows that had existed between previously smaller fields were removed. Barley crops were planted. The monstrous brick walls of the new house sprang up as if by magic overnight. What appeared to be a half a mile of gingerbread fretsaw work arrived at the beginning of July, along with big iron pipes for the plumbing, a boiler for central heating, six elaborate mantelpieces, and two claw-footed bathtubs, painted gold. By the end of July, Maurice and Caroline were installed in their new home, the huge shadow of which, at twilight, seemed almost to reach the steps of the Ballagh Oisin.

The young couple's departure from the hotel was met with general relief. There had been several monumental disagreements during their stay there – the furnishings of the interior were not, apparently, up to Caroline's standards. Complaints concerning washing with a pitcher and a bowl could be heard some mornings when passing by the door of the couple's room, and the lack of a private bathtub was a subject that was often raised. When the windows for the new house were delivered and proved to be pointed not curved, Caroline reacted with angry tears, blaming her husband, his parents, even a couple of guests for the mishap.

There were two or three uncomfortable visits from Mister Gilderson himself, who had managed to outlive his third wife (mother of Caroline) by seven years, despite the fact that his frame was twisted by the arthritis that, he claimed, was made much worse by the presence of lighthouses like the one at the end of the small island just off the end of sandy Tremble Point. Lighthouses, he insisted, lured his ships into the path of destruction while, at the same time, they interrupted the currents of fresh air that he believed bought relief to his arthritis. "And," he once announced, shifting his limbs on the velvet chair that had been offered him, "they accelerate my gout."

"Poor Papa," said Caroline.

The other thing that Mister Gilderson despised was discovered when, in attempting to dispel the tense silence that followed,

Maurice described a spectacular storm in which he had been caught the previous winter. Gilderson had no tolerance for any story relating to weather in general, and snow in particular. "Do we really have to listen to one more tale concerning blizzards, squalls, drifts, ice, or falling barometers?" the older man said with irritation. "I will not hear of any reference to carriages abandoned by the side of roadways or ships being frozen in harbour. And, please refrain from any mention of November." Weather was, to Gilderson's mind, the enemy of business. Like a relative who had caused him embarrassment, he did not wish its name to be spoken and wanted its picture turned to the wall. Annabelle knew that November was the month when, for reasons of safety, all ships, except Gilderson's steamships, went into retirement until the spring breakup. Several tragedies had occurred during this month, tragedies that, according to her father, Gilderson had measured purely in terms of loss of cargo and vessels with no apparent thought for the attendant loss of life. She looked at him with amused disapproval, then said, wickedly, "I quite like November. Things settle down and become quiet on the island then. Not so much coming and going. You can turn your mind to other things . . . reading, art."

Oran Gilderson, who had ignored her until this moment, turned in Annabelle's direction, as if trying to determine just who she was. When, after a moment or two of concentration, recognition dawned, he smiled, nodded his head in a conciliatory fashion, and said, "Indeed, yes, reading and art, wonderful pastimes for a woman. But I, madam, am a man of business."

Before she began the journey back to Timber Island, Annabelle took her nephew aside to offer a warning. "Weather isn't the only culprit," she told him. "Greed can be an enemy of business as well. Remember that."

During the next two or three years it would happen that Maurice would prosper to such an extent that not only were his own parents impressed by his successes but he almost won the favour of his father-in law. Barley rose to a dollar a bushel, and more and more of Gilderson's ships sailed back and forth across the lake carrying the golden cargo to the American market. Caroline added a conservatory to the house and a trellised gazebo to the yard. In the course of one year she bought no fewer than twenty hats, each piece of headgear more flamboyant than the one that had preceded it. When she became pregnant, one of the larger bedrooms was turned into an elaborate nursery, and soon that nursery contained a squalling baby boy who would eventually become my father and whom Maurice decided to call Thomas Jefferson Woodman in deference to the Americans whose thirst was making them so rich. Some of these Americans patronized the Ballagh Oisin, but these were Americans with modest incomes, usually of Irish descent, attracted to the hotel by its Gaelic moniker and its views of a lake that reminded them of the sea.

Even Annabelle had to admit that things were going well. The spoiled Caroline had taken, with surprising enthusiasm, to motherhood. Maurice had been sensible enough to hire men knowledgeable in the ways of farming operations while he was kept busy by the very gratifying pastime of keeping the books and investing the returns. Branwell painted all winter and amused and saw to his guests all summer. Everyone doted on the child, whom they called T.J. for short, and when this child began to use language, Marie revived her stories, bringing into the occasional evening the wolf, her slaughtered parents, her own trip to Orphan Island, the epidemics that swept through that institution, small white coffins arriving on a dark brown sleigh, the delivery of stone angels, and a number of other wonderfully terrifying circumstances that might occur on the road from childhood to adolescence.

*T*here weren't many clients any more – the timber business being what it was. Annabelle mostly busied herself with annotating her splinter book, with painting, and, when the season permitted, she worked on what was becoming an impressive series of flower gardens near the house. Still, over the course of the next few years, she returned to her father's office every now and then to record transactions concerning the salvage enterprise in one of his ledger books, an enterprise that had, in recent months, begun to pick up somewhat. When she was in the office she still some-times made half-hearted, unsuccessful attempts to sort out everything her father had left behind. She had not been able to force herself to roll up the maps of the bogs, however, and they had become such a permanent – though dusty – feature of the place she began to look on them as a sort of parchment carpet. On one afternoon in August, she had brought a good-sized feather duster with her so that she could clean up a bit. Perhaps, she mused as she worked, this is how entire civilizations become buried. Dust that is not removed might, over the course of time,

245

accumulate to such an extent that eventually all architecture would be buried: columns and amphitheatres, temples and palaces. Sooner or later everything would succumb. If, in a thousand years, an archaeologist visited Timber Island, what would be left for him to dig up? Not much, she decided, a few stones from the foundation of the big house and bricks from the chimney, an anvil from the smithy, perhaps. By the time the word *anvil* entered her mind Annabelle had stopped dusting and was looking out the west window toward the quay. Various sails and funnels were in view and among them she was surprised to see the sail of Branwell's small boat, which was approaching her docks. She was glad to know he was on his way to the island: he hadn't visited in months, and she, having resolved to pay more attention to salvage operations that had been left in her care, had several times postponed her planned visit to the hotel.

When she saw him alight at the quay, she stepped outside and called his name. Shortly thereafter her brother was standing quite still in the open doorway of the inner office, stunned by the sight of the maps all over the floor.

"Maps of the bogs," Annabelle explained, not waiting for the question. She picked up the duster, bent over Gortatlea Bog, and brushed the dust from the beautiful colours.

"The villainous Irish bogs."

"The very ones."

Branwell began to weave around the topography in the direction of his sister. "He kept these maps." He studied each map for several minutes and then, as if exhausted by the information they imparted, he collapsed in Cummings's chair, which Annabelle had brought from the outer office after her father's death.

Remembering her own visits to her father's inner sanctum, the coldness of the surroundings and the coldness of the welcome, she wanted any visitors who came her way to at least be able to sit down. As an older woman, and, though she wouldn't have admitted this, a lonely one, she wasn't adverse to a bit of conversation.

She asked her brother to stay for an evening meal, and offered him a room for the night. Then she began to speak about the maps. "Look at this," she said, pointing again to the map of Gortatlea Bog. "Or this." Her toe touched the centre of Glorah. "He loved all of this. It's obvious. Why did he want to destroy something he thought so beautiful?"

"People do what they have to," her brother said quietly, "and sometimes things are destroyed in the process." He began to pull on his right ear. "Poor Father," he said. "He likely didn't even know that he loved looking at landscape, figured it was only useful if you could exploit it in some way or another."

Annabelle wondered if in fact persistence was part of the explanation she was looking for. Was it the knowledge of something you have loved continuing to exist after you have left it behind that had caused such fury in her father? Branwell was still pulling on his ear and looking out the window. Annabelle could see that though the revelation of the maps had moved him, he was nevertheless preoccupied by something else. "What is it?" she asked finally. "What's on your mind?"

"Worry."

Annabelle waited. Then, when nothing further came from her brother's lips, she asked him what it was that concerned him. "Sand," he replied. "Maurice's foreman has told me that the soil is changing. He says it's turning into sand."

"But that is nonsense," said Annabelle. "Soil doesn't just spontaneously turn into sand."

"Yet it seems to be so. Caroline is in a state because her flowerbeds are beginning to be filled with sand and her lawns are not growing properly. There is a different kind of tough grass coming up and it is sparse, with a lot of sand showing through." He sighed and looked at his hands, which were clenched in his lap. "And that's nothing compared to the sand around the hotel," he said. "There are dunes gathering beside the porch."

Annabelle tried to call up this image of the porch, but could picture only white rocking chairs, swept steps, tidy lawns.

"Well," she said, "perhaps that's only natural that this should happen. Tremble Point is situated on the sandy end of the County, after all. Maybe by next year things will have returned to —"

"You have no idea," Branwell interrupted, "what this is doing to Marie. There is sand some mornings in the corners of the guest rooms. Sometimes it gets into the bread she bakes or, worse, into her sauces. Almost always it is sprinkled on the top of her lemon meringue pies. It is bothering the guests. Some are leaving early. And Marie . . . it's as if she is carrying the weight of this somewhere near her heart. She doesn't really complain, but I can see it in her face, I can see it in her eyes."

"Marie does not complain? About something this serious?" Annabelle recalled the fearless, outspoken little girl from orphanage, the strong young woman Marie had become. "Something is terribly wrong, then, and she is remaining silent so as not to make things worse."

Branwell nodded in sad agreement.

On her last visit Annabelle had noticed something she couldn't identify that seemed to be missing from her friend's expression, and from her gestures. She had never known Marie not to be quick in her movements and certain in her speech. Now all energy seemed to have vanished from her character. She had invented no new recipes as far as Annabelle could tell, and no matter how Branwell teased, she could not be coaxed into defending the politics of Quebec, a subject that would have always elicited passionate declarations from her in the past, sometimes in English, sometimes in French. It was as if an essential component in her proud bearing had faltered and this frightened Annabelle. What faltered in Marie would falter in Annabelle as well.

"Is there a chance that the foreman is mistaken?" she asked.

Branwell shook his head. "He says it has something to do with the rotation of crops."

"But Maurice — and everyone else for that matter — has been growing nothing but barley. No one is rotating crops."

"That's it exactly. They haven't been rotating crops. None of the barley farmers along our stretch of shore have been rotating crops and now the soil is depleted. They were making pots of money," he said bitterly. "Why would they want to change?" Branwell lifted his arms into the air in a gesture of desperation. "All this sand," he whispered, "all this sand because of people's obsession with money."

Annabelle stood in the centre of the room, bogs all around her. For the first time she thought about the tidy lush landscapes of her mother's past, and for the first time she found herself hoping that these landscapes were still there just as her mother

had described them to Branwell, each field in place, crops rotated
or left fallow every year or so. The oak her mother talked about
came into her mind and she glanced out the window searching
for the tree in her own yard, as if for reassurance.

She turned to the Branwell. "You must tell Maurice to sell
immediately," she said.

"He's been thinking of politics," Branwell ventured, without
much enthusiasm in his voice. "He's joined the Tory party, so I
suppose that's a start." He drummed his fingers on his father's
desk. "How can I convince him to sell? I wanted him to rotate
the crops two years ago. I wanted him to sell out last year. But it's
clear that nothing I say will move him."

"He'll listen to Marie. He'll listen to his mother."

Branwell looked embarrassed. His hand moved again toward
his ear. "Marie tried to speak to him," he said, "but Caroline
would hardly let her raise the subject. She became quite hysteri-
cal." He paused. "It's only Caroline that he listens to now."

"Why doesn't Maurice just put his foot down?" Annabelle
could feel an angry flush travel up her neck and flood her face.
Weakness, she thought, was the answer to that question. Weakness
combined with ambition and greed. Spinelessness and, of course,
the chains of romance.

Branwell shrugged and shook his head. He rose from the
chair and began to pace up and down the room. "The hotel is
Marie's life. The only life we know, the only life we have. But my
son, our son, is so wrapped up in his marriage, and so controlled
by his father-in-law, he has given no thought at all to what is happening to his mother. She feels that she's lost him. She suspects

that we have lost the hotel. It's as if she is being depleted along with the soil."

"Depleted?" she said. "Marie?" Annabelle didn't want to imagine this.

Branwell said nothing.

"Do you remember," Annabelle asked eventually, "do you remember the time father took you with him to pick up the figureheads?"

"I remember that it was a long, long journey, and that we travelled by coach." Branwell paused, shook his head. "And I remember the figureheads. But that's about all."

"He wanted you to see the workshops," said Annabelle. "You were seven years old. It was the only time that he ever, ever considered doing something that might be of interest to a child. And it *is* wonderful, when you think about it, that there were men in Quebec who devoted their lives almost entirely to the carving of mermaids." She stepped carefully around the maps and took two wax models from the shelves. "Look," she said, "look at these models."

Her brother glanced at the figures in her hands. One was made in the likeness of Napoleon, the other was a bare-breasted woman. "It's not likely," he said, "that Father would have allowed Napoleon to be fixed to the prow of one of his schooners. I remember a woman similar to this, though, and some kind of animal . . . a griffin, I think."

"I expect he brought the models home simply because he liked them. But all that's gone now, anyway," Annabelle murmured. "Along with everything else." She returned the models of the figureheads to the shelves. "What do you think would have happened to those young men who were trained to do nothing but carve figureheads?" she asked Branwell. "Once the ships that bore them were scuttled? No one knows the moment when something that seems permanent will simply cease to exist." She thought of the last day in the sail loft, of the sea of canvas that was abandoned there, seams half-sewn, threaded needles halted in mid-stitch. Her father, she remembered, would not allow the half-completed sails to be removed. "They'll find out they're wrong to bring all the ships to full steam," he had insisted. "And we'll need the canvas for the return to sail." But the needles had rusted and eventually the thread had begun to fray, to rot.

"What *I* remember," she told Branwell, "was that you had been made to sit between the life-sized mermaids in the coach on the way back while Father and a griffin faced you." Annabelle smiled, picturing the scene: the patriarch, the small frightened boy, two mermaids, and a griffin enduring the bumpy track and the deteriorating weather of a mid-nineteenth-century November.

"The money Father left to Maurice?" she asked suddenly.

"He still has some of it, apparently . . . enough, I suppose, to survive."

"Good. Then he must sell immediately. Move down the lake a bit to the next County. Set himself up in another house and run for office." How she longed to voice her opinion of her nephew's wife, but instead she said, "Caroline will be content to be the wife of a politician once she knows there is no other choice. You can count on that. She'll like the power, the attention. How's her father's company faring through all this, by the way?"

Branwell sat down again. "Almost completely out of business," he said. "Or at least out of the business of transporting barley. The Americans slapped an enormous tariff on his shipments last month. On everyone's shipments. They want to use their own barley now . . . and barley," he lifted his eyes to his sister's face, "the price of Canadian barley fell to twenty cents a bushel last week." He raised one hand, then let it drop. "He still builds ships, of course. Gilderson was clever enough to change to steam early on. And steamships will go on forever."

"I doubt it," said Annabelle, removing a ledger from the edge of Dereen Bog and watching the map slowly curl back into a cylindrical shape. "Nothing goes on forever."

$\mathcal{A}$s an old man, during his last visit to the hotel, while he and Branwell were sitting on the porch on a summer's night, Joseph Woodman had put down the paper he was reading and had turned to his son. It's odd, he had said, but we have no raft on the river tonight. Not one raft. And Branwell, who by then had nothing at all to do with the timber business, had experienced, to his astonishment, a feeling of loss so profound that tears jumped into his eyes, for it was the first time in decades that, when the river was open, that no Timber Island raft was making its way to Quebec. The cargoes of logs, you see, would have been arriving at the quay less and less frequently, the numbers of coureurs de bois thinning out as the men drifted to more dependable forms of employment. Branwell reported in his journal that while he and his father sat on the porch, one of the season's spectacular full moons was hovering over the dark water and because that water was so uncharacteristically still ("nary a zephyr disturbed the serene silence," he wrote), the silver path to the shore was like an invitation to walk on the lake. It was the beginning of the end,

and both men knew it. Old Marcel Guerin was climbing the stairs
to the sail loft less and less often to repair ropes and canvas
because there were fewer and fewer sails on the lake. Shipbuilding
of the kind for which Timber Island was famous was almost at a
standstill. The steamers with their plumes of black smoke marked
a horizon that was once busy with barques and schooners. And,
most tragic of all, the last of the great forests were down.

Until that moment, though, there had seemed to be a never-
ending supply of wood from those forests and this inex-
haustibility had suggested to Branwell that one raft or another
would be present on the river for all the summers to come. Only
much later in life was he able to realize that, even in a colony whose
wealth was founded entirely on the slaughtering of wild animals
and the clear-cutting of forests, there were moments of pure
magic. His journal, when he was home, had been filled with
announcements pertaining to the arrival of ships whose names
put one in mind of a courtly procession of gorgeous women: *The
Alma Lee, The Hannah Coulter, The Minerva Cook, The Lucille Godin,
The Nancy Breen, The Susan Swan, The Mary Helen Carter.* Travelling
downriver, he had been witness to spray in the distance and the
men kneeling and reaching for their beads in the remaining calm
minutes before the short, terrifying journey through the Coteau
Rapids. And then there had been the evening meal on the river, the
men singing and, the following day, the French villages along
the shore coming into view, steeple by steeple.

Now, Branwell and the white-haired Ghost were sweeping
sand from the same porch on which his father had made his sad
declaration. But this was an act of futility. The sandy fields were
full of the scant beginnings of starved crops of barley that would

never ripen. Just that week three farming families nearby had left
their houses, their ruined land, and had moved out of the
County, heading for the city and the hope of a factory job.

"Horses don't like sand," said Ghost. "The going's too tough
for them. I'll have to have to find some place more hospitable
to horses."

Branwell wasn't listening. He was thinking instead about an
anecdote told to him by his father when he was a boy. He could
see in his mind's eye the Windsor chair that his parent had occupied and the glow of a pressed-glass oil lamp, so the story must
have been told to him in the evening, probably in winter, he
decided, as the old man was so busy in the summer there wouldn't
have been time for the kind of reflection the tale required.

The elder Woodman, who had been young at the time when
the story took place, had been in Ireland, standing on the edges
of Knockaneden Bog. "A dreary waste if ever there was one," he
had commented, staring at Canuig Mountain when he noticed a
surprisingly large procession making its way down the incline.

"What the devil is that?" young Joseph Woodman had asked
the man who had conducted him to the vicinity of the bog, in
order, he was to discover, that he might see the remains of an
interesting buried trackway recently uncovered by turf cutters.
The trackway, his father had assured Branwell, was nothing of
the kind, was just a scattering of stones that the Irishman
believed was proof of an earlier civilization when roads had
flourished in the district.

"That," Joseph Woodman's aged companion had told him,
pointing up the mountain, "is the funeral procession of a man of
only forty some years of age, called O'Shea, and him the last one

being brought out of there. The last man being brought down out of Coomavoher," he said. "All the rest gone away or dead before him. And isn't the place only ruins and vacancies now with him gone."

Everything in the Iveragh was ruins and vacancies as far as Woodman could tell.

"And I remember," the old Irishman had said, "when he went in there after marrying a woman who had the grass of three cows from her father, he went in with a wardrobe on his back, straight up the mountain with a wardrobe on his back. He was that strong." The speaker had crossed himself and added, "Heavens be his bed."

His father had smiled. "Now that is the definition of avoidable difficulty," he said to his son. "Who but a fool would choose to live in such a wild, inhospitable place? No one but an Irishman would endeavour to haul furniture to such a grey, destitute, though" — he had admitted with an uncharacteristically dreamy look in his eye — "in certain lights, beautiful mountain." From where he had been standing, he assured Branwell, he had been able to see traces of neither grass nor animal. This young O'Shea should have forgotten about the woman and her cows, his father insisted, should instead have walked in the opposite direction and got out of the place altogether, unless of course, he had been able to do something about draining the godforsaken bog, the vapours from which had undoubtedly floated up the mountain and killed him.

Branwell remembered this story now as he and Ghost continued to sweep, sand crunching under their feet when they moved and filling in the areas they had cleared just a short while

before. His father, he realized, would have met a courteous people
in Ireland, a people delighted by the appearance of a stranger,
eager to relate their own history that, not being able to write,
they would have carried with them – letter perfect – in their
minds. They would have had the whole of their vast territory –
thousands of acres – in their memories: each rock, each bush, all
hills and mountains and the long beaches called strands. They
would not have understood (and, according to his father, could
not have understood) the idea of maps, maps like the ones
Annabelle had shown him, and probably would have been suspicious of the notion that all known things could be reduced to
a piece of paper no larger than a tabletop. They had named
everything already, and from the sound of the names his father
sometimes recited angrily, wistfully, the poetry of the naming
had entered their speech. Ballaig Oisin was such a name.

"Ballaig Oisin," he said, leaning on his broom. "Who but a
fool would endeavour to remain in this impossible place just
because it is beautiful under certain angles of light?" It was especially beautiful right at this moment when the dunes were
painted mauve and pink by the lowering sun and the water
beyond them was blue and black satin topped by white lace,
made so by the same wind that was bringing sand into the interior corners of his hotel. In the bay, a stranded schooner tilted
sideways, its bow driven deep into one of the new invisible sand-
bars just beneath the surface of the water. Even the lake itself
seemed to have joined this conspiracy of relentless sand. For all
he knew it could be turning itself into a desert.

"I've seen that boat," Ghost nodded in the direction of the
abandoned schooner. "I've seen that boat unfurl its sails and

cross the bay in the middle of the night. Could see all the passengers too, and the crew, stretching out their arms and calling from the deck."

Branwell raised his eyebrows and looked at his friend. "You dreamed that," he told him. "Everyone on that ship waded to shore. In another week they could have reached land without getting their feet wet."

"Dreamed it . . . saw it . . . makes no difference. A ghost ship is never a good sign."

Branwell could hear the sounds Marie was making in the kitchen, cleaning up after the evening meal she had prepared for the three of them. It was autumn; there were never many guests remaining in the hotel in this season, but Branwell had every reason to believe that, next summer, there would be no guests at all. The Ballagh Oisin was finished. He was certain of this.

"You'll be here for a while yet," said Ghost. "You'll stay here until your son moves and gets settled up in that big house on the hill."

There were times when Branwell felt that Ghost's telepathy was intrusive, but he had learned, over the years, to trust what the man had to say. "What hill?" he asked. "What house?"

"Thirty some miles to the west," said Ghost, his eyes narrowing. "Near a village called Colborne named after colonial administrator and rebellion crusher John Colborne, a merciless old powermonger if there ever was one. But that's the way things unfold. Your son will be a merciless old powermonger as well. There is no stopping destiny." He paused for a moment. "I think there is another hill in his future as well, in Ottawa. He's going to be a relentless, old political ranter, as far as I can tell."

Branwell laughed wryly, and for the first time in days.

"Yes, sir," said Ghost, reading Branwell's mind, "a henpecked man in politics is a force to be reckoned with."

The next morning when Branwell ventured out to the stables he found Ghost saddling up the white horse that had been given to him by the family as a Christmas gift just two years before and that, proud of his sense of humour, he had called Spectre. His carpetbag was packed, and his mandolin was tied to the pommel of the saddle. "Taking her away from this," he said, stroking the animal's muzzle. "It's back to Baden for us. There's a new tavern right across from the station where I can entertain, and I might get some kind of work out at Fryfogel's, though the old man's dead and the place is no longer an inn."

"How do you know he's dead?" Branwell was aware that the question was ridiculous as soon as it was out of his mouth.

Ghost didn't bother to reply but said instead that two of the sons, fair to middling farmers, now lived there with their wives and children, in the rooms of what had been the inn.

They walked with the horse out of the darkness of the stables into the vivid autumn light. Choked by sand, the dying trees in the vicinity of the hotel had shed their leaves in midsummer, and now their leafless limbs threw tangled shadows over the surrounding dunes. "Well, I wish I could offer you something here," said Branwell. "But, as you can see, there's not much hope of that. So I guess I'll say goodbye, then. I suppose I'll miss you, though."

"Not for long, you won't," said Ghost. "The walls out at Fryfogel's aren't painted yet, remember, and now you're going to need the money." He mounted the horse. "See you in the winter!" he called over his shoulder as the horse struggled through the sand in the direction of Maurice's monstrous brick house (which sported a large For Sale sign on the yard fence) and the sand-covered road that led to a more stable world.

"Not in the winter!" shouted Branwell. "I'm never going back there in winter."

"Oh yes you are!" the Ghost shouted back. "You can be sure of that."

Branwell watched what remained of the road until Ghost was out of sight. Then he turned to face the hotel. Some of the white paint had been scoured from the exterior by the sand-laden wind, and the worn grey clapboard was showing through. And then there was Marie's pale face at the kitchen window. He raised his arm to wave to her. She did not wave back but turned away, instead, and disappeared from view.

$\mathcal{A}$nnabelle, despite her fierce independence and her absolute practicality, was assaulted by passion in midlife, assaulted and imprisoned for a brief time until sorrow released her. Yes, even Annabelle was caught, likely while looking in some other direction altogether. It began at sunset one early evening in the autumn of the following year. There was a cloud, engorged by sun, hanging like fire over the ships at Kingston pier on the mainland. She gathered together her watercolours and sketchbook and walked outdoors, delighted by the apparent effect of fire on pale brown sails. This was an atmospheric opportunity. She would have to be quick to capture it.

Yes, this had been the summer when everything fell into ruin: the hotel, Caroline's gazebo, the price of barley, the summer that Maurice, in spite of his wife's resistance, had finally gone ahead and put his house up for sale. Annabelle had just returned from the Ballagh Oisin and her clothes still danced on the line outside, shedding sand as they were "aired." All day long she had been worrying about Marie, who had been filled with distress at the thought of everything she and Branwell had so carefully put together being taken slowly, painfully apart.

Who would have imagined, though, that Annabelle would count herself among those who stumbled, who risked a complete collapse? She was just over forty years old and looking forward to a life spent earning a modest living and painting the decaying hulks in Wreck Bay, as well as the healthier ships that were across the water in Kingston Harbour. Moreover, she had been visited by the sin of pride. Despite her former dislike of it, she had been pleased by her mastery of the salvage business, delighted, in fact, by the independence it afforded her. She even dared to hope that she might be able to help her brother and her friend when the time came, as she feared it would, for them to leave the hotel.

What made her soften, then, and agree finally that Mister Gilderson could bargain with her for the island? Was it his own decline, his own loss of authority? Perhaps she wanted to see him sitting on the other side of her desk, his fortune diminished, his ability to bully those around him subsiding. Perhaps, despite her father's dying words, she believed that it would be impossible for her father's old rival to carry out his plan to purchase the property and what remained of her equipment. Perhaps she wanted to see him humiliated, grappling with that impossibility. She believed that she hated him.

But there was something else as well. She had to admit that, when all was said and done, she wasn't entirely against selling to Gilderson. In fact, it would have given her some satisfaction, a little taste of power in the face of her now safely dead but still strangely controlling father. Though gone now for years, he continued to speak — often, in fact — in her mind, dispensing advice

and admonitions. She had never been afraid of him, and she
wasn't now, but occasionally she felt he was voicing his disapproval as he had attempted to do in the past. "For God's sake,
don't sell to that bandit Gilderson!" Annabelle could imagine
her father shouting these words, flushed with rage, glaring at her
from under his thick eyebrows that resembled grey broom straw.
Though his rival had been a decade younger than him, and would
therefore to his mind be permanently undereducated and inexpe-
rienced in the ways of lake transport, her father had always
believed that his own business was threatened whenever Gilderson
turned his attention to the eastern end of the lake.

Gilderson and his servant were lodging in the ancient and no
longer entirely satisfactory guest house that Annabelle herself,
having no domestic staff of her own, had prepared for him.
Shortly after his arrival, she had conducted him to the office
where she had talked to him at length about what remained of
the business. Later, while he was making a slow, private inspec-
tion of the island, she had prepared an evening meal of mutton
stew, a meal they took together in the parlour while the servant
ate in the kitchen. Annabelle had had difficulty concentrating
on the polite conversation concerning Branwell and Caroline
that the occasion seemed to demand. Along with her father's
voice, an absurd list of all the goods Gilderson had trafficked up
and down the lakes was building itself in her mind: barley, cabbages, weather vanes, sets of china, hacksaws, buggies, furniture,
whisky, horses, human beings. What a lot of *things* there are in
the world, she thought, and more all the time. Oran Gilderson,
she realized, was a master of displacement, and now by the looks
of things, it was she who was going to be displaced.

After dinner, he asked if he might smoke, and when Annabelle said by all means, he poured a small amount of golden tobacco out of a leather pouch and firmly pushed the flakes into the bowl of his pipe. He turned his chair away from the table and toward the window, then leaned forward to strike a match on the bottom of his boot. This match, though Annabelle didn't yet know she would want to save it, was destined for her scrapbook, her splinter book.

Gilderson gazed with thoughtful satisfaction out the window. "Good," he said finally. "Not a single lighthouse in sight."

"There are several in the vicinity, however," Annabelle told him. "Two on either side of Kingston and one on Insignificant Island. Did you not see them on your walk?" She had painted all three at one time or another, always under stormy conditions and with a ship, sometimes two, smashing into the nearby rocks. "They can be seen quite clearly from several spots on Timber Island but never from the house itself."

Gilderson puffed away without comment for several minutes. "I was not looking at the view on my walk," he said. "I was searching for equipment." Then he stood and walked to the fire, where he began to remove the remaining ashes from his pipe by knocking it against the grate for what seemed to Annabelle to be an exaggeratedly long time. Eventually he turned to Annabelle and told her he would not be purchasing her property. She did not ask why he had suddenly taken this position, but he told her anyway. "Too many lighthouses in the district," he said, "and, despite what you may think, lighthouses are dangerous for my ships."

What nonsense, thought Annabelle, and then, He's had to sell almost all his ships anyway. "Very well," she said, gathering the dishes from the table and heading, though the wreaths of smoke left in the air by her guest's pipe, for the kitchen. Gilderson took his leave and walked off in the twilight toward the guest quarters. When he was gone, Annabelle gathered her camp stool, sketchbook, and brushes and went outside to capture the light.

So she would not be displaced after all. The island would remain in her possession. Whatever possibilities the sale had presented to her — a small house of her own, perhaps some travel — now faded and withdrew. But these had never really taken solid shape, anyway, in her imagination, beyond the images of the deck of an oceangoing vessel and a simple porch unsullied by fretsaw work. She let these pictures disappear from her mind without a great deal of regret and concentrated instead on the ships she could now see swaying in the distance and on the strange colour of the light from which the warmth seemed to be leaking minute by minute. The sky that had been orange was now violet, and the lake, which was quite still, had become not silver exactly but rather pewter-coloured, there being no glitter on its surface.

She felt his hand on her shoulder before she paid any attention to his voice, probably because the quay upon which she sat had always, in the past, been filled with male voices, French and English voices, voices she had very early on learned to ignore. A male hand squeezing her shoulder was an experience so new that it might have been a bolt of lightning judging from the effect it had on her system.

Annabelle stiffened, examined the hand that had so unexpectedly come to rest on her person, and noted with relief that the fingernails were clean. She turned on the stool then and looked up into the not altogether unattractive but very hairy face of Oran Gilderson. His moustache, she realized, was stained yellow as a result of his fondness for tobacco. There were two deep furrows that ran from his cheekbones to the beginning of his lavish, well-kept, but far too long beard, furrows that could only have been gouged by a grimace of some sort visiting his expression over and over. There was a full crop of grey hair in his nostrils, also showing a jaundiced tinge. She decided to concentrate on her painting.

"I like a woman who can do dainty things," Gilderson said, referring, she supposed, to the watercolour on her lap. "Do you sing as well?"

"No," said Annabelle. She was mildly offended by his reference to her picture as something dainty. And the man had been into the whisky; she could smell it. Still, there was the extraordinary warmth of his hand on her shoulder and this, like some unlikely force of gravity, bound her to her place.

"A widower is a very lonely man. A widower whose daughter has left him is lonelier still," said the voice behind her.

Annabelle had absolutely no experience with this kind of talk. Her father had reacted to neither her mother's presence nor her absence except with a kind of unvarying, vague irritation. Branwell had remained stubbornly silent on the subject of male affection of any kind, and Maurice . . . well, Maurice was, as far as she could tell, so frightened of his wife, and so in love with her, that had he an opinion on the subject it would be unreliable at best. The man's fingers were beginning to explore her collarbones, his other hand having now come to rest on the opposite shoulder.

Annabelle rose quickly to her feet, upsetting the stool as she did so, and letting the sketchbook fall from her lap. As she began to limp away from him, Gilderson followed, caught her arm, then embraced her and pressed a quantity of whiskers and a mouth smelling of tobacco and whisky into her face. It was almost dark. Annabelle used more force than she knew she was capable of to push the man away, then walked, with as much speed as possible, back toward the house. He was calling her name and shouting sentences that she could have sworn included the word *marriage*, but she was determined not to pay any mind.

Once she was safely behind the locked door, she peered furtively out the window, just in time to see a silhouetted Gilderson begin to walk unsteadily back to the place where he would spend the night. There was a certain poignancy about the curve of his back and the careful determination with which he measured each step that softened Annabelle. He is getting old, she thought, and he will get older yet. Then, just as she thought this, Gilderson stumbled, lurched forward, and fell on his hands and knees, and something in Annabelle stumbled and fell with him. She brought her hand up to her mouth as if to prevent herself from crying out. It seemed to take him an extraordinary amount of time to get to his feet. He was like a bear that had been shot and had not quite realized that his wounds were fatal; Annabelle half-expected him to throw back his head and roar. It occurred to her that she should be leaving the house to see whether he had broken any bones, but she found it quite impossible to move, and eventually she perceived that he was once again stumbling through the increasing darkness toward the guest house. Would he spend the night tossing in an agony of remorse and embarrassment? she wondered. Not likely, she concluded, probably in the state he was in he would be snoring as soon as his head touched the pillow.

In the middle of the night, Annabelle sat bolt upright in her bed. Had he really used the word *marriage* and, if so, in what context had he used it? She wished she had listened more carefully now, in order to have caught exactly what he had said to her. Annabelle lit the lamp – there was to be no sleep for her that night – and looked first at one of her shoulders and then at the other. Perhaps she hadn't heard him clearly. It could have been that he was simply inquiring about a carriage to meet him in Kingston the following day. But no, that was not likely because, like all shipbuilders, he would detest roads and railways and would insist on travelling, as much as possible, by water. She crossed her arms over her breasts and put her own hands on her shoulders, trying to determine how these bony protuberances would feel under the touch of another. Bony, she decided, was the only adjective one could apply to such shoulders, bony and old. Her heart, on the other hand, was behaving like a young trapped animal, restless, pacing, eager to get out.

The next morning everything in the house and outside its windows seemed just slightly unfamiliar, as if a series of minor alterations had taken place in the physical world overnight. Not since she had been young had Annabelle looked at objects with such intensity: the hairbrush on her dresser, the leather of her boots, the veins in her own hands as she laced up these boots, the cloth-covered buttons on the pale blue dress that she removed from the wardrobe, each chip and crack in the ironstone dishes she assembled on the kitchen table (two place settings for breakfast,) the dull sheen of an unpolished silver spoon, the oily yellow of the butter, the blue tinge of the milk. Waiting at the parlour window, from which the guest house was visible, she became absorbed by the dusty, disintegrating tassels on a worn velvet curtain. What could be the purpose of tassels on parlour curtains? The shadows of the leaves on her mother's oak tree trembled on the carpet at her feet. What exactly was the purpose of that tree? While she was pondering such questions she saw Oran Gilderson emerge from the guest house along with his servant, who carried a valise in his hand. Without looking in the direction of the house, Gilderson walked as briskly as his age would allow toward the quay where the skiff in which he had arrived the previous day was anchored. A murky blend of anger and disappointment was awakened in Annabelle by this sight. This was followed by a sense of distress so overwhelming that she was affected physically, could barely manage to remove herself from the window. For the first time in her life she went back to bed in the morning and stayed there until midafternoon.

This was to be the beginning of a spate of days so disorganized that Annabelle would not have been able to fully recall them in the future, had she the inclination to recall them, which would be far from the case. She lit no fires, she cooked no meals. When she ate, which was rarely, she picked up an apple in passing, or a crust of bread, perhaps some cheese. She made no drawings, and beyond fixing a particular match to a page in her scrapbook, she did no work of any kind. Weeds were appearing in her vegetable garden, flowers in the parched plots bordering the house died of thirst in the dry autumn heat. The bed into which she flung herself at any hour of the day or night remained unmade.

She neither dressed nor undressed, wearing the same blue cotton shirtwaist she had put on the morning of Gilderson's departure. As the days progressed, the stains under the arms of this dress darkened and the cuffs at her wrists became more and more soiled. She did not wash; her fingernails became filthy and cracked. It was as if she had forgotten about her body and its functions altogether, as if her physical self had become simply a bothersome bundle that, as the result of an evil spell, her racing mind was required to haul around with it wherever it went. And in this racing mind sat Gilderson, as grim and pompous and unpleasant as ever, but tenacious – the idea of him like a warm hand glued to her shoulder as she moved from place to place. She was always moving from place to place because except for the few hours when she fell into the delirium that she now called sleep, she could not stop walking.

She walked through all the rooms of the house, up and down the halls, up and down the stairs, including those that led to the attic where Marie had once lived. She walked in and out of the guest house. "Lonely man, lonely man," she whispered, looking at the faintly greasy dent his head had left in the feather pillow on the unmade bed. She walked around and around the circumference of the island, pausing only to glare at the distant lighthouses she had in the past been quite fond of. She began to play counting games: mentally cataloguing all the door latches on

the island, for example, latches attached to the doors of the
buildings that still stood, then picking through the collapsed
wreckage of those that had gone down during one of the previous winters and finding a surprising number of latches there. She
repeated the process with hinges and porcelain knobs, and then
with panes of glass, broken (in the case of fully abandoned
buildings) or otherwise. This inventory required a great deal of
concentration; these phenomena, after all, had all been rejected
by Gilderson, just as she herself, she now believed, had been
rejected by him. Her table remained set for breakfast: two knives,
two spoons, two forks, two folded linen napkins, her mother's
best cups and saucers.

The curious thing, she would soon come to realize, was that
her opinion of the man had not changed one whit. She knew
exactly what he had been, and what he would have been had a
reversal of his fortunes not taken place. She knew that he had
abused his employees, misused the landscape, greedily hoarded
his wealth, and had cared not a fig for any other human being
with the possible exception of his overindulged daughter. She
had not even considered what they might talk about had they
been given the opportunity to do so on a regular basis. And yet
this did not prevent her from going over and over in her mind the
conversation they had engaged in during the one meal they had
shared, searching for a hint of affection in remarks such as
"damn fine potatoes!" or questions such as "Have you much
trouble getting supplies from the mainland in winter?" She was
hoping to find a key to his behaviour, to what it was that drove
him out the door of the guest house with the object of placing
his hand on her shoulder. The other curious matter was that she

was able to think of such things while, at the very same time, counting the number of pieces of scrap lumber left lying about on the island, scrap lumber that Gilderson was clearly not interested in.

Throughout all the walking and counting and listing Annabelle became gradually convinced that all through her adult life there had been something lost in her that now, as a consequence of one masculine touch, had been found, and that having been found she was now going to have to come to terms with it one way or another. Even though the lost thing was now found, she was never able to bring clearly into focus what the lost thing was, only that it had been discovered far too late. Sometimes she was grateful for this. At other times she was angry. She knew that it had something to do with the two place settings that she had been unable to remove from the kitchen table, and something to do as well with the dent in the guest-house pillow, but her mind would take her no further than that. Her thoughts skimmed past the complexities of her condition and insisted instead on increased motion, this nonsensical accounting.

In the midst of her counting exercises, or while she was walking vigorously from one end of the island to the other, she would now and then stop for several moments and look toward Kingston. If she saw a skiff approaching she would scrutinize it intently and, once she had determined that it was not the skiff she was looking for, she would crouch behind a convenient bush until the vessel drew up to the quay, deposited whatever it had on board, and withdrew. Often what it had on board was the post: odd bits of business she should have been attending to but, during this period, had no interest in whatsoever. Sometimes the skiff contained a person who would walk up to the house and pound on the door until, confused by her absence, they too would withdraw, though not before puzzling over the damp letters that had been left in the open box situated near the water. It was only during these spells of concealment that Annabelle became aware of herself, the fact that she had not bathed, or changed her clothes, or cleaned her house, or picked up the mail. She would huddle in a kind of fever of shame behind a cedar bush or a gooseberry bush, as if her previous self had joined with the visitor and was judging her condition. It was only then that it occurred to her that, had the gentleman she was looking for magically appeared, she would be in no state to receive him, only then that she admitted that she was never again going to have to receive him.

Still, the idea of his arrival, the reception of a guest, set off another bout of industrious activity and, after pulling from the cupboard bottles and powders and cereals and sugars that had not seen the light of day since Marie had departed for the hotel, Annabelle began to bake. Various small insects had died in the flour, the vanilla had become a gummy paste, and the sugar had transformed itself from crystals to a solid lump, the baking soda had almost disappeared, but none of this stopped her. She had fresh butter and she mixed all of the ingredients she could find into its greasy texture along with several jars of preserves she found in the cellar. Then she added a quantity of water and poured the mess she had made into round cake tins, square cake tins, cupcake tins, and finally onto a number of cookie sheets. As she gathered together the kindling and split logs in order to light the stove and heat the oven, she became aware that she was weeping, and weeping the way a child weeps, loudly, and for effect. Once she heard herself, she stopped and concentrated instead on placing the racks in the oven so that she could push almost all of the tins inside it.

The temperature inside the room rose. Annabelle sat perspiring beside the window looking at the lake.

Finally a skiff she recognized, though not at all the one she was waiting for, was seen on the horizon, coming from the open lake and not from the direction of Kingston. It annoyed her that Maurice would arrive at this moment as if he knew she was not herself and was consciously intending to invade her privacy. Perhaps he had been sent to spy on her. Well, he wouldn't find her, she would remain hidden, and he would go away again. She looked at her forearms, which were almost unrecognizable: reddened by sun, covered with flour dust, and laced with scratches from long periods of time spent in the centre of bushes. She remembered the man's fingers on her shoulder, the Masonic ring, the grey and black hairs that grew just above the knuckles.

It was the look on Maurice's face as he approached the house that caused Annabelle to become instantly sane. As if she had snapped shut a book she had been reading – a fantasy about a foreign country, perhaps – and the world of numbered things she had inhabited for the past few days closed with a bang and her previous life opened before her in a violent rush. She forgot all about the latches and doorknobs and piles of discarded lumber. She forgot all about Gilderson and his big warm hand and her own bony shoulders. She forgot all about the baking. She gazed with horror at her unkempt flowerbeds and vegetable garden. Then she looked again at Maurice's face, and the last vestiges of trance drained out of her. Even from this distance she could see he too had been weeping; there was sorrow in the way he carried his body, even his hands appeared to be sad. Annabelle rose to her feet and called her nephew's name. She was certain that he had come to deliver some terrible news. Marie, she suddenly knew, was dead.

When after a while they pulled away from the quay Annabelle remembered the small, dark figure she had seen arriving in the sleigh boat all those years ago and the Gilderson daydream fell forever from her mind. She realized, just for a moment, that in recent days while she had been wandering around her empty house and vacant island half-crazed, almost as if she had been acting out the silly Lady of stupid Shallot, Marie, her better, more beautiful self, lay trembling on the edge of death. Annabelle was filled with grief and shame, and fully herself again. She recalled her friend at the orphanage talking about the carved angels walking on the snow. Marie was not the dying type, they had agreed on that distant afternoon.

She would bring her back to the island to be buried. She would have a small white angel carved for her grave. What would any of their lives have been without the quickening that an orphan had caused in the only world that Annabelle had ever known?

$\mathcal{B}$ranwell remained at the Ballagh Oisin for another year and a half after his wife's death. Alone and miserable, he responded only now and then to messages from his sister, who begged him to return immediately to Timber Island. This was something he had decided he would never do for, despite the fact that his dear wife was buried there, he would not allow himself to be a grave-stander. His father, he remembered, had often carried on about the senselessness of an Irish poem entitled "I'm Stretched on Your Grave," and somehow the idea of the futility of such gestures had stuck for all these years in his mind. Even Marie would not have approved of him moping around her headstone under the spell of what his father would have called "Irish behaviour." No, he would leave the tending of the grave to poor Annabelle, who had once told him she had always believed that Marie was her other, more beautiful self.

Branwell spent his time, instead, aimlessly sorting through his wife's few possessions: her dresses and coats, hairbrush and mirror, odd bits of jewellery, hairpins and nets, pots and pans,

and a variety of other cooking utensils, her small collection of
pine butter moulds (she had been touchingly vain about the look
of her butter that she had churned herself), things he had barely
paid attention to until now. He believed that something should
be done with all of these abandoned objects, but he had no idea
what, and knew, in any event, that the sand would claim everything in the end.

When the winter arrived he was grateful for the heavy snow
the season invariably brought with it because at least in winter he
didn't have to spend all his time watching sand and, unlike sand,
snow could be kept out of his rooms, his clothing, his bedding,
his hair. It could be shovelled, thrown to one side, arranged in
piles that, more or less, stayed in place. He could open his door,
walk to the lake and back, and an hour later, his footsteps would
still be visible, small blue pools filled with shadow. This was
strangely comforting in the face of what seemed to be a complete
erasure of everything he had worked for and everything he had
loved. He found it hard to remember that there had been a time
when he had loved the beach and the dunes, the soft feel of sand
under his feet, the ribs of sand he could see when he had waded
through the shallows to bathe. He had also forgotten that the
proximity of this beach, those dunes, had been one of the elements
that had made the Ballagh Oisin so popular during the summers
of the past. Sand was the enemy, had always been the enemy. He
was certain of this. It was as if he was living in the bottom half of
an hourglass in which, as the days passed, he was being buried alive.

For the first time in his life he had begun to pray. In the
evenings he would pluck Marie's rosary from the nail in the wall
where he had hung it the previous evening, and then he would

whisper the words he had learned all those years ago at the
orphanage just before his wedding, words he had never voluntar-
ily used since. He liked the repetition of the name Mary, and was
moved by the knowledge that his wife's fingers had travelled over
the surface of the beads that his own fingers were touching now.
It was one of the ways that he felt he could speak to Marie, but
in the end, like all his other attempts to reach her now, this would
become unsatisfying, and one winter night he would not remove
the rosary from the wall and fall to his knees near their bed. The
beads would remain hanging near the wardrobe until the sight of
them alone became too painful a reminder. Then he would take
them down and place them in the small ivory jewellery box that
would itself become too painful a reminder until it was finally
consigned to a dresser drawer.

His sister wrote to him often, but he rarely answered —
sometimes he didn't even bother to open the envelopes. His son
wrote less often, and these letters, though always opened and
read, were never answered. Branwell could tell that Maurice was
suffering from the loss of his mother, yet, in spite of this, he
found that he was unable to write with words of consolation.
He would never be able to accept the idea of his son's greed, his
weakness, his role in the wreckage, and any correspondence
between them could only be a reminder of all that.

As it turned out, things would unfold just as Ghost had
predicted. Maurice would run successfully as a Tory for the
Northumberland County seat and would spend his time travelling back and forth from that County to Ottawa, while his wife
presided over the building of another, even larger, brick house
situated on a hill overlooking the town of Colborne. When Old

Gilderson finally died of a heart attack (perhaps brought about by the shock of his son-in-law's election to public office), he would leave just enough money for the building of the vulgar turrets and arched entranceways of which his daughter was so fond. There would be a ballroom on the second storey with a glass floor through which the light from the belvedere would shine. The property on which the house stood would be called Gilderwood, in memory of Caroline's doting father. Branwell, after receiving this information, might have looked out his north window, where in the distance he would be able to see the first house that Maurice and Caroline had built, a house that would eventually be sold, at a great loss, to American summer people.

As far as Branwell would be able to tell, no reversal of fortune was ever going to take place. On spring, summer, and fall mornings he awoke to a fresh drift of sand on the front porch. During the autumn that followed Marie's death, dunes had completely swallowed her flowerbeds at the rear of the house — having already destroyed, in summer, those at the front. Pillows of sand sat on the seats of the wooden rockers that Branwell did not bother to put away for seasonal storage as he had in the past. The boat house in which he had stored such things was half-buried in any case; there was no hope of opening its doors. The three canoes and four rowboats that he set out at the beginning of each summer had been rarely used and had disappeared under so much sand he could not now be entirely certain of where he had last seen them. The vacated stables were rendered entirely inaccessible, and Branwell was forced to enter through the hayloft in order to dig for the firewood he had stacked in a corner of the ground floor. Sand accumulated on the hotel's windowsills and inched up the glass. Each day it was becoming more and more difficult to open or close the front door and, increasingly, lengthy ribbons of sand had slipped under this door and into the large entrance hall.

Whether the well had dried up was irrelevant in that the pump that surmounted it had utterly vanished. Three times a day, with sand capsizing like miniature avalanches under his feet, Branwell was forced to trudge with two galvanized pails down to the lake and back again in order to have water for washing, drinking, and cooking. Not that he cooked much anyway, living mostly as he did now on carrots and potatoes and sometimes an egg or two, all boiled in one pot on the top of one of the Quebec heaters. He had trouble even looking at Marie's beautiful cook stove, The Kitchen Queen, which stood unlit in the kitchen, its decorative features and its copper boiler cold and unpolished. Furthermore, the last time he had opened one of its ovens, Branwell had been appalled by the sight of the tiny dunes that had formed inside it, and the excess sand that descended like a pale brown curtain to the floor.

Word of Marie's death had apparently been passed from tavern to inn to tavern, in a westward direction, and had finally reached Baden about a month later. The first letter Branwell received from Ghost had mostly concerned this sad event and was filled with his memories of Marie's kindness, her spirit, and her outstanding cooking. Branwell eagerly opened every letter he received from his friend whose unpronounceable first name was printed neatly on the back flap of each envelope as Gzsrzt

Shromanov and then translated in brackets ("Ghost"), as if to make clear which of the many men of Branwell's acquaintance who were named Gzsrzt might be writing to him at this time.

The strange thing about Ghost's letters was that they were utterly reflective in nature and referred to events that had already happened rather than those that were about to occur. When Branwell wrote to inquire about this, his friend replied that not only had he never fully trusted the future tense in written rather than spoken English but he believed it was bad luck to commit to writing anything at all pertaining to predictions. *Destiny*, he wrote, *has always been suspicious of notation. Destiny has never taken kindly to anyone that has kept a written record of its intentions.* He described instead the fine new Baden tavern and its splendid stamped-tin ceiling that had no cracks in it and was full of decorative swirls. He made reference to the health of Spectre, who was flourishing, he said, in the company of the various other horses that were temporarily housed in the tavern's stables now that there were enough settlers on the Huron Road and the surrounding concessions that *a good quantity of horses were needed to get people to the places where the railway, mercifully, wasn't.*

As all delivery vehicles and the rural post had given up trying to negotiate the dunes months before, Branwell had to stumble through one mile of sand and down two miles of decent road into the town of West Lake in order to purchase supplies and to pick up his mail. The trip was made considerably easier in the winter because the sand was itself buried by drifts, and because of the snowshoes he had purchased, years before, after his visit to Baden. On one such trek, during his second winter as a widower, he made the return voyage with a sack of potatoes, several loaves

of rapidly freezing bread, a freshly killed and also rapidly freezing chicken on his toboggan, and two letters in the pocket of his
coat. The tops of his ears were frostbitten. There was not much
to look forward to – beyond fried chicken – at the end of this
particular journey.

One letter was from Annabelle, who was passing on what
Maurice had told her about the death of Gilderson: the date,
the place of his internment, and other details about the old
scoundrel that Branwell forgot as soon as he read them. The
other was written in an unfamiliar hand and was postmarked
Shakespeare, Ontario. The naming of places in this Dominion, he
thought, was becoming increasingly preposterous. Branwell tore
open the envelope, tossed it into the fire, and began to read the
sentences written by Peter Fryfogel, son of Sebastian and current
owner of the elusive Fryfogel Inn. Two charlatans, painters of
naked women, had arrived in Baden at the request of an otherwise
solid and successful citizen who was building a beautiful mansion
right in the centre of town. This had reminded Peter that his late
father had always wanted murals painted by the good and honest
innkeeper, Branwell Woodman, but, if he remembered correctly,
circumstances had prevented Mister Woodman from reaching
the inn the one time he had been in the district. Would he once
again consider taking up the task this winter when there would
likely be few tenants at Mister Woodman's lakeside hotel? Please
advise and etc. Branwell read the letter twice, a bit confused that
Ghost had predicted nothing about this possible commission in
his letters, until he recalled that any reference to the painting of
murals at the Fryfogel – if in fact this painting took place –
would have required the written use of the future tense.

Branwell opened the drawer of the desk at which, in the past, he had carried out the business of the hotel, riffled through a quantity of correspondence and sand, and finally found some paper that was blank except for the printed illustration of the Ballagh Oisin in better days. He unscrewed the top of a pot of ink and sand, dipped his pen, and began to answer in the affirmative fully aware, as he did so, that while he was obviously fulfilling Ghost's prediction, he was also writing a letter of farewell to his cherished hotel. Once he began this second journey to the west, he knew he would not be returning. The sand had won; he would abandon the Ballagh Oisin to its fate.

In fact, Branwell *would* return, but this would not happen for several years, and it would happen only once. As a much older and much crankier man, Branwell would insist that his son, Maurice "Badger" Woodman as he liked to be called, with whom Branwell had been living unhappily for some years, accompany him in the cabriolet on a journey back to Tremble Point. "I want you to see this," he would say, having secretly never fully stopped blaming his son for the greed, for the barley, for the sand, for the death of his wife, and knowing full well that whatever it was they were going to view would not be an improvement on what he had left behind on this February day. When they arrived at the spot, they would have to climb a dune in order to enter the hotel by the door that had led to the upper veranda. They would crunch along the sandy second-storey hall as far as the central staircase, which Branwell would begin to descend, stopping on the fourth step down. The sand would have almost entirely filled the first floor by then; only the turquoise skies of Branwell's murals would be visible. Branwell would think then of all that was buried: sofas, tables, chairs, umbrella stands, mirrors, door stoppers, Marie's copper pots, the cook stove, and he would turn to his son, who remained blinking at the top of the stairs. Shaking his cane at him he would shout, "You are a creator of deserts!" On the way back to the cabriolet, descending the dunes, Maurice, the now influential politician, dressed in his waistcoat and top hat, would become caught in a slide and would fall directly on his backside.

But now, during his last few days at the hotel, Branwell became involved in a frenzy of essentially useless activities. He touched up certain areas of the murals that had become chipped and cracked over the years, he cleaned out the closets, and shook sand out of the bedclothes stored in the linen wardrobe. He puttied several loose window panes, oiled hinges that had become tight and difficult, took the carpets outside and beat them, and, as a last gesture to Marie, he polished up the Kitchen Queen. Then, after packing a few items of clothing in a leather valise and putting all of his paints and brushes into a wooden box, he placed these two pieces of luggage on top of a drift just beyond the porch. When he re-entered the hall, he looked for some time at the panoramas he had painted. Then he turned away from the fantasy of his landscapes and swept a quantity of sand — and himself — out the front door, leaving the broom standing upright in the snow like a scarecrow, or a kind of sentinel, guarding the empty hotel.

7he new Baden Tavern was made of brick, not logs, its windows were surrounded by decorative moulding, and there was a large wood-burning furnace in its deep cellar. These architectural details would be the only differences, as far as Branwell could tell, that would enable him to separate his current stay in the district from the one he had endured ten years before. Each day, he pulled aside the burlap curtains in his room and stared, as he had in the past, into a sea of swirling white. Each evening he fell asleep to the sound of howling winds tearing around the snow-bound village, and each night he was awakened intermittently by the moan of train whistles. Kelterborn was gone; Lingelbach, the present owner, was so like Kelterborn, both in his taciturn manner and in his physical appearance, that he hardly qualified as a noteworthy change.

Ghost, however, who had wandered all over the townships, insisted that there *were* changes. More than one track, a proliferation of new farms, villages like New Hamburg to the east and, now that the Irish had arrived in droves, places called Dublin and St. Columban were appearing to the west. "My father would have been beside himself," Branwell told his friend, all the while thinking as he had in the past, Why these European names? Almost everyone had horses and buggies now, Ghost explained, and several blacksmiths shops had opened as a result. The gorgeous mansion going up across the street was said to have ten marble fireplaces, all made in Italy, and the two painters Fryfogel Junior had referred to were, indeed, painting naked ladies on the walls, "ladies so real you almost thought you could touch them." He paused here, closed his eyes for a few moments, then said that he didn't see Branwell painting naked ladies in the future, mores the pity. "General stores in every village," Ghost said, "and churches everywhere. An undertaker. A tombstone maker."

"I imagine I'll have to take all this on faith, though," Branwell said. "I've never been able to see anything but the inside of a tavern, a different tavern, yes, but still a tavern much like all the others."

Ghost pointed heavenward, explaining that none of the other taverns had tin ceilings like this one. "Not a crack in it and there never will be a crack in it. Even if the tavern fell down there would not be a crack in that ceiling."

Branwell looked at the ceiling, the ceiling Ghost was so fond of. The decorative swirls were confined to borders that surrounded flat square panels like an embossed baroque frame. He wondered briefly about the machine that would be required to make such a thing as a ceiling. Must the tin be heated or was it soft enough to be pushed into the shape required? Nonetheless, to his eye, there was a monotony about the resulting effect, exaggerated by the rather dirty pale yellow paint that covered it, or perhaps it was white paint, discoloured by the pipe smoke that, he was beginning to discover, filled the barroom day and night.

Ghost asked about Branwell's financial situation, which, admittedly, was shaky at best but which he hoped would improve once he got out to Fryfogel's.

Lingelbach, who was pretending to be absorbed by the task of wiping down the bar with a damp cloth, moved closer to the side of the room where Branwell sat with Ghost. "Road's disappeared," he offered.

Again? thought Branwell. What was it about him that made particles of almost everything want to accumulate wherever he went? What else could possibly happen to him? He half-expected a plague of sawdust, or of iron filings to appear in his future. He wouldn't have been surprised if brimstone began to descend from the sky. Lingelbach was speaking again. "You'll have to pay me," he was saying to Branwell. "There's the room, the board. You'll have to pay me one way or another."

On the fourth day of the storm Branwell descended the stairs at the tavern to be confronted by a strange scaffolding made up of two tall stepladders placed about six feet apart with a couple of wide pine boards resting between them. Ghost, who had clearly been supervising the placement of this scaffold, took Branwell by the arm. "I see pictures on this ceiling," he said, "and," he nodded his head in the direction of the bar, "so does Lingelbach. We both see you painting these pictures, starting this morning."

Branwell had no desire to paint a ceiling. He was tired, sad, and slightly disoriented by being in the company of others after his solitary life in the hotel. He thought about snow falling on the roof of his old home and wondered how the shingles would hold up if this storm were to travel eastward. Looking at the scaffolding, he said, "I'm not Michelangelo, you know, I'm not Tiepolo."

"Who?" asked Ghost.

"Who?" echoed Lingelbach, once again pretending to be absorbed in sponging down the bar. When Branwell answered with nothing but a sigh, the owner of the establishment added philosophically, "No matter, whoever they were, they would have had to pay for room and board."

Maintenance, thought Branwell, is so central to human life, it's a wonder the very enormity of it didn't cause hopeless exhaustion in those who thought about it. Maintenance and money. There was a price to pay for sleeping at night and a price to pay for waking up in the morning. There was a price to pay for shaving your face and cutting your hair, for the clothes on your back and the food that you ate. And there was an even bigger price to pay, as far as he could tell, for having experienced happiness. I've lost everything, he concluded.

"You haven't lost me," said Ghost, reading his mind.

When he wasn't eating or drinking, Branwell spent his remaining few days at the tavern lying on his back. As his friend had predicted several years before, paint did indeed drip into his eyes as well as into his moustache and onto his face. But there was one comfort, and that comfort had to do with weather. Branwell painted nothing but scenes relating to summer: a still millpond at twilight, a farmhouse with buggy tracks visible on a road leading to its door, a few sunny water scenes punctuated by the curve of a sail, several waterfalls.

"I see *another* waterfall," said Ghost enthusiastically as he watched from below, "a much larger waterfall that will be painted by you in the future. I see Niagara." And then, in his new self-appointed role as supervisor, "So you can use turquoise . . . so show me something else! I see *other* colours! I see flowers. Paint some flowers every second square!"

The aesthetes from across the road took a break from their trompe l'oeil efforts to inspect, scoffed at Branwell's little land-scapes, and went away. The blacksmith arrived, announced that tin was not a real metal, that it would rust in a decade, and that therefore all of this painting was a waste of time, and then he too went away. Branwell lay on his back for several afternoons, a brush in his hand and unsolicited memories of his childhood in his mind. He remembered an iceboat moving across Back Bay, snow falling on a young oak tree in the yard, a girl arriving at the wrong door in late winter. All this while he continued to paint a warm season, flower by flower.

After a few days of intimate engagement with the tin ceiling, having slept late because there was no wind rattling the sashes of the window, Branwell was awakened by a spear of sunshine touching his face. He lay quite still, waiting for the wind to pick up, waiting for the light to soften as snow entered it. But the spear remained crisply defined on his pillow and the sharp, ferrous smell of water was in the air. When he opened the cur-tains he was delighted to see that the icicles hanging from the eaves above the window were releasing glistening drops of water from their tips, but even more exciting, the entire village was

chiming with a sound he had never before heard in this district —
that of sleigh bells.

He was packed and downstairs in a minute and was standing
halfway up the stepladder placing tubes of paint and brushes
back into the wooden box when Ghost entered the room.
"January thaw in February," he said. "Better get out of here
before Lingelbach gets back from the store. You're not going to
finish the ceiling."

This seemed self-evident to Branwell, but he told Ghost
that he would get back to it after he finished the commission at
Fryfogel's.

"Doubt that," Ghost replied. "I don't think I'll be seeing you
for a couple of years."

"Why not come out to the inn? It's only a few miles."

"The current Fryfogel thinks fortune telling is un-Christian
and, for some reason, Spectre doesn't like his horses . . . maybe
they are too pure. Besides, a January thaw in February is always
short-lived. Don't forget about Niagara Falls, though. I see it
painted overtop a fireplace in a room upstairs on the brookside
of the inn. And a mountain scene would be good too, there being
no mountains in this district. Paint a moonlit mountain scene in
another room."

And so, time, it seems, will always apply its patina to human effort,
and paintings completed on walls are destined to be altered,
damaged, or erased. Stains blossom, cracks appear, and the men of
maintenance arrive with trowels and plaster. Electricity and central
heating are invented and installed. Meadows and rivers, mountains

and night skies are stripped away, concealed, or scraped off. Walls are broken into, the pipes of indoor plumbing are forced into the structure, then begin to decay or burst suddenly in the midst of a deep freeze. Further surgery is required. Each decade insists on its own particular changes.

A few years after Branwell had put the finishing touches on his *Niagara* and his *Moonlit Night*, the Fryfogel, having already undergone the hardship of trying to compete with something as relentless as a railroad, would begin to experience difficulties of a different nature. Peter Fryfogel would die and be buried next to his father in the small family plot to the west of the inn. There would be disputes among various heirs about ownership, and a series of "cautions" would be instated against the property. Eventually, parts of the inn would be leased to spinster sisters trying to make a living by serving home-cooked meals to motorists on what was now a paved highway between Guelph and Goderich. A cairn would be erected nearby to mark and memorialize the blazing of the Huron Trail, now more than a hundred years old. Halfway through the twentieth century, the provincial government would decide to widen the highway and would expropriate much of the front yard. A decade after that there would be an attempt to reopen the building as a hotel, but that attempt would amount to very little, the private company involved would decide to sell the property to the County Historical Society. Various pieces of the adjoining farm property would be subdivided and sold. Heritage easements would be applied for by the Historical Society and would be approved. A drunk driver would lose control of his car and mow down the tombstones in the family plot. Governments at all levels would become more interested in business than in history, and money to keep the inn standing would be in short supply. Squirrels would invade the attic and chew holes through the roof, rats would enter the cellar kitchens, fifth- and sixth-generation pigeons would roost under the eaves, but even so the inn, now entirely emptied of both people and furniture, would continue to stand, its small paned windows rattling each time a tractor trailer roared past its beautifully proportioned Georgian front door.

With each change of ownership — and sometimes even without a change of ownership — a new layer of patterned wallpaper would be slapped over both the mural of Niagara Falls in the upper room on the brookside and the mountain scene across the hall. Finally, the fractured wall paintings would be covered by no fewer than ten layers of paper flowers and paste and the landscapes would be forgotten altogether. And, in the end, a tenant suffering from the effects of a particularly cold winter would punch a stovepipe hole into the wall above the fireplace in the upper west room, little knowing, as he did so, that he had completely destroyed Branwell Woodman's carefully rendered moon.

A Map of Glass

She stepped into the elevator with her husband and decided not to speak. She would not answer questions, she would not offer explanations. This was a tactic she had used often in the past, a predictable symptom – something she knew would reassure rather than alarm Malcolm. When the steel doors opened to her floor and she walked down the corridor by his side, she continued to keep the silence. Although, if asked, she would not have been able to say who was in the custody of whom, she felt as if they were a jailor and prisoner approaching a cell. When they reached the correct number, she placed the key in the lock, opened the door, and walked into the room with Malcolm following close behind. "Why did you do this?" he asked. There was bewilderment, not aggression, in what he said. She knew he didn't expect an answer.

Without looking at him, Sylvia quickly undressed and slid into the bed, rolling onto her side and closing her eyes.

She knew that he was standing at the end of the bed looking at her, knew that this would go on for some time. Finally, however, she heard him open the bag he had brought with him, and then the sound of him undressing and preparing for sleep. "Tomorrow," she heard him say as he lay down, leaving, as always, a respectful amount of space between them. She was kept awake for a while by the worry that, now that Malcolm had come, she might not be able to retrieve the green notebooks or gain one more day with Jerome. She wanted to give him the sheets of paper on which she had been writing these past few nights – a parting gift. And she wanted, even for just one more afternoon, to say the name Andrew aloud. How could she abandon that pleasure, that pain? The bright afterimages from the night street unsettled her as well, remaining on the edge of her consciousness like small flickering insects floating near the bed, as if they wished to attach themselves to her body, her mind.

When she woke the following morning she decided to relent somewhat, spoke when she was spoken to, and allowed Malcolm to guide her downstairs to a restaurant she had not even known was a part of the hotel.

"We'll leave after breakfast," he said, once they were seated at a table.

"Not yet," she said, "wait one more day."

"All right then," he replied, indulging her as he always did once she began to speak after a bout of silence, "we'll be on vacation. We've never been on vacation before and I don't have to be back until tomorrow." He raised a gleaming white napkin to his mouth, then folded it once and placed it again on his lap. "There are good museums in this city. You are at home in museums."

"Yes," said Sylvia, knowing that she was being granted a deferral, "yes, I am at home in museums."

✕◦

Jerome had begun to read aloud from the notebooks soon after Mira had returned from work. He had been a bit unnerved by his own curiosity, his eagerness to discover what Andrew Woodman had written, and was surprised as well by his desire to say aloud the words that were written on the page so that Mira could hear them. She had been distracted at first: searching for food in the refrigerator, washing an apple at the sink, leafing through the envelopes and flyers that had come in the mail. Then, for several minutes, she had walked back and forth eating the fruit as he read. When he looked up, he could see her looking closely at the skin of the apple, trying to avoid biting into a bruise. Gradually, though, he could feel her becoming focused, attentive. In the end she sat down at the edge of the couch and placed her legs over his lap. He rested his arms on her thighs and turned the pages, one by one.

Later that night they ate a spaghetti dinner by the light of a candle stuck into a Chianti bottle – an artifact, Jerome told Mira, that Robert Smithson would have been familiar with in the 1960s. Everyone had them, he said, all the beatniks, and then the hippies. There are probably photographs, he said jokingly, of the major figures of those times posing with or near their Chianti candleholders: Ginsberg, Ferlinghetti, Jim Dine, Smithson, Robert Rauschenberg, Frank Stella, Jack Kerouac. Those were the days, he explained, when the major figures in the arts had been as concerned about their personas as they were about their art so they would have had themselves photographed in any number of bohemian situations. That's all gone now, he continued. Ego no longer has a role to play.

"I thought you said that the art object itself was finished." Mira leaned forward to pour herself another glass of wine. Some of the red liquid splashed onto the table near her sleeve, but she seemed not to notice. Jerome could tell that, after the first glass, she had become a bit wobbly, a term she used to describe the affect of alcohol on her system. He looked at the beautiful curve of her mouth in the candlelight, her smooth brow. He watched her face change as a thought developed in her mind. "It's odd, don't you think," she eventually said, "that even though now there is no one there at all, a hundred years ago people were making objects on that island – watercolours, ships, rafts. What happened to everything?"

"Lots of it just floated away, I guess. Sylvia told me that sometimes several rafts were chained together so as to get more timber to Quebec." Jerome began to mop up the wine with his paper napkin. "I've always liked the notion of sequentiality." He turned, tossed the napkin across the room, smiled when it landed in the sink, then picked up a fork and curled some of the noodles into the bowl of a spoon, a way of eating that Mira had found quite amusing the first time he demonstrated it to her.

"Is sequentiality a word? I don't think it is." Mira turned her head to one side and partly closed her eyes as she often did when she was questioning something. "Perhaps we should look it up," she added.

"I've always been interested in the idea of floats," said Jerome, ignoring her reference to vocabulary. "You know, the kind you see in a parade. I love the idea of placing some kind of construction on a platform and hauling it down the street. Then the art would pass by the viewer, you see, instead of the other way around. You could do the same thing with rafts, but maybe the rafts themselves would be so visually exciting that nothing else would be needed. Sylvia told me the logs were tied together with withes: birch saplings crushed by a roller then twisted into a kind of cord. Even the materials used to construct the rafts were trees. The whole thing was about trees . . . well, dead trees." While he was speaking he thought about the broken shards of ice that had approached the island. He remembered how excited he had been when he thought a quilt had been trapped in one of them. Why, he wondered now, why had he been unable at first to see what was really there?

"Mmm," said Mira, "trees." She was fiercely urban, wasn't interested in trees in the wild unless they had somehow to do with Jerome, with one of his "pieces." Jerome was secretly delighted by the way certain subjects intrigued her simply because they pertained specifically to him – though it was unlikely that he would ever admit this. She once told him she would never tire of his maleness, the pale colour of his skin, the peculiar ways in which his mind worked.

The cat, who had become thoroughly spoiled, had leapt up on the table. Mira stopped eating long enough to return the animal to the floor.

"When you do that," said Jerome, "it's as if you are pouring him onto the floor, it's as if he were a great big jug or as if he were water being poured from a great big jug."

"He is a great big jug, aren't you, Swimmer?" Mira bent down to caress the animal's head.

After finishing the meal, they stood side by side at the industrial-looking sink, their hips touching, their hands busy washing and drying the few dishes they had used. Jerome had flung a tea towel over his left shoulder, a tea towel that he would forget about until it became time for bed. Even a night when he and Mira simply went to sleep was a night to look forward to: the warmth, and the shape of her body beside him, her face just barely discernible when he woke in the dark. She slept so deeply it was as if she were somehow working at it, as if she were a small steady engine purring beside him all night long.

"You know," he said to Mira, "I have come to like Sylvia. I wasn't sure . . . didn't quite know what to make of her at first."

"I think she is a bit like an avatar for you," Mira paused. "A sacred visitor disguised as someone else."

"Yes, sort of like that." He remembered Mira telling him about avatars in the past. But he couldn't be certain of what she had said, and didn't want to ask.

Later, when Jerome joined Mira in bed, he found her with one of the notebooks open, reading ahead: her legs were stretched out straight beneath the duvet and her elbows were resting on the bones of her hips while her hands held one of the green journals. He was very fond of the expression of almost puzzled absorption she always assumed when she was reading; it made her again seem mysterious, distant, a string of thoughts and images running through her head. It seemed to him that there was a kind of trust in the act of privately reading in another's presence, the same kind of trust that must exist in order for two people to sleep together night after night in the same bed. Part of that trust was that the other person would not break into the experience. But this time he wanted inclusion.

He settled down beside her.

"Lots about rafts," she told him.

"Read it to me then."

Mira flipped back four or five pages and began to read aloud. The rafts, a long river, a small boy, the dark facade of an old orphanage were escorted by her voice into the room. Jerome saw all these things while sleep attempted to rise up to meet him. Eventually Mira crept out from under the duvet, pulled a skein from the bag that held her knitting supplies, broke off six inches of red wool with her teeth, then placed it on the page and closed the notebook. "I can't help remembering what you said about this place . . . how the buildings were deserted, falling down."

Jerome looked into the distance for a while, then turned to Mira. "Too bad," he said. "Too bad there isn't some way of making a time-released film of an abandoned building decaying and then germinating, day by day, over the period of, say, a hundred years. It's strange, now that I think of it, how much attention is always given to construction when decay is really more pervasive, more inevitable."

"Decay and change," said Mira. "People moving from place to place, leaving things behind."

Jerome had in mind a photo of his parents and himself, one taken formally in a photographer's studio when he had been about four years old. His parents had been young, smiling, quite beautiful really. There had been no trace of what was to come. There was always the sense that no matter how perfect the moment, change is always hovering just outside the frame. People will remove their arms from the shoulders of their companions. The group will break up, go their separate ways.

It was one o'clock in the morning, and he was exhausted. There would be no more talking tonight. He raised his body slightly, twisted his torso, and extended his arm to turn off the light. Mira rolled toward him, placed one knee between his legs, then bent her head under his chin, her face against his chest. They would sleep in this position, barely moving all night long. "Krishna," Mira whispered. It was a joke they shared about Krishna, how he had been so beautiful that all the milkmaids had fallen in love with him. Jerome knew he was not the most beautiful person in this relationship, in this bed, and he was far from godlike. If anything, he resembled more a tattered, starved saint: thin, almost defeated, trudging back from the wilderness.

✗

In midafternoon Sylvia was staring at a miniature bronze figure, not three inches high. A bending saint, she thought, a saint bent under the weight of his sorrow. *Sleeping Apostle*, the card next to the object read, but Sylvia knew that the small man was not sleeping. The attitude his tiny body had taken spoke of a hard awakening followed by a collapse into sorrowful reflection. His head was cradled in his arms, his knees were drawn up to his chest; anguish was evident everywhere – even in the folds of his clothing. He was Andrew the last time she had seen him: Andrew huddled in a corner of the room. Andrew shrinking. Andrew unreachable.

She was at home in the museum, at home with this.

She had not been at home in the first museum they had visited, a large stone building that one approached by climbing an imposing staircase in front of which hovered crowds of children and various men with carts selling balloons, hot dogs, candy floss. Inside, she found herself frightened by the geological exhibit that included a huge mechanized globe that opened to reveal the construction of the Earth's centre – the construction of the underworld, she thought – and dark, narrow, claustrophobic passages lined by not quite real rocks. Later there were the bones of dinosaurs, suits of armour, weapons, shields, wrapped mummies, and several improbable dioramas depicting life in certain ages: stone, bronze, Aboriginal, pioneer. Her own age, or at least the age that had encased her life, seemed never to have been inhabited, and was illustrated here by a series of roped-off rooms containing too much furniture. *A Victorian Parlour*, a sign in front of such a room read. *Do not enter. Do not touch.*

Her husband had peered intently at each exhibit and had fished for his glasses in order to read the typed explanations that hung in glass frames on the adjacent walls, but she knew he was just trying to humour her. These attempts to feign absorption in that which he believed might interest her were something she was well used to. Like an adult in the company of a child at a puppet show, he was mainly intrigued by her response to whatever it was he was showing her. He monitored her slightest shifts of mood and attention and, as a result, it did not take him long to sense her distrust of the place he had chosen. She was thinking about the smallness, the innocence of her own museum, its pioneer tools and Native arrowheads, its one "special" exhibition of labels from the County's now defunct canning factory. Julia, she remembered, had once asked her for a map of the museum, but she had talked her through it instead. "First case," she had said, "pine highchair, wood stove, patchwork quilt, hand iron, empire sofa." Julia had nodded; she had lived with all of this. Even the canning labels had been easy to explain: "three tomatoes, two peaches, an ear of corn." What had been more difficult had been answering Julia's questions about why one would put such labels in a museum. "Because they are finished," she had finally said, "because we are through with them."

Now in the second museum, the large gallery of art, Sylvia found that she wanted to move closer and closer to the smallest objects. When she came to the apostle, she wanted to reach behind the glass and unfold the delicate figure, to open the tiny arms. She wanted to lift the chin, examine the face.

Several minutes passed, then Malcolm touched her arm, as she knew he had learned to do years ago when he sensed she was starting to disappear. The touch was brief, his hand remaining in place just long enough to get her attention.

"You've had enough," he said. "Let's go back to the hotel."

Sylvia did not answer but pulled away from the object and followed her husband as he walked through room after room toward the entrance that would now be the exit. She was both mildly relieved and faintly put off by the way he so easily took stock of her levels of energy, as if he carried with him at all times a device for measuring the temperature of her moods. As she emerged into the light and descended the stone stairs she was aware of two things: the sound of Malcolm's footsteps beside her and the dependency descending like a familiar cloak over her spirit. There was warmth in the cloak, but it felt wrong for this season. She knew that from now on there would be moments when she would want to remove it from her shoulders.

Since she had checked in a few days earlier, Sylvia had turned on neither the television at the far side of the room nor the radio beside the bed. She had been marginally aware of red lights — pulsing on the one hand or deliberately announcing the passage of time on the other — which seemed to insist that something should be done, that the status of the objects they were attached to should be changed in some way or another. But the newness of her rented space had been entertainment enough for her: the framed serigraph of haystacks and distant water that called to mind Tremble Bay near where the Ballagh Oisin had been situated, the reflecting surfaces of furniture dusted by an unseen stranger when she was elsewhere, the pile of the carpet forced upright each day by a vacuum cleaner that she neither heard nor saw, the way each trace of her own occupancy had been silently removed from the bathroom — damp washcloths and wrinkled towels replaced by their pristine doubles, the wastebasket emptied. Each time she opened the door she would stand listening to the low, thrumming noise of the hidden machine that heated or cooled the room — a constant purr that bled into the sound of the city traffic beyond the walls. Were it not for Julia's map, lying each evening on the desk just as she had left it, she would have barely been able to believe that she had spent the previous night sleeping in the smooth bed or had bathed that morning in the gleaming tub.

All of this contributed to her increasing belief that consciousness began again in the evening, that the dark, not the light,
was the new beginning, the awakening, after hours of day-lit
dream. It was like an empty canvas on which the same painting
could be rendered over and over again. Her grief, especially,
seemed to have been washed and ironed during the day so that it
could be presented to her again each evening, clean and fresh, the
colour of it slick with newness, arresting, impossible to ignore.

And now her husband, walking into this new space with her,
silent, perhaps secretly angry, his trench coat open, his gloves in
one his hand, a small encased umbrella in the other. He pulled
the hotel parking stub from his pocket. "Too late to go back
today," he said in a flat tone she could not interpret. "We'll head
out after breakfast, first thing tomorrow morning." He stepped
toward the window, pulled aside the curtain, looked briefly at the
brick wall. "Not much of a view, I didn't notice that last night.
Or this morning, for that matter."

"No," said Sylvia.

He turned back toward the room and began to move in
Sylvia's direction but stopped when he saw Julia's map on the
table. "You've been working on a tactile," he said. "I didn't notice
that either. But that's good. At least that's something. I can't
remember, did you tell me what this one is?"

"No," said Sylvia. "No, I didn't tell you."

Still standing near the door, she knew the deferral was over.
Suddenly she didn't know how to move into the room, how to
become comfortable with the curtains, the furniture. She stood
near the closet, running one hand across her hair, her other hand

moving up and down the opposite arm under her coat, pulling up the sleeve of the wool cardigan she was wearing.

Malcolm took off his own coat and dropped it, along with his scarf, on one of the beds. "I wonder," he said, "if maybe there aren't some other things you haven't told me, Syl. This running away, for example, this disappearing act, perhaps you could tell me what this is all about."

When she didn't answer, Malcolm crossed the room and quite gently removed her coat, hung it in the closet, and then retrieved his own coat from the bed. He had some trouble with the hangers, but eventually both garments hung side by side like two people waiting in one of the queues Sylvia had seen at street-car stops since she had been in the city. She lifted one arm and moved her fingers over the soft, skin-coloured fabric of her husband's trench coat, forcing herself to think about the naming of colours. Julia had once told her that there was a theory that the Greeks and Romans were "blind to blue," that although the colour was everywhere around them they couldn't see it at all. She then asked her to describe the difference between azure and cerulean, and Sylvia had remained speechless, realizing that the task was impossible. Perhaps, Julia had continued, perhaps colour could somehow be transposed into touch. Were there not, for example, warm and cold colours? Blue, Sylvia had said, might be smooth, like skin touching skin. But it's a cold colour, Julia had reminded her, laughing.

"I thought you said you would never want to go to the city on your own," Malcolm was saying. He was sitting in the chair beside the desk now, turning a postcard of the hotel around and around in his hands. He was looking directly at her with an expression on his face she did not recognize. She wondered if he felt fear, if her act of truancy had shaken his trust in the predictability of the condition. "C'mon, Syl," he said softly, "at least come in and sit down."

She walked as far as the bed and sat down, keeping her back straight, her attitude formal.

"Good," said Malcolm, "that's more like it."

More like what? a much younger Sylvia had often wondered whenever an adult spoke these words. More like the past, she thought now. Something about perching on the edge of the bed made Sylvia feel like a child, not like the child she had been necessarily, but more like the anxious girl she had once seen in a reproduction of a painting by Edward Munch. "It wasn't so bad," she said, looking at her hands clasped in her lap. "The train wasn't so bad. I slept most of the way."

She recalled the uniformed man staggering down the aisle, shouting the name of the city. It was odd to think that she hadn't known Jerome then, and now she had revealed the most intimate sides of her secret self to him and had given him access also to the pages of Andrew's past, the last evidence of his living hand.

Malcolm was speaking again. "It wasn't about him," he was saying, "was it? This inexplicable behaviour wasn't about him, I hope, because, if it was, I should know." Malcolm cleared his throat and began to tap the corner of the postcard rhythmically on the glass surface of the desk. "I thought we were all finished with that," he said.

"We are all finished with that," said Sylvia. "All finished."

Malcolm shook his head, then placed the postcard flat on the desk. "Oh, Syl," he said quietly.

Sylvia gazed at her husband. He looked smaller than he had in the past, diminished, as if he had discarded certain parts of himself in the few days she had been absent from his life. She recalled how certain, how strong he had been the night he had found her staring and rigid at the kitchen table, the newspaper article about Andrew in her hand. "These things happen," he had told her, after he had read the piece, "these tragedies."

"Tragedies," she had repeated. And then she said it. "I loved this man."

"No," he had said. "No, that can't be right. You are confused," he had said. "You've never been able to know anyone. You wouldn't have been able to . . ."

"I was able. He didn't know, you see. He didn't know about me."

Malcolm had become very silent, had slowly pulled up a chair beside the one in which she was sitting. She had not looked at him, but had been able to hear the sound of his breathing.

"You'll forget all about this," he had said finally. "We won't speak of it, and with time you'll start to forget."

"He forgot," she had answered. "Andrew forgot."

"We won't speak of it," Malcolm repeated, gently lifting the paper from her hands.

"You didn't ever believe me," Sylvia said now, "when I tried to tell you. Everything went wrong because you hadn't heard, you didn't believe . . ."

"Syl," Malcolm said quite sharply, "listen to me, listen to *me* now." He spun the swivel chair suddenly in her direction. "We've been over and over this. You know that, Syl, everything, everything was fine. With each passing month you made such progress. And I, I was happy, I was *proud* of the progress you were making."

Progress, she thought, pride. She stared at the mirror that faced the end of the bed in this disinterested interior and watched her mouth tremble. When the feeling was at its most critical she stood, picked up a chair, turned it to the wall, sat down, and began to concentrate on the texture of the plaster that had been slapped on the surface in such a casual manner it suggested interiors so foreign that she could not name them. Spanish, perhaps, or Italian, maybe Irish. The stippled effect looked not unlike the bubbling ridges of cold white mountains on one of the tactile maps she had made for Julia, a map of a polar region. She would think about Julia now, instead, how she had liked the idea of the cold, the ice – something in the landscape she could feel. There were scrapes and dents on this wall, a mark here and there that had not been removed by the dust cloth of the anonymous cleaner. Someone might have risen to their feet with such velocity that the chair they had been sitting in struck the wall. Someone else had likely swung a suitcase into the room with such recklessness a tiny plaster hill had been knocked from the surface as they did so. In the past she would have objected to even this insignificant example of change. In the past the sameness of any room would have been what calmed her. But now she found herself consoled instead by the thought of Julia and by this evidence of human spontaneity. How had she been so utterly altered?

"What are you thinking about?" asked Malcolm. She could sense that he was drawing nearer.

"The wall," she answered. "I'm thinking about the wall."

He was standing behind her now, his hand on the back of the chair, near her shoulder blade. "C'mon," he said, his hand touching the wool of her sweater, not reaching her skin, "let's go downstairs. Let's get something to eat. Forget the newspaper, at least for now. We'll go over all of that again, later, when you are feeling better."

The wall was approaching and withdrawing as if it were peering at Sylvia, then turning away with distaste. But gradually her head cleared, her vision became less blurred. She rose to her feet, turned, and faced her husband. "Why do you think I'll be feeling better?" she said. "How can you know that?"

For the first time there was real irritation in his voice. "What do you think all of this has been like for me? I was frantic with worry. If one more day had gone by, if they hadn't traced your card, I would have had to go to the police and then where would we have been?"

"I don't know, Malcolm, where we would have been. I never know, do I, where we have been, where we are now. Perhaps you should tell me, perhaps you should explain it all to me." Abruptly, she remembered that she had not yet put the *you are here* marker on the map she had been working on. She had always used a particular type of small mother-of pearl button for this, but she had forgotten to pack the button jar when she left the house. Often the button was placed in a parking lot, but there was no parking lot at the lighthouse. The end of the lane would have to do.

"You can't seriously believe that I shouldn't have been worried," Malcolm was saying. He had moved away from her now and stood at a distance where he could see her face. "You've never been away overnight on your own. You barely know the people in the next town, never mind in the city. You were missing. I would have had to report you as a missing person."

"A good description," she said to him, "a very good description of me, don't you think? Haven't I always been a missing person?"

Malcolm's expression darkened. Sylvia knew that she had hurt him, that soon he would begin to defend himself. "Remember this," he said. "I'm only trying to look after you, the way I've always looked after you. I don't understand this tone in your voice. I don't understand what you think you are doing. You have no one but me to care for you."

"I have some friends here," Sylvia interrupted. "I have a friend here."

Malcolm shook his head. "Who are these friends? How can I possibly believe in them? You don't make friends . . . you've never been able to —"

"There's Julia."

"Yes, Julia," Malcolm said vaguely. "But when I called her she wasn't able tell me where you were. You were in distress, quite possibly in danger, but Julia wasn't in a position to help me find you."

Sylvia turned away from the wall, rose from the chair, and walked across the room to where her suitcase rested on a luggage rack. "Yes," she said. "Yes, let's get something to eat." She opened her suitcase, unzipped a small quilted case, and lifted a string of pearls toward her throat. As if by instinct, Malcolm moved behind her and closed the clasp at the back of her neck, again without touching her skin. These were her mother's pearls, her grandmother's pearls. Perhaps they had belonged to her great-great-grandmother.

"We'll talk about this later, when you feel better," Malcolm said again. After putting on his jacket and before opening the door, he turned in Sylvia's direction. "I was convinced that we had it all sorted, Syl," he said, "convinced that you finally knew the difference between what goes on here," he moved his fingers toward the top of her hair, careful not to touch her head, "and what goes on out there," he swept his hand through the air that existed between them.

Sylvia had no answer for this, knowing that what he referred to was his reality and as such had nothing to do with her. His "out there" would be so much different than hers. "How do you know for certain," Julia had once asked her, "that what you see is what other sighted people see?" "I don't know for certain," Sylvia had answered. "I never have."

As they walked down the hotel corridor, however, she touched her husband's arm, wanting him to know, by this gesture, that there was no malice in the words she was going to say. He had taught her this, how to touch someone softly, when trying to make a point. It had not been easy for her, this reaching toward others, but she had learned to do it.

"Julia couldn't tell you where I was, not because she was unable, but because she didn't know," she said. "Still, if she had known she likely wouldn't have told you anyway."

"No," said Malcolm after a few silent moments. "No, probably not."

They stepped into the elevator, the arrival of which had been announced by a startling bell. "You see," Sylvia continued, "like you, Julia is not a believer . . . with this difference . . . she doesn't believe in the condition . . . my condition . . . she doesn't believe in it at all."

She looked at her husband's profile, to see how he was responding to this information. He was standing with his hands clasped behind his back and his head lowered. She was almost certain that there was no expression at all on his face, not even an expression of disagreement or disapproval. It was as if he hadn't heard the words she had said, or perhaps had heard but didn't believe in them.

Later that evening, when she walked into the bathroom to prepare for the night, she saw that evidence of her husband was everywhere: his toothbrush, his travel case, his razor, his brush and comb.

Such familiar objects.

Lying on the bed after undressing, she willed herself to consider Malcolm, who lay, as always, with his back to her, sleeping in the almost purposeful way of a physician whose rest is often interrupted. The room was merely pulsing now in the faint city light that the curtains could not entirely extinguish: things were better. She began mentally to go through the shelves in her husband's study, book by book, recalling how the different colours of the spines had pleased her once she had become accustomed to the newer volumes placed here and there among the older texts left behind by her father. As a kind of lullaby, she allowed a list of titles to run through her mind. *Clinical Gastroenterology, Pathological Basis of Disease, An Index of Differential*

Diagnosis, Medical Mycology, The Metabolic Basis of Inherited Disease, Principals of Surgery. She went to sleep comforted by the thought that someone, anyone, had taken the trouble to attend to a tragic alteration of the body, as if they had wanted to draw a map of its regions, then explore its territories.

After dinner she and Malcolm had walked into the alley and she had showed him the door she visited each day. "He is so young," she had told him. "Only a boy in many ways."

She watched Malcolm as he took in the graffiti, the name Conceptual Fragments. Though he had said nothing, she sensed his distrust of such things. "I still don't understand," he said. "Who are these people? What do they have to do with you?"

They were standing by the drainpipe that Sylvia had examined when she first reached the city. It looked darker somehow, and small icicles had formed, like teeth, around its mouth in the evening cold. The sound of a streetcar and laughter from a group of people passing on the sidewalk had become more than noise, seemed to have taken on a physical presence. "He found him, Malcolm, he found Andrew," Sylvia said at last. "Jerome, the young man who lives here . . . he found Andrew's body in the ice." Sylvia glanced toward the door and lifted one hand almost as if she were going to touch it, then let her arm drop. "I think he was the right person, the right person to find him," she whispered, speaking to herself now, knowing that what she said was true.

"Oh," said Malcolm, placing his gloved hands in the pocket of his trench coat. "Oh, so it's that. I suppose you were after the details." He coughed, then took Sylvia's arm and began to lead her back toward the hotel. "Well," he said, turning away from the alley, "at least that's all over now."

"No," she said calmly. "It's not over. I won't leave this unfinished, I just can't do that. I am going back tomorrow. I said I would and I will." She stopped walking. "Alone," she added.

He remained silent, but she could tell the stubbornness, the refusal was gone from him. It's the leaving, Sylvia thought, he knows I can do that now, just walk away. "You'll have to get in touch with the office," she said, "to tell them you won't be there tomorrow. You'll have to get someone else to be on call. I will leave the hotel after lunch. You can pick me up here at this door at five."

"This is all very unsettling," he said, but once they were back in the room he immediately picked up the phone to make the necessary arrangements for his absence. Then he smiled at her in a resigned, fond, and faintly condescending way. I'm doing all this for you, the smile said, I am doing all this because of your condition.

His patience, she decided, was a burden: not for him – for him it was second nature – but it was a burden for her. She wanted to throw it off, be done with it. She was tired, she suddenly knew, of taking all the responsibility for it.

*O*n Saturday mornings Jerome and Mira almost always ate a late breakfast at a nearby café where they could order brioche or biscotti and read the weekend papers left behind by previous customers. This was a lingering luxury, ending only when they decided how they would spend the afternoon, whether they would go to a gallery where a friend might be performing or exhibiting, watch a film, or simply explore certain unfamiliar neighbourhoods in the city, cameras in hand, seeking new images. They rarely returned to the studio on Saturday during the daylight hours, wanting one day in the week where a kind of fluidity would determine their actions. Sometimes a casual group of mutual friends or acquaintances would gather around them, expanding and contracting as they moved from place to place. The appearance of Jerome's work in certain magazines or in the arts pages of newspapers had made him more socially sought-after in such places than he had ever been in the past, and often he and Mira had hardly settled in at a table when they would be joined by other young people dressed in the customary dark clothing.

He was not entirely at ease with this. Not being much of a talker, he was never quite sure of what would be expected of him by way of conversation and was grateful for Mira's poise, her curiosity and genuine interest in people: in what they were think-ing, doing, how the small dramas of their lives were unfolding. He generally left the talking to her, but listened, nevertheless, intrigued by the way Mira hid or revealed her cleverness, deferred or brought her thoughts forward into the path of the talk. But he frequently felt ungainly, awkward, as if his legs were too long to fit comfortably under the table, his voice either too loud or too soft.

Today, however, they had arrived at the café early enough that no one they knew had, as yet, emerged from the badly heated studios or cheap apartments they called home, and he and Mira were able to sit near a window, talking quietly.

"Look," Mira was saying, "you can see the top of Sylvia's hotel from here. We could call her, you know, or drop by."

Jerome did not respond.

"She doesn't know anyone else in the city," Mira said. "What is she going to do all day?"

"The map, remember," Jerome answered.

Mira was gazing out the window, looking with concern at a couple of half-grown stray kittens who were gnawing on a dis-carded hamburger bun lying on the sidewalk.

"Don't even think about it," Jerome said to her. "One cat is enough."

"Okay," she said, turning back to him, "let's go home. I think we should finish reading before tomorrow. And anyway," she said, looking around the half-empty café, and then at the partially eaten pastry on her plate, "I'm finished. I've had enough."

Something echoed in Jerome as Mira spoke. It was his mother's voice, speaking these exact words – I'm finished. I've had enough – late at night, when his father had not been home for two days. She had been talking to herself, or perhaps to her husband whose inebriation wouldn't have permitted him to hear her even if he had been in the room and not in a bar God knows where. The despair in her voice had both frightened and infuriated Jerome; he had wanted to shake her, he had wanted her to forget about his father and his troubles because despite what she was saying, whatever announcement she thought she was making, he knew she hadn't had enough. His father would return, beg for her forgiveness and receive it, and the whole cycle would begin again, maybe in a matter of weeks, maybe not for a month. He was fifteen years old the night he heard his mother speak these words, believed he hated his father and, in a curious way, also his mother, hated their weaknesses. He wanted them out of his life, out of each other's lives, or failing that he wanted them to go back to the life they had lived while they had all still been in the north.

"What are you thinking about?" asked Mira, leaning forward to shake his arm gently. "Where have you gone?"

"Nothing," said Jerome. "Nowhere." But he knew exactly where he had gone: back to the disappeared world of his child-hood, the place he couldn't stop revisiting. Quite often, in recent months, when he had been attempting to complete some ordi-nary task, he would visualize the long dark avenue of an airshaft he had peered down as a child. Never permitted to enter the mine itself, he had found the shaft housed in a small unlocked build-ing just beyond the perimeter of the site. Terror-stricken and fascinated, he would slip through the door and gaze into a depth of blackness, experience the warm draft on the skin of his face, the pull of the underworld.

His father would have engineered that shaft, all other ventilation shafts, as well as the shaft that was the route to the underground. The tunnels that followed the threads of gold that branched like a central nervous system through the solid yet vulnerable rock would have been designed by him as well.

Those were the good years, years when alcohol was a companion, an equal, not a master. Everyone was young; the northern Ontario settlement was a wilderness adventure, the mine a miracle unfolding so far from the rules of ordinary life that no rigid social order was born in its wake. Uneducated immigrant miners and labourers mixed with the collection of necessary professionals assembled by the company. Bosses strolled through the underground labyrinth with the men. A pipefitter might become godfather to the son of an accountant. The doctor might serve as best man at the wedding of a sump-pump operator. Legendary parties celebrated such weddings and christenings (the dog sled delivering the whisky driven by the mine manager himself) or bloomed on nights when there might be nothing more to celebrate than a record freezing temperature or the fact that the mail had finally got through after a blizzard.

And in the midst of all this there was Jerome's handsome, laughing father, architect of the underground: a singer, a dancer, the last man still dancing at dawn.

Jerome had but the faintest of memories concerning this period, but his mother had resurrected fragments of the narrative after his father's death. The time his father had insisted that all the girls at the brothel attend the manager's Christmas party, the time he had arranged for three famous rock bands to be flown in by a squadron of bush planes, the time he had offered to be Santa Claus at the school and had been so exhausted by the previous evening's revelry he had fallen asleep under the Christmas tree. This was the carefree, madcap side of booze, a sort of good-natured jig on the part of the Grim Reaper performed in advance of sharpening up the sickle. It had infuriated Jerome that his mother took such obvious pleasure in recounting these episodes, as if his father's intoxication was a life-enhancing achievement rather than the hot destructive windstorm that he remembered devouring everything in its path. But he loved her, and was also grateful, therefore, for these brief sessions when she was free of pain. He had kept his expression neutral, smiled or laughed on cue. He had pretended to listen with eagerness.

"What's *wrong* with you today?" Mira was asking. "You've barely spoken since we got up."

"Nothing's wrong," Jerome said. He began to fish in his pocket for money to pay the bill. These coffee bars, he thought, these pretentious places. "Let's go back," he said to Mira. "If you want to finish reading those notebooks, then we'll finish reading those notebooks."

Walking toward the studio Jerome fought off the dark image of the air shaft and attempted to enter the moment, to be a man in the company of a young woman on a Saturday morning in an interesting part of town. But he knew this wasn't working. Mira was looking at him intently by the time they entered the alley, a number of unspoken questions were in the air, and he could feel resentment rising in him. He wanted to hold on to the privacy of his mood. Her intuition, and her concern about this, was an intrusion.

Still, once they were inside, and before he had arranged himself on the couch again with Mira, he had begun to soften.

"Let me read it this time," he said to her.

Mira opened the book to the spot where she had placed the piece of wool the night before. Then she handed it to Jerome. He scanned a few lines, then said, "She will probably go, once we've read the journals. She only asked for a few days, after all." The feeling he experienced when saying these words was tinged with something he couldn't identify. Anxiety. Sadness. Fatigue. Maybe guilt. For a moment he wondered who was leaving whom.

"*Summer after summer,*" he began, "*beyond the bright windows of the Ballaig Oisin . . .*"

Jerome put the notebook on the table and looked at Mira. "I don't know," he said. "I don't know what to do about her. I might be about to let her down, somehow."

Mira moved closer to him. He could feel the slight expansion and contraction of her ribs, the rhythm of her breath. "It will be okay," she said. "For now just keep reading."

Jerome leaned forward, picked up the notebook. "*Summer after summer,*" he began again.

"*A*ndrew always said there were people who were emplaced." Sylvia was standing now, speaking to Jerome's back while he was busy at the counter making tea. The green notebooks lay on the crate that served as a coffee table but, as yet, Jerome had made no reference to them. Walking that morning from the hotel to the alley, she had been lit with anticipation, hungry for Jerome's reaction to Andrew's words. But once she had entered the studio, she found she couldn't bring herself to ask the question, to expose the hook in her mind.

"It seems that those who are emplaced are made that way by generations of their people remaining in the same location," she continued, "eating food grown from the same plot of earth, burying their dead nearby, passing useful objects down from father to son, mother to daughter. He said that I was like that to such a degree I was almost like an anthropological discovery. Or perhaps an archeological discovery; something, more or less preserved, more or less intact. I was so emplaced, you see, that it was an adventure — almost an act of heroism — for me to leave the

County, travel thirty miles to his hill. Without him . . . without the lure of him . . . I never would have done it."

Swimmer had jumped up on the crate and draped himself in a casual manner over the notebooks.

"He also told me that there was always a mark left on a landscape by anyone who entered it. Even if it is just a trace — all but invisible — it is there for those willing to look hard enough. He said this elsewhere, of course, not just to me, said it in lectures and wrote it in his books before he retired and became silent and all but forgotten. But what about his own trace?" Sylvia asked suddenly, a hint of anger in her voice. "When he disappeared no one looked for him, looked hard enough, long enough. We knew it would come to this, they likely thought, a huge final disappearance at the end of a series of lesser disappearances."

"Maybe they did look for him," said Jerome, "maybe they just didn't know where to look. Perhaps you were the only person who knew where he might have gone."

"And yet I didn't know," said Sylvia. "I didn't know where he had gone. But he was walking toward the past, I think. Does that make any sense to you?"

"It makes sense to me now. I . . . both of us read what he wrote." Jerome handed Sylvia a steaming mug. "Because I'd been out there on the island surrounded by the remnants of what had existed in the past, it was astonishing for me to have it all reconstructed, to have it come to life, or come back to life." Jerome stood in the middle of the room while the slim ribbon of steam from his own mug rose toward his shoulder. "And I was a bit surprised." He sat on the end of the sofa nearest to Sylvia's chair and

placed his tea on the table. "I was surprised by the humour. I
would have thought him to be more consistently serious."

"He *was* serious," said Sylvia, "but he loved humour, loved
laughter. I always thought that Andrew would remember forever
how I laughed when I was with him, I, who so rarely laughed. But
perhaps to him I was a woman who laughed often, one who was
light-hearted, easy to know."

Jerome smiled. "We liked the story," he said, "but somehow
it made me think that everything in the world is just a mirage,
just a suggestion, gone before its graspable. I think I already
knew that, some part of me already knew that, the part that
avoids" – Jerome searched for the word – "stasis, stability, that
emplacement you just spoke of. Stability seems to me, sometimes, to be just another way of saying the end."

"Stability was what I always wanted," said Sylvia, "More than
you know."

"Perhaps. But you . . . you lost someone. And I'm worried." He
cleared his throat. "I worry about that." He paused. "About you."

"Oh, don't," said Sylvia quietly. "You're so young. And all of
this . . . it's well . . ." For the first time it occurred to her that she
might have troubled this young man. "You'll forget this," she said.

"No. No, I won't." Jerome looked solemn for a moment,
then glanced at Sylvia and smiled. "I won't want to forget. Not
the story. Not the things we've talked about." He moved over
to the couch and slowly sat down. "And the truth is, I want to
know, I guess I always wanted to know what happened to him.
And now I want to know about you. You keep saying you lost
him twice."

"Yes, twice." Sylvia sat in the chair and placed her mug on the table. "It is a miraculous truth," she said to Jerome, "that the same man who introduced me to sorrow by walking away from me would also be the man who, years later, would introduce me to redemption simply by turning around and walking back. It was like a resurrection, really . . . or so I thought."

Sylvia glanced at Jerome. One half of his face was lit by sun from the window. His eyelashes cast a faint shadow on his cheek.

"The side porch of the house where I live was glassed in long ago," she said, "probably at the end of the nineteenth century. In the intervening years it has been used first as a sunroom and then as a mudroom for the wet shoes and galoshes belonging to my father's winter patients. There is something called a health clinic now, where my husband and another doctor share an office and examination rooms, so there are no longer any galoshes, no longer any patients, only me, alone each day, wandering through the rooms.

"I had begun to use the glassed-in porch to grow geraniums, the only plant with which I have had any success whatsoever." She laughed. "They remain blooming, despite my lack of botanical skill, for three seasons out there. In the winter, of course, they are brought indoors – though Malcolm is put off by what he calls their musty scent. I, however, believe that the plants have no smell at all. I enter and vacate the house through the glassed-in porch, walking past this unnoticed odour whenever I go out, and whenever I return from wherever it is that I have gone."

She had always liked the way that the aging parts of a geranium plant could be so easily, so gently detached from the rest of the plant. No cutting, no snapping: they gave themselves with grace to the experience of being discarded, to the idea that the plant on which they flourished would contain not a hint that they had once been part of its physical composition. She remembered that on the spring morning when she heard the phone ringing deep in the centre of the house she had left the sunroom with a geranium leaf still between the thumb and forefinger of her right hand and had begun to walk through the indoor rooms, past all the family furniture, toward the sound.

In the silence that followed the conversation, she had turned away from the wall that held the phone and stared out the north window at the lilac bush in the middle of the yard. The tree was about to bloom and she could recall thinking, How strange it was that the tight, stiff skeletons of the previous year's blossoms were still on the branch and that they had looked similar to those that were about to flower. The few remaining dead leaves had a dusty grey hue, as if they were not leaves at all but rather old bits of faded cloth left unprotected in an attic. She recalled the dust that had covered the plastic flowers, on the table, long ago, the last time she had seen Andrew. She recalled some of the words he had said: *stop . . . this . . . can't.* How had she been able to walk past the memory of words such as these?

"A single phone call," she told Jerome now, "and Andrew and I began to meet again after years of silence, even though as the great-great-grandson of the Timber Island empire he should have been aware that to do so was to attempt to bring the timber raft back to the island, to sail backwards and with great difficulty upstream." She paused, her head to one side. "Were we wrong in our desire? I have no answer for that question. But once we began seeing each other again, I believe we both knew we would have to see it through that place where we would be carried separately back downstream so far apart we would be unable to wave, to shout."

"Why?" asked Jerome, "Why would it have to be like that?"

"Time," said Sylvia. "Seven years had gone by. When I went to meet him at the cottage I came to realize that no one had been near the place for a long, long time. In the past, you see, the table would have been littered with papers covered by his handwriting and on the floor near the desk there would have been small, irregular towers of journals and books. There had been time. There had been change."

"Yes," said Jerome. "There would have been . . ."

"I was tremendously nervous and began to talk and talk. I told him about the museum, about how now that the last of the old families were leaving the County, we were receiving so many donations that we were likely going to have to rent warehouse space. As it was, the basement of the building was filling up with parasols and baby buggies and high button boots and silver tea sets and crochet work and coal oil lamps and strange pioneer tools: planers, clamps, lathes, all the things Gilderson's ships would have brought into the County. He was looking at me closely as I spoke and I became self-conscious, unable to finish the sentences I was so earnestly beginning.

"'This is what makes me happy,' he said. 'This is making me happy.'

"I should have asked, What is making you happy? Us being here again together? The fact that I will be cataloguing objects? You not working? Looking into my face? But instead I turned away, began to gaze through the window at the struggle a tree seemed to be having with the wind. And he walked away, then turned back, and took my hand. Just the slightest pressure, the most casual touch – his sleeve brushing my arm as he passed me in the room – would cause a kind of sorrow to fall over me like rain, and then I would put my arms around him and everything in me would open."

How silent Andrew had been during this reunion, though he had said her name while they were making love.

"He embraced me with such a sense of ease," she said to Jerome, "such an air of familiarity that, in a way, time evaporated. Neither one of us said the word *change*, as people so often do in such situations. Change seemed to be irrelevant to us. What was relevant was the buried past, the dark painted hallways of the hotel under the dunes, the wrecks that littered the floor of the Great Lakes, what I had learned about the sagging timbers, the aged grey-coloured straw of the increasingly abandoned barns in my County. His ancestors. Mine.

"But in the months that followed, I should have reached across the dead blossoms of the previous season and touched his older face. I should have spoken his name. I should have at least said, Where have you been, where have you been, my love? I should have asked, Why, why did you leave me? I should have asked, Why, why did you leave the young woman that I was then? And why have you summoned the older woman that I am now, and why has she so spontaneously responded to the summons? But I couldn't do it. I received not the slightest hint of permission to ask these questions. Not from him. Not from myself."

What had made her again take such journeys away from her backyard and kitchen, away from the familiar patterns of her dishes, the sheets and towels that normally touched her body,

away from the easy cadence of a shared daily life toward tension
and deceit and a growing knowledge of inevitable bereavement?
She had called it love, of course, but perhaps that was just her
way of disguising something deeper, something darker, a desire
to put everything solid and respectable at risk. Andrew had
always been less reflective, and therefore, she supposed, more
honest . . . more honest in that he resisted any attempts at interpretation, refused to name their connection at all.

"No," she said suddenly. "I believe . . . I am certain that I loved
him, or at least I loved the version of him that I was given. I loved
that fragment of him that I was given. Only now and then did we
speak of our connection and then almost always contentiously.
When I felt him drifting far from my shore, as I sometimes did,
I would want some kind of declaration, some sort of explanation.
He always resisted this, often with cruelty. But there was a great
deal of tenderness as well. Yes, there was tenderness. And when
we spoke about history, about the past, about the generations of
his family, and about mine, about lost landscapes and vanished
architecture, there was . . . I still believe this . . . quite a lot of joy."

Sylvia was remembering the rasping texture of Andrew's
unshaven face against the palm of her hand, or grazing the skin
on her stomach, the heels of his hands pushing into the muscles
of the small of her back. Had he known even her name the last
time they had clung together like that? Were his expressions of
passion a request for response or were they cries of alarm at an
act he did not recognize and would not remember, an act of love
lost forever the minute it ended or perhaps even while it was happening? For the first time she attempted to struggle away from
the anguish thoughts such as these carried in their dark arms. She

wanted to come back into this room, back to the young man to whom she had been speaking, wanted to greet even the offensive tubes of artificial light that flickered over his head. But when she looked up, Jerome was gone.

His absence was temporary, however. He walked back toward her from the inner room and carefully laid six black-and-white postcards in a line on the floor at her feet. "This is all that I have from my early childhood," he said, "all that is left."

Sylvia was careful not to pick up the cards, change the pattern, the sequence he had chosen. She leaned to one side and dug in her handbag for her glasses, then bent forward and looked. The head frame and outbuildings of a mine, a log house situated on a point of land that reached into a lake, a partly built town site with a new church and evidence of a forest fire blossoming on the horizon, several men standing beside a dog team with the message *4 feet of snow, 38 below zero !!!* written beneath them, a trio of miners posing in a rough-hewn underground tunnel, one man pouring liquid gold from a furnace, the town site now fully developed with a drugstore, soda fountain, small frame hotel.

"Its all gone now," said Jerome. "The mine closed and everything disappeared. It had hardly begun and then it was over. There is nothing left, nothing at all." He was silent for a moment. "They said there was no more gold. But the truth was that my father made a mistake. His mistake closed everything."

Jerome was hunkered down quite near her. She could see that there was a moth hole in the shoulder of the sweater he was wearing and that his blue jeans were worn at the knees. Mothers, she knew, sometimes attended to things that needed mending.

"The mistake," Sylvia said. Malcolm had taught her that one need not always use the interrogative. Sometimes a repetition was enough encouragement, and she found herself wanting to know.

Jerome pointed to a man on the fourth card. "You see that miner?" he said. "That was the miner who died, fifth level down, one level too far. His name was Thorvaldson." He turned the card over to check the list of names on the back. "Yes, from Iceland. The men came from all over northern Europe, you know, and from Cornwall and Wales. There was a rock burst. Everyone else — my father included — got out."

"I'm sorry, but I know nothing about mines . . . your father was a miner?"

"No, he was the engineer, so he should have known, probably did know. The veins . . . the veins of gold became larger at deeper levels, but everything would be less stable. The mine closed after that, the community disintegrated."

"Because of the miner who died?"

"Because the company bosses finally became aware — as a result of the burst — that they weren't going to be able to get any more gold out of that ground."

Jerome stood and began to walk back and forth across the concrete floor. "My father smashed the glass of the frame that held his diploma. He tore up the diploma itself and tossed it the fire. I remember this. He was drunk, of course, enraged. My mother and I were terrified. He never went near a mine again — no one would have hired him anyway. We moved to the city, or at least to the edge of the city. He worked for a while making geological maps for a metallurgical company, then, when his hands began to shake too much, as a janitor for the same company, and, finally, he didn't work at all."

The term *alcoholism* slid into Sylvia's mind. It occurred to her that like so many things that can go wrong, the word started with the letter *a*.

"I'm sorry," she said to Jerome.

"What's to be sorry about," he replied. "*He* was the one who made the mistake." Jerome's anger was so visible that Sylvia, who had rarely experienced anger, could feel it hissing in her own blood. Her fear of the fluorescent lights began to return. She wondered about the lighting in the mine, and remembered a photo she had seen of men with lights, or was it candles, in their hats. "People do what they have to do," she said, something she remembered Branwell saying in Andrew's writing. "And," she said, recalling the story of the timber, the barley, the sand, "and they almost always go too far."

Jerome bent down and snatched the cards from the table, as if he were a gambler sweeping up a suit of cards. "Did he have to drink so much that you could smell it coming from his pores day and night?" he said. "Did he have to take us down with him?"

"Yes," said Sylvia. "He probably had to do all of that."

"Did he have to kill my mother? The whole thing, the drinking, the humiliation, the crummy apartments, his sordid death, all of it killed her . . . and not quickly either . . . it killed her by degrees. She didn't last two years after he was gone."

"No," said Sylvia uncertainly. "He didn't have to do that. But she, she likely had to die for him."

Jerome stood, postcards in hand, looking directly at Sylvia, and she willed herself to look back. The air was thick with anticipation, as if anything at all might happen and she was momentarily aware of the risks two people took simply by being alone together in a room. Murder, love, collision, caress, were they not all part of the same family?

Jerome turned away. "I'll take these back now," he said, looking at the postcards in his hand. "I'll put these away."

When Jerome returned to the room, his expression was neutral, removed. He sat on the couch and folded his arms over his chest. "My childhood," he said. "I don't know why I brought it up. It's all over anyway. It's finished. I shouldn't have bothered you with any of it."

"Please," Sylvia said, leaning forward. "I wasn't bothered. I'm glad you told me." She smiled. "Now I will be able to remember that I knew you," she added, then looked away, feeling almost shy. "How little, in the final analysis, we really know about another person."

Jerome raised his eyebrows at this and nodded. "But, still," he said, reconsidering, "after reading Andrew's journals, I think maybe landscape – place – makes people more knowable. Or it did, in the past. It seems there's not much of that left now. Everyone's moving, and the landscape, well, the landscape is disappearing."

"Have I mentioned that the old cottage was approached by way of a grove of trees?" Sylvia asked. "These were planted a century ago to line the driveway that swung up toward the mar-vellous entranceway of Maurice Woodman's old house. Andrew and I would have to walk past the lightning-struck burnt foundations of that house in order to meet."

In the early days, she'd often had to walk though a herd of staring cows as she moved along the edge of the hill. There was always a soft wind, an echo of the breezes that would have touched the shore of the prehistoric lake, and she had always stopped to look at the view, which included the village below, rolling farmland and woodlots to the west, the charmed surface of the lake in all directions, and the arm of her peninsular County bending around the waters at the eastern horizon. Then, after passing through the dying orchard, and walking farther, she would begin to sense a shift in the land underfoot, as she moved past the scattered fieldstones, and in some spots the vestiges of the walls and crumbling mortar that were the last remains of the foundation of the great burnt house, the grassy basins of its cellars and kitchens. Andrew had done some digging in these basins and had come across a few ceramic marbles, ones he believed that his own father, T.J. Woodman, must have played with as a boy, and a porcelain cup and saucer, miraculously undamaged. But most exciting to her were the large, smooth, oddly shaped pieces of melted glass, which he had come across, evidence that the rumour about the glass ballroom floor was true.

"It was *true?*" exclaimed Jerome when she told him all this. "The artist Robert Smithson would have been fascinated by that. I keep thinking all the time about a piece he made. It was titled *Map of Glass*, I've never known if he meant a map of the properties of glass, or if was referring to a glass map, which would then be, of course, breakable. But even he . . . I don't think even he would have thought about melted glass. A ballroom with a glass floor, on fire and then *melting*. That's just wonderful!"

Sylvia laughed at Jerome's reaction. "Andrew told me that lightning striking sand can cause glass to form spontaneously. I never knew that, did you?"

"No," said Jerome. "No, I never knew that."

"Once, toward the end of that last summer, Andrew said that he wanted me to think about the great cities of Earth, to think about them not being there any more, about them never having been there at all: the forests of Manhattan Island, the untouched riverbanks of the Seine or the Thames, the clear water moving through reeds near the shore, the unspoiled valleys that existed before agriculture, then architecture, then industry changed them."

They had been looking through the windows of the cabin into the forest as he spoke and occasionally deer would drift by, soft and brownish grey, between the tall trunks of the trees. Andrew once pointed out that the earth colours of their coats echoed a patch of yellow dried grass, or a pale grey log, brown bark, or the rust of fallen pine needles.

As he had told her this, every part of her was touched by his voice. There had been the warmth of his skin against hers, and the delivery of syllables all through the sunny afternoons. Later when the rains came, the sound of water falling through the holes in the roof into the pans they had placed here and there on the floor was like punctuation marking the cadence of his speech.

"You, Jerome, may never know what it is to enter another kind of partnership, what is given to you in such circumstances. Somehow, neither person leaves a footprint, casts a shadow. We remained utterly unrecorded, unmarked."

You, she remembered Andrew once saying, playfully bumping his shoulder against hers, *all the time you come to this place, climb this hill, simply because I am here. I don't want to leave you,* she had said. *But you have to,* he had replied. *You have to leave me so that you can come back again.*

He had begun to seem older, softer in body and in spirit, vague in some ways, and therefore kinder. His moods were no longer as swift and sharp in their arrivals and departures, and his love for her — if that's what it was — carried with it no unsettling urgency. Yes, he was kinder, and she, for her part, felt a depth of tenderness for him that at times almost overwhelmed her. It was like a long silken banner or a column of smoke drifting in a warm wind, this tenderness she felt, something hovering above them that changed the air. The months would pass, autumn would arrive, and things would become confused, painful between them as he began to become lost. Once, as she walked away she turned to wave and she saw him framed by the open cottage door. There he was, standing quite still on the stoop, as exposed as she had been all those years ago when they had met on the edge of traffic. He raised one arm: a gesture of welcome and warning and farewell. The sun had come out in late afternoon and the surroundings were starkly lit. His eyes were almost closed. He was wincing in the face of the glare.

"There was warmth," Sylvia said, "and the sense that while we held each other we were, in turn, being held by the rocks and trees we could see from the windows and the creeks and springs we could sometimes hear running through the valley. And then there was the view from the edge of the hill, a view of distant water and far shores, and a few villages positioned like toys around the bay."

For just a moment it occurred to her that she might actually have died, that she and Andrew might have somehow died together and that all this recounting of facts and legends to Jerome – combined with her life in the hotel – was the fabric of an afterlife that would go on and on like this, day after day, for eternity. Then she remembered Malcolm and how he had now entered this afterlife.

She placed the mug of tea Jerome had given her on the floor. "By early autumn he had begun to say odd things, things I knew he had never said before; at least he had never said them before to me. He began to speak about people I didn't know as if I knew them. Sometimes he was quite passionately angry with some person or another and he would pour his heart out about this without explaining who the person was, or even what the situation was that caused the anger. I would listen; I would listen without questions because I couldn't bear to interrupt in any way this miraculous openness: I was so eager for any kind of information that might deepen my knowledge of him. As the autumn progressed, though, the anger was starting to spread, and by November it was beginning to include me. But then it would vanish as soon as it arrived. He would simply stop in midsentence and embrace me. Once or twice he wept at that moment. And," Sylvia paused here, unsure whether to mention this, but wanting to articulate it so that it would be real, a fact, "often, during those last months, often he wept when we made love."

Jerome was staring at the wall, embarrassed likely. To him she would have been always a much older woman, one with few rights in the territory of sexual love. She must remember that.

"It wasn't until then," Sylvia told him, "that I fully realized that not only had the inside of the cottage deteriorated but the gate that I remembered at the top of the lane was gone altogether and the cows were gone as well. What had been pasture was now scrub bush, almost impassable except for one narrow, winding path. The surviving orchard trees were choked and twisted and the view was visible only in certain empty spots. I barely knew where I was. I couldn't recall the wind that was tossing the trees; my memories of this forest had to do with seasonal colour, never with motion." Bright green of spring, the bruised white of winter, she thought, wondering where the line had come from. In the past, she had believed the trees had been entirely still, a stage set, frozen in time.

Arriving one November morning, she had taken off her coat, had laid it over the back of a wicker chair that was grey with dust. The room had been cool and there was a faint smell of mice beneath the stronger smell of wood smoke. *Aftermath* was the word that crept into her mind; the windows were foggy, clouds of dust had gathered under the furniture. Cobwebs swung from the beams. This was the territory of aftermath.

Annabelle's painting was askew on the wall. She had walked across the room to straighten it.

"Annabelle's painting," she had said.

He hadn't replied, had moved instead — just as he always had in the past — slowly across the room toward her.

"In the beginning there was this difference between us, Jerome: I believed that anything that I permitted to happen to me would go on happening . . . forever. He, being fully engaged with human life, believed, I think, that when something stopped happening, it was over. Not that it wouldn't happen again, just that this particular session was over, and that there would be something else taking place, something else that was equally worthy of his attention. His view of life was sequential, symphonic. But I could tell this view had changed."

Near the very end before he had stopped talking altogether, Andrew had spoken about nothing but furniture. These were the only nouns that appeared to interest him. At first Sylvia had thought he was speaking metaphorically, something he had often done in the past. "Look at the . . . table," he would say, when they stood near the window, surveying the view of the lake, "look at the mirror." A table laid out before them. A mirror of the sky. It made some sense to her. She didn't question it, or him, or the fact that he was not saying the lake was like a mirror, like a table under the sky.

"How did you lose him?" Jerome was asking.

Sylvia sat entirely still, her face averted. "How can I describe those last meetings to you, Jerome? I who had spent years attempting to interpret his most fractional gesture, his most subtle shift of mood, would find him tremendously altered: unshaven, unbathed, sometimes, even after I'd arrived still expecting me, sometimes not, but in either case, utterly unprepared. Once, as I stepped though the door, he said, 'Can I help you?' with a kind of cold courtesy, as if I were a salesperson or a pamphleteer. At times he would look at me with longing for minutes at a stretch, then turn away as if in disgust, or he would swiftly take himself to the opposite corner of the room where he would all but growl at me in anger, refuting every sentence that I spoke.

Each phrase began with the negative. 'Don't talk to me about the trees,' he would say. 'You know nothing about the trees.' Or, 'It's not your lake, don't speak of it.' Often he said, 'We can't go on with this.' His tone would fill me with fear, but the reference to 'this' could cause temporary relief. 'This' was the word that made reference to our connection, our communion. 'This' meant that we weren't finished. Not yet.

"I would remind him of the stories he had told me, attempt to bring the lovely talk back into the room, but he would deny that he had ever told me such stories – 'You have invented those,' he would say – and would refer instead to problems he was having with people I had never heard of. They had stolen his wallet, his life, his soul. They had abandoned him in alleyways or on park benches, cast him adrift in a leaking vessel, denied him food and water.

"He would pace like an animal around the room, then peer at me with great suspicion. 'I am willing,' he would say, 'to resolve this here, now, but . . . What?' he would plead. 'What is it?'

"'Tell me about Annabelle,' I would say, 'about Branwell.' I wanted the family history or, failing that, his descriptions of geological formations, his descriptions of strata.

"'We will stop,' he said. 'We will stop.'

"Then he would cross the room, bury his face in my neck, pull back and show me his face, torn by grief." Sylvia hesitated, almost unable to continue. "That was when I knew that emotionally he had fully entered me, and that from then on his grief would be my grief, his story my story, his enormous waves of feeling, my feeling. I had felt almost nothing until him, and now I would continue to carry all of the rage and terror and anguish that he would leave behind, that he would forget. And shortly after I understood this, he asked the terrible questions. 'Could you tell me your name, your date of birth? Could you tell me who you are, what you are doing here?'"

She had known then that her horses were finally and wholly smashed, that all the objects in the house that had held her had crumbled into dust. No words were possible then. No words at all.

"Sometimes, early on," she told Jerome, "during our first long season, Andrew and I would meet accidentally on a street corner or in a shop. He was still mapping the County then, recording abandoned houses, or those that had evolved into ugly attempts at modernization. Often he was searching for things that had completely disappeared: a burial ground connected to an early settler, a scuttled ship, a hotel eclipsed by a moving dune of sand. These quests would bring him into Picton, to the registry office or the library with its haphazard archive, and once or twice a year, we would encounter each other without preparation, without warning.

"Always, I reacted to his appearance with panic, believing that I was the casualty of some terrible mistake, that I was wreckage. And yet somehow I would be able to speak, to exchange greetings, and to my later sorrow, to behave the way Malcolm had taught me to behave with all the other strangers whose paths intersected my days and evenings, in spite of my terror, my sense that everything had gone wrong, was lost, irretrievable, that there was only unfamiliarity and fear. For days afterwards I would be certain that this encounter, this distance and awkwardness, was the truth, and I would be certain that this was all we were to each other: exchanged civilities in the vicinity of traffic, indifferent, removed, suspicious of each gesture. There was no sweet secret, no complicity between us; nothing belonged to us — not the present, not even the past. He became a man walking away from me. He became a man I had never known. That November, remembering those times, it seemed as if they had been a terrible premonition of how things would end between us, with this difference: *I* became a woman *he* could not remember. A woman he had never known."

Sylvia was sitting upright in her chair as she said this. Jerome was looking at the wall. "That's terrifying," he said.

"Yes, I became afraid, afraid that we didn't exist." She paused. "That perhaps we had never existed. And then last year, in early December, I drove along the lake through one of the season's first heavy snowfalls in order to get to the hill, to get to him. By the time I arrived the weather was so bad I could barely see; it was as if the landscape itself were being eliminated. I remember thinking as I struggled through the wind along the edge of the hill that this was the first time I had been unable to look at the view before walking into the interior, before entering his embrace, though I was, by then, certain of neither the interior nor the embrace. I had been taking all the responsibility for some time, making all the appointments for our rendezvous, moving through the relationship in the way that, in recent months, I had learned to move, trying to ignore his lack of participation. I was carrying a bag of food in my arms because I knew there would be no food. I was carrying several things in my mind, things I wanted to say to him to try to bring him back to me, because I knew by then that he was going, because I feared, by then, that he was gone. As I walked past the foundations, I saw that the indentations that marked the ancient cellars and kitchens were filling up with snow, as if the last vestiges of the old house were finally being folded into the white landscape. The door of the cottage was ajar. There was no smoke coming from the chimney. I could find not a trace of him – not a trace of us – anywhere." Sylvia stopped, lowered her head.

"But still I waited, as I had always waited. I sat on the chair with the torn rush seat and remembered our clothing tossed there by arms much younger than the ones that lay, useless, in my lap. I ran the ancestral stories over and over in my mind. And then I saw Annabelle's scrapbook lying beside two green leather journals on the table. I opened the velvet cover and read the captions Annabelle had written to describe the fragments she had pasted in it. A piece of parchment from a map of the bogs, lace from the collar of the first good dress Marie had been given as a child, a ticket to the Louvre museum found in Branwell's desk drawer, the last rose of summer 1899, that fateful match that had lit Gilderson's pipe, lake-bleached splinters stolen from the hull of several timber carriers, bark from the recently felled cedar tree the men always erected in the middle of a raft for good luck, the sole of a shoe washed up at Wreck Bay – probably belonging to a drowned sailor – and still he did not come. Yes, these were the things I looked at while the knowledge of his permanent absence grew in me, and the light in the cottage grew darker, and the light in the sky grew dimmer.

"I closed the scrapbook and slipped it into the bag I had brought with me. Then I opened one of the journals and saw his handwriting. It was the ink on the page that made me want to take them with me, that last trace of his moving hand. Outside, the storm had moved to another part of the province, or had sailed over the lake to the country on the other side. The air had cleared and there was still a trace of a red sunset in the western sky, though not a whisper of it on the grey winter lake. As it had the first time that I had climbed that hill so many years before, deep snow slipped over the tops of my boots and scalded my legs as I walked toward the car. The storm had left a piercing wind in its wake and the newly fallen snow was beginning to arrange itself into a series of drifts. My footprints couldn't have lasted longer than a half-hour. Had Andrew come the following day there would be nothing to tell him about my approach, my retreat. But I knew he would never again walk through the orchard, enter the cottage, light the stove. I knew he was gone."

For the first time, Sylvia rose from her chair and began to walk back and forth across the room as she spoke. Jerome watched her move from place to place. "How might we have appeared, I wonder, to someone observing us from off stage: a man, a woman, alone together in a broken-down cottage?" There would be the glances, smiles, the long silences, and the sessions of speech that would pass between them, the unconscious gestures: he leaning toward her, she touching his wrist, placing her hand on the side of his face. They would curl together on the bed, for hours at a time, sleeping. They would often touch, sometimes casually, sometimes passionately. They would approach each other, withdraw, and eventually separate, permitting concession roads, fields of grain, entire townships, a body of water to come between them. Strings of migrating birds would emerge, like dark sentences, in the sky, as the season changed, the years passed, and the lake altered under varying degrees of light. And finally, finally, they would forget; forget, or be themselves forgotten.

By now Sylvia was standing in the part of the room where Mira so often worked on her performance pieces. There was still a small amount of sand on the floor, and each time she stepped forward or back it crunched softly under her feet.

"I often ask myself what river, what lake or stream the ice came from. I am for some reason anxious for this piece of the puzzle though it makes, I know, absolutely no difference to the outcome or even to the explanation. I've had the maps out, you see." Sylvia, standing entirely still, was visualizing every bend in the shoreline, each creek that fell into the Great Lake, lakes rising like rosary beads from the tangled string of a northern tributary, the whole watershed. "I want to know how long the journey was," she said to Jerome. "I want to be able to mark the point of entry, the port of embarkation. I want to be able to add some information to the long, sad message of Andrew's silence."

"Poor Jerome, I thought, reading your name, learning your age, and the fact that the sail loft had been given to you as a studio in which to make your art. Poor young Jerome. He would have dropped the brush, or pencil, or whatever was in his hand and he would have descended the stairs of the sail loft, then he would have moved out through the soggy late-spring snow and down to the dock.

"The ice would have been dark blue with a grey tinge . . . am I correct? It would have been feathered at its edges with snow, a frosty, almost decorative edge receding a little because of the water that would be nuzzling it like an animal. The figure frozen in it would appear to be halted forever in the attitude of one who is about to rise from a bed or from the grave, a figure interrupted forever in the midst of an act of resurrection. The arms would have been outstretched, I think, as if about to receive a blessing, a vision, the stigmata, or perhaps simply a lover."

Sylvia paused and looked away from Jerome, toward the wall. "Simply a lover," she repeated.

"I had seen him like this, you see," she continued, still not looking at Jerome. "I had seen him in morning, in afternoon light, partly rising from a bed with his arms outstretched, his lower torso buried in white bedclothes, his expression benign, tender, as I walked toward him, his entire self exposed. I had seen all this in him, and he had seen all this in me, and yet each time there would come the moment when we dressed, gathered together the few belongings that we had brought with us, and prepared to leave."

Sylvia, as if finishing a performance, walked back to her chair.

"Not ever, not even at his weakest moment, did he ask me to stay, although once I remember, once he said, 'Don't go yet, not quite yet.'" Her voice began to break. "I will always, always keep that memory."

Jerome had moved swiftly, soundlessly, from the couch and was sitting on the table directly in front of Sylvia. Here he was able to lean toward to her, to be within reaching distance. He took both her hands in his and held on to them.

An hour later, Sylvia and Jerome were standing side by side in front of a drafting table slowly, deliberately, going through the photos Jerome had taken on the island. "I finally began to develop them," he told her, "just this week." He moved one photo to the front of the table. "In the mornings," he added, "before you arrived."

Just after Jerome had shown Sylvia some of the "Dugouts" that would be used for his *Nine Revelations of Navigation,* and after he had found in himself the courage to point out the place where he had found the body, they heard the front door open and a few seconds later Malcolm and Mira entered the studio. "I was just putting the key in the lock when he walked up behind me," Mira said. She looked serious, worried. "He says he's your husband."

"Yes," said Sylvia, "he is." She stood to one side and stepped back so that she could see all the photos that were laid out on the table, and so that Jerome could point to them and tell Mira what they were. There was a calmness in her now that she realized was in opposition to the tension that had entered the room with Malcolm. "His name is Malcolm. And Malcolm, this is Mira and" – she turned toward the young man – "Jerome."

Jerome turned slowly, a photo of a milkweed pod still in his hand. Then he carefully put the picture down and, without making eye contact, walked across the room to extend his hand, a hand that Sylvia now knew well, having held it and then watched it move from one black-and-white landscape to another. Malcolm shook hands and then said that Sylvia had told him that this was an art studio. He looked around the room, clearly searching for paintings.

"The art is different than you might think," Sylvia told him. "Jerome takes photos and makes things out of doors." She gestured toward the collection on the table, then looked at Mira, who was removing a grey pea jacket and hanging it on a nail beside the door. "Mira does a kind of dance . . . a mysterious performance."

"This is the island," Jerome said to Mira, who had moved toward the table. "This is what I was doing on the island."

The girl bent over to look at the pictures more carefully. "Yes," she said, "yes . . . this is good."

Once they entered the living space, as Mira called it, Sylvia and Mira sat on the couch while Malcolm continued to stand near the door. Jerome walked over to the crate, lifted the journals, placed them in Sylvia's hands. "Don't forget these," he said.

"We loved them," said Mira, placing her hand on Sylvia's sleeve, "those stories. But what happened to Branwell . . . and Ghost?"

"What stories?" asked Malcolm before Sylvia could answer.

"Just some notes," said Sylvia, "that I found somewhere. That's all . . . all it is. I read them at night, when you were on call or when you were sleeping so you didn't . . . well . . . you didn't know about it." She saw her husband flinch when she said this. "I don't mean that I was keeping it from you, exactly, no, I wasn't doing that. It was just something that was private, known only to me."

"And now known to these two strangers," said Malcolm.

"Not strangers. Not now."

"No, I suppose not." He glanced at Jerome, who, like himself, had remained standing. "I hope this wasn't too disturbing for you."

"Disturbing?" said Jerome. "No, it wasn't disturbing."

"It was fine," said Mira. "It was good. It was all just talking . . . and interesting." Her hand was still on the older woman's arm. "What are you going to do, what do you want to do now?"

"I'll go back, I suppose," said Sylvia. She raised one hand and touched the top of Mira's head. "You have such wonderful hair."

Mira stood, took Sylvia's hand, and helped her rise from the couch. "Come into the bedroom," she said. "I'll show you the new fabric that I bought. And I have some borders, just some scraps really, that would be good, I think, for those tactile maps you make."

"Wait a minute," said Malcolm, "shouldn't we be going?"

"I don't think so," said Sylvia softly, "not yet, not quite yet."

Jerome could sense Malcolm's irritation as Mira drew Sylvia out of the room. The older man looked around the space for a while,

then turned toward him. Jerome was leaning against the wall farthest from where the doctor stood. The man's coat remained
fastened, his scarf tied, and Jerome could tell that he wanted to
be gone, that this was not the kind of interior in which he felt
comfortable. He had looked at the fluorescent lights and the
cement floor with distaste the minute he had come into the room.
Jerome could imagine him wondering how the hell his wife had
managed to spend so much time in such stark surroundings.

"So it was you who found the Alzheimer's patient, the one in
the ice," he said to Jerome. "They often get lost like that and come
to a bad end. It's always a tragedy . . . but what can anyone do?"

Jerome remained silent.

"I've often wondered if they think they know where they are
going when they wander off, if they have a destination in mind,
and then forget all about their original intention. But by that
stage it's almost impossible to determine what is in their minds.
Must have been a shock for you to find him like that."

"Yes," said Jerome, "I was out there alone . . . but fortunately
I had my cellphone with me. I went —" He stopped speaking.
Why was he revealing this pointless information? He didn't like
the direction the conversation was going but did not know how
to introduce another subject.

"I suppose she . . . I suppose Sylvia told you that she knew
him, this . . . Andrew . . ." Malcolm paused, trying to come up
with the last name.

"Andrew Woodman," said Jerome. "His name was Andrew
Woodman."

"That's right, Andrew Woodman. I suppose she told you she
was his lover, had been his lover for some time."

"I don't think we should talk about this," said Jerome, his eyes narrowing. "Whatever Sylvia said, she said it to me . . . in private."

"Well, he wasn't," said Malcolm, "he wasn't her lover. He would never have known her, never have met her. She read about him, about the discovery of his body, last year at the same time that she read about you. It happened like this once before: she collided with someone on the street, and he was her lover too, though she claims it was the same man — one lover encountered several times."

Jerome turned away from Malcolm, then looked at him suspiciously from the corner of his eyes. He totally distrusted this man, believed he could sense the anger brimming in him, though his manner was friendly, polite. From the next room he could hear the sound of Mira's voice, and he wished that she were here with him.

"It's the condition," Malcolm continued. "It sometimes manifests itself this way in a kind of hallucinogenic imagination. It's quite rare, but it does happen. It's a sort of inversion of the way the symptoms usually appear. Sylvia is particularly interesting for this reason. And she is, has always been, such a reader, she has trouble, you see, separating reality from what happens in books. We avoid films for this reason." He smiled. "Not that there are many films to avoid where we live."

Jerome was aware that his heart had begun to pound disturbingly. More than anything he wanted to be apart from this man, away from the things he was telling him. "Would you like to sit down?" he asked, indicating the chair. Sylvia's chair, he thought.

"No, no . . . thank you. We'll have to be going. It takes a couple of hours to get back to the County. And we'll be wanting to get back early. Sylvia will be quite tired" – Malcolm looked around the studio with what Jerome believed was disapproval – "after all this."

During the silence that followed, Malcolm walked around the room inspecting the various images tacked on the wall. He stopped when he came to the reproduction of the Flemish painting. "Is this one of yours?" he asked.

Jerome did not move from the place where he was standing. "No," he said, "that's a poster of a Patinir, *Saint Jerome in the Wilderness*, sixteenth century, couldn't possibly be mine." There was a hint of contempt in his voice. This man knows nothing, he thought, and then, for just a moment, he remembered Branwell's distant blue landscapes.

"I know so little about art," said Malcolm, as if sensing the route Jerome's mind had taken, "but what with Sylvia and my practice I haven't the time to explore much of anything else."

Surely this man in the flawless trench coat, the expensive silk scarf, the ridiculous toe rubbers didn't expect sympathy. The very notion that this might be the case set Jerome's teeth on edge; he had no time at all for sympathy-seekers. He recalled his father's whining, his pleading, his uncanny ability to make his mother really believe that everything – the drink, the disappearing money, the unexplained absences, the sudden bouts of abuse – was her fault and, by association, by the mere fact that he was her son, his fault as well. His mother had trained him early on, so early on he had no memory of the training, to step carefully around his father in certain moods and at certain levels of inebriation. As a young child he had feared all this. As a teenager he had hated it. Now, suddenly, he remembered his father baiting his mother across a table filled with the dinner she had cooked to please him, and how, unable to bear one more minute of it, he had sprung to his feet prepared if necessary to beat the weakness and cruelty out of him. But his mother had intervened, had taken his father's side, and, by the time Jerome had exploded out of the apartment, his mother was holding the sobbing broken man his father had become in her arms, apologizing for her son. "Your son," was the way his father had always put it when registering a complaint, overlooking, it seemed to Jerome, the fact that he was his son as well.

Jerome became aware that Malcolm had begun to speak again. "She confessed her imaginary life to me after she read the item in the paper, after she had read about you," he paused, cleared his throat, "and about him. She couldn't stop herself from speaking, actually, couldn't help but confess; she was that distraught. Just because it didn't happen does not mean that it does not, at certain times, seem real to her . . ." For the first time Malcolm showed some emotion, there was a tremor in his voice. "She has suffered a great deal."

"Yes," said Jerome. He was standing as far away as possible from the man, his arms crossed protectively over his lower ribs, his head down. Not since he had been a teenager had he shown such visible signs of sullenness, and he was peripherally aware of this and oddly embarrassed by it. Sensitivity, he thought, yes, his father had also been able to manifest sensitivity when it suited him, when he had something to gain from it. Any sign of male adult tears caused Jerome to close down completely; he had no faith in these displays. Only Mira's tears could move him, but even then, even with her, he could feel his guts clenching once the tears began. He could feel himself wanting to escape.

He decided to speak. "It seems to me," he said coldly, "that you are suggesting that she, that Sylvia, is telling lies."

"Oh no," Malcolm raised one hand in protest, "she believes, sometimes, that these episodes really took place. But it's impossible." He reddened slightly. "You must understand," he said, "she has no real physical, *we* have no real physical life. It's simply not possible, not with the condition. I accepted that when I married her." He looked at Jerome as if gauging whether to go further.

Jerome was damned if he was going to continue this conversation, going to ask about their physical life, or demand that this doctor explain the ridiculous condition he had been making reference to.

"I love her, you see," the doctor continued, "and that includes accepting everything she is. Everything that is wrong with her."

"I don't think there is anything wrong with her," said Jerome. "I just don't believe that. None of this is her fault." He turned and walked into the other room, where he found Mira bent over a stuffed plastic bag and Sylvia sitting on the futon, her lap filled with colourful ribbons and scraps.

Both women looked up when he entered, Mira with a length of sparkling rickrack hanging from one small delicate hand as if she had been caught in the act of inventing lightning.

They were about to depart. Malcolm stood by the door clasping the fabric-filled plastic bag as if it were a large belly that he had

miraculously grown in the last few minutes. Jerome was still refus-
ing to look at him.

Sylvia was bending over the handbag into which she had
placed the journals. She was looking for something, a frown of
concentration in the centre of her forehead. Swimmer, unnoticed
by her, was threading in and out between her legs. "Oh, here it
is," said Sylvia, pulling out a thick envelope.

Jerome approached her then, took her arm, and walked her
to the opposite side of the room where the drawings she had
noticed were pinned on the wall. He had added two or three to
the set since then and on a bench beneath these were some of the
photographs he had taken on the island – developed just that
morning before Sylvia's arrival. "You haven't seen these ones yet,"
he said. "This is what the floor of the island looked like," he told
her, "up close, under all that snow."

"What's this?" she asked, peering closely, then pointing to
the feathers and the blood.

"Just a bird. Swimmer ate most of it." Cock Robin entered
his mind. "Swimmer killed him, not a sparrow."

Sylvia smiled, and as she smiled Jerome leaned closer to her
and whispered, "Don't go back with him. Stay here, stay anywhere, but don't go back. He's got it . . . he's got *you* all wrong."

"Does he?" asked Sylvia.

"He doesn't believe you. He thinks you are inventing everything."

"Oh, that," said Sylvia, smiling again. "Yes, it's just like that.
Nothing harmful really, just the way it is."

"You could stay in the city," Jerome persisted. "If money is a
problem you could probably get paid for making those maps."

"Not very much," said Sylvia, still smiling. "It's mostly volunteer work. No, no I have to go back."

"Why?" asked Jerome. "*Why?*" In the background he could hear Mira laughing at something Malcolm had said. Little did she know, he thought. Everything in him now wanted to protect this woman.

"Because people do what they have to."

"Just tell me one thing," said Jerome, his eyes burning, "just one thing then."

"Yes?"

"Was there ever a condition?"

"Oh Jerome," said Sylvia softly, sadly, "there is always, always a condition." She turned slowly away from him and walked across the room to join her husband at the door.

Just before stepping over the threshold, Sylvia handed the envelope she had been holding to Jerome. "The answer to what happened to Branwell and Ghost is in this envelope. Or, at least the way I imagine it. It's not long, but still a kind of final chapter, I suppose."

They drove out of the city with excruciating slowness in the thick of rush hour, silence a third but strangely benign presence in the car. Once, when they were halted by gridlock on a major thoroughfare, Malcolm pointed out a garbage truck inching down the opposite side of the street, stopping every twenty feet or so to pick up trash. "What the hell are they doing collecting garbage at this time of the day?" he asked with irritation, not expecting an answer.

Sylvia glanced over her shoulder to look at something as ordinary as a garbage truck, even though her thoughts were still with Andrew, still with the way she had been able to reconstruct his mouth just a few minutes before, the curve of his brows, and how this reconstruction had felt smooth and inevitable, like recalling with pleasure piano music or an old poem one had memorized in one's childhood. She was about to let her mind slide back into Andrew's embrace when something caught her eye. A young man, holding on to a steel bar with one hand, rode on the back of the truck, and each time the vehicle stopped he swung easily down to the pavement, picked up a plastic bag with the sweep of an arm, then tossed this bag over his head into the bin, the motion so fluid and filled with such grace, it was as perfect as a dance. Sylvia was able to watch this young man, this repeated gesture, for three of four minutes until the truck moved beyond her peripheral vision. The thought struck her that if she and Andrew had had a son early on, he would have been about that age. By twisting in her seat she might have been able to see more of the dance, but the traffic had begun to move again, the light had changed.

"Youth," she thought as she was driven away, "how beautiful."

$\mathcal{M}$ira was holding on to Jerome as he wept, shaking in her arms like the child he had never permitted himself to be. Her own eyes were filled with tears, but she would not let herself go fully into his sorrow. This was his territory, his arena; he had opened the door to show her, but he did not want her to enter these dark spaces and she knew this and loved him harder for it.

After Sylvia had left, he had kicked a cardboard box across the room and punched his fist through the temporary wall that marked the bedroom space. "I want her to get *away!*" he had yelled at an amazed Mira. "I want her to be finally free of it!" Mira, her eyes wide and mouth partly open, had remained standing as if she would be glued forever to the time when a young man she thought she had known had punched the wall.

"She wasn't your mother, Jerome," she had said quietly.

"You know *nothing* about my mother," he had shouted, and then, once he had seen and fully registered her shocked expression, he had added more softly, "but, goddamn it, she was another chance."

He had told Mira then about the nights he had spent listening to his father roam the apartment like an angry nocturnal beast, the sounds of bottles breaking, his father collapsing on the cold tile of the bathroom floor, the smell of urine and vomit. He told her about the long absences, the lost jobs, the threats, the promises, certain humiliating appearances at school functions. He told her about his mother's withdrawal, how eventually by the time he was eleven or twelve he couldn't reach her even when she was in the room sitting by his side.

"There was never any past for her," he said. "It was all eaten away by my father's addiction, which was so huge a part of her life that everything else paled in comparison. She never told me about the farm where she grew up, she never told me who her people were, where they had immigrated from, why we were sort of Catholics, why she had called me Jerome. There were some old dishes around for a while that she said had belonged to her grandmother, but he destroyed them . . . he destroyed them on purpose. I think he broke them to smash up her past, to shatter anything that didn't relate specifically to him. There were no photo albums, no pictures of anything at all."

He told her about looking down from the balcony at the twisted and wrecked shape of his bicycle in the dirty snow, and then that same shape in the dead spring grass, each day after school, until one day when he looked it was gone. It was after he spoke about the bicycle that he had begun to weep.

His tears unlocked Mira and she went to him and held him as he cried, the sobs coming out of him in long, shuddering gasps. "Who threw your bicycle off the balcony?" she asked. "Who threw it into the snow? Was it your father?"

"Yes," Jerome whispered, "yes." He pulled away from her and placed his head in his hands. "I was trying to smash it up, just trying to smash it up. He came out onto the balcony . . . drunk, horribly, staggeringly drunk. He pulled it out of my hands and threw it off the balcony. And that was when he fell." Mira could feel the tears on his face, could hear the bewilderment in his voice as he said these words. "He lost his balance, and he just fell over the railing."

Mira wrestled her way back into his embrace and held on to him with a force she wouldn't have thought possible in the past, held on to him while he cried like a broken child.

When it was over, they both fell asleep sitting upright on the couch, their heads touching. Swimmer, who had hidden behind the refrigerator when he saw that Jerome was angry, joined them once he was certain all was safe, walked around Jerome's lap three times in a circle, then settled in and went to sleep as well.

Mira wakened first and gently leaned forward to retrieve the folded pieces of paper she had placed in the exact spot where the journals had lain on the crate in front of the couch. Jerome rolled his head back and forth against the quilt, then sat up and massaged his head with his hands.

"Okay now?" Mira's hand was on his neck.

"Okay."

"Do you want to go out and get something to eat, or do you want to read this first," Mira held up the folded papers, "and then go out."

"Read it," said Jerome. "We'll go out later."

Swimmer jumped more noisily than usual down to the floor. If they weren't going to continue sleeping, he wasn't going to stay.

Mira began:

Branwell despised almost everything about the pretentious house that his son's wife had built on the hill. He hated its stamped brass doorknobs and its carved oak newel posts, he hated its decorative plastered ceilings and its bogus venetian chandeliers, he hated its patterned carpets and its heavy, ornate furniture, he hated the opaque glass ceiling that was also a ballroom floor, and he hated almost everyone that danced on that floor. He did not despise the property because, as I would later discover each time I visited Andrew there, the property was undeniably beautiful. He did not hate the view from the hill because, in certain lights, he almost believed he could see the Ballagh Oisin rising from the sand far off on the peninsula at the eastern end of the horizon, and because the view, too, was undeniably beautiful. And, most of all, he did not despise his grandson, T.J., who had inherited his own father's obsession with grandfathers and, as a result, was beginning to show an interest in colour and shape.

Andrew told me that probably Maurice — the Badger — would have been forced to take the old man in to live with him at Gilderwood upon his return from southwestern Ontario. Then, not much later, he likely commissioned a series of murals from his father for the great downstairs hall. Perhaps he hadn't really wanted the paintings but had hoped that his father's melancholy would abate if he gave him something useful to do.

Branwell's melancholy had not, however, abated and evidence of this fact was painted on the walls of the central hallway of the house. The dusky, fortified European cities were reproduced there, or at least some of them, as were the sins of the artist's son, in a horrifying array of colours. A variety of animals decked out like Maurice himself, in the usual parliamentary garb of frock coat and top hat, were depicted writhing in the flames of hell as punishment for their sins. A well-dressed horse, for instance, was being broken on the wheel, a huge yellow frog in a top hat was being plunged by a demon into a cauldron of boiling oil, and a great red bear in a waistcoat and pocketwatch was being dismembered alive. There was absolutely no trace of the distant blue landscapes of his early works, some of which can still be seen in the odd old house in the County.

When Branwell began this Allegory of Bad Government *(a parody of the name of a Sienese fresco he had read about), T.J., delighted by the various animals in the piece, had been permitted to assist, and had spent some days colouring a waistcoat or a top hat. Minister Badger Woodman, as he was now famously called, had apparently wondered about the subject of the mural his father was painting in the front hall, but, having a literal mind, was completely unable to interpret the symbolism that Branwell was striving so diligently to convey. Caroline, beyond commenting on the suitability or lack of suitability of the colours, would have given the mural barely a glance. Subjects other than herself did not interest her.*

Branwell had not heard from Ghost in more than two years. It was now the end of one appalling century and the beginning of another, though looking at the serene view from that hill, it would have been almost impossible to believe that entire ecosystems had been eliminated never to return, and that in Europe, home of all those defensive and defended cities that had so disturbed Branwell years before, various leaders were preparing to embark on a series of wars more horrifying than anything the young Branwell could have imagined in the attic of

Les Invalides and, in fact, more horrifying than anything he could think of while standing on the edge of a hill, the panorama from which resembled more than anything the beautiful turquoise landscape he had carried with him for most of his adult life.

August is the month of lightning on the Great Lake Ontario and the shores that surround it. Often, one can stand at the lake's edge in the evening and watch sheet lightning move like a distant beautiful war along the seam of the horizon where water touches sky. But it is the other kind of lightning I am referring to, the kind that is built from heat and moisture, the kind that is a companion to storm. In some ways, this kind of lightning is like the approach of someone significant in your life: a friend, a lover, an enemy. You see the lightning, then you count out the beat of the distance until the thunder comes. Julia says that it is the interval between thunder and lightning that is the closest she comes to being able to see weather. When the interval closes, the meeting takes place and the lightning strikes.

No one in the large house was hearing thunder or listening to intervals, as all were soundly asleep. Ghost, however, galloping on a white horse down the King's Highway toward the village beneath Gilderwood Hill, was measuring the distance of the storm on the one hand, and the distance he must cover on the other. He knew what was going to happen. He hoped he would get there in time.

When he arrived at the top of the hill the fatal strike had already taken place, the fire had begun and flames were emerging from attic windows. By the light of these flames Ghost was able to see that two or three people were standing out on the lawn dressed in nightclothes — servants, likely, who would have inhabited the attic and who would have felt the strike and fled the house. They had left the magnificent front door open in their flight.

Ghost, seeking Branwell, and seeking also someone close to Branwell, did not dismount but rode his white horse right through the entrance, down the hall past Allegory of Bad Government, *and straight up the wide stairs. In Branwell's bedroom, Ghost leaned down from his horse and lifted his friend out of the bed by his nightshirt. "Get on the horse," he shouted, "but there is someone else. Who is it? Where is he?"*

Branwell was convinced that he was dreaming, and the smoke that was blossoming in the upper air of his room did nothing to dispel this conviction. Nevertheless, he knew the answer to Ghost's question. "T.J.," he said. "In the next room."

And so the child that would become Andrew's father burst out of the burning house and into the safety of the landscape riding with two white-haired men on a white horse backlit by red and orange flames. And Andrew — the future — was riding that white horse as well, along with his life and what that life would do to my life and all the other lives it would touch.

Andrew told me that if you now asked anyone in the village below the hill about the house they would talk about the lightning strike, the fire, the subsequent loss of life, and the glass ballroom floor. They would talk about the painted hallways, and about a rumour that suggested that someone had once ridden a white horse up the central staircase. They had forgotten all about the subject of the murals, they had forgotten about the rescue, they had forgotten all about the boy who had been raised by two old men in a cottage that was still standing on the property.

Perhaps, Jerome, all of life is an exercise in forgetting. Think of how our childhood fades as we walk into adulthood, how it recedes and diminishes like the view of a coastline from the deck of an oceanliner. First the small details disappear, then the specifics of built spaces, then the hills fall below the horizon one by one. People we have been close to, people who die, are removed from our minds feature by feature until there is only a fragment left behind, a glance, the shine of their hair, a few episodes, sometimes traumatic, sometimes tender. I have not been close to many people, Jerome, but I know that once they leave us they become insubstantial, and no matter how we try we cannot hold them, we cannot reconstruct. The dead don't answer when we call them. The dead are not our friends.

All of this is terrible, unthinkable. But, it is not as terrible as being forgotten by the man you love while he is breathing the same air, while he is standing in the same room. He has forgotten you and yet some part of him remembers that he should touch you, and he does this, but as he moves against you he no longer speaks your name as he plunges his hands into your hair because he has forgotten your name. When he undresses you he registers surprise that your flesh is imperfect. He has forgotten your age. He has forgotten the many years that have passed since he first desired you, and the suffering during those years that has changed your face, the texture of your skin, the curve of your spine. The accumulated absences, the accumulated distances — he has forgotten all of these. He thinks that it was just yesterday that you collided near the stop-light of a town whose name he can no longer recall. He thinks the smooth legs that took you to the dunes above a buried hotel are the same legs that brought you back, years later, to the meeting place, the room in which you have fallen over and over again onto a bed whose springs are now rusty, whose mattress is now filled with dust. He has forgotten the love. His body knows what to do, but his mind has forgotten, his heart has been stilled.

I have scraped my memory like a glacier through my mind, with as much cold rationality as a person like me is able to muster, trying to deter-mine, trying to remember when each story was told to me. What was outside the window when Andrew spoke of Annabelle? There is a flicker of white, but whether this is the white of trilliums on the forest floor or the white of snow floating though the pines I can't now say. Perhaps it's the continuous white of cotton sheets that stays with me for, during the hours we spent together, we clung to that bed as if it were an island and we the only two survivors of one of Annabelle's marine disasters. And what age were we at this time or that time? What made him decide that we needed a particular story on a particular day or during the course of a particular year? Was his hair brown, or grey or white, as he spoke the words? In the end, though, it does not matter, just as it does not matter that although I believed that he had returned because — miraculously — he wanted to begin again, he had really returned because he had forgotten that we had ever stopped. What matters was the miracle that we ever met at all, the miracle of the life I never could have lived without the idea of him, and the arm of that idea resting on my shoulder.

All the while I have been talking to you I have been listening for the sound of Andrew's voice, because they are his stories, really, these things he told me. But now I have to admit that I have been listening in the way I listened to a stethoscope that belonged to my father. When I was a child, I removed it from his office so many times that eventually, as a kind of joke, I suppose, I was given an instrument of my own for Christmas. I loved the rubber earpieces that shut out the noise of the world. But, even more, I loved the little silver bell at the end of the double hose, a bell I could place against my chest in order to listen to the drum, to the pounding music of my own complicated, fascinating heart.

Jerome remained silent while Mira folded up the papers and placed them on the arm of the couch. He was trying to remember the last time he had been read to, who had done the reading. It would have been during his childhood, but the feeling associated with the faint memory was good, warm. There had been an encircling arm, so it would have been early on – his early childhood. Sometimes there had been stories, he suddenly knew, sometimes poetry.

"God," said Mira. "How sad, how terribly, terribly sad. Do you think we'll ever see her again?"

" 'The boy stood on the burning deck,' " said Jerome quietly " 'when all but he had fled.' "

"Jerome . . . ?"

"Wait," he said, not looking at her, then slowly turning, his eyes wide. "I think it was him."

Mira was searching his face.

"I think it was him." He closed his eyes, then opened them again and grabbed Mira's arm. "It was my father," he said with amazement, the shock of something resembling pain, or perhaps joy, making it necessary for him to have to steady himself. "He read to me," he said with wonder in his voice. "It was my father who read to me."

He leaned back to allow the memory to take shape and could hear the sound of his father's voice reading a story about a toy canoe launched at the head of Lake Superior, not far from where they had lived in the north. The small watercraft had been taken by currents of water far from its birthplace. Moving through one Great Lake after another, past cities and farms in the company of freighters and pleasure boats, tumbling over the falls of Niagara, rotating in whirlpools, passing perhaps Timber Island, reaching the St. Lawrence River, floating under the bridges of Montreal and Quebec City, it always carried with it the certain knowledge of the eventual salt sea as a desired destination. What had happened then? What had happened once this tiny object reached the desired destination?

It could only have been overwhelmed, Jerome decided, swallowed up — destroyed, in fact — by the enormity of its own wishes.

ACKNOWLEDGEMENTS

During the four years that passed while I was writing this novel, a great number of people helped and encouraged me, both personally and professionally. In particular I would like to thank Mieke Bevelander, Pat Bremner, Anne Burnett, Liz Calder, Adrienne Clarkson, Ellen Levine, Allan Mackay, Ciara Phillips, Emily Urquhart, and Tony Urquhart. Pertinent bits of valuable information, or inspiring thoughts, were provided by Mamta Mishra, Rasha Mourtada, and Alison Thompson, as well as by archivists at the Library and Archives Canada and the Marine Museum of the Great Lakes at Kingston, Ontario. Without Pat Le Conte I would not have been able to finish the novel in comfortable surroundings. Without the luck brought to me by a certain multiple of three, there would have been much less joy.

Several publications were also very important to me, especially John K. Grande's essays on earth sculpture and the two wonderful volumes describing the Calvin Timber Business on Garden Island: *A Corner of Empire* by T.R. Glover and D.D. Calvin and *A Saga of the St. Lawrence* by D.D. Calvin. The imaginary timber empire described in the central section of *A Map of Glass* is very loosely based on the Calvin business, but all characters and events are purely fictional. Another book I found helpful was

Great Lakes Saga by A.G. Young. The phrase "the ugliest species of watercraft ever to diversify a marine landscape" used on pages 157 and 169 was borrowed from this volume.

I would also like to thank the Canadian National Institute for the Blind (CNIB) for information concerning tactile maps and the Perth County Historical Foundation for information on the Fryfogel Inn.

I am very grateful to Heather Sangster for her careful attention to details.

I would like to thank my much loved late father, Walter (Nick) Carter, who was a benign, careful, and highly respected mining engineer and prospector, and whose affection for his profession led to my own, admittedly now diminished, knowledge of the mining world.

Finally, a special thank you to my editor, close friend, and best adviser, Ellen Seligman.